THE BIRD WOMAN

She slipped from the branches of a willow and alighted on the ground. For the first time, I saw a creature I had heard men discuss only in hushed whispers, a creature feared and loved by all males who had seen her (because they feared the love she inspired), a creature with white hair and dark eyes and a face like an omniscient child. I saw a woman who personified all the naive dreams and yearnings I had ever entertained toward godlike womanhood. I saw the bird woman.

I wanted her forever. We all did. But none of us would have her—besides, at that moment she was our only hope of finding the monster who threatened the immortality of us all...

AN EAST WIND COMING

ARTHUR BYRON COVER

A BERKLEY BOOK
published by
BERKLEY PUBLISHING CORPORATION

AN EAST WIND COMING

A Berkley Book/published by arrangement with
the author

PRINTING HISTORY
Berkley edition/November 1979

A portion of this
book has appeared
in *Heavy Metal*, Vol. III,
No. 2, June 1979.

ISBN: 0-425-04439-4

A BERKLEY BOOK ® TM 757,375
Berkley Books are published by Berkley Publishing Corporation,
200 Madison Avenue, New York, New York 10016.
PRINTED IN THE UNITED STATES OF AMERICA

While this novel was being written, my father, Dr. William A. Cover, passed away at the age of sixty-four. Like many sons, I learned my father had meant more to me during his life than I had ever realized. This novel is dedicated to his memory.

Many friends aided me, in one way or another, during the writing of this book. The world of letters may condemn them forever, but I appreciate it. However, if I were to begin to list all those who contributed, it would run to approximately twenty pages; the successful completion of such a list would not endear me to my agent, my editor, or my publisher. I hope my friends will know who they are and will accept my thanks.

There's an east wind coming all the same, such a wind as never blew on Earth yet. It will be cold and bitter, friend good doctor, and many of us may wither before its blast. But it's fate's own wind, nonetheless, and a cleaner, better, stronger civilization will lie in the sunshine when the storm has cleared.

—the consulting detective

CHAPTER ONE

1. *I am the wolfman!*

And the forest, which had been filled with the chatterings of insects and birds, was stilled by that dreaded cry. Silver owls did not rustle their wings as they remained perched on the limbs of elm and maple trees. Red crickets, normally the most talkative of creatures, lapsed into an unaccustomed silence. Beasts of prey—and prey—halted, not daring to move their paws for fear that they would crackle dry leaves or snap twigs; and those sounds, so meaningless and commonplace during other times, would guide the creator of that cry to his feast.

I am the wolfman!

The cry was softer this time, almost piteous; and it seemed to the more intelligent animals that the creature experienced a measure of regret as he broadcast his boast throughout the wood.

I am the wolfman!

The words were whispered now; and the silver owls, who possessed remarkable insight, imagined the creature in an uncharacteristically introspective mood, drooping his shoulders and hanging his head, lamenting the fate which had made him

1

the victim of dark forces nurturing his savage impulses. For once there had been a time when the wolfman had not been feared.

As the wispy clouds were gently parted by cool winds, the full moon glowed, illuminating pathways, clearings, and treetops. Animals who had paused in the open now faded into the woods as silently as they could. No one could be sure that the wolfman was far away, because his cry echoed; it did not seem to diminish with distance, but to grow instead, as if his fierce joy and pathetic sadness endowed his lungs with an impossible strength. The animals did not feel secure or safe when they were no longer bathed in silver light; the mere act of hiding did not protect them from the wolfman. But there was something comfortable about being enveloped in the darkness, about not being touched by the light that had created the wolfman.

Finally, standing on top of a grassy mountain overlooking the forest, silhouetted by the impassive moon, he uttered one last cry.

I

He clenched his fists, his claws digging into his palms, and threw back his head to stare at the sky.

am

His voice, which spoke only four words, was softer now, though its volume was no less. His black lips were drawn back, snarling, pressing tight against his gums.

the

And he inhaled, standing on the front pads of his feet, flexing his muscles, imagining his blood—red and warm—flowing through his arms and legs.

wolfman!

His cry concluded triumphantly, all traces of self-pity having vanished, overwhelmed by a sudden satisfaction in the knowledge that of all the unique animals in the forest, none was his equal. Very little other knowledge, true knowledge rested in his mind (though occasionally disturbing flashes of well-articulated thoughts occurred to him, only to be totally forgotten in an instant); his actions were dictated by his instincts, which were capable of instructing him how to overcome every challenge and how to satisfy every craving. Now he craved food and, growling, he loped toward the forest.

The wolfman had claws nearly a decimeter long, on both his hands and his feet. His body was covered with brown hair. As he leisurely prowled the forest, his thick arms dangled and his hands often scraped the ground like those of an ape. He had red eyes, a flattened nose, long ears, and a dimpled chin; when he closed his mouth, the tips of his two canine fangs protruded over his lower lip. His face was not quite so hairy as the remainder of his body; about his nose and cheeks was a hairless patch of thick brown skin. His one article of clothing was a tattered pair of green corduroy trousers.

Game was abundant this night, and the wolfman felt a craving for a splendid feast, but not for food which he could hunt and kill in the forest. When he detected the scent of a doe, which he could outrun easily and which would prove to be no challenge, he ignored it; and he ignored other game, so much game that the silver owls, who were always present at the site of death, were confused and upset. Something was not normal this night. The animals of the forest had grown reconciled to the forays of the wolfman during the full moon, and now something new was wrong. Although it was usually contrary to their dispositions to be concerned for the welfare of others, the animals were afraid for the wolfman's latest prey; they sensed that his character had undergone another radical alteration which, though it might not affect the equilibrium of their lives, would have a disastrous effect on the balance of life elsewhere.

Soon the wolfman effortlessly ran through the forest, navigating the ground as if he had explored it all carefully in the past, as if he had noted every fallen log, every bush, every rock, every hole, every crevice. He did not pause to rest. Some force—not his instincts, which merely guided him—urged him onward, and he leaped over streams, darted under low-hanging branches, dashed through clearings, and weaved through clumps of trees, his primitive mind trusting entirely to that mysterious force.

Eventually he passed out of the forest and entered a land of many strange wonders, wonders which he invariably disregarded because he was so intent upon reaching his goal (whatever it was). He did not possess the subtlety of mind to appreciate the beauty of the waterfall which poured down a jewel mountain reflecting the stars and the moonlight; at the base of the waterfall, mist hung in the air; and when he bounded over huge jewels in the river, the droplets clung to his fur, causing it to glisten as if a frightful vision had streaked it white.

He was not overwhelmed by (because he could not comprehend) the massive canyons whose walls were actually invisible force fields preventing entry into another dimension. He was not distracted by the eerie sight of a sector of space in that dimension trapped underneath a barren plain of earth. Nor did he feel peaceful and serene when he ran through fields of tall grass which appeared to be tan in the blanching glow of the moon. He felt only excitement as he impatiently traversed those fields, toward the waiting golden city which beckoned on the horizon.

The wolfman suppressed the urge to utter his dreaded cry as he approached the golden city. His stomach gnawed; for a moment he regretted bypassing all those opportunities to feast in the forest, where the game had been plentiful, but the thought faded like so many others before it. He realized (as well as he could realize anything) that the choice had been his, and that if he had gorged, he would have been too sluggish to travel to the city, where awaited the meal he desired above all others.

He silently ran past several empty wooden or brick houses which formed a feeble barrier between the fields and the city. Then he entered a magnificent neighborhood of golden apartment complexes. The urge to utter his cry and to kill simultaneously was almost too potent to resist; but though he had never before required caution during his brief lifetime as a hunter, his instincts warned him that caution was required now. Carefully avoiding garbage cans which, when struck, would create a dreadful clammer, and avoiding parties of eternal children absorbed in their inane games, the wolfman stalked the golden city. He could have killed anytime; he was undetected. He could have burst into an apartment or crashed through a window; he could have slain the first prey he saw. Any one of over a hundred android eternal children could have been his. But the mysterious force informed his primeval intelligence that here was not the proper site, that elsewhere was more appropriate. Though the wolfman's hunger was without parallel in his fleeting memory, he chose to ignore it, to follow the will of the force instead. Besides, the thought of so many creatures who could conceivably retaliate in such close proximity disturbed him. His instincts instructed him to fear these creatures who enclosed themselves in shimmering gold.

Soon he found himself in a neighborhood which was the exact duplicate of the other, save that it was empty. Now his hunger was overpowering, too great to be regulated by practical concerns. He still would not kill while there were several of these creatures together, but he had no qualms about slaying a creature who was alone. Both his instincts and the mysterious force seemed to agree on this matter, and they directed him through the empty neighborhood whose unnatural silence distressed him.

However, after a short time he scented the creatures again, in yet a third neighborhood, much more crowded than the first. The wolfman could not mistake the almost tangible feeling of *loneliness* in the atmosphere. It did not matter who was in close proximity to whom in this third neighborhood; all these creatures, even when touching, were *alone*. The wolfman did not ponder upon how he knew this sophisticated fact, upon how he sensed a feeling which previously he had been unequipped to understand; his was not a questioning nature; it was enough that he knew. Without realizing the implications of it, he had somehow become familiar with these creatures he had thought so alien to him. And his familiarity breathed in him a supreme confidence similar to the one he habitually carried with him in the forest.

Indeed, the neighborhood, though it shimmered gold, resembled a forest, a jungle. It offended the wolfman even as he exalted in it. The streets were cracked, in disrepair; clumps of weeds crawled through holes and clung to the concrete like strong green spiderwebs. The streetlamps were few and dim; underneath several lay pieces of glass. Windows were boarded; fire escapes and railings were rusty; a sink outside a building had a leaky faucet. The neighborhood also resembled a forest in that it was allowed to take on its own character, though some ghostly thought informed the wolfman that the creatures could mold their environment to their liking if they chose. When the wolfman observed the creatures, either singly or in groups, as he searched for the proper victim, he detected their sense of desolation, their lack of purpose, their despondency—all mirrored and reinforced in the neighborhood they inhabited.

Goaded by both his hunger and the fascination born of an unsuspected kinship with these creatures, the wolfman hunted for many hours. Often he did not care if he was detected, and he traveled entire blocks via the rooftops, jumping from building to building, or he ran down dark, deserted streets and alleys.

Finally his instincts informed him that an entire area was virtually deserted; and he waited on top of a two-story building for an unsuspecting creature to pass beneath him.

His patience was rewarded sooner than he had hoped. After fifteen minutes of waiting, he heard the rhythm of slow footsteps gradually becoming louder. He stifled the urge to growl in anticipation.

The creature was a female. She had a lean body, brown eyes, and black hair cut just above her shoulders. She wore a beige raincoat, though the sky was still clear and the light of the full moon was almost undiminished by the glow of the golden city. Her hands were in her pockets. She watched her feet as she walked, unmindful of any obstacles which might be before her. For an instant the wolfman felt a twinge of pity as his red eyes glowered upon her features; she suggested a fragility which stirred something in his stomach, something other than hunger (or a hunger of a different type), something which he repressed immediately as he reminded himself that he was the wolfman. That he desired a feast. That all irrelevant concerns must be put aside as he fought for his survival in this strange golden city.

The wolfman jumped toward the sidewalk, not five meters in front of the creature. He snarled as she stepped backward and screamed. He imagined his claws ripping into her, as they had ripped into prey so often in the forest; and it seemed that already her blood was warming his mouth, that already he was leaving her on the sidewalk, her unwanted parts torn from her body and left for the scavengers. As she closed her eyes, paled, and began to swoon, he leaped toward her, preparing to rend her with an upward sweep of his claws as she fell. He uttered his cry.

I am

And he felt his body crackle as if he had suddenly stepped into the fires of a volcano. He did not feel pain, not as he was used to experiencing pain, but it seemed that his body had been split into a million different bloodless parts.

the wolfman.

He concluded his cry in the forest. He did not know how he had arrived back in the forest, and he did not care. He had become mad, a vessel of rage; and his primitive mind vowed that before dawn he would slay many animals, that it did not matter if he feasted or not, so long as animals were dead and all knew he was the most fearsome prowler in the forest. Growling, he stared at a tree.

I am the wolfman.

A silver owl, it seemed to him, returned his stare with approval.

2. *An account from the good doctor's notebook:*

The consulting detective and I stood over the fallen body of the godlike woman. A lackluster yellowish beam radiated from the streetlamp near us, as an oppressive fog crept over the shabby golden buildings which formed the district known as the East End. The consulting detective was clad in his renowned tan caped-back overcoat and his tan deer-stalker cap, whereas my apparel included my familiar gray greatcoat and top-hat boiler. My friend and I had been strolling through this decrepit district, lamenting the fallen state of the ill-starred denizens, when we happened upon the rather appalling sight of the wolfman, who normally frequented the forest to the south, attacking the ace reporter. I must admit, the horrendous vision dulled my mercurial reflexes. I was so overcome by the awesome knowledge that a godlike life weighed in the balance that I hesitated; and if I had been alone that precious life might have been lost, for the wolfman had justly earned his reputation as an atavism. However, I was not alone, for my existence derives much of its justification from my presence at my friend's side. And the consulting detective acted quickly, to say the least. He teleported the wolfman back to the forest where he belonged, knowing that the atavism would not think to teleport back to the city until the coming of dawn, when his intelligence and better nature would return.

The smoke emanating from his pipe bowl like that from a stone chimney, his gray eyes appearing to have vanished in the eerie effect of the dim light and the fog, the consulting detective said, "Quickly, examine her! She may have come to harm!"

"Oh, yes," I replied. "Foolish of me to forget." I knelt and felt the pulse at her neck. From my fingertips flowed vibrations which penetrated and inspected every organ of her body. Ignoring the pleasant thought of inspecting her under more favorable conditions (often I am not discreet, and proper thoughts occur to my undisciplined mind at improper times), I closed my eyes and concentrated. After five seconds had elapsed, my fingertips picked up the rhythm of responding vibrations. I looked up at my friend, whose face was totally dark now, a black object outlined by the inefficient streetlamp. But I did not need to see his face to know the concern reflected there. "She's fine," I said. "As I suspected, she just fainted from the surprise. And with good reason, I might add."

My friend took his pipe from his mouth. "Fortunately, I'm aware that life's full of little surprises. Consequently, nothing surprises me. Otherwise the young lady's troubles would be of a physical character."

"Precisely the wounds most easily healed," I replied, creating a bowl of warm water beside me. I dipped my fingers into the bowl and flicked drops of water at her face.

"I'm well aware of that too," he said softly, as if my observation was not one that he cared to endorse.

Before we could carry the discussion to its inevitably anti-climatic conclusion, the ace reporter groaned, rolled her head to either side as if she was asleep on a bed equipped with luxurious pillows, and fluttered her eyelids so that the lashes appeared like tiny wings in flight. Save for a certain hollowness about the cheeks, her oval face was swollen with hints of baby fat, providing her with the best of both youthful innocence and mature worldliness. I smiled at her, more at her lovely features than to reassure her that all was well, I'm afraid. Although her complexion was quite pale, she managed to smile bravely at me as I helped her stand. "You, of all people," she said, laughing weakly. "I haven't seen you for literally ages." Which was literally true. "And I should have expected you too," she added to the consulting detective, who nodded politely and stared at her coldly as if she was an artifact. "I suppose you saved me?" she asked, looking in my direction, preferring my warm personal manner to the consulting detective's cool professional one.

"My friend did. He teleported the wolfman to the forest."

She laughed again and clapped her hands once. "That was certainly a judicious course of action. Exactly what I should have expected. Well, where have you guys been keeping yourselves?"

"We're stay-at-homes," said the consulting detective, his eyes twinkling as if he had told a little joke. Some joke. Save for occasional ventures to remind himself of the flavor of fresh air, he had stayed at home for millions of years, waiting for a knock at the door.

"I guess you are," said the ace reporter in a sing-song voice. The consulting detective's eyes ceased twinkling and hardened with concern. Then all her attempts at shrugging off the episode with the wolfman failed; she grasped my forearm with both hands. "I—I'm glad you decided not to stay at home tonight."

I embraced her. She cried on my shoulder as I glanced at the consulting detective, awaiting whatever silent instructions he might decide to give me concerning the best method of handling the situation. He puffed on his pipe and smiled; he bobbed on the balls of his feet; his manner seemed to say, "You're the ladies' man; you handle it." And my expression, I am sure, seemed to reply, "Yeah, but you're the cool professional. What am I supposed to do?!"

After a few moments, however, the ace reporter cleared up that little dilemma, by sniffing twice, wiping her eyes, and biting her lower lip. She allowed her right hand to drop from my shoulder, but her left hand slid down my arm and encircled my elbow with an electrifying grip which sent waves of warmth cascading through my system. Now that her emotions were nearly under her control, I was once again tempted to extend her an invitation to visit my office the next day for a complete checkup. She looked at the sidewalk. "I suppose something good can come of all this."

"And what is that?" asked my friend in a comforting, patient tone.

"I could write an interesting story for the paper."

However, her tone betrayed her. I glanced at the consulting detective; he scowled at her, informing me (thanks to my encyclopedic knowledge of his gesticulations) that he too realized that she had no faith that her story would be interesting. The consulting detective closed his eyes as if his mind had entered another world; he said, "Will you write the story? I read all the papers, and the good doctor and I would find an account of the pertinent facts written in your own uncommon style extremely valuable."

She turned away from both of us; and though I could not see her face, I knew that she was disconsolate from the manner in which her shoulders slumped. "There ... probably won't be a story. Nothing I've written lately has been good. Not even updates of previous features and fillers. I've lost the touch."

At that moment my friend's cool professionalism flew apart, vanished, disintegrated, as if it had never existed; and he became the consulting detective I love best—the moral force of a civilization personified in a man of passion. It's not an easy job, I assure you. His gray eyes ablaze like hot coal, his teeth clamping so hard on the pipe stem that I feared it would break, he strode to the ace reporter, grabbed her shoulder, and spun her about so roughly that I feared he had reduced himself to ungentlemanly methods to convince her of the error of her opinion. His face was as pale as hers, not from the horror of a recent experience, but from frustration, from the dreadful knowledge that his attempt to brighten her disposition and to provide her with hope would no doubt fail. He said, "You've lost the touch because you believe you have, and for no other reason. If you would only believe, then you'll regain it. Like that!" He snapped his fingers. "You may think that it's asking a lot to request that you simply *not accept* a problem which has been building up for a few million years, and possibly it is. I might concede that point if you carefully constructed a logical, airtight case for it; I repeat, I *might* concede the point. But I cannot stress too strongly that that's your one solution. Once you convince yourself to begin thinking a new way, then many of your difficulties will become virtually non-existent. The only person who can truly give your life meaning is yourself. You *can* regain the touch . . . if you want to. If you sincerely want to."

After the conclusion of the speech, the ace reporter smiled feebly and said, "I suppose that is possible. I mean, I have all eternity before me. Anything is possible."

The consulting detective sighed, withdrew his pipe from his mouth, and tapped the bowl on the streetlamp. He had said similar words to a goddess, while upon a previous case, and she had not believed him either. "Yes," he said in a defeated voice. "Anything is possible." Now not even he could contest the inevitable. The article would not be written.

I pursed my lips and scraped the sole of my right shoe over the sidewalk. The three of us stood there under the misty glow of the streetlamp for a silent minute, a minute pregnant with unspoken embarrassment. We did not know what to say or to do next. The ace reporter was doubtless attempting to conceive of a method of expressing her appreciation and then to take leave of us. I did not want her to go. It seemed that the fog was becoming thicker, the air chillier.

Finally I said, "Uh, er, do you live around here?"

The ace reporter blinked; I imagined that her eyes had metamorphosed into glistening crystal. "Here in the East End? No. But I come here often, especially since I stopped writing. The neighborhood seems to suit me, somehow."

"May I offer you advice?" asked the consulting detective.

"Besides that which you've already given me?"

"Yes." He refilled his bowl, staring at her with stern eyes all the while. She had done nothing to deserve such a heartless stare, and so it took her several moments to reply:

"Go on. I'll listen to whatever you have to say. Especially since I owe you my life, for what it's worth."

"And I realize you believe that its value is minimal. Very well. That problem will take care of itself in time. However, should you desire that time, my advice is: don't live here."

The ace reporter laughed with incredulity. "How did you know I want to move here?"

"A logical conclusion, derived from obvious deductions. But I emphasize, should you live here, your life will be in danger again."

"My word!" I exclaimed. "How can you say these things? We've no indication that..."

"From the wolfman?" said the ace reporter. "That was a fluke. He probably won't leave the forest during the full moon again for several million years. Besides, I'm capable of taking care of myself."

"Trust me!" snapped the consulting detective. "You know I don't issue warnings lightly. I've never been known to sprinkle my remarks with casual riddles. I mean exactly what I say. Soon the inhabitants of this wretched glittering slum will encounter a dire danger. I don't know the nature of the danger, but the indications are unmistakable. Don't live here. I didn't rescue you so you could waste your life!"

"All...all right, I'll do as you say," said the ace reporter, clearly disbelieving him, clearly thinking that he had become prime fodder for the heinous experiments of the shrink—a disreputable godlike man who was only too glad to perform experiments, any time, anywhere.

"Promise?" asked my friend, his eyes blazing like huge stars.

"P-promise."

"Cross your heart?" he asked, grabbing her shoulders.

"Cross my heart," she said meekly, overcome by the repressed intensity of his voice. She made the appropriate gesture as he released her shoulders.

"Excellent," he said simply. They both were silent for twenty seconds, while she wildly stared at him as if her fate at the claws of the wolfman had been the lesser of two evils. I confess, I could understand how she had arrived at that opinion; I had no conception of what my friend was talking about. "I shall hold you to that promise in the future," he said.

"Sure. It's okay by me," she said. "Well, uh, thanks for saving my life. It's been swell. I've really got to be going now." And without another word, without waiting for us to reply, the ace reporter whirled and disappeared into the fog. His face totally stoic, as if his outburst of emotion had occurred weeks in the past, the consulting detective puffed his cherrywood pipe and stared at the fog until we could no longer hear her footsteps. He had assumed the likeness of a man who had recently taken on a heavy burden.

It had heretofore been my custom to wait patiently until the consulting detective felt the proper time had arrived to explain the unexpected and accurate observations which caused so many, myself included, such consternation. But upon this occasion, his observations were, to my mind, merely unexpected. And, I feared, just a teensy-bit irrational.

"Friend consulting detective?" I said.

"Yes, friend good doctor?"

"Might I inquire . . . ?"

He laughed. "Of course, of course. I realize what you must be thinking. Do not be concerned. At least, do not be concerned for me, but for the wretched creatures in this East End." He gestured at the buildings I could barely discern through the fog. "All will become clear to you in good time, my faithful friend," he added, affectionately putting his hand on my shoulder. "My mind has been preoccupied with this enigmatic neighborhood for many weeks. Whenever I ponder the events I fear to come, I realize that the battle for which I've prepared for eons is nigh. And through it all, friend good doctor, I can depend upon only one thing."

"And what is that?" I asked, my words strangely catching in my throat.

"Why, your friendship," he said cheerfully. "Your friendship, of course. Surely it was obvious."

He turned away from me and began walking the deserted streets. I walked beside him. He said, "I shall explain everything, but as I do so, I think we should stroll through this receptacle for wasted souls. It creates the atmosphere."

And we talked.

However, before I can relate to the reader the words we spoke before the coming of the dawn, I must engage in that rather odious necessity, the expository lump (or the expository limp, as the Big Red Cheese called it during a rare moment of jest in his noteworthy *Treatise on the Godlike Narrative*, perhaps his *magnum opus* with the most *magnum* of all).

Possibly I was in Cleveland on the day it began, but I don't know; I recall only that I've no reason to recall Cleveland. Disregarding such convoluted paradoxes, on that fateful day two powerful beings, acting on an impulse which can be explained only as one of the continual pranks the universe plays on innocent beings, transformed mere man into godlike man, conferring upon him great powers and immortality. (Incidentally, this metamorphosis occurred soon after a disaster of an unspecified nature which wiped out the majority of mere man's numbers, thus accounting for the fact that Godlike Earth does not now house a population of several billion.) It would have been logical to assume that a race with our powers would claim the universe as its home, not one paltry planet. But three beings with a unique vision—the demon, the lawyer, and the fat man—embarked on a quest to grant godlike mankind the mixed curse of depression, in the hopes that depression would give individuals of our race the proper incentive to realize their full potential. In the course of their quest, our three heroes lost their most prized possessions—their fame and glory. This excruciating setback did not deter them; they remained steadfastly devoted to their cause. They encountered the (insane? deluded?) other fat man, who lived in an ivory tower in a field of black orchids and who confided in only two servants. This other fat man claimed responsibility for causing godlike mankind to remain stagnant on Earth, and for providing us with the desire to assume new identities at the expense of our true ones. His motivation was to acquire an ordered environment which left him free to tend to his greenhouse. I must say that our three heroes did not take him seriously; and to this day it has never been satisfactorily proved that the other fat man (who eventually left Earth to explore the universe with his servants) was merely a weird bird or indeed the secret ruler of godlike mankind. To draw this section of the odious necessity to a brief conclusion, it will suffice to say that our three heroes succeeded in depressing their race, but life remained the same. They had achieved their goal but not their desire. Apparently mere man possessed other qualities which his godlike scion should emulate if he was ever to secure his rightful destiny. Our three heroes decided that a revival of sexism (of which I have never approved) was in order.

And upon that rather discordant measure, enter the consulting detective! They enlisted his aid in determining why fully half the race accepted sexism with glee, while the other half regarded it with loathing. This line was *not* drawn at the sexes, with the males for it and the females agan'it. The consulting detective and I traveled to a parallel universe where my friend loved the enticing Clam of Catastrophe, who in the human guise which she preferred was one of the superior women it has been my incredible good fortune to meet from time to time. (Perhaps one day I shall see her again, and the consulting detective and she will resume their aborted affair. It does not seem likely, but as my friend observed at their parting, they have all eternity before them, and anything is possible. I trust this is true.) The consulting detective learned what I'm proud to say I knew all along—that sexism is a degrading perversion of love; and he convinced his employers to explore love rather than to exploit the objects of their affections, which they have been doing since with varying degrees of success. They have not yet learned what mere man instinctively knew, but they expect a revelation at any moment. No doubt when it arrives, it will unexpectedly; and it will make a considerable difference in our lives.

Or it might not.

Their dreams—now, our dreams—may have turned into pathetic delusions, for recent events have presented us with undeniable evidence of a profound alteration in the godlike condition, an alteration decidedly for the worst, of which nothing can convince me bodes good tidings for my narrations to come. The one joy I derive from this grim development is that, happily, it signals the termination of my odious necessity; and I may set forth on my account of an expository lump of a more dramatic nature.

The consulting detective was a godlike man who seldom took exercise for exercise's sake. He looked upon aimless bodily exertion as a waste of energy, and he seldom bestirred himself save where there was some professional object to be served. Then he was absolutely untiring and indefatigable. Save for the occasional use of cocaine he had no vices, and he only turned to the drug as a protest against the monotony of existence when cases were scanty (which was most of the time) and the papers uninteresting (which explains his concern over the ace reporter and her missing touch). This night we had rambled about together, in silence for the most part, as befits two godlike men who know each other intimately, apparently aimlessly; yet he had insisted upon remaining in this unappealing new neighborhood. At first I thought he had been seized by one of his frequent moods of melancholia, and I had resisted the urge to examine his spleen. But now I realized that he had had some definite purpose in mind.

I could not fail to notice that my friend's eyes belied his casual, relaxed demeanor, that he was suppressing a restless excitement, that he seemed to be already taxing his incredible deductive abilities to their utmost, though there was still no client, no case, no emergency. If I had detected the identical symptoms in another individual, I would have declared him to be a victim of nervous energy, of hypertension; but this was the consulting detective, and he was not like other godlike men. As I prepared myself to comment on his superficially contradictory behavior, he surprised me yet again, by answering my question before I could voice it. "Indeed, you know me too well," he said. "Indeed, I am at work, hard at work, though on the surface of things, at least, there appears to be no need."

"Has something occurred of which I'm unaware? Perhaps some article in the papers which I failed to take important note of because it seemed trivial?"

"No. Nothing as simple as that."

"Then tell me. My curiosity isn't my subtlest characteristic."

He took his pipe from his mouth and smiled wryly, as if some dark, secret, yet pleasant memory had beckoned his attention.

"Do you recall our conversation with the lawyer last month, when he informed us that the love of his life, that charming woman Kitty, left him?"

"Humph. Indeed I do. But I attached no importance to the event, for whenever she returns to him, it seems she leaves him immediately afterwards." Upon reflecting the substance of my answer, I confess to a certain degree of cynicism. Perhaps my reader will regard this as understandable, though I do not expect him to condone it, when I remind him that in my previous narrative, I revealed that Kitty was my first, my truest love. Some wounds never heal, not during all eternity.

"And do you also recall that he was inexplicably worried about her—he admitted as much himself—and feared that she may have come to harm because he could receive no word from her? A frustrating and confusing position for a godlike man to find himself in, especially one with his connections."

"Yes. He wanted you to seek her out."

"Exactly. A case made to order for my abilities. Yet I refused."

"I recall being puzzled, and the lawyer was extremely upset. In fact, he gave you some rather explicit advice concerning the best available aperture in which to insert your organs. If you're thinking of taking his advice, I would consider your activities in poor taste."

"My taste would not be put to the great disadvantage as that of my victim, but put your mind to rest on that score. On that fateful day when I get around to performing my masculine duties, it will be in the missionary position and no other. However, after he stalked from our apartment, nearly upsetting my chemical apparatus in the process, I succumbed to a bleeding heart, and requested that the universal op fulfill his request."

"The universal op? Did he not assist the demon, the lawyer, and the fat man on their little, uh, problem concerning the acceptance of sexism before they engaged your services?"

"Yes. He is an extremely competent officer. Were he but gifted with imagination he might rise to great heights in his profession. However, I did aid him to the extent that I suggested he begin his investigation in the East End, and after he had heard my reasoning, he agreed wholeheartedly."

"Why don't you take up the search? Surely with your superior abilities..."

"Friend good doctor, I've made several suggestions since, which the universal op has carried out with his customary competence. The results have been, in some respects, superior to any that I might obtain, doubtless due to the fact that his peculiar talents are best suited to this type of case. I'm ashamed to admit, though, that the most desirable result—that of discovering Kitty's whereabouts—has yet to be obtained. No, friend good doctor, I fear more important matters require my attention."

By this time we had reached the shabby park of the East End. A broken drinking fountain emitted streams of water at irregular intervals. The wind carried a newspaper page down the sidewalk, and the page appeared to slither like a legless spider as it scraped the concrete. Dry clumps of leaves on the ground rustled as a rat, fleeing our presence, rushed under them in search of shelter and protection. A park bench rested at an angle, one of its legs having been broken off and never having been reattached. One tree, much taller than its fellows, rose high toward the sky, the fog causing it to resemble an intelligent beast looming over two helpless, defenseless creatures, namely us. I could not fathom how the inhabitants of the East End, seeking solace from their squalid surroundings, could find it in this shoddy excuse for the beauties and comforts of nature.

"At least I have a grip of the essential perimeters of the case to come," continued the consulting detective. "I shall enumerate them to you, for nothing clears up a case so much as stating it to another person, and I can hardly expect your cooperation if I do not show you the position from which we start. Besides, I have carried this burden alone for far too long, and I find that I must confide in a friend."

He rubbed his chin thoughtfully. "The first indications that something frightening was brewing came to me when we became aware that many godlike men and women, for no apparent reason, desired to create and to live in this slum. Not a single inhabitant can satisfactorily explain its appeal, yet all seem drawn toward it. This time there is no mysterious other fat man manipulating them. There is another cause, the clue to its nature provided by the fact that each of them, regardless of the specific outlook dictated by their identities, has lost faith in the basic benevolence of life. In truth, they've embraced their *lack* of faith with what can be described as only a demonic zeal. As I've said, the East End creates the proper atmosphere.

"I believe that they are suffering from delayed effects of sexism, of depression, and possibly of other phenomena logically developed from the first two. Negativism is perhaps an apt term."

"But is this not what our three friends have desired?" I protested, raising the point I thought most likely others would make.

"I think not. You yourself attempted to treat some of these people. You said they were merely suffering from an overdose of the humors. Need I remind you that your treatments failed? No, something far more sinister is transpiring. This East End is but the most obvious cancerous growth of negativism. What sort of godlike man was the wolfman but a year ago?"

I snorted in a kind of laughter as I thought of him. "Why, he was an amusing little beast, not too forceful, yet direct and engrossing in his way. During the full moon he was content to lounge in the fields and peek at the naked sheep. He uttered his cry after viewing a particularly naughty scene."

"Would you say he was harmless?"

"The shepherd didn't think so. He clothed his flock to discourage the wolfman. However, that sneaky little voyeur found the sheep's garters and black stockings to be the quintessence of erotic fashion. And who knows? Perhaps sheep like to 'do it' in public. Yes, I would say the wolfman was harmless."

"And what is he like now?"

"Well, he's an annoyance, to say the least."

"You've an incredible gift for understatement, friend good doctor. The wolfman is an 'annoyance' to us, but to the animals in the forest he's an executioner. While in his human guise, he is racked with guilt over the animals he has wantonly slain, and he fears for what he might do in the future. (And his fears are entirely justified, in light of recent events.) However, he does nothing about his problem. Although his life is one of misery, he accepts it as his lot. He has no faith. In short, he is negative."

"I seem to recall that you've had similar moods," I said, smiling to myself.

"My melancholia is not unrelieved by bouts with good faith and optimism," replied the consulting detective off-handedly. "The wolfman is but one example of many. Because he cannot cope, his joy has turned into relentless despair. The same applies for those who live here, in this neighborhood."

"But the fat man is of the opinion that these adverse forces—possibly combined with the might of love—will create a leader who will spark a new era for our race. They are incentive."

"Doubtless there were mere men who broke the chains that shackled them, who saw no reason why they couldn't live in the reality of their dreams, who believed they could shape the world to their vision. For such men, there was no gap between ambition and accomplishment. There is no reason not to assume that these incentives will provide us with a similar leader, with a godlike man who will give us the stars."

"Then what is the nature of your complaint?"

"Precisely this: while we await this leader, what of the *common* godlike man? What of those who perceive life as a series of insolvable problems, one after another, with no respite between them? The common godlike man is being slowly ground into the earth, my friend. A tremendous wieght has descended upon him; and he cannot throw it from his shoulders; he cannot exalt under its pressure. The strain is beginning to tell, and I fear that our race will undergo much suffering as we await the key to our destiny, as we race from philosophical point to philosophical point, vainly searching for an answer that may not exist. Friend good doctor, you and I can live under such a strain, for we were built to do so. In fact, we can conceive of no other existence. But, I repeat, what of the common godlike man? What of him?"

"Are you implying that our three friends have been totally wrong? I freely admit that sexism is abhorrent, but . . ."

"I'm implying nothing, for I've not trained myself to answer such questions. However, perhaps they erred in selecting negative traits to add to the mixture in their attempt to rejuvenate our race. Perhaps, perhaps, perhaps; I cannot say because I simply don't know. I can and will say this, however: it is my unshakable belief that the common mere man fared no better than the common godlike man. I believe that the average mere man was fully aware that on the cosmic scale his life was weightless. That he would never fully touch the hearts and minds of others. That regardless of what he did and thought, he would never succeed in obtaining his goals. He lived from day to day, vainly reaching out for intangible objects he could not grasp.

And ultimately, all he had to look forward to was death—the conclusion of his meaningless struggles. What good is faith under such conditions?

"I believe that occasionally there arrived a mere man who felt that the only method of giving his life meaning was to perpetuate the negativism he quite correctly sensed about him. Who felt that he had to strike back, to tear down, to destroy. Who could express himself only in the most primitive fashion. Who killed. That is all his life meant to him: an opportunity to take the lives of others for whatever perverted pleasure he gained."

I must say that I was aghast at the consulting detective's remarks. I had never seen him personify the moral substance of a civilization with such fervor. "And you believe that a similar godlike man will exist here?"

"I believe it. The incident of the wolfman was but an overture. For the first time in our history, we will be faced with murder."

"What about the cigar-smoking frogs?" I inquired.

The consulting detective rolled his eyes toward the sky. "What about the cigar-smoking frogs?" he asked, not attempting to conceal his impatience and disgust.

"They've tried to kill godlike men."

"Oh. Well, that doesn't count."

"Why not? An attempted murder is an attempted murder."

"The frogs are stupid; they never succeed because that dynamic administrator of Africa, the duck, keeps them well under control. No, I was speaking of an intelligent murderer, a godlike man who desires to kill not because he's an atavism, but because murder provides him with a means of establishing his imprint upon the godlike race. I was speaking of a man hopelessly oppressed, whose very existence had become a prison, a man created and fostered by surroundings such as these."

By now we had returned to the streets, and he gestured at the buildings. At the opposite end of the street, a godlike man aimlessly walked about, as did we, and he pretended not to take notice of us.

"Death will be his solution," said my friend. "Death will provide him with meaning."

"I must say, you're expecting the emergence of a monster."

"Exactly. What do you think of my theory?"

"Humph. It is all surmise."

"But at least it covers all the facts, and make no mistake, I was discussing facts. When new facts come to our knowledge which cannot be covered by my theory, it will be time to reconsider it. At present we can do nothing but what we have been doing."

"And what is that?"

"Exploring every street, every alley of the East End. For here, I believe, is the battleground upon which our war shall be waged, where we shall oppose this monster, as you call him, who in turn opposes all that we and our three friends stand for. We've erred in the past, and we must assume the responsibility. When this monster arrives, we will have been in part accountable for his existence. We must err no more. It will be our duty to combat him. I believe that I was born to combat him; that is my destiny."

My friend spoke no more as we continued our distasteful exploration of the East End; and indeed, to my mind, he had spoken more than enough. But though his words had not been free of the emotionalism he normally disdained, I could find no fault with his basic logic, try as I might. For though I've always attempted to perceive the world in an optimistic light, that early morning I was forced to admit that there was a darker side to my character, one of hate and fear, as there is a darker side to all godlike characters. And I could not with certainty proclaim that if my life had been different, if I had not been blessed with the friendship and the trust of the consulting detective, that I would not have metamorphosed into the monster who would slay those who had done him no harm. Indeed, I was seized by a dreadful premonition that my friend's words would prove to be truer than he knew.

And now, with the second and hopefully more dramatic expository lump drawing to a close (an occupational hazard of beginning a narrative *in medias res*, I suppose), it will suffice to add that despite my qualms, despite the ill tidings for the future, my steps were filled with purpose, my spirit with exuberance, and my heart with faith. For it was my destiny to aid my friend regardless of what transpired, in victory or defeat, even if my aid consisted merely of remaining at his side. And I resolved always to do this. For the oppressive fog, the chilly night, and the dimly lit streets were my elements as well. I too had been born to combat the monster. I too was firmly on the path of my destiny.

CHAPTER TWO

1. On the northern fringes of the East End, striding the polluted river between the boundaries of the city and the fields, stood a rusty iron bridge, a bridge whose existence was totally unnecessary, for godlike men could teleport from one bank to the other, and eternal children delighted in swimming the murky waters. There were no roads on either side of the bridge. The ancient structure appeared to be the sole survivor of an age which had passed long ago. Like the river, it could have been cleansed by any godlike man should he have felt the inclination to do so; yet somehow it was indisputably correct that the bridge be rusty, just as it was correct that the river be polluted with trash and foul-smelling chemicals (though no one knew, or cared to know, the source of the contamination).

As the sun rose, its bright rays dissipating the fog and providing the city with a faint gleamer of beauty, the lawyer walked under the bridge on the bank near the expansive fields. He carried his sword cane on his shoulder, as a gentleman might carry his umbrella, or as an exhausted soldier might noncha-lantly carry a primitive weapon in the spirit of the fatigue following a battle, as if he required a weapon through force of habit despite the unlikelihood of further violence. His clothing was, as usual, immaculate, tastefully selected; he wore a black derby, a red vest, a ruffled white shirt, and a black suit. Once observed, it was impossible to imagine him wearing different attire. The lawyer took pleasure in this fact, which is why he never wore different attire (save for those occasions which required no attire at all). His clothing conformed to his conception of his personality: cheerful, with an aura of dark majesty; worldly-wise, with more than a hint of somber philosophy and intelligence.

However, this morning the lawyer felt that the environment, which suggested waste and despair, was more suited to his disposition. For eons his sole goal in life (to which all others had been means to an end) had been to secure the affections of Kitty. Upon those frequent occasions when Kitty preferred to bestow her warmth upon another, his goal had been to repossess her affections, to win her back. Now he was once again without her; and now there was no villainous third party; now there was not even a Kitty to dream of. The lawyer could not accept the possibility that their torrid, eon-spanning affair had reached a conclusion without a resolution. He thought that he believed that even a resolution which cast him from her life forever was preferable to this limbo, but of course this was not the case. She had cast him aside, seemingly forever, countless times. But . . . now there was no Kitty, no hopeless odds to overcome; there was nothing. And so he wandered the area about the unnecessary bridge, gazing across the river toward the eternally dying East End. His eyes, which had once sparkled with the anticipation of experiencing his most private dreams, were now dull, as if all spirit had faded away. His lean, handsome features were slack with the sorrow of depression. The memory of her haunted him, and it seemed that he saw the vision of her reflected in the water, that he caught her scent among the odors of the chemicals, that he sighted her far away, in the city, wandering to a destination he could not conceive.

His only hope was that he would hear the gunsel (righthand man of the fat man) whistle, signaling to him that the universal op had word. He was convinced that the consulting detective could have found her by this time, even if she had chosen to flee to a parallel universe; but at the moment the lawyer was forced to depend upon and accept the second string.

The lawyer sighed. His mind was so occupied with dreams of Kitty that he did not note the object falling from the bridge into the polluted river. He did not hear the splash. For several moments the lawyer stared at a tin can bobbing in the current, rushing toward the ocean. During those moments it seemed that all existence revolved about that insignificant tin can. The lawyer identified with it. This morning he could identify with anything, providing that it had seen better days. In this respect, the lawyer was not hard to please.

Nor was he hard to surprise. He had seen many stranger sights than the dirty hand—draped with vines, ascending from the water like a wisp of smoke from an eerie submarine fire— but his mind had dwelt upon the mundane often lately, and consequently he was unprepared for the norm. The hand grasped the tin can and crushed it, with the unhurried execution of a man casually crushing trapped cockroaches. The lawyer deliberated over the possible reactions expressing surprise (he could never be sure when godlike eyes were upon him) before selecting the one which seemed most applicable to the situation: his lower jaw dropped and his eyes bulged, as if a tremendously heavy anvil had fallen from the sky and painlessly landed on his foot.

The hand tossed the tin can away with an admirable air of self-assurance. Faster than the eye could follow, the hand disappeared under the water. A minor turbulence marred the river's steady flow, and when the hand reappeared, it was clean and free of vines. The lawyer was not so surprised to see that the hand was attached to an arm; nor was he surprised that the arm's owner was in the process of departing from the river. The arm was clothed in a loud yellow sleeve. Eventually it was painfully apparent to the discerning eye that the loud yellow sleeve was part of a loud yellow suit.

The lawyer conjured a pair of wire-rimmed sunglasses, which he carefully designed to give himself the proper aristocratic air. "There. Now I can look at you."

And what he saw was the godlike man known, understandably enough, as the man in the yellow suit. The lawyer thought the title charitable. The godlike man standing on the water, holding his arm in the air as if he was asking the lawyer permission to go to the bathroom, should have been known as the obnoxious man in the extremely loud yellow suit. But questions of fashion aside, the newcomer was a dashing figure. His dark complexion complimented his brown eyes. His brown hair was gray at the temples. He was but a few centimeters taller than the lawyer, though his shoulders were much broader and his torso wider. His mouth, which was slightly effeminate, curved itself into an enigmatic smile which accentuated his narrow, square chin and his high cheekbones. A scrawny vine was draped over his shoe. The man in the yellow suit lowered his arm and bowed, as if he was attempting to impress a beautiful woman with his chivalry and grace. He said, "Now that I'm no longer submerged, I can look at you too. Quite a coincidence, don't you agree?" He walked across the water and onto the bank.

As he had the misfortune to be standing downwind, the lawyer deadened his sense of smell. "Actually, I don't care what it is. Where did you come from?"

The man in the yellow suit raised his eyebrows and pointed at the bridge without looking at it. "From over there."

"I know I'm going to regret asking this, but what were you doing there?"

"Committing suicide."

The lawyer pursed his lips and nodded thoughtfully. "Okay, I'll play your silly game. Why were you committing suicide?"

"Haven't you heard? There's no point in living. Everybody's talking about it. It's the latest rage. So I woke up early this morning, thinking that since life was useless, there was no point in going on. Since I had always wanted to drown—to reunite myself with the source of life—I could see no good reason why not." He extended his arms as if he had brilliantly executed a speech on the stage. "And so—here I am!"

"Some inner sixth sense is compelling me to tell you that as a suicide, you're an utter failure."

The man in the yellow suit closed his eyes and frowned as if the lawyer's words had shattered the framework of his life. Sighing, he wiped the water from his face. "Yes. I admit it."

"Then why don't you return to the river and finish the job? I want to be alone."

"You've the appearance of someone who wants to be alone." He knotted his brow, rubbed his chin, and frowned as if he was grappling with a complicated paradox. "Getting any?"

"Let me put it delicately: those occasions which require no attire at all have reached the epitome of infrequency."

"Then you're always alone."

"You could say that. The love of my life has vanished and no one can find her."

"How interesting. I've the opposite problem myself."

"Oh?"

"The woman with a black veil has been pursuing my enticing bod for eons. I think she thrives on rejection."

The lawyer nodded again. "This woman and I have a lot in common. There's a lot of rejection to thrive on. Is her pursuit the cause of your, ah, attempted suicide?"

"Not a chance. I wanted to die for the same reason I decided to live: because I felt like it. A whim, you might say. I do everything because of whims. I've rejected her for so long because that whim has lasted longer than most, that's all."

The lawyer took several steps from the man in the yellow suit, who was rapidly becoming an individual he did not want to stand near. "Doesn't that attitude cause you to be inconsistent?"

"Friend lawyer, true consistency is found only in your social life."

"That wasn't nice." Tiring of the conversation, the lawyer turned on his heel, twirled his sword cane, and began to walk away. When he allowed his sense of smell to function again, the wind carried a particularly potent whiff of chemicals to his sensitive nostrils, and he grimaced in disgust. Yet he too did not want to restore the river to its former purity, much as he yearned for it. His adept mind was beginning to bring its vast resources to bear upon that intriguing contradiction when a treacherous sledgehammer blow struck him on the back, sending him plummeting toward a huge mud puddle. The lawyer was unaware of his impending fate, however, for simultaneous with the blow, a galvanized steel bucket descended upon his head, severely diminishing the range of his vision.

This unexpected chain of events so befuddled the lawyer that he did not send the bucket to the anti-matter universe until he had wallowed for several seconds in the mud. An expression of great weariness passed over his features as he sat up, looked at the man in the yellow suit, and said in a defeated voice, "Now what did you do that for?"

"Just a whim."

"What a peculiar person," said the lawyer aloud to himself.

"You're not angry, are you?" said the man in the yellow suit, grasping the lawyer's hand and pulling him to a standing position.

"I most certainly am," said the lawyer as he sent the filth on his attire to the anti-matter universe, becoming once again quite immaculate. "I'm contemplating the most horrible revenge imaginable."

The man in the yellow suit raised his left eyebrow.

"I'm going to heartlessly thrust you into an environment which no godlike man can cope with," continued the lawyer. "Soon you'll fear for what little sanity you've remaining. Random event will follow random event. To the uninitiated, the conversation will seem like a string of *non sequiturs*. Oh, I'm going to thrust you into the hothouse, all right. It will be the perfect opportunity to see if your whims are made of strong stuff."

"If you're talking about the East End, I've already been there. I adjusted with no difficulty."

The lawyer grinned. "I don't doubt that. No, my revenge will be much more despicable. Clean yourself. I'm going to introduce you to my friends."

2.　*An account from the good doctor's notebooks:*

The demon's castle lies like the boss of a shield in the fields near the golden city. I could spend many pages describing the interior of that magnificent structure, for every vast room possesses a distinct indentity, and the castle itself reeks of an hypnotic air of evil which appeals to me despite my better nature. Indeed, were I to describe in detail the castle, my verbiage would slow my narrative to the pace of an inflicted snail. And since no author of sea stories worthy of attention has allowed himself such indulgences, I shall follow this example, and confine my description to the room of the castle which, upon first glance, seems utterly out of character—the locker room. However, after I had been many hours in the company of the demon and the fat man, I realized that the presence of a locker room was singularly logical, to say the least.

Unlike more functional locker rooms, it does not lead to a football field or a baseball diamond. The only exit leads upstairs, and the locker room itself resides under the moat. However, the water rapidly spurting out of the showers invigorates these tired immortal muscles with zest, and the steambath's effectiveness is unparalleled in the history of our race. The steel lockers contain many sneakers, gym shorts, and G-strings, none of which I have ever had an occasion to model. (The fat man, however, wears such an outfit when he exercises by performing a series of deep knee-bends.) The long wooden benches are uncomfortable until one grows used to the positively unique pleasure of "roughing it." It is no wonder that sexism enjoyed such a vogue in the past, if it mainly consisted of personifying a pioneer spirit by sitting on benches and discussing objects (of all kinds) close to the heart. Often I have almost succumbed to the temptation of relating incidents from my amorous past, but again, that is not germane to my tale. In conclusion, I must add that the floors are green tile, that the lower two meters of the walls are painted dark gray, and the remainder of the walls and the ceiling are light gray. If not the proper atmosphere in which to discuss the destiny of a race, it is the one I have become accustomed to.

Lest the reader think I am too easily pleased, the locker room has one unfortunate drawback, and that is that it is not conducive to relaxment after spending a long night awake. I sat on a bench as if I had been nailed there, my arms straight and my palms on my knees. As I listened to the consulting detective, smoking his pipe and leaning against the wall like a shadowy figure in a dream, recite his deductions concerning the true import of the East End in words nearly identical to those I have already related in this chronicle, I kept my eyes open with the utmost difficulty. Not only was I tired, but listening to the same pedantic metaphysical reasoning for the second time from my friend, normally a lively conversationist, bored me out of my skull.

The fat man nodded gravely at each conclusion my friend reached. His girth was so vast, his motions so ponderous, that even his lightest, most frivolous gestures were grave. He resembled a massive toadstool as he sat on the bench; the poor wood creaked every time he twitched a gigantic buttock. Occasionally he ran a meaty palm over his balding head; often he pursed his lips, the slightly pink skin resembling fungi on an albino oak. As grotesque as he was to look at, his amoral personality and his ability to find humor in the most pedestrian of subjects made me anticipate his presence. This morning he wore his favorite gym shorts and sneakers. Doubtless his white socks were reeling under the pungent odor of his feet. His white T-shirt clung tightly to his fluctuating torso.

At first glance the demon did not appear to be listening to the consulting detective. He was masquerading underneath a stoic facade, even as did my friend, when in reality he was tingling with excitement. My friend's words discussed a situation close to the demon's heart. For the demon was a shallow personification of evil. His spirit, despite his protestations to the contrary, was not malign. Like an eternal child, he was fascinated with the *appearance* of evil, with its physical manifestations, especially if they were satanic in origin. In days past, he had resembled an actual demon from the place of torment itself; he had been fully five meters tall, with four nostrils, a beak, and a penis which could put that of many a mastodon to shame. Now he was nearly as human as the rest of us, with a penis of a relatively normal size which was always emphasized by his tight (and I do mean *tight*) trousers. His green clothing was invariably a shade darker than his green complexion. His pointed ears, his red eyes, his white eyebrows, and his leering smile—all were indicative of his fascination with evil.

He concealed his excitement at the substance of the consulting detective's words by engaging himself in activity. At first he created water for the black orchids in pots on the sole shelf in the locker room. Then he opened a closet door and dragged forth a tub of lemon cookies. He halted the tub before a simulacrum of a man which was more than a mere duplicate; although it could not think, move, or age, although it had never been alive and never could be, its interior performed many of the functions of a live godlike body, and resembled it in many other ways. Most importantly, its bloodstream was warm, and the blood rushed through the simulacrum as if it was in a perpetual state of exertion. The simulacrum was not in the locker room for decorative purposes, or to display the demon's ingenuity, but to provide an appropriate home for the demon's pet—a tapeworm.

As soon as the consulting detective had concluded his discourse, the tapeworm stuck its head out of the simulacrum's anus and said in what possibly is the most offensive, grating voice I have ever heard, "Where's my lemon cookie?"

The demon grinned as if he had unleashed some terrible monster upon the unsuspecting world, and indeed, so great was my loathing for his pet that I considered it nothing less. The demon reached into the tub and tossed a lemon cookie to the tapeworm whose mouth (?) caught it with a sucking motion, like that of a vacuum cleaner. Suddenly the cookie disappeared into the tapeworm, creating a tremendous bulge like that in a snake who had just swallowed its meal. The tapeworm said, "Gee, thanks," and then crept into the anus, the bulge stretching the elastic sphincter muscles until they almost lost their natural tension. I remember thinking, *That's all we need: a simulacrum with the runs.*

Making a mental note to sell the idea to the Big Red Cheese the next time he needed a plot for a story, I asked the demon, "And what do you think of my friend's deductions?"

"I hope he's telling the truth. This foul villain sounds interesting."

"You wouldn't think so if you happened to be one of his victims," said the consulting detective.

The fat man laughed, the ripples of his stomach being positively seismic. "My dear detective, I think you are taking your conclusions much too seriously. As the good doctor so graciously pointed out, it is all conjecture, and until something happens, it is nothing more."

"Possibly," said the consulting detective simply. I could tell that he regretted informing the demon and the fat man of the situation, yet I knew, as he knew, that he could not have refrained in good conscience. "But whether or not you believe me is immaterial. The demon's answer is conclusive proof, despite its flipness, that he accepts the possibility of what I say. I submit: that should be enough to force you to suggest certain, ah, precautionary steps."

The fat man smiled, the ends of his mouth fairly disappearing under the blubbery weight of his cheeks. "I think you have already refuted any argument I could make to the contrary, sir. I congratulate you."

The consulting detective bowed with what I can only describe as eloquence; an abiding respect existed between him and the fat man, the kind of respect that exists between equal minds, regardless of the direction of their creative energies.

"I do agree there's truth in what you say," said the demon, forcing a crumbling lemon cookie into the simulacrum's mouth, "but as to how much truth..." His task completed, his point seemingly made, the demon shrugged.

It was painfully apparent by the somnambulent manner in

which he puffed at his pipe, by the way his eyes casually inspected the smoke drifting about his face as if it concealed the solution to some significant riddle, that the consulting detective was disappointed in the lackluster greeting these vaunted minds had made toward his theory. No less than I. However, it must be said in the demon's and the fat man's defense that my friend's conclusions were totally alien to the accepted thinking of eons, and that to some extent it was to be expected that his thoughts be saluted with tolerant amusement, which is how godlike mankind once saluted a certain quest for depression. Successful revolutionaries always become the establishment eventually; it is a sad thing. The social realism of my explanation aside, I began to fear for the boredom quotient of this section of my memoirs, and was considering editing it out entirely, when I was saved by the unexpected entrance of the lawyer and the man in the yellow suit.

Without so much as a perfunctory nod, the lawyer marched until he stood but a meter in front of the consulting detective. "I've an overwhelming urge to tell you that I think you bear a startling resemblance to pig innards!"

For a terrible moment I shuddered as my friend's eyes glared until I was afraid their red color would match that of the demon's; for that moment he hovered over a landing site of incredible violence, and I steeled myself, awaiting him to answer the lawyer with a verbal attack unparalleled in the history of our race. He could have done it too. Instead, he controlled himself. I realized (as did the lawyer, who stared at his softening, glistening eyes) that his anger did not stem from the lawyer's unwarranted attack, but rather from a sincere feeling of guilt that he was unable to take up the chase. After all, it was almost unthinkable that when the game was afoot, the consulting detective was at home, nursing a sore toe or something else equally mundane. And what passed between the consulting detective and the lawyer was a bond as great as the mutual respect between him and the fat man; yet this bond was one of sadness, of sympathy. The lawyer's anger evaporated, and he turned away, saying meekly, "Forgive me. It was just a whim, that's all.".

The man in the yellow suit smiled, as if the lawyer's words were of substance, though for the life of me I could not guess why. The fat man's face was stoic; I was of the impression that he did not care to reveal his feelings, assuming that he had feelings on the matter in the first place. And the demon, who normally did not pass up an opportunity to rib his diminutive friend, stared at him with sadness; and I realized that he too shared his friend's pain, for he had been one of the many to "steal" Kitty from the lawyer in the past.

"I'm sorry," said the lawyer, pretending to inspect the growth of the black orchid. "It's just that I don't know what to do with myself. I feel like I'm half a man."

"Then take heart," said the fat man. "You're still twice the man Kitty is."

"Two times zero is zero," said the demon, smiling. The lawyer wrinkled his nose like an offended cat; and the man in the yellow suit silently clapped his hands.

"That's not fair!" exclaimed the lawyer. "I'm emotionally stricken! I'm down; I'm really down! How can you say you're my friends, when you know I'm down?"

"When I know a man's down, I have a whim to kick him," said the man in the yellow suit.

"My word!" I exclaimed. "Why?" For I was never particularly adept at riddles or cryptic sayings.

"Because then he has a chance to rise above us," said the consulting detective, who was a student of such riddles for some reason.

The lawyer stared at the ceiling as if he expected a new arrival descending from above to help him. "That doesn't make any sense. I'm not prepared to cope with this."

"You were correct," said the man in the yellow suit. "This environment is frightening. However, I'm fitting right in."

"Congrats," said the lawyer. He turned toward the consulting detective. "I must explain myself. It's not that I don't like the universal op. It's just that . . . that . . ." He faltered; he could not find the proper words.

"It's just what?" asked someone in a muffled voice.

We turned as one toward the doorway, and we saw the godlike man known as the universal op.

Upon inspecting this gentleman, it was not difficult to determine why the lawyer felt short-changed that the universal op was searching for Kitty, and not the consulting detective. The public, not unnaturally, goes upon the principle that he who would aid others must himself be whole, and looks askance at the deductive powers of the man whose own face is beyond the reach of his persona. For the universal op was truly faceless. He possessed no mouth, no nose, no eyes, no cheeks, and only the bare outline of ears. His was a smooth mug, to say the least, and there was not even a wrinkle on his forehead.

There was nothing else exceptional about him. He had short black hair. He wore a plain blue suit. He possessed a physical strength greater than the average, and he moved quickly and gracefully, yet these advantages were offset by the fact that he chose to inhabit an eternally forty-year-old body with a soft gut—an extra two decimeters on his waistline. The universal op, indeed, seemed to carry age and the weariness of age with him. If ever there was a godlike man ripe for the East End, it was he. And yet he did not choose to live there; because as long as he worked, or there existed the possibility of work, he had a reason for living. The personal cost of that work—the toll on his spirit—made no difference to him, for he also carried the air of a godlike man who had lost all of true importance. He did not inspire confidence, that is true, because he was an individual who asked for nothing and got it. The lawyer required appearances to see him through his ordeal, appearances the universal op was not prepared to give.

"Have you found her?" demanded the lawyer in a voice which had become nearly as grating as the tapeworm's.

The universal op shook his head. He turned his blank face toward the consulting detective. One was aware of his regret and defeat by his slumped shoulders, his languid economical movements, and the tone of his muffled voice, which seemed to originate in a dreamworld near our own. "I've stirred things up all over that ghetto. I stayed up the night checking out my last leads. The gunsel's watching a few people I talked to, just to see if they were lying, but we don't expect nothing. Got any new ideas? Cause I sure don't."

"I've none," said the consulting detective after a brief pause. "There's nothing else we can do."

"Except wait," said the universal op. "Which amounts to the same thing."

"What?" exclaimed the lawyer. "I can't believe you fools are going to give up, for no good reason! Why, it goes against everything you've ever stood for!"

"Whatever that is," said the universal op.

If the lawyer had heard, he gave no indication. "It just

occurred to me—the true, legitimate reason why you're giving up. I think you two are shams, that as detectives you're utter flops. I've been a regular zany to entrust Kitty's welfare to you. I'm doubtless a much better shamus than the two of you put together."

An astounding retort came to my mind; I opened my mouth to deliver it, and thus seal my position as one of the great wits of our race. But the consulting detective halted me with a gesture, thus once again consigning me to oblivion. (I would record the retort here, so that all would know that it would have been immortal if it had had the opportunity to live; but it seems that it has slipped my memory. Should it come to me, I shall not hesitate to add it to this chronicle. Doing so would do much to enrich verisimilitude, which a great number of godlike narratives have been lacking of late.) My friend said to the lawyer, "Those are grievous charges you bring against us. I'm sure that the universal op's feelings are as wounded as mine."

The universal op shrugged. "Who gives a shit?" he inquired. A colorful chap, in his own way.

"I'm prepared to disprove your charges," said the consulting detective. "A few moments ago, in an introspective mood which I assume was accidental (for it made you careless), you mentioned that recently you didn't know what to do with yourself. I'm prepared to prove that not only do you know what to do with yourself, but also that you've been doing it, whenever the opportunity presents itself." With disarming intensity, he smiled. "How do you relate to those fruits, you inimical person you?" My friend never was good at street language, but at least he was improving.

"Ha!" exclaimed the lawyer gleefully, as if he had been patiently waiting for eons to utter that single syllable in an appropriately melodramatic situation. He stepped backwards into the tub, overturning it and himself. Sitting on the floor, he said, "Try it if you dare!"

The consulting detective shrugged. He raised his eyebrows. To the others he appeared characteristically devoid of emotion, but I could tell that he was struggling heroically not to smile. "Every night you arrive at your room in the castle, and you are drained, spent. But most of all, you are alone and in need of comfort. And the one person who can comfort you under these adverse circumstances is—yourself." He paused, and then spoke not to the lawyer, but to the assemblage who by this time had guessed the substance of his words and were suppressing their laughter. "In a true test of my deductive abilities, I proclaim, here and now, for all to hear, that this worthy gentleman sitting on the floor has spent many pleasurable hours . . . twanging the wire." He spun about and faced the pale lawyer. "Admit it, you degraded individual. In the privacy of your bedroom, armed with but a volunteer hankie, you fondle your one-eared elephant!"

The lawyer stood slowly up, fixed his large blue eyes on us with a strange wild stare, and then pitched forward on his face among the lemon cookies which strewed the floor, in a dead faint.

The fat man threw back his head and roared, his stomach threatening to split like the earth during a quake. The man in the yellow suit and the demon too were weak with laughter. Even the universal op, I believed, was chortling beneath his blank face.

"Goodness," I whispered. "How did you arrive at such an amazing conclusion?"

"A lucky guess," the consulting detective whispered in return, so that the others could not hear. "It just seemed probable."

The demon snapped his fingers and the tub righted itself; the lemon cookies floated into the tub. Now that none of the precious snacks of that slimy invertebrate could be damaged, the demon condensed the space between the water molecules in the air and directed them with a cruel celerity at the lawyer's head. Sputtering and cursing, the lawyer shook his head and sat up. After drying himself, he again stared at the consulting detective from his vantage point on the floor; he stammered, "How did you know? How could I have possibly given myself away?"

"Ahem, er, ah, well, scientific deduction is, ah, easy when you know how. In your instance it was simplicity itself. In fact, now that I've had an opportunity to ponder the matter, I confess surprise that you had, uh, shall we say, covered your tracks so ineffectively."

"Tell me, man," said the lawyer. "If at all possible, I must avoid this embarrassment in the future."

"Yes. I can sympathize. Well! Your undoing was caused by what to the untrained eye is insignificant. Yet to an individual such as I, who has devoted a good portion of his immortal span to observing the peculiarities of social realism, the giveaway was obvious. One of the characteristics of the habitual masturbator is the strengthening, tightening, and overall disproportionate growth of the *pronator quadratus*, a small quadrangular muscle situated at the distal end of the forearm beneath the tendons of the *flexor digitorum profundus* and the *flexor pollicis longus*. Friend lawyer, the *pronator quadratus* of your left wrist illustrates such an unnatural growth. Should you continue to indulge in sexual self-gratification, I would recommend that you become a switch-hitter." The consulting detective looked at me, lifted his shoulders slightly, raised his eyebrows, and presented me with a confused expression for the merest trace of an instant; his gesticulation eloquently inquired, "Do you think they bought that?"

The lawyer certainly did. Standing, he quizzically inspected his left wrist. The consulting detective's answer had given him the raw material for a host of questions, questions which he fervently desired to voice, refraining from doing so in the interest of remaining in blissful ignorance. I could not help but notice that halfway through my friend's explanation, the demon ceased chuckling and covered his left wrist with the fingers of his right hand; subsequent chuckles were forced. The smile of the man in the yellow suit suddenly resembled a decal ironed on his face. The fat man glanced several times at his massive lap, where rested *both* his hands.

The consulting detective placed a palm on the lawyer's shoulder. "Don't look so dejected, my friend. I was only having a bit of sport at your expense. Masturbation is nothing to be ashamed of." His eyes glowed, and a wry smile came to his face. "Truth be known, there are infrequent occasions, perhaps once every hundred years, when the urge nigh overwhelms me, and I spend a few pleasant minutes roaming with my midnight rambler."

"You do?" asked the lawyer, unable to conceal his joy at having found a kindred soul.

"Yes. And so does the good doctor."

I began, "Well, that is to say, I..." but then I decided that silence was my best recourse.

"And so do these fine gentlemen—even, I wager, the universal op," continued the consulting detective. "There are times when they discover that they must go it alone, and they do not impress me as souls who will be hampered by conventional morality when there's a little pleasure to be gained. Isn't that correct, gentlemen?"

For several moments no one answered, and all knew that the silence was an affirmation of his thesis. Finally, drawing himself to his full height, the man in the yellow suit said bravely, "Yes, but isn't that what life's all about?"

His logic escaped me. "Eh?" I inquired in a stunned voice.

"Beating off!" he answered. "Both figuratively and metaphorically speaking. How can we be ashamed of masturbating, and how can women, when for all our struggles, for all our hopes and goals, for all the love and hate we sow, in the end it may be only so much sperm on the wall?"

The lawyer nodded thoughtfully. "You know, I never looked at it that way. Hey, guys, he could be right."

"If life is best represented as sperm on the wall, then you're dried up," I said. "From previous dealings, my friend and I know you've no ideals, no interior logic. No wonder your life seems useless and wasted, for without ideals it's impossible for a godlike man to live rewardingly, to, uh, fertilize the lives of others." I smiled, quite pleased with myself, and I looked about at my friends while awaiting for them to express their heartfelt approval.

"Don't mind him," said the consulting detective, tilting his head in my direction. "Sometimes he gets carried away." He turned to the lawyer. "I fear that I must call a halt to this buffoonery, friend lawyer, and finally tell you why I've thus far refused to search for Kitty. In fact, should I prove to be correct, her disappearance should assume a position of relative unimportance to all but you. Friend universal op, you should pay close attention also, for I believe that you too shall play an important role in the events to come." And he proceeded to elucidate in great detail his theory about the monster he would challenge in the East End. If the reader found himself bored, his attention wandering and his emotions yearning for action, while perusing my narrative wherein I delivered my expository lump, then I cannot sympathize. For he did not have to listen (or more precisely, read) the same words *three* times, unless his attention span and memory are short. (Should that be the case, there are many narratives woven with considerably less skill and less respect for the reader's intelligence than my humble offering. In particular I recommend the Big Red Cheese's *Polk Salad Days Are Here Again*.)

The man in the yellow suit appeared to be contemplating the consulting detective's words as objectively as he could, which was not very. As for the universal op—who can say? If he ever had any true emotion, an ability to listen to a hair-raising theory as if it were other than a laundry list, then he had lost it long ago; or he had thrust it into a hidden chamber in his heart where it could not affect him or his world. If I had sincerely, with great feeling, told him that I wished him happiness, he would have been confused; for happiness and sadness were not concepts in his world. The usiversal op merely *is*, and as long as he *is*, then that is enough for him.

As usual, the lawyer's emotions were quite plain. At the conclusion of the consulting detective's discourse, the lawyer's shaky legs carried him to the bench opposite that of the fat man. His sword cane resting beside him, he placed his hands on his knees and looked down at the floor. He said weakly, "What if this person you speak of has done away with Kitty?"

"Have no fear on that score," said the consulting detective briskly. "If my future foe had slain Kitty, he would be proud; he would glorify in the fact. He would want us to know all his horrible deeds and he would dare us to capture him, knowing that his freedom to commit similar deeds in the future would be torturous for us. No, have no fear, my friend. Wherever Kitty is, she is physically well."

The lawyer, who had received very little comforting news during the past few weeks, seemed to be somewhat reassured. However, that assurance was not fated to last long, for the man in the yellow suit said, "You've made an erroneous assumption."

The consulting detective whirled and fairly shouted, "Explain yourself! How can you, having devoted your life to the pursuit of an idiosyncratic vacuum, hope to add something of import?"

"Don't be touchy, and hear me out," he said with a dignity I would not have expected of him. He realized the seriousness of the situation and had chosen to act accordingly.

Quite admirably, my friend readily admitted that he had been wrong to make such an unwarranted outburst. Explaining that he was under something of a strain, he apologized profusely and added that he could not afford to disregard any opinion from an intelligent individual.

The man in the yellow suit said, "This man might be extraordinary, your antithesis, as you claim. However, what if he is of the common herd? What if he is but an average godlike man who suddenly has the urge to draw attention to himself, and then who drifts back into the crowd, until the urge overwhelms him again? What if he is not a monster *per se*, but a downtrodden individual who has taken a wrong step and cannot find his way back to the proper path? A common man who, like myself, finds himself outside the mainstream of society? There is a bond between this man and me.

"But society has always accepted me on my own terms, whatever my terms at the moment happen to be. What if this man lacks the talent and charisma to be accepted? What if he's hated godlike mankind for eons? Then two things are obvious. He is not the antithesis of you, but of me. And secondly, he will be unpredictable, more dangerous than you've ever suspected."

"Are you implying that this common monster has slain Kitty and simply not called attention to the fact?" asked the lawyer.

The man in the yellow suit did not reply.

"It is possible," said the consulting detective. "Friend lawyer, I owe you an apology. I never considered that. Damn! How foolish of me! If I continue to think in such a muddled fashion, I have lost—we all have lost—before the game begins." He looked at the man in the yellow suit, frankly respecting and reassessing him in a new light. "My friend—if I may call you my friend—you've taught me a lesson today. I assumed that my foe would be as logical in his twisted way as I, and you've shown me that I've ignored the logic of illogic. When the game begins in earnest, I would consider it a great honor if you assisted me."

"I will," said the man in the yellow suit.

"You're cordially invited to remain with us in the castle," said the demon. "You're interesting, and I suspect there are bonds between us as well."

"A magnificent suggestion!" said the fat man, slapping his hand on his thigh; the sound was like a thunderclap. "Should life be but a spurt of sperm, you might find yourself sperm on the ceiling!"

"I will stay. The notion appeals to me."

"Excellent," said the demon. "And now, if you good people will excuse me, I've an important rendezvous." He walked straight out of the locker room, as if we did not exist. He seemed unusually anxious during those last moments with us, but my mind, at least, was mulling over other, darker matters; so I took little notice of his uncharacteristic affectations.

"You will find that there are many pleasures here," said the fat man. He pushed a silver button on the locker behind him. Then he looked at me. "Friend good doctor, what of you? Will you remain with us for a spell?"

"I don't know. It depends on ..."

The consulting detective walked past me, past the simulacrum, and to the black orchids on the shelf. He plucked an orchid, looking down at the abyss of black. It was yet another new phase of his character to me, for I had never before seen him show any keen interest in natural objects.

"What a lovely thing a black orchid is!" he said, leaning his back against the wall. "There is nothing in which deduction is so necessary as in the mysteries of life itself. Philosophy can be built up as an exact science by the reasoner. Yet, there are aspects of life which the reasoner cannot hope to explore, and one such aspect is death. Our highest assurance of peace in death seems to me to rest in black orchids. All other things—violence, age, fatigue—are really necessary for death in the first instance. But this black orchid is an extra. Its smell and its color are a promise of peace in death, not a condition of it. It is only goodness which gives extras, and so I say that we have much to comfort us in black orchids."

For several minutes we silently gazed at the consulting detective. The universal op, normally untouched by such thoughts, was as affected as we, and he sat beside the lawyer on the bench with a weariness that made me pity that noble, poor faceless man. I wondered: if he was to die in the days to come, would he acquire his face? Would he realize that it was inside him all along, residing in his spirit, waiting for the moment during which he would uncover it? The consulting detective had fallen into a reverie, with the pedals of the orchid between his fingers. The reverie was not broken until the beautiful woman summoned by the fat man entered.

I write that she was beautiful though I cannot be sure with absolute finality. She wore a nearly transparent green gown that presented me with an utterly enticing view of her wonderful breasts, each equipped with a nipple resembling a huge vanilla drop, and of her dark pubic hair that loomed like a thicket in the realms of my oral fantasies. She carried herself with dignity, shamelessly proud of the effect she was having upon us depraved gentlemen. She certainly had enough alluring qualities to be called beautiful, but again, I cannot be sure. For as she walked to the beaming fat man, I could not fail to notice that she wore a paper bag over her head. Two slits for her eyes had been carefully cut from the bag, but that was all I could see of her face, and I could not summon enough presence of mind to peer through the bag. Perhaps I was too afraid of being disappointed.

"Enough talk of death," said the fat man as she sat on his lap, her arms entwining about his neck like pale milky snakes. "It is time for an affirmation of life. It is time for love."

Despite his sorrow, the lawyer smiled at the fat man's attitude, which was simultaneously repulsive and childishly endearing. The man in the yellow suit appeared to be wondering, at last, exactly what he had gotten himself into.

"I don't need love nearly as much as I need z's," said the universal op. "I think I'll be going."

"Uh, I would like to echo those sentiments," I said.

"If you're waiting for me," said the consulting detective, "you're falling behind."

And so we left them. At our apartment, I could not sleep for several hours, as much as I required it. The consulting detective injected cocaine, and that disturbed me, I suppose. But his addiction did not disturb me to the degree as did the expository lump. Though I had been bored with it, it would not leave my thoughts, and when I finally did sleep, I feared for what I might learn upon awakening.

3. The demon stood in the fields near his castle. He squinted when he looked at the hazy yellow sun hanging in the sky like a fragile bulb; the harsh light forced him to lower his eyes. For a moment he watched the breeze fan the yellow-green grass, and he sniffed when the pollen began to irritate an insignificant but inconvenient allergy he had never been able to rid himself of, despite all his vast powers. He closed his eyes, and felt himself succumbing to the weight of a spell. His experiments in the nature of love had led to a result which once he would have considered impossible, utterly beyond the range of probability; yet as he stood there, feeling like an outsider from his own home and all that he had known, he could not deny the effectiveness of that spell, nor could he deny the exquisite delight of his captivity.

He became weary. He sighed, staring at his green hands, a small part of him hoping they had the power to grasp the invisible shackles bonding his spirit. That small part of him was convinced that were it not for the spell, his spirit would be unconquerable, unquenchable, that there lay within him the ability to achieve things that would pale his previous, not inconsiderable accomplishments. The demon wished that small part of him would grow, like an appealing fungus, and saturate his spirit, so that he once again might be free. However, as he stood there, basking in the tenuous heat of the early morning sun and hearing the breeze rustle the grass like tender fingers caressing his white hair, he also wanted to control his rebellious nature; he did not want emotional freedom, for he would have found it useless; his imaginary achievements were meaningless in the context of this spell. Despite his qualms, despite his anxieties, he felt a peace within that could be compared to the peace he experienced in the bed of a woman after he spent his passion.

The demon was confused. He had never spent his passion upon the weaver of the spell. So why should anticipatory qualms gently obtain the peace when, theoretically, only direct action, manful dominance, and a probing member could fill the bill? Something was amiss—at least, the demon tried to convince himself something was amiss. Yet he could not rid himself of the notion that although the universe might be in a sorry state, as the consulting detective implied, things were proper and orderly and indisputably correct when it came to the universe of his heart.

The demon shrugged. There was no help for it. Even if there was help for it, he would have denied it.

He teleported himself from the dawn to the night of Africa.

The moon did not hang in the sky like the flimsy sun; it had the appearance of an eternal object, if not the reality. It never moved, had no phases, no periods of invisibility; it was forever. The demon felt its cold light wash over him and fill his heart; though the peace had not left him, he felt like a totally different entity in the jungle; he felt that all the old elements of his body and personality had rearranged themselves in a small but vastly consequential way. A portion of his former demonic zeal emerged from behind a previously unnoticed barrier, and he realized with a smidgen of incredulity (he was too preoccupied to experience more than a smidgen) that he was actually relishing the forthcoming encounter with the uncertainties of love. He imagined, as he had imagined in the past, that this encounter might be memorable. After all, there was always the distinct possibility that his activities might proceed upon a definitely masculine line; the weaver of the spell might melt in his arms, succumb to nameless passions manifesting themselves somewhere in the vicinity of her groin, and yield herself to his roaming hands, his puckering lips, and his puckish staff of life. She was but a godlike woman, with relatively normal needs and desires (so far as he could discern); it was a matter of time, and matters of time never disturbed him.

But what did disturb the demon was the undeniable fact that his fantasies and passions were right and proper, entirely in order with the scheme of the universe. They were not tainted with the cruelty and the perversity that he had grown fond of back in the good old days when he was a sexist. Ah, if only he could love and leave this godlike woman! How much more confident and comfortable he would be! But there was no hope that he could coldly use this woman as a vehicle for his fiendish desires; it simply was not in the equation.

Oh well, thought the demon, *you can't have everything*.

The demon had not teleported to the usual bypaths of Africa taken by godlike men, the duck (dynamic overseer of this exotic land), and the cigar-smoking frogs (a peculiar native tribe). Indeed, the demon had teleported himself to a site singularly appropriate to the situation at hand.

For the moonlight washed over the dense forest like a tasteful strobe, causing tiny particles of silver to dance like elfish phantoms on leaves otherwise blackened by the shadows of night. Here the silence was not disturbed by a lonely breeze, but by the chattering of golden metallic insects, the purrs of giant kittens, the buzzing of tiny elephants with dragonfly wings, and the humming of singing flowers. Every cell of this Africa teemed with a tender and joyous life that fanned, rather than diminishing, the demonic zeal he yielded to as he contemplated his love. As he walked to the clearing which was their prearranged meeting site, he could not fail to be affected by the beauty of a bundle of phosphorus flowers illuminating the sparkling rubies and diamonds scattered among the grass. Nor could he be unimpressed, try as he might, by the soft texture of the wide pentagonal leaves brushing his face as he walked under a low branch. The very air reeked a purity challenging his nature; yet the challenge seemed apt as he inhaled the sweet smell of bananas, roses, and damp leaves. Overhead birds sang in melodious voices which stirred unnameable feelings in his breast. He could not see the birds; it was too dark, despite the moonlight, and the birds were concealed in the foliage; but he knew he would see many soon, for there was a godlike woman who frequented their company, who alone of his race could answer them in their unique voices, who seemed to have been created not by her own wish-fulfillment when she was a mere woman, but by a benign force greater than all the great forces he had previously encountered.

She was the bird woman, and it had been she who had conquered him so decidedly, so mercilessly, so effortlessly. It had been she who had conquered him upon a whim, who had initially looked upon him with favor, who had entered his heart (reversing the process he usually preferred).

And as the demon pushed a branch from his eyes and stepped into the clearing, he saw her. He saw her bathing in the moonlight like a spirit dancing on the particles in the air of a sunlit room. He saw her reclining on a slope, in the grass, her eyes turned toward the sky, her soul flowing in an ether he could not hope to grasp. He saw her surrounded by birds, birds of all colors, sizes, and voices. A tiny red bird with long feathers and a disproportionate purple beak was perched on her outstretched hand; it tilted its head this way and that, staring into her eyes, as if it too was mesmerized by her presence and confused by her demeanor. Doves, toucans, auks, passenger pigeons, scarlet-winged tanigers, whooping cranes, penguins, cardinals, and bald eagles—all these and more were interspersed with the birds that had always been native to Africa, with birds so beautiful that they had never been given names in godlike man's history.

As beautiful as the birds were, they could not compare to the beauty that caused the demon to feel so lightheaded that he was forced to steady himself by leaning against a tree. For several moments he remained silent and still as he attempted to become unimpressed with the vision before him. He had almost succeeded when, as if she had known the treachery of his demonic heart, the bird woman caused her companions to be silent with a wish; and she answered them in the voice of a bird.

And the demon's treachery dissipated like gossamer, as he had known it must. Her song by itself was not enough to weaken his resolve, but when it combined forces with her beauty, he was lost, tangled in a snare of loveliness. He consoled himself by thinking that any male with a functioning apparatus would be tangled.

The bird woman had long white hair that fell past her shoulder blades; several wayward strands rested upon the curves of her breasts. Her clothing—an unadorned bodice that hung at her upper thighs and had but one shoulder strap—was composed of the web fluid of jungle spiders, who also were her friends. All the animals of Africa (including, presumably, the cigar-smoking frogs) were her friends. She had dark eyes that alternated colors between blue, brown, and black, depending upon the angle light struck them. Her oval face and slender, curved body had pale skin resembling the skin of death in the moonlight; yet this unfortunate paleness did not detract from her beauty; instead, it added yet another intriguing ingredient to the mysterious brew. Her pert nose and her round cheekbones that allowed no gauntness to manifest itself despite the lighting or angle of her profile also contributed; as did the slight pinkness of her lips, and the unnaturally perfect shape of her tiny ears. But none of these were as important as the fluidity of her movements; when she moved her arm, signaling the red bird to depart so that another might take his place, the demon could not be sure there was friction between her arm and the molecules of the air.

The demon had always considered himself a connoisseur of feminine beauty; but never before had he encountered an object so inexhaustible, so profound (and disturbing) in its implications. He could have leaned against the tree all night, satisfied his time was well spent, but he was drawn to her, not only by her beauty and her spell, but by some indefinable characteristic of her spirit. It was not sufficient to watch her from afar. Like the birds, he wanted to be close to her.

He walked through the clearing, displacing as few of the little creatures as possible, and sat by her side. She seemed to acknowledge his presence with an approving glance, but the demon could not be sure, so quickly did her attention return to the white falcon perched on her forearm. With her right finger she touched its beak, as if she were petting an eternal child. The falcon croaked, and she answered the bird with a song.

But there was no song for the demon. He sat demurely, his

knees drawn to his chest, and his arms wrapped about his ankles. Soon the circulation in his buttocks became retarded; however, he would not squirm to restore it. He had a hundred things to say to her, all of them (he deemed) important enough to justify the interruption of her rapport with the birds. He strained a hundred times to force the words through his mouth, but the sentences which seemed so eloquent to his fevered brain would not come; which was just as well, he thought, for he feared their poetry would become stunted and pathetic when molded with the concrete of language. He could not convince himself of the naturalness of the silence between them, nor could he convince himself of the naturalness of verbal communication. Finally he did speak, softly, haltingly, with words that approached what he felt in his heart. He said, "Cease... now cease, tyrannous love. You change my happiness into intense distress; you remove from my heart its repose and calm."

The bird woman abruptly concluded her song to the falcon. For a moment she seemed irritated, if the squinting of her eyes and the tightening of her lips were any indication. She lifted her arm a centimeter, then lowered it two centimeters, and without delay, the falcon rose into the air. As the falcon sped to a limb to rest, the rustle of its wings drowning the chirpings of the birds, the demon feared that his worst trepidations had come to pass, that he had needlessly angered the bird woman. When the falcon alighted, and the limb had adjusted to its weight, all in the clearing were silent, and the only sounds were the dim hummings of flowers, and the gentle rumblings of kittens roaming the forest. The demon's muscles tensed, and he wanted to lean away from the bird woman, in the hope that the extra miniscule distance between them would protect him from her anger. But when the bird woman turned to him, her expression softened, and the cool abyss of her eyes, which had been solely reserved for her birds, was directed at him for the first time that night. This heartened the demon, and he continued: "For me there is no rest, no hope; only death can console my fierce torment and distress. Only death... and this horrid shelter, this silver jungle. In you, then, I take refuge from terrible caverns, silent horrors, and solitary retreats. Cease to rend my breast, to pierce my soul. Begin to love me."

The bird woman stared at him more in the manner of an affectionate animal than that of a godlike woman. The demon feared that she did not comprehend his words. If true, he could easily forgive her, for he did not comprehend them himself. He spoke of death, and in all his evil pursuits he had never thought seriously of death. Yet this unthinkable end, this abrupt termination of existence was somehow part of his tortured spirit. As he timidly returned the bird woman's stare, he realized belatedly, that she did understand. The words pitifully expressing his longings had somehow reached her. He waited for her reply; but she rarely spoke the language of godlike men, and now her words were not the words of speech; instead, the demon detected her hand moving almost imperceptively toward his hands about his ankles.

Perhaps he had finally cast a spell of his own, though this had not been his intention. He knew that to speak further would mar the spell, but he felt socially obligated to speak. The silence was too agonizing. He said, "Keep your electric eye on me, babe; put your ray gun to my head. I'll be a rock-'n'-rollin' bitch for you."

He smiled when the bird woman grinned as she leaned to him. Their mouths were almost touching, but she could not resist grinning. The demon was elated; she was a normal godlike woman after all. At least in some respects.

They made love throughout the African night, under the eyes of the birds; and the moonlight cast a shimmering veil on their activities. The demon's vision could not quite penetrate the veil. Each delectable view of the bird woman's body, each caress upon her ivory chin, each caress she granted him in return (invariably causing a shudder of a thousand dancing needles reducing his sensations to an unreliable series of pleasurable impressions), each damp kiss they shared, each drop of his sweat (the bird woman did not perspire), each climax—all were vaguely unreal; the demon could not accept that he was actually fulfilling the passions which had obsessed him for so long. (He was comforted by the suspicion that the bird woman had no difficulty accepting it.) When they lay side by side, in the African dawn, the demon looked back upon the events and discovered that he could not quite recall several memorable moments of love-making (they had seemed memorable at the time). And when they had parted, the bird woman mysteriously disappearing into the jungle verdant, the demon teleported to the fields near his castle; watching the blazing red sun dip like a fiery pearl sinking into a vessel filled with a thick liquid, he felt the love-making events merge into a hazy dream. He wondered if he had ever actually touched her, if he had been deluded by the spell, a victim of her obscure purposes. He burned with a passion not yet diminished.

A single wisp of cloud glowed across the tip of the sun. The demon scowled. He had been drained of all emotion and sensation while pondering the dream, but now he felt his passions surging inside him, and for a moment, a brief transitory moment, he believed that he had never seen everything so clearly before. The demon concentrated; he envisioned the bird woman's love as rain. The wisp of cloud blackened and expanded. Winds from the west caused the cloud to billow, to roll across the dark blue sky like a specter; the foundations of the earth itself groaned under the weight of those mighty winds. The demon opened his mouth, closed his eyes, and lifted his head to the clouds; a thunderous moan throbbed in the sky . . . and in the demon's heart. As lightning crackled, its sole purpose apparently to deafen the denizens in the city of godlike man, the demon drank the water from the clouds. He drank the cool, cool rain, the love of the bird woman; and still the passions were not diminished.

4. The woman without a nose looked at herself in a broken hand-mirror; she stood under a streetlamp in the East End; the pale white glow of the lamp, interlaced with the curious, languorous silver rays that had descended over the city after the rain clouds had blown away, enabled her to view her countenance from an objective distance that she had never before achieved. She felt like an entirely different person examining . . . the woman without a nose.

She wondered why she had molded herself without a nose. (She assumed that she had been the one to mold herself; she could not imagine another taking such an interest in her that he/she would condemn her to an eternity of loneliness.) She wondered why she had not utilized her own powers to create a nose. She could have created a fine nose, an exemplary nose. Her nose would have been capable of complimenting the extraordinary range of facial expressions she commanded whenever the mood struck her. It would have been pert, noble, with just a touch of flatness to it, enough flatness so that it would have been one of her most distinguishing features, but not so much flatness that it would have rendered her nostrils too large and unsightly. Her nose would have concealed the ugly hole in the center of her face. She wondered why she did not create a nose right now, while she was thinking of it; why, she could create a magnificent nose, a nose that would be the talk of all godlike mankind. Right now. She knew she could create it right now.

But somehow it did not seem worth the effort.

Even if she had a nose, it would not solve her other problems (though she knew, with all her heart, that her lack of a nose was somehow related to her other problems). Perhaps she had lived with her problems for so long that she was afraid of another way of life.

She had no friends, no acquaintances. She had spent eons secluded away in her apartment. Occasionally she dreamed of a godlike man who sensed the warmth and sincerity of her godlike spirit; this man, who had never seen her, would divine the location of her apartment through the inner sixth sense everyone knows true love grants those who are worthy; he would politely knock on her door; when she answered, he would not be offended or disgusted at the unsightly hole in the middle of her face, nor at any of the innumerable imperfections of her body; instead he would toss his hat on the nearest chair and, without pausing to shed his overcoat, would take her in his long, strong arms, lifting her from the floor without exerting a portion of his inexhaustible powers; and he would kiss her without a word of greeting, and they would make love, succumbing to nameless passions and to the most disgusting thoughts. When he fucked her in the mouth, he would expel come with such force that her throat would be clogged, and she would choke, and she would feel the hot come slip down her trachea as well as her esophagus. Sometimes she imagined that the godlike man was attracted to the hole in the middle of her face, and that he caused his erect prick to shrink proportionately so it could be inserted neatly into the hole.

Perhaps that was why she had not created a nose. If she had a nose, she would lose this most secret of delights, this most personal dream, while she waited for the one godlike man who would make the years of loneliness worthwhile. But in the meantime, there was this misery, this unending misery that even the delights of her fantasies could not relieve.

She put her mirror in her faded blue purse. She realized she had not smiled at herself in the mirror; she usually smiled at herself because if she did not, no one else would. However, she did not want to be reminded tonight that five of her front teeth were missing. She wore two flannel petticoats under her ragged brown skirt to insulate herself from the cool wind that capered through the streets and between the buildings like an intelligent, ominous presence. She walked aimlessly through the streets, avoiding others who, like herself, had been drawn to the East End for reasons they did not care to know. Her free hand held her black straw bonnet on her head; sometimes the wind unexpectedly accelerated. Three times that night she caught glimpses of her reflection in puddles rippled by the wind, and she wondered why she had allowed herself to become overweight. Some women were attractive because they carried a few extra pounds, but those women were not as short as she.

The woman without a nose felt no desire to return to her new apartment in the East End. It was small and cramped; the walls were cracked and cockroaches lived in the kitchen. She hated living there, but she believed it singularly appropriate that she lived in a place she hated, a place that increased her misery. As long as she was miserable, she knew she was alive.

Once the woman without a nose tripped in a crack on the street. She did not fall; she merely twisted her ankle slightly. For several minutes she concentrated on the pain edging from her ankle to her knee. She did not neutralize the pain, though she wished it would end; she concentrated helplessly, believing there was no point in comforting herself. Three people, as alone as she, walked by her at different times, but they did not comfort her, though it was well within their power. The woman without a nose averted her eyes from them, and they did likewise. After the pain subsided, she vaguely considered returning to her apartment. However, there she could only sleep or practice her facial expressions in preparation for the day she got a nose. But she would never have a nose without losing her most secret dreams. She did not want to continue this eternal compromise; nor did she wish to change her life, for she would lose too much regardless of her new direction.

She believed herself temporarily reconciled with the great paradox of her life; she would accept it, at least for another couple of eons, because to deny it would be the equivalent of admitting that all her past suffering had been for nothing. She would also continue wandering tonight through the East End, for many of the same reasons. She would pretend that the decrepit buildings, the chilly wind, the dim streetlamps, and the stark decor soothed her soul and enabled her to endure these tortoruous hours. And as she walked, her mind was numb; not one thought occurred to her that she could remember a minute after its passing. She hoped (without fully forming the thought) a singular event would happen, an event which would irrevocably alter everything she knew.

And that is what she hoped when she saw the godlike man enshrouded in black standing next to a picket fence, the faded green paint chipped and peeling. She could not make out his features or his dress; it seemed that he deliberately existed in a haze, vibrating his atoms on a plane that made it impossible for her to detect the particulars of his build or countenance. She could not see him staring at her, though he undeniably was; for she could feel the power behind the eyes, the soft white heat of his emotions. She was aware at once that his purpose in frequenting the East End differed from her own.

Something light and wonderful happened inside her when she thought that she might be the object of his purpose. She was not afraid of disappointment, for she had not had the occasion to be disappointed. Never before had her hopes had substance.

She smiled, unmindful of her missing five teeth. She hesitantly walked toward the enshrouded figure, her steps quickening and steadying when the man reached to her with a hazy blackened hand.

CHAPTER THREE

1. *An account from the good doctor's notebooks:*

We were seated at breakfast, my lover and I, when I heard a telepathic message from the consulting detective. It ran this way:

Have you a couple of hours to spare? Have just been summoned to the East End in connection with a dreadful tragedy. Shall be glad if you will come with me. Air and scenery miserable.

So I found myself and the consulting detective standing over the fallen body of a godlike woman for the second time in thirty-six hours. When alluding to the air and scenery, my friend had indulged in his usual habit of grossly understating aesthetics. The air fairly reeked of misery, and the mere thought of the task before me filled my heart with pity—directed, I'm afraid, more at myself than at the unfortunate creature on the bloody sidewalk. She lay near a ramshackle picket fence, her hand nearly touching the gate, as if she had hoped to find relief and succor in the deserted apartment complex beyond the dry grass. All the surrounding apartment complexes were deserted; there had been no aid for her on the block, no one to hear her screams (indeed, if she had screamed). This was one of the most

foreboding neighborhoods of the East End, and for the life of me
I could not understand why any godlike woman would wander
down this street. However, there were many, many things I
could not understand, nor was I especially anxious to come to
grips with the problems.

His pipe smoking like a miniature volcano, the consulting
detective stood next to the gate, his feet at the hand of the
godlike woman. His eyes glowered. He was not affected in the
least by the disgust and fear which assailed me. Although
nothing about him had changed, I could scarcely recognize him
as the friend with whom I had shared many leisurely eons. No,
he was a machine primed for action more than a godlike man.
Every cog of thinking apparatus was working overtime; his five
senses—and perhaps more—were relaying to his brain every
detail of the scene before him. He had no use for emotions which
would only impair him; therefore he could not allow himself the
luxury of grief and pity. The inhuman shell he had cast about
himself upset me, yet I could well comprehend the necessity for
it. Doubtless he would have performed my impending task
himself, and performed it as well as I, but I was the professional,
and he probably felt that the professional touch would yield
more detached results.

I was not at the site of the crime for three minutes when I
commenced my task, but before I narrate the grisly details, I feel
that I must expound upon our comrades and the crowd, as their
reactions to this initial crime will have some bearing on the
narrative to come. It takes more time to tell it than it did to see it.
In addition, my task was not something I like to think about,
and I would like to put it off for as long as possible.

Actually, the crowd can be disposed of immediately, since it
consisted of a menagerie of approximately fifty godlike men and
women, all inhabitants of the East End. Normally each
individual possesses a unique and separate identity, but though
the appearance of each member of the crowd was distinctive,
their spirits merged into one mass, hollow at the center, numb
and confused, forgettable in the extreme. I paid the crowd little
attention, at the time unconcerned with its innermost reactions
to the crime.

The fat man, the demon, the lawyer, the universal op, and the
man in the yellow suit formed an interference between the crowd
and the corpse. Acting under the consulting detective's

instructions, they insured that no member of the crowd came too close and interfered with our work. I could not see the gunsel (I have never seen the gunsel), but my instincts informed me that he was either in the crowd or in an otherwise empty apartment overlooking the site; as always, he was watching and waiting, but for what and for whom, I cannot say.

The fat man and the demon, who often react similarly to identical environmental stimuli, were shocked, as were we all. However, their interest manifested itself most actively. Though something terrible had happened, something *exciting* had happened, and like readers who finish a book at one sitting, they could not wait to learn what would happen next. I did detect that sometimes the demon lost his train of thought, and a film dropped over his eyes; as excited as he was about the impending possibilities of the next few days, another subject had cast a deeper hold on his imagination.

The lawyer watched the crowd as if he was caught in the grips of a horrendous vision. His usual eager, if incompetent, self had been dealt a cruel blow. When his attention wandered, it was not to the consulting detective and myself, nor to the hypnotic corpse, but to his attire. He nervously breathed upon and shined the handle of his sword cane; he pulled down the hem of his black coat; he adjusted the length of his shirt sleeves at his wrists. It did not take the training of a consulting detective to know that he was thinking of Kitty; the timing of her disappearance had now become even more inopportune.

I have implied that the universal op was shocked by the crime. I trust this is so. Beneath his smooth, featureless face, he is doubtless as human as any of us, and I speak of his nobler virtues and his feelings for the welfare of others because of my deep respect for the godlike man. In truth, his mannerisms implied no shock, no concern. He was as cool, as detached, as the consulting detective; perhaps more so, because he achieved these ends with no apparent effort.

I have stated that the consulting detective was professionally detached; I have implied that other members of our select cast have viewed various aspects of the scene as if it were a dream. The man in the yellow suit watched us and performed his job as if he were *himself* a dream. I had never before seen a godlike man so wedded with unreality; you could picture him as unreality personified and you would not be picturing an abstraction. I suspected that he saw more, knew more, than even the consulting detective, but I also suspected that the details of his vision, if known, would have yielded few practical results. The aura about him diminished as time passed in the East End, and my third suspicion is that the details of the vision—his additional insights into our predicament—were lost to him.

Having made these observations, perhaps in the hope they would increase my intestinal fortitude, I sighed and knelt beside the woman. Her skirt was crumpled about her waist. Blood, now dried, had soaked the skirt and drenched the sidewalk in the area between her legs. Blood was smeared across her face and still seeped through the wounds of her throat. Vibrations rippled from my fingertips, and the answering vibrations were jagged and disharmonious, each break in the rhythm informing me of another outrage done on the poor unfortunate's body. Her face had not yet become stiff; a curious lifeness remained on her features and, most importantly, on her glassy eyes—open, staring and blank. Feeling as if she were still staring at the murderer, it increased my already considerable discomfort to be kneeling above her. My keen eyesight and encyclopedic anatomical knowledge quickly catalogued her surface injuries, though I confessed that at first her curious lack of a nose confounded me. But as I could detect no trace of an incision about the hole in the center of her face, I deduced that she had been disfigured because she had wanted to be. My examination concluded, I closed my eyes momentarily and felt the muscles of my waist harden. When I stood, all my muscles were tense; I turned away from the corpse, my heart relieved that I would have a respite before I looked at it again.

My friend the consulting detective gestured to the universal op. The three of us stood close to the corpse; we spoke in low tones, though there was nothing to prevent any member of the crowd from hearing the conversation by increasing his aural faculties if he wished. The consulting detective said, "Well, friend good doctor, what is your report?"

I cleared my throat. "I doubt if I can add anything to what you've already observed, but, as the eternal children say, here goes nothing. Below the left jaw, at the ear, there begins an incision eight and one half centimeters long, apparently made with some sort of supernatural knife. I found no evidence that the victim was able to repair the damage; all her wounds were of a permanent nature, incapable of healing. Another incision, two centimeters below the first but shorter a centimeter and a half at the left side and ending seven centimeters below the edge of the right jaw, has reached the vertebrae." I cleared my throat again; I had difficulty forming the words.

The consulting detective was silent as he waited for me to continue. I suppose I could say that he was not exactly sympathetic under the circumstances, but when I take into account his urgent need to receive all the information I could give—perhaps every second counted!—his silence, his refusal to push me before I was prepared to recommence, was indicative of more than adequate understanding. The universal op said in a muffled voice tempered by a tenderness I could not interpret as genuinely understanding, "Take it slow and take it easy."

"I've no choice," I said. "There are several slashes down the right side of the body and across the abdomen. Most of the blood has been absorbed by her clothing. The wound from under the pelvis to the right side of the stomach is irregular, unlike the wound under the right rib cage. The omentum has been stabbed several times. In addition, and this might be important as you form your psychological profile of the inhuman monster, the vaginal area has been stabbed twice. I might venture an opinion."

The consulting detective, whose eyebrows had risen at the word "vaginal," nodded his assent.

"The monster probably will direct his violence solely toward women. The wounds at the vagina can't be considered strictly functional, that is, if his motivation is simply to kill. He directed not only his violence at her vagina, but his hatred, if you can understand the distinction."

"Thank you, friend good doctor," said the consulting detective, "but I can understand the distinction quite well. And you're correct in stressing its significance. As you suspected, I already knew all you've told me, but I hadn't noticed the wounds of the vaginal area because, frankly, I hadn't thought to look. You shame me."

"Please . . ." I began.

He silenced me with a gesture. "This is the second error I've made concerning the psychological profile of my foe. I've become so intent upon perfecting my methods—the logical deductions gained from the observations of trivialities—that I'm overlooking the obvious. I trust you've memorized all you've told me in greater detail, that you can write it up for me so I can examine it when I wish."

"Yes, of course. Does that mean I can disturb the body now?"

"Yes," he said after a pause.

I turned and knelt. I closed her eyes. The look of peace on her face, the erasing of her fear and hatred, was more in my mind than in the reality, I'm afraid.

"What shall we do with the body now?" asked the universal op. "We should dispose of it somehow, since we've no more use for it."

"I say," said the man in the yellow suit, descending from his clouds and stepping between the universal op and me, "wasn't there a ceremony of some sort for the deceased in the days of mere man?"

"Knowing them, there were several," said the demon, his little display of wit returning a portion of the satanic gleam to his eyes.

"What do the cigar-smoking frogs do when a fellow dies?" I asked.

"They eat him," said the fat man.

"I suppose we might as well start right now," said the lawyer. He pressed the button on his sword cane; the blade protruded with a metallic hiss and he stepped toward the fallen woman. "I'm famished! I'll take anything but the liver. I hate liver."

The consulting detective gently touched the lawyer on the shoulder, halting the little man's relentless progression toward his culinary delight. "I think that with our inherent resources, we should be able to think of a more dignified method to dispose of a body."

The lawyer blinked several times at the consulting detective. "If you say so, but I'm really hungry. I could eat a horse."

"And you'd probably enjoy it too," said the consulting detective. "No, I believe the corpse should be turned over to those who were once her friends."

"Why?" said the lawyer. "Let 'em find their own frigging food! Who do they think they are anyway?"

"They are not a bunch of anyways," said the demon sternly.

"Huh?" inquired the lawyer.

"I'm afraid you don't understand," said the fat man. "No one is going to eat the corpse of this wretched creature. The cigar-smoking frogs are not the proper role model for our race."

The lawyer shrugged; I believe that to this day he has not fully comprehended our reasoning process.

The fat man said to the consulting detective, "I've already sent the gunsel in search of this creature's friends. It took him but a few moments to learn she had none."

The consulting detective's professional attitude melted; his shoulders slumped; all the energy and fire smoldering in his breast were displaced by a weary, hollow sensation. He gazed at the corpse. "Why does fate play such tricks with poor, helpless worms?"

The fat man sighed, his vast shoulders sinking like two deflating lumps. "Perhaps we shall learn. In the meantime, I suggest we consign the body to the fires of the antimatter universe."

The consulting detective nodded. "That is appropriate, especially since those fires were the weapons used to slay her."

The fat man raised his right eyebrow, which probably caused him to expend considerable energy. "Oh?"

"Later the good doctor will assist me in deducing the exact design of the knife; for now I can merely say that its blade was forged from the fires of a sun in the antimatter universe."

"My goodness!" I exclaimed. "How did you know?"

"From the singed cells in the interior of the incisions. That explains why the victim could not repair her wounds. Her atoms had been reduced to nothingness, and though she still had the power to create new atoms to heal herself, so great was the pain that she was unable to concentrate on the act. She had not the will."

"I daresay no one would have had the will," I said.

"Exactly. Not even myself," said the consulting detective. "Another might have healed her, but she was pitifully alone. And now that her wretched soul has fled . . ."

"Are we to assume that if one of us is cut by this ripper, then he's as good as dead?" asked the universal op.

"Sure. Unless he's very fast," said the man in the yellow suit with a sardonic air.

I frankly admit, I was aghast at both the question and the answer. The thought that I might be personally endangered by the murderer had not occurred to me; and if that was not a sufficient blow for my self-assured mind to reel under, the man in the yellow suit's casual acknowledgment of the possibility—not only to others, but to himself as well—with a statement calculated to reduce the concept to its most base triviality was staggering. I would have never thought on my own accord that I might meet my ultimate destiny as a butchered heap on a sidewalk in squalid surroundings. I was about to belittle that acceptance when the consulting detective, nodding grimly and filling his pipe dangling like a broken limb from the right corner of his mouth, said, "Should the event arise, strive to keep your wits about you and teleport to your nearest companion. It shouldn't arise, because I am instructing each of you not to be alone while in the East End at night, but merely because an event shouldn't arise doesn't mean it will not."

"Teleportation under such circumstances will be difficult," said the fat man. "The, ah, ripper's victim might find himself a showering horde of independent atoms."

"He might," said the consulting detective, "but the alternative is certain." Somewhat needlessly, I thought, he pointed his pipe at the corpse.

"*Yeech,*" said the lawyer. "If we're not going to eat this thing, let's get rid of it before it ripens."

"I agree with your sentiments, friend lawyer," I said, "though I find your tact to be vaguely analogous to that of a rabid mastodon."

My little joke—humor comes to us on the most unlikely occasions, I've learned—brought forth giggles from several members of the crowd; the giggles were laughter in spite of itself; instantly the crowd (which evidently had increased its aural faculties to satiate its morbid curiosity, as I had suspected) embraced its previous somnambulistic mood.

"Who would care to do the honors?" inquired the consulting detective.

"I would," I said.

"I thought as much," said the consulting detective.

I allowed myself one last lingering look at the godlike woman's wretched remains. Beads of perspiration, caused more by the stark sun than by the anxieties assailing my spirit and inner security, rolled down my temples and the bridge of my nose. I was not sickened by the corpse; instead I was gripped by an infinite sadness; and for a moment I imagined I was that wretched heap, and that I was somehow staring at myself. I scowled. The corpse disappeared. Normally such a disappearance is instantaneous; nothing remains behind, not even for a moment. However, I somehow thought it appropriate to delay the teleportation of a few atoms, and I shaped them into three tiny stars of yellow light, which, in their turn, diminished until they blinked out, following their fellows into the antimatter universe. It eased my anxieties to create a moment of loveliness from what had been so repellent.

The blood on the sidewalk disappeared with the corpse. Like the crowd, my companions and I milled about, each of us (with the likely exception of the consulting detective) wondering what we should do next. Yet we would not wander on the site where the corpse had laid; it remained in our minds. Many members of the crowd strayed away; clearly they would learn nothing more, and there was nothing more to see. The others watched us, waiting for us to do or say something. The consulting detective had lowered his eyes to the sidewalk; he would not face those who tarried. Normally he was a godlike man indifferent to the masses; but this time he seemed acutely attuned to their needs, as if he believed his search for the murderer was but a minor skirmish in a greater battle.

Soon the fat man embraced the same attitude; however, unlike the consulting detective, he possessed a wealth of experience in manipulating both the masses and individuals. If he had been with us on the night we had saved the reporter from the wolfman, he doubtlessly would have purged her of her negativism, at least for the nonce. Unheeding of the tremendous pull gravity exerted upon his flimsy flesh and vast girth, he drew himself to his full roundness. "My friends, I wish there were words which would comfort you," he began in a voice burdened by a weight of an entirely different sort, a weight I had not suspected him of carrying. "But to say all will be well would be to lie, and though I've no objections to telling a few whoppers now and then, especially to alluring ladies, this is hardly the proper occasion. You see, I would be caught; you would know I lied." He paused, perhaps expecting to hear a titter of laughter lightening the mood; when his pause was greeted with silence, he continued unflustered, recovering his verbal fumble with a dexterity of confidence. "I can state truthfully that we shall do our utmost to capture—and to punish, if you should so desire—this ripper, but I fear that ultimately our success will not comfort you, that while we might alleviate your present concerns, we would fail to solve the problems which have led you to create and dwell in the very environment which has provided the ripper with his opportunity. In other words, we cannot soothe your spirits." Again he paused, dramatically this time. "Unless you take the first steps. Unless you look into yourselves with objectivity. The ethical structure of the universe, such as it is, differs for each individual; therefore, each individual must rearrange his own. If you can see where I'm coming from."

I could, but the audience could not. Blank is not the word for the faces in the crowd; despite their noses, mouths, dimples, and ears, the faces might as well have been as sandpaper smooth as the universal op's. "I believe you've won a convert," I whispered to the consulting detective.

The fat man pursed his lips, which protruded from his immense cheeks like a singular sprout growing in the walls of a chasm. He realized that he was not reaching them. They were too far away, but I could not help but admire his attempt. He said, "My friends, regardless of my eloquence, regardless of how I mask my meaning with the considerable poetic license I usually reserve for the personal glories of romance, I cannot hide the truth. I can say it a thousand times, in a thousand different ways, but the gist will remain: the only person who can help you is yourself. You must follow your path alone, and you must take what solace you can."

A dark-haired woman carrying a rusty, blunted sword said, "But no one cares for us! No one cares what happens to us! No one cares what happens to me!"

"Oh, but I do," said the fat man, and it would tax my already taxed remarkable talent to communicate to the reader the sincerity, the depths, the concern, the warmth, and the compassion the fat man also uttered with that simple reply. Never before had so few words said so much; yet, never before had so much failed so miserably, because we all knew at once that the dark woman had remained untouched. "And you would find that others care, though perhaps you'll find it sooner if you would care for them more than you care for yourself."

He turned on his heel as if he had been jerked about by an earth tremor. He walked past us, stepping over the site where the corpse had lain, and continued walking, away from the crowd. I had never before heard a godlike man say such hokum with such seriousness, and as if he had read my mind (which is possible), he winked at me while passing me, applauding his own magnificent performance.

For several seconds we watched his figure recede; perhaps we were waiting for it to diminish. Then, almost as a unit, we followed him, and began our trek from the East End. The depressing aspects of the neighborhood were not quite so effective in the daylight, though the grime upon the street often caused me to wrinkle my nose in dismay. Dancing rays of sunlight poured over the golden buildings, and yet the sunlight reflected from those walls of gold became drab and lackluster. The East End shimmered with vagueness. Had it not been for the sorry condition of the thoroughfare (which constantly brought my thoughts to reality), I would have believed I was walking in a dream. However, it did not occur to me to repair the cracks in the sidewalk, to kill the weeds, to wash away the dirt, though it was well within my abilities to do so without effort. Something about the East End was indisputably correct, and it would remain correct until more pressing problems were solved.

After we had strolled for fifteen minutes, and neared the deserted neighborhood bordering the East End like a buffer between dimensions, the consulting detective said, "My friends, we now must make plans and take precautions. We've many theories to choose from, thanks to our friend in the yellow suit, and what we choose will also influence our course of action."

The universal op said, "I find it hard enough to tackle facts, friend consulting detective, without flying away after theories and fancies."

"You are right," said the consulting detective demurely. "You do find it difficult to tackle the facts."

The universal op shrugged and shook his head; I could almost imagine him grinning at the verbal sally which had shattered his defenses.

"What are we to do if the ripper is my antithesis?" asked the man in the yellow suit.

"Until we know for certain what he is—that is, until we've actually crossed paths with him—we should leave metaphysics aside. It won't aid us in our search at any rate."

"But philosophical forces in opposition are fated to meet; it is the metaphysical way of the universe; the history of life is the history of conflict."

"That may well be," said the consulting detective curtly.

"However, the conflict between illogical rationalism and logical anarchy is one thing; and the conflict between the ripper and his victim is quite another. Until this fiend is defeated, we must take care to insure that all our theories have practical results. It must never be said that a life was lost while we sat at home pondering what good comes from lost lives."

"In that light, may I add to my previous theory?" I asked.

"Of course."

"I believe the ripper is a man driven to make his foul crimes as public as possible. Despite previously expressed fears over the fate of Kitty, you can expect no anonymity from this man. He will kill again at the first opportunity. He will dare us to capture him. He would slay right under our noses."

The consulting detective, creating a wire gizmo which he used to clean the sludge from his pipe bowl, nodded; he slowly closed and opened his eyes. "Exactly my opinion. This overconfident man will flaunt his destruction of the social order. He will provide us with several opportunities to capture him, at least in retrospect. He is predictable only to a degree; there's no telling what he might do next or when he'll do it. However, I am of the firm opinion that his crimes will be committed at night."

The lawyer twirled his sword cane. "He may be a defecator."

The consulting detective's eyes now burst wide open, as if someone had taken his photograph while using a camera with a five-hundred-watt flash cube. "A what?" he managed to inquire, hoping to mask his incredulity.

"A defecator. Someone who turns traitor." The lawyer smiled to himself, satisfied that he had made his point. Then his expression assumed that of a man who, while admiring the fit of a new tuxedo as reflected by a mirror, realizes that he has forgotten to put on his undershorts. "I said that right, didn't I?"

The demon cleared his throat, raised his eyebrows, and turned his head slightly to the left. A comment formed in his mind, I am sure, but he did not reveal it because the content would have been superfluous to what conclusions we had reached concerning the lawyer's pitiful education.

The fat man smiled. "Friend lawyer, even those who are most pure are defecators upon occasion, though the truth might upset them. I think we can safely assume that the ripper is working for himself, for his own pleasure. In any case, that is irrelevant to capturing him."

"Exactly," said the consulting detective. "And we must do the work ourselves because, frankly, of the entire race, only we are capable of functioning at peak intensity. We're the cream of our race; even when grappling with depression, we do not succumb to the disease which has caused those poor souls to take up residence in the East End. I can depend only upon you six."

"And the gunsel!" interjected the fat man.

The consulting detective nodded. After he refilled his pipe and mentally ignited it, he said, "Conceivably, the ripper is an individual of whom we've been unaware; if that is true, then we will capture him only when he tries to kill again. However, we must search out those godlike men who are most likely, psychologically speaking, to vent their internal frustrations upon others. We must interview as many as possible during the day, follow up every clue, whether it seems promising or not. If necessary, we must interview the entire race, in the hope that the ripper accidentally gives himself away."

The demon rubbed his narrow chin. "That won't be easy. He's undoubtedly a clever gent."

"His intelligence is of the first order," said the consulting detective. "At night we must patrol the East End. We must maintain the vigilance. And we must travel in small groups to decrease the likelihood that one of us will face the ripper alone. The gunsel will be our wild card. Of us all, he has the only genuine tracking experience."

The demon cleared his throat. I detected a curious reluctance on his part to speak, as if he was preparing to expose some secret which would somehow lower our estimation of him as a satanic being. He said softly, with but an approximation of the iron will and self-assurance which was his normal metier, "I'm, ah, passingly acquainted with an individual who might prove to be a more adept tracker than the gunsel." He scowled, a significant thought coming to his mind, and then cupped his green palms around his mouth. "No offense, kid!" he yelled, the echoes gradually fading like idyllic dreams during a rainy dawn. "You're still tops in my book!"

The neighborhood was silent for a few moments heavy with suspense. Then, without preliminary so that I might adjust to the sudden onslaught of sound, the gunsel whistled shrilly, signifying that he held no grudges against the demon.

The consulting detective ignored the byplay. He said,

"Excellent, friend demon! Who is this godlike man? Will he be willing to offer his services?"

"Well, first I'm obliged to tell you that the, ah, individual I've in mind is, oh, of the female persuasion."

"Now that's what I call excellent!" I exclaimed.

The fat man rubbed his hands and swayed his hips. "I concur, friend good doctor. It's about time I had something lovely to look at. My eyes have had a terrible day. My soul is starved for beauty."

"Careful, friend demon," said the lawyer, grinning rudely. "I just might snake her."

The universal op, usually indifferent to our conversation when it turned to the direction that makes the world go round, said, "You'll crawl after anything with a snatch." It did not take much to disgust the op sometimes.

The consulting detective, suddenly ignoring a great deal of byplay, said, "Her persuasion is immaterial. If she can be of service, I would be honored to make her acquaintance. But . . . ! The disease of the soul we're battling has thus far affected women most strongly. Though I surmise she has not been affected, what are the possibilities she will be in the near future?"

"None," said the demon. "As far as I can tell, she's immune to every disease civilization has to offer—good and bad." He smiled weakly, thrust his hands into his pockets, and then looked straight ahead, subtly signaling that he no longer wanted to discuss her. I must say, he was certainly mysterious about the young lady. I knew at once that he had fallen for her like a swarm of dwarf stars. If he had not acted so mysteriously, I might never have known, for when he is in his right mind, the demon is a consummate performer. "I'll arrange a meeting for this afternoon—if I can."

"Five will be best," said the consulting detective, "for that is when we'll meet to discuss our strategy for patrolling the East End tonight. This morning, over a hot breakfast, we'll discuss who shall be our first suspects."

"Hey, what about Kitty?" asked the lawyer.

The consulting detective put his hand on the lawyer's shoulder, this time comforting the little man as one would comfort an ailing eternal child. "Don't fret, my friend. Her disappearance hasn't slipped my mind, though it might appear that way. We'll keep our eyes peeled for clues, and you'll help us search for Kitty as you help us search for the ripper."

"The East End might be a good place to start," said the man in the yellow suit.

"Indeed, that's where you and the universal op will search," said the consulting detective. "You'll search separately, during the day, but I believe neither of you will be in danger. You two have the closest affinities to those depressed denizens."

The man in the yellow suit grimaced; he was not sure he liked having an affinity with the residents of the decrepit district. If the universal op regretted the comparison between his personality and that of the despondent dwellers, he did not show it. Typical.

By now we were well within the deserted, preserved neighborhood surrounding the East End. For a time I had not noticed the alteration, so intent had I been upon the conversation. This neighborhood too shimmered with gold; and the thoroughfare was in remarkable condition; the sidewalks were scrubbed and immaculate. Even the sunlight glittered with gaiety. Nevertheless, the silence hung over the buildings, the grass, the trees, the macadam, and the lamps like a suffocating plastic bag. It was difficult to pretend there was nothing missing. I breathed easier when we had walked the four blocks of this bordering neighborhood; after three blocks I could already hear the dim laughter of eternal children at play.

"Aha!" exclaimed the consulting detective as we paused to watch several eternal children swing on a Jungle Jim (we realized that we needed more contrast in our lives). "A newspaper stand! Just what I need to take my mind off things for a while!" He strode to to green metal stand like a music lover darting across the room to remove a needle caught in a plugged groove; but as he reached down to the latch, he saw something through the dusty glass which caused him to pale. His eyes widened; he exhaled in shock, wheezing; he slowly brought his right hand to his heart; I think he was also dizzy. "What cruel trick is this?" he asked the sky. "These are yesterday's papers!"

"Oh dear!" I said. "What can the matter be?"

A trace of color returned to his cheeks as he ignored his disappointment and self-pity, as he coldly considered the ramifications of his discovery. "It can only mean—dare I say it? dare I even think it?—that the debilitating erosion of the soul has struck not only the ace reporter, but the entire newspaper staff as well." He sucked in his lips, nicking them with his teeth, and inhaled. Finally he said, *"Poot!"* with all the loathing and ferocity he could muster.

Then he abruptly calmed; his tensions spent, he did not seek to refuel them. "Oh well, I suppose I'll have to do without for the duration. It's a shame, a damnable shame. We could have used the cooperation of the medium to our advantage."

"In what way?" inquired the fat man gravely.

"I think it's important that the people be aware of our efforts in their behalf, whether they reside in the East End or not. Additionally, they must be informed of all the facts, of the danger the ripper presents to society as a whole." He emptied his pipe by tapping it against the newspaper stand. "Someone might inform us of a valuable clue. Or we could ask for the editor's cooperation and distort a story to goad the ripper into making a mistake. The uses of the newspaper are endless. Besides, you know as well as I that there are times when a newspaper is the handiest thing around when duty calls and you need something to read quickly."

"Everything you say is true," said the fat man, pointing to the sky. "That is why I've no objections to helping you."

"Why, that would be greatly appreciated, indeed," said the consulting detective warmly. "What do you propose to do?"

"Become the editor. It has been some time since I drank from the heady cup of power."

2. The editor puffed his cigar. When this failed to satisfy him, he inhaled it. When he thought he would vomit, he created and swallowed a heartburn tablet. When the tablet failed to tilt the chemical balance of his stomach into the base category, he stuck his finger down his throat, figuring that he might as well go ahead and vomit and get it over with. He leaned over the empty trashcan, his right elbow supporting him on his desk and the edge of his buttocks in danger of slipping from his swivel chair, so the act would be at least reasonably sanitary. But his finger was too short and meaty to do more than cause him to cough. Withdrawing his finger, acutely aware of the pressure of extra blood in his face causing the skin to redden, the editor lit another cigar. He leaned back and put his feet on his desk. He figured he might as well relax. However, he could not relax; he was too bored; there was nothing to do. He could do whatever he wanted, but he could think of nothing; he could not even make himself vomit. He believed that somehow his plight symbolized the predicament of modern godlike man in today's hung-up society. (Or was it flipped-out society? He could not be sure.)

He wore his usual, boring attire: a brown suit, a brown tie, and an unbuttoned white shirt with thin blue vertical lines. He thought, *If I came to the office wearing nothing but a pair of panties, would anyone notice?*

If he had worn the panties today (and he had been sorely tempted, for some reason, to finally succumb to this fantasy he had nurtured for eons), no one would have noticed. No one was there to notice anything. The editor was the only person in the ten-story newspaper building. It was not the fact that he was alone that bothered him (he had always been alone in one fashion or another); it was the *emptiness*. The clutter outside his office, the messy desks of his staff, the half-full cups of lukewarm coffee, the trash on the floor, the scattered remains of every edition for the last two weeks, the switched-on fluorescent lights—none could compensate for the absence of life. He had not realized how much the knowledge that others were in the building and working, especially the reporting staff outside his office, had soothed the ache of loneliness. It had been soothed to such a degree that he had forgotten its existence. And now he realized, with a shattering glimpse beyond the veils he had woven to bluepencil portions of his perceptions, that he had ached forever. He had always felt this way. What's more, he had tried everything (including a few positions that compromised his integrity as a man) and nothing had worked. Save for the cigar smoke slowly curling toward the air vents which did not compensate for the silence elsewhere, the atmosphere was tinged with a dull dreariness that threatened to, but never quite did, take on a yellow color. His office and the staff room, even the ceiling and floor, seemed to waver in and out of reality. The only way he could be sure that they were actually there was to touch them; not only was that impractical (though it would at least keep him occupied), but he feared that even then he would still be deluding himself.

He did not understand how he had become so literally (as opposed to metaphorically) alone. It seemed that just a little while ago there had been reporters pecking away at rickety typewriters, smoking sissy cigarettes, and avoiding work. Perhaps less reporters than normal, but he had chalked that up to just another sign of the times. He could not remember exactly when he had become alone, exactly when the transition from metaphor to reality had taken place. Had it been late yesterday afternoon? Or early this morning? Did it matter? After he had pondered those questions for a sufficient length of time, he wondered if there was any point to making a distinction between literal and metaphorical loneliness. From there, his lightning-quick mind shifted to the next logical problem: was there a point to anything? And then: was there a point to contemplating the pointlessness of it all?

Wow, he thought, with but a fraction of his former enthusiasm, *what a great idea for a feature story. The philosophy page has been a little drab of late. Of course, so has everything else*. He tried to think of a feature writer who could whip up a story about the pointlessness of life (though it stood to reason that if life had no meaning, there was no point in writing the story in the first place). He did not have much time to think when he heard some very strange noises in the street below.

At first the editor thought his mind was playing tricks on him ("joshing," he preferred to call it). However, the noises persisted until he had no choice but to ignore his doubts and to proceed like the unthinking men of action in the office who, unlike him, always got the girls. Once his course was charted, he proceeded without delay, the calculating smoothness of his motions impressing even him. If only the girls in the office could see him now! They would be impressed too! Not every godlike man could make the simple motion of pushing a swivel chair backward and then turning toward the window such a delightful, graceful ballet.

What the editor saw made him forget all about congratulating himself. (And just in time too, for he was beginning to wonder if there was any point in congratulating himself.) Though the vision provided him yet another opportunity to question his perception of reality, his mind was quite occupied with comprehending it. After a few moments he recognized the man-mountain on the street five stories below. It was the fat man; it could be none other. The editor relaxed. Where the fat man was concerned, anything could happen; the question of reality was immaterial.

The fat man's activities confirmed this observation. He wore his most pristine white suit; he carried a car door under his elephantine left arm. Whenever he spied an attractive young godlike woman, he whooped, hollered, and whistled; he stomped his feet as if he wanted to cause an earthquake; he beat upon the car door with his right palm, creating an annoying hollow thump. The purpose of all this escaped the editor. It appeared that the fat man's activities were supposed to attract godlike women to his mammoth body; yet they invariably ran away; and the fat man seemed to take a perverse pleasure in his failure. The fat man pranced up and down the sidewalk, smiling like a gremlin to himself; his shoulders were flung backward, his hips swayed as he walked, and his spine was curved, creating a curious awkward motion and causing his buttocks and thighs to appear arthritic. The editor pondered this peculiar vision. He could only conclude that this was what the fat man had meant when he stated during interviews that he enjoyed "strutting his stuff for sweet young fillies." The purpose of the car door eluded the editor, but there were some things godlike man was not meant to know.

Finally the editor decided that perhaps the fat man was trying to draw his attention in addition to displaying his wares. It made sense in a convoluted way, because the fat man disliked the direct approach. The editor opened the window. Puffing his cigar, he said, "Hey you! Got a license to peddle that stuff?"

"Certainly!" boomed the fat man. "I took my last shot this morning. How's tricks, chief?"

"Don't call me chief! Come on up here; I want to scare myself."

The fat man blinked out of sight. The editor turned to see him sitting comfortably in the William Morris chair, his white Borsalino resting like a giant egg shell on his knee. The car door was propped against the wall.

"You don't need me to scare yourself," said the fat man. "You've already accomplished that most adequately."

The editor blew a smoke ring. "Am I to assume that your cryptic remark is somehow supposed to bring us to the heart of our discussion?"

"If you wish. However, in my opinion, you've already assumed too much—about love, life, and the universe."

"That takes a lot of assumption."

"Which you've done without compunction." The fat man smiled slightly; the editor could not be sure if he raised his eyebrows to accentuate the point, but he thought he detected a slight movement in the forehead region.

The editor felt a weightlessness in his midriff; he experienced the beginnings of dizziness and sickness, though he was neither. He was positive that the fat man was unaware of any alteration in his gestures or inflections, but he could detect them. He was apart from himself, watching himself; simultaneously he felt blind, as if he had never seen anything and never would. "That's ridiculous! I'm an old newshawk, and old newshawks never assume."

"That's an assumption."

"This is not the heart of our discussion!"

"You made *that* assumption; not I."

The editor wondered when he would wake up and begin today.

The fat man continued, "Friend chief, you've made innumerable assumptions about innumerable matters. When was the last time you've examined your role as an old newshawk? When did you last wonder if there was any purpose to your dreary routine? Every day you wake up at six—only mere man would have been stupid enough to awaken so early with regularity—and teleport to your office. You don't have a day off, which means that thus far you have spent your eternity at this desk, handing out assignments and rewriting poorly phrased articles. You've never interviewed an illustrious godlike man personally; you've been content enough to delegate personal social experiences. Why, I have it on the impeccable authority of my gunsel that when none other than the Big Red Cheese visited these offices, you were too flustered and timid to speak to him. Not a week passes that you do not devote a major feature to the exploits or writings of the Big Red Cheese, and yet you had nothing to say to him. Your medium is the essence of communication, true, but you yourself are incapable of taking part in the most valuable communication of all—those private moments of transitory pleasure that occur when two godlike men of extraordinary talent meet."

The editor wondered if he should defend himself against the unwarranted verbal onslaught. Then he realized that he could not defend himself. Not only would the fat man give him cause to regret it, but he had nothing to defend himself with. He knew that every word was true, even as something unnatural and black rose up in his spirit to deny them.

"Your sex life is indicative of your entire existence," said the fat man. "The temporary relationships, which should seem alternatively sweet and bitter, are bland in the extreme. I can understand why you haven't seen the light and become a sexist. To do so would require strength of will, a delight in power for its own sake. But you drift from liaison to liaison, knowing that not a one has made a significant difference in your life, that it wouldn't matter if you had been chaste for eternity. For you, poontang is a means to fill the hours between office hours, not an expression of your individuality and masculinity. I pity you, friend chief, for the man who doesn't partake of the spiritual delights of poontang is a stone drag." The fat man licked his lips. *"Umm-doggies!* Just thinking about it unhinges my jaw for action, and indeed I would teleport myself to the demon's castle, snap my fingers at the lady of my choice, and whip on her a slice of ye olde tubesteak, had I not more important things on my mind."

"My sentiments exactly," said the editor angrily, the black force inside him taking root. "I've had more important things on my mind."

"For all eternity? No, I think not, friend chief, for all on your mind is the perpetuation of your personal prison."

"I've a newspaper to run!" said the editor, slamming his fist on the desk, on his pack of cigars.

The fat man allowed the editor a moment in which to anguish over the damage. "Tut, tut, this display of temper is unseemly, but at least it's a step in the right direction. My friend, life goes on about you. The newspaper is an excuse, a surrogate existence you use to convince yourself that you've tasted experience. You've imposed a tiny, insignificant order on the universe, in the belief that chaos is something dangerous and obscene. You reject the pain of chaos, hoping somehow to discover pleasure. Chaos and pain are nothing to be feared. Quite simply, they are the true order, and they are waiting to embrace you."

"You're saying life is absurd! I reject your opinions; I'm not interested. Now get out of my office!"

"My friend, you may not be interested in absurdity, but absurdity's interested in you."

"In me? Why?"

"It's interested in us all. The best you can do is forestall it, but ultimately it *will* embrace you, and there will be nothing you can do about it. In fact, throughout my monologue I've detected a slight alteration in the manner of your gestures, a sign that old habits are dying, that deep inside you, you realize the truth of my words. Chaos is in the process of embracing you. A new insight is coming to you. One day soon you will see more than you've ever seen, know more than you've ever known, and feel more, much more than you sense through your fingertips. I cannot tell you what you will see and know; the experience is unique, evading the concreteness of words as a slippery fish falls through clumsy fingers. You might even say it's mystical. I know godlike men who purport at objectivity sneer at the mystical, but such men never affect the truth, the reality of what the awakened mind perceives."

The fat man leaned forward, his meaty wrist resting on his knee; for a moment it seemed that he would topple over like an axed tree. "You've spent your eternity making trivial choices. Every day you arrive here and make decisions which ultimately affect no one, for they're soon forgotten in the wake of more trivial choices. Exercise your power of judgment upon yourself. You must embrace freedom, even as it embraces you. For that is what chaos truly is: freedom. All the consummation requires is the triumph of your will."

The editor did not speak. For several moments he expected the fat man to continue, until he realized that it was his turn to speak (at last!). But he did not know what to say; there were too many choices. However, the black force inside him no longer resisted the words. Finally the editor said meekly, "What am I supposed to do?"

"Why, exercise your freedom! Leave this office and never return. Find a new life. Better yet—*make* one! Leaving this office will be but the first major step, but subsequent ones will be much easier. And as long as you never weaken and accept a drab pattern in place of this drab one, then you'll never lose this freedom."

"But what about my responsibilities?"

"As the universal op would say: Fuck your responsibilities!"

"Who will edit the paper?"

The fat man smiled, more to himself than to the editor. "For the next few weeks, I will. I have need of it. Now, before you begin to suspect my motives, I must remind you that had I wished, I could have seized this hallowed office by brute force. But there was a victory to be won, a failure to be avoided, and a virus to destroy, so I chose this method."

"And what virus is that?" asked the editor cynically.

"The virus of your spirit. You were caught too deep in its throes to notice that it had infected you and your reporters. And as for your absent reporters . . ." The fat man waved his hand by way of completing the sentence.

The editor asked, "And how do you propose to run this paper without reporters?"

The fat man snorted in pleasure. "My gunsel has various methods of persuasion at his disposal. They left for the wrong reasons; you must do likewise—for the right reasons."

"Now that all the loose ends of my life are tied up, I'm to just leave? Forget about my social obligations?"

"Absolutely. Just get up and go. Teleport away if you want to be fancy about it, but go, my man, go! Godlike mankind is engaged in the midst of a great war against an unseen and unknowable foe, and it can be won only in each individual's heart. Social obligations are of no consequence; they are *never* of consequence; they are only prison bars. My friend, assert your will. If ever there was anything you wanted to do, anywhere you wanted to go, then do so. An eternal life doesn't mean you've more than one; you've only one, and you must live it to its fullest. I can't say more, though I've tried again and again. I can only impress upon you that you must not be like mere man. Can you think of the countless millions of them who wanted to live, who so desperately wanted to live, but who never had the opportunity, who never had the will, who died never knowing they could have been truly free? Think of them; think of their meaningless morals and social obligations. Think of the great, never-ending pain they suffered to avoid minor, transitory pain."

"And that's all it will take?"

"No; it will take more, much more. I know what you're thinking. Somehow the mere act of walking out that door should be more dramatic, more visual, more hypnotic. It should be something you'll look back on with visceral excitement. Well, it won't be like that, because life's not like that. And make no mistake, this isn't a contrivance of fiction, but life itself. Nevertheless, at this singular moment, the universe is turning around you. For the moment, the eyes of unseen spirits are upon you; and what you do will affect not only what you do in the future, but those unfathomable spirits. But I digress; forget them. Think of yourself. Go. This is your moment, and whatever misfortune may befall you in the future, none may take it from you."

Again, the editor was silent. He tapped a pencil on the desk four times. He mentally lit a cigar. Then, he rose, slowly, with his new cigar dangling from his mouth and his palms resting on his desk. And though he rose like a man shouldering a tremendous burden, in reality he felt a burden diminishing. The blackness inside had smothered him, but never had the taste of cigar smoke been so tangy; never had the air smelled so clean.

3. *An account from the good doctor's notebooks:*

An anomaly which often struck me in the character of my friend the consulting detective was that, although in his methods of thought he was the neatest and most methodical of godlike mankind, and although also he affected a certain quiet primness of dress, he was none the less in his personal habits one of the most untidy men that ever drove a fellow-lodger to distraction. Not that I am in the least conventional in that respect myself. The rough-and-tumble work in Cleveland, coming on top of natural Bohemianism of disposition, has made me rather more lax than befits a medical man. But with me there is a limit, and when I find a man who keeps his cigars in the coal-scuttle, his tobacco in the toe end of a Persian slipper, and his unfiled newspaper articles transfixed by a jack-knife into the very center of his wooden mantelpiece, then I begin to give myself virtuous airs. Our chambers are always full of chemicals and of relics which had a way of wandering into unlikely positions, and of turning up in the butter-dish or even in less desirable places. So the reader may well understand my consternation and indignation when, soon after we had returned to our apartment to lay the groundwork for the investigation, the consulting detective casually walked to the coat rack and purposefully picked up his tan cape-backed overcoat with two fingers. For three excruciatingly long seconds he held it, its hem six centimeters from the floor. Then he dropped it.

I must say, an irrational redness flared in my mind, and I felt personally affronted; the place was already in such a state of disarray that I was loathe to invite feminine companions for a visit lest I once again be subjected to that ridiculous remark, "What a mess! Oh well, I suppose it's typical of you free-wheeling bachelors." I managed to restrain my temper quite admirably until the consulting detective performed the identical action with my gray greatcoat. Now the irrational redness flowed up my neck and face. "I say there, just what do you think you're doing? I've got a heavy date picking me up tonight."

"I'm afraid there won't be any heavy dates until this affair is wrapped up, old friend," said the consulting detective as he walked to his room, taking long, determined strides. Though the majority of his energy was taken up with whatever obscure scheme was forming in his mind, he did not conceal his amusement at my indignation, which I took pains to control when it dawned on me that perhaps there was a legitimate reason for his shenanigans. I was too shocked (and angry) to inquire about the reason when he emerged from his room carrying a box of old clothes. Some of these he ripped, others he allowed to remain intact, but all of them he strewed throughout the apartment. The light in his eyes gleamed with a pleasant blaze; I think that he actually enjoyed himself; like that of an eternal child, the consulting detective's nature was more attuned to making a mess than in maintaining neatness.

Eventually satisfied that the decor was sufficiently disastrous, he lit a rare cigar and seated himself on the couch. The lazy smoke lingered around his mouth and nostrils; the ashes he flicked onto the floor, not even making a pretense of reaching to a tray. I watched him for some time, vacillating between ire and curiosity, pretending to examine my notes for one professional paper or another, until my curiosity—and my confusion at his smugness—got the better of me. "I give up. Would you please tell me exactly what's going on?"

"The greatest philosophers of mere man couldn't do that," said the consulting detective. "But, if I will be permitted to drift from the sublime to the mundane, I myself am currently awaiting the arrival of our first suspect."

"Eh?" I attempted to summon a more eloquent reply, but I discovered that I had summed it all up admirably.

"Why should we search for him when there are more than adequate means of drawing him to our quarters?"

"Who are you talking about? And if news of this mess gets into the social columns, I'm going to have a lot of embarrassment to endure."

"We'll have the fat man kill the story," said the consulting detective, smiling. There came a knocking at the door. "Ah! He has arrived!" Standing, he flipped the cigar into a glass of warm water on the dining table. The hiss of the extinguishing stogie was vaguely analogous to the hiss in my reddened brain. He opened the door and gave entrance to perhaps the most unusual godlike man of all. I confess that I had not thought of this individual for many years, not since I had last invoked his name to frighten a flock of eternal children disturbing a moment of privacy with a, ah, friend.

He was the tatterdemalion. His body was composed entirely of moldering rags; how he breathed, how his circulatory system functioned (or how he endured without one), how and what he ate, and how he maintained the incredible concentration that must have been required to stabilize a body so remote from the prosaic laws of science, I've no idea. The rags were all colors, but they were tinged with grime, giving each shade a common denominator of brown. He was only a meter tall, yet his shoulders still slumped, and his dangling arms were disproportionate by a few extra centimeters, giving him the appearance of an ape sculpted from materials found in a junkyard. His face was that of a demon—but the fangs bent at the slightest pressure the more tightly wound lips put upon them when he closed his mouth; the points of his long ears were in constant danger of drooping like damp flowers; the reptilian layers of skin on his face, composed as they were of additional layers of rags, did not appear coldly inhuman; as to how they actually appeared, I am at a loss to explain. His eyes were two deep black holes, containing none of the articles I normally associated with eyes; his breathing created an eerie distant wheeze; how he saw with two black holes for eyes and why he needed to breathe and how he made those wheezes and how he spoke—these and many other aspects of the tatterdemalion I am also at a loss to explain. He certainly peaked my medical curiosity, and had I the time, I would have barraged him with questions concerning his unique physique. But it was the consulting detective's show; other questions were to be asked, other matters were to be considered.

The tatterdemalion picked up a rag and inspected it. He held it close to his black eyes. "This isn't quite dirty enough, but it will do," he said in a voice so inhuman, so different from any I had ever heard, that to describe it would be like describing a new and terrible color bearing no relationship to the colors known by my audience. He turned to the consulting detective. "Thank you, sir, for these rags."

My friend gestured at the room. "You may take whatever rags you desire."

The tatterdemalion nodded politely. "It isn't often that people give them freely. Sometimes I'm able to intercept them on their way to the antimatter universe, but usually I lose those."

"All I ask in return is a few answers."

"Answers? I would gladly give you answers, but I know little. Only my collection of rags."

"These answers fall well within your realm of knowledge. The first question is the most obvious: why do you collect rags?"

The tatterdemalion looked to me. I could not read his expression, for he was incapable of facial expression. I believe he was looking to me for a possible explanation for the sudden interest of a fellow godlike man in such a lowly personality. I had no notion myself, until it occurred to me that it was not unlikely that such a person, apart from society and possessing little self-esteem, might strike back against others, thinking in his own demented way that he was avenging real or imagined hurts a world had heaped upon him. When that revelation came to me, I averted my eyes from the tatterdemalion, to betray nothing of my friend's motives.

"I've never given the matter much thought. They comfort me somehow."

"If I were to tell you that you collect rags because they're worthless, because you believe yourself to be worthless, what would your reaction be?"

"I-I don't know. I suppose I am worthless."

"Why?" asked the consulting detective.

I braved a question when the tatterdemalion could not answer. "Do you collect discarded material items because you believe yourself to be discarded?"

The tatterdemalion shook his head. "I don't know. I don't think of myself as discarded. Why are you asking me these things? I don't like to think about these things."

"We wouldn't subject you to these questions if we didn't feel it was important," said the consulting detective a trifle impatiently. "We don't enjoy hurting others for any reason."

"I know that, sir."

"I don't know if you really do. Unfortunately it is immaterial. What do you do with yourself besides hide in your lodgings—wherever they are—with your collection of rags?"

"Nothing." It seemed to me that a touch of bleakness, the first trace of traditional human characteristics I could detect, had found its way into the tatterdemalion's voice. The little creature stood before us like a lost entity; I knew that immediately upon his exit, it would be difficult to imagine that he had ever stood there, so alien, so small, so convinced of his insignificance.

"If you did consort with society, with other people," asked the consulting detective, "what do you believe you would have to offer them?"

"Nothing."

"What have others offered you?"

"Only rags. Just rags. It's all I want."

"Why rags," I asked, "when you could create beautiful jewels and metals, or flowers, or entire landscapes? You have within you the ability to do anything you desire or to create whatever you want. You could even create your own rags. Why collect the discardings of others?"

The tatterdemalion did not speak for several moments. When he did, the bleakness I had suspected previously had blossomed in that inhuman voice; the pathetic sadness of it eclipsed all other qualities, until it permeated our chambers like an odious infection. At that moment I would have done anything to ease the heart of the tatterdemalion; I even would have indulged in the unmanly gesture of embracing him and holding him as one does an eternal child; but the intensity of the sadness was such that it riveted me to my chair. Additionally, I was aware that nothing, absolutely nothing could be done to alleviate the tatterdemalion's sadness. Any attempt to ease his pain would only have resulted in more pain. He said, "Because nobody wants them. Even objects with no heart and no feelings should be wanted by somebody. There wouldn't have been any point in their existence in the first place if somebody hadn't wanted them. And people, when they're done with them, just throw them away. And I'm thinking that it's not right for nobody to want those rags. So that's what I do; I keep them."

Sighing, the consulting detective again gestured at the roomful of rags. "The cigar in the glass is a bonus. Take it."

"Thank you, sir. It's not often that people are as thoughtful as that." He walked to the table, reached up, and took the cigar from the glass, his rag hand absorbing quickly a great quantity of the warm water. He inspected the cigar. "Yes, when this dries out, it will do nicely. Thank you again, sir."

When the tatterdemalion had left with the latest additions to his rag collection, I walked to the window so that I might watch him shuffle away below. Soon he turned a corner into an alley, and he was gone from my sight. Several people were on the street, walking to and fro, and not even the eternal children had noticed him. The consulting detective put his hand on my shoulder. "I know what you're thinking, old friend," he said, "but some souls are fated to be doomed, and we can do nothing. I suppose we must accept it." He paused to take his pipe from his mouth; suddenly his eyes blazed; he had shaken off the despondent mood the conversation with the tatterdemalion had fostered upon him. "While some forms of doom are acceptable, others are not. Come, friend good doctor, we must get to work. We must save what souls we can."

4. Seven days after the creation of godlike man, a spiritually ambitious young gentleman and his equally ambitious wife (they had always prided themselves on possessing the healthiest souls in the neighborhood) simultaneously attained a degree of development which has not been equaled since. Indeed, their achievements ranked so far above all godlike mankind that even if others had been able to totally perceive them, no one would have ever learned exactly who they were, what they had been and what they had done to reach that exalted state. We may call them, for lack of more accurate terms, the eighth-dimensional man and the eighth-dimensional woman; and though we cannot communicate accurately how they pictured life, how they thought and spoke, how they lived, and how they looked, both to their eyes and to the eyes of others, we may approximate these things, if the reader would keep in mind that the words are, at best, analogies which ultimately correspond to reality only by default.

They were gray shadows that crept over the world of godlike

man; though they had not the powers to travel vast distances instantly, they had not the inclination, and were unaware of their loss. Nor did they travel in space, though they did not require oxygen; for them there was no difference between the warm safety of a planet and the cold, inhospitable vacuum of space. They did not perceive themselves as shadows, but as coolly glowing wisps of light, with the most minute substance. It was to the rest of the world they were shadows; and they saw the world as a shadow; they discerned objects and locations only with an effort (which usually was not worth the trouble; mundane existence was of little interest to them).

Their only emotion, the one source of their knowledge, was their love. They experienced no ennui, no doubts, no fears; in their pure state, they had no past and no future; there was only the endless pleasure of their love. Sometimes a godlike man saw, for an instant, two curious shadows drifting in the sky above a golden city; sometimes the shadows dove like dolphins in a gossamer ocean; and sometimes they dove into one another, merged, and separated, each whole, but enriched by the other. The godlike man forgot the shadows; he could not perceive them enough to take full note of their presence. He remembered a vague uneasiness, a moment filled with a loss he could not pinpoint, could not comprehend. Not in the wildest flights of his imagination would he have guessed that what he saw was two of his fellows engaged in an eternal act of loving—of foreplay, consummation, and a subsequent peace that permeated the loving when it began anew. Sometimes, while a godlike woman was making love in her dark apartment, and she opened her eyes as she caressed her partner's hair and back, she saw two flickering shadows deeper than the darkness flow through the ceiling. She experienced a momentary dissatisfaction that all the exemplary love-making in the universe could not ease. (And exemplary love-making was pretty hard to find; most godlike women had to settle for merely adequate love-making. Eternal life had created in man an unfortunate disinterest in certain nuances of living.) But that dissatisfaction usually passed as her partner, sensing her disappointment, jabbed and grunted and in general carried on like a savage so that he might ignore the ugly insecurity that dampened his confidence.

The eighth-dimensional man and woman were unaware of the disquiet they caused the spiritually impoverished; indeed, they were unaware of almost everything. Time itself was meaningless to them; they did not know if they had reached their exalted state seven days ago or seven million. And what did it matter? When they dove into each other, the gray universe exploded into colors upon colors—created by two hundred twenty-seven thousand, nine hundred and forty-six primary colors in ever-changing cascading patterns that hypnotized and bewildered. They were an integral part of the patterns; as the universe changed, so did they. But the colors were the lesser joy. The sensation provided the greatest pleasure. They felt themselves fall apart into separate atoms and molecules; and then they came together, as one entity, merging their minute substances and their minds until they were one body with one thought; and there were no secrets, no reason to conceal one closet of the mind for the sake of privacy, no distance between their personalities. They, of all their race, experienced a union which was literally that.

Small wonder that when they took time out from their mutual ecstasy to think of the shadows below, it was with a mixture of pity and wonder. Pity that the shadows were trapped in one trivial plane when there were an infinite number to explore; wonder that the shadows did not appear to yearn for those infinite planes; wonder that the shadows did not constantly strive to reach for the levels of existence so near the remorseless cold of reality. However, there was not much opportunity for pity when there were so many phenomena of love to experience. In fact, it was remarkable that they sometimes thought of the shadows at all. The love filled their entire beings, until they thought of one another as love personified, until they could not imagine another emotion as part of their psyches. They had literally achieved what the poets of mere man had only dreamed; and their lives were warm and comforting. When they thought of the love they had known in the world of shadows, they wondered how they could have ever called it love. It had been more a scenario of dissatisfaction than an epic of bliss; the history of their former lives was a never-ending list of meaningless bickerings, the insecurity of feeling unloved even while consummating love, unperceived distances between them, and the continuous threat of the relationship severed if any one of innumerable occurrences came to pass. Now they had escaped all that; now their lovemaking was free of residual guilt of the pleasure of their bodies (a guilt fostered upon them by an unenlightened society, usually the odious villain in the internal drama of spiritual struggle). No longer did they have to cope with the icky slipperiness of sex. No longer did they have to cope with the trials and tribulations of washing stained bedsheets before the folks came over for a visit, premature ejaculations, periods, and the disconcerting scent of sweaty armpits during orgasm. Why they had put up with all that mess and fuss they could not understand. Now they were free from worry; and that freedom provided them with the opportunity to discover... themselves.

Small wonder that when the eighth-dimensional man sensed that the eighth-dimensional woman was losing her hold on the higher planes and was beginning to return to the world of shadows, he began to worry.

At first the change was barely noticeable. He did not know if it had initially manifested itself in her body while they merged together, or in the back of her mind, in some secret compartment that still yearned for the mundane, that had become frightened of the universe of visions they had entered. He knew at once that if this doubt was not unchecked, then it would exaggerate until she experienced anxiety at the sight of every new color. Eventually she would fear losing that which was of no consequence. Having found her purpose in living, she would renounce it because she would believe one such as she could never truly have a purpose. The eighth-dimensional man had seen the same phenomenon occur a thousand times in the world of shadows; self-doubt invariably caused the victim to indulge in self-fulfilling prophesies. And others achieved all they had ever dreamed, and then uselessly set more "unobtainable" goals for themselves, guaranteed to put a strain on the fuel pump, just to avoid the false dilemma of stagnation. *Ha!* said the eighth-dimensional man to himself. *It's absurd to think that nirvana brings stagnation. It can't happen.*

He would have informed his wife of this undeniable truth, but though he could speak to himself, he could not speak to her. Previously this unfortunate shortcoming of their spiritually elevated beings had not impressed him as a shortcoming. There had been no need for them to speak to each other; all the communication they had required was satisfied by the interplay of their substances when they merged. But though the pleasure of their mystical sexual activity was undiminished, the eighth-dimensional man knew that the wedge had been forced between them. It was a matter of time in this timeless world.

He did not allow his worry over the impending loss of his wife to cause him to doubt himself. He *knew* that nothing would cause his hold to slip from this immortal plane. Even without the lovemaking, there still would be the eternal peace, the beautiful colors, the self-sustaining energy, the wonderment of discovering nuances of the soul. All these could be enjoyed without company, though company was certainly a plus, no matter how you looked at it.

As time passed, he sensed her distance widening and widening. He wondered what the reason could be; it could not possibly be himself; it was physically impossible on this plane for lovers to play the game of making each other miserable. Despite his attempts to maintain the constant ebb of ecstasy which had made his life a veritable encyclopedia of bliss, his body became permeated by a bittersweet sorrow which he eventually identified as the emotion that overcomes the soul when an affair is drawing to a close. He had never before thought of his relationship with the eighth-dimensional woman as an affair, not even when they had lived in the world of shadows. Although he recognized that his reaction was essentially protective, shielding his spirit from her vicious pessimistic onslaughts, the knowledge was not comforting. Nevertheless, when his love finally slipped from the higher plane and became part of the world of shadows, he did nothing to keep her with him, though he sensed that his efforts would be successful for a time.

Thinking that perhaps his solitary situation would grant him new perceptions and insights, he attempted to experience anew the glory and peace of his achievement. His attempt lasted six hours; it was undramatic, to say the least, and all he learned was that his peace had been forever tainted by the loss of her. Somehow nirvana was unimportant alone; he had shared it with her too long. He decided, much to his surprise, that his policy of *laissez faire* had been an abject failure. He was also surprised to learn that one who had shed nearly all his personality and its affiliated fears could feel like a total nerd. There was but one solution: to search her out and help her shed the shadows she had embraced.

This did not take as long as he had guessed. After making the strenuous effort to reorient himself to the shadows, so that he might discern them with some degree of accuracy, he found himself drawn to a certain sector of what attempted to be a glittering beautiful city, but which in his definition of reality was a drab construction of inconsequential lifeless buildings, little toothpick boxes. He sensed an onslaught of pessimism resembling that of his wife, but which was infinitely more powerful. Though he basked in the warmth of colors, seeing only vague outlines of dark shadows, he felt the cold like distant waves of absolute-zero blasts. He was finally drawn to her, as if some portions of their spirits would always be merged; the parting could never be complete. He found her in the coldest sector of the city, and when he saw her sitting alone in an apartment, he experienced a yearning, an acceptance of his failure to keep her, that somehow protected him from the cold, enabling him to come closer to the shadows, to see and hear her more clearly.

It had been eons since he had pictured her as corporeal in his expanded mind's eye. And he never would have pictured her as an older woman; to his spirit, she had always been a drink of youth. Yet there she was, it could not be denied, and she was middle-aged. She had the power to make herself young again, as young as seventeen if she wanted, and she thought it more appropriate that she be nearly forty, with wrinkles about the lips and eyes, thick veins showing through the skin of the neck, and thin dry hands. Several strands of dark gray were interwoven in her black hair. The texture of her skin was not as smooth as the eighth-dimensional man would have liked; he did not remember it as so stretched and haggard about the neck and chin. He did not like to see her wearing that drab yellow skirt, that white blouse, that bra (he had always thought bras looked ridiculous on younger women; *but*, he reminded himself, *my love isn't young anymore*). And she had never before worn stockings or high heels; he wondered why she had chosen to. The most confusing aspect of her appearance was her wide eyes; once they revealed the wild, youthful spirit she had known, and by rights they should have, regardless of her age. Now her eyes revealed youth in an eternal state of expiration; something inside her was always threatening to die; and though she had given up the fight long ago, though she wanted it to die, it remained alive, its refusal to wither constantly torturing her. The eighth-dimensional man felt an alien coldness rise in his heart and attempted to reach through the mystical planes toward her. Though the cold was pleasurable after a fashion, born from a pity in his heart rather than from the oppressive universe, the eighth-dimensional man feared what might become of his spirit upon reaching her; so he squashed the cold and tried to be objective about what he felt. However, all his considerable objectivity could not prevent him from marveling at her sitting there, in the center of the living room, without a table beside or in front of her, with her hands demurely in her lap, her head bent slightly downward, her eyes staring blankly at the floor, doing these things as if they were all that ever could be done, as if there had never been anything else to do or think of. So unlike the woman he had known. He never could have imagined her becoming so unlike that woman, a woman who had caused the universe to spin like a carousel around her. Yet . . . there she was. She might as well have never loved, thought, or believed, for all the benefit those past activities did for her present situation.

Someone knocked at the door. The eighth-dimensional woman arched her eyebrows, her curiosity briefly returning to her a trace of her former vivacity. She opened the door and when she saw the peculiar visage of the gentleman standing before the threshold, she inhaled sharply, holding her hand over her mouth.

"Can I come in, miss?" asked the universal op.

"Ah, yes," said the eighth-dimensional woman, after pondering the matter for a few seconds. "It's just that . . . you startled me."

"I understand," said the universal op, rubbing his smooth chin. His featureless face seemed to be unnecessarily lingering on the woman's wide eyes, as far as the eighth-dimensional man was concerned.

"Would you care for some coffee?" At once the eighth-dimensional woman grimaced. "Oh, I'm sorry. You obviously can't . . . I mean . . ."

"Forget it," said the op. "I'll absorb some when I get home. It looks strange, so I always eat and drink alone."

"I really am sorry."

"Like I said, forget it."

"Would you care to sit down?" she asked, gesturing to a couch.

"Yeah. That'll be all right," said the op, sitting and crossing his legs. He waited for her to sit in the lonely chair before him; then he said, "I would appreciate it if you would answer some questions, miss."

"I've no objections, though I don't know what I can tell you about anything."

"Let me be the judge of that." The op withdrew a holophoto of a dapper young godlike man wearing a derby and a black suit. "Ever see this bozo before?"

"No."

The op leaned back, still holding the holophoto to her. He made a sound as if he was pursing a set of lips deep in his skull. "Do you find him attractive?"

She tilted her head. "He is rather cute."

"That's the one thing you could have said that could convince me you're telling the truth. The best thing Kitty ever said about him was that she wouldn't kick him out of bed. Of course, she was never known to kick *anybody* out of bed, regardless of provocation or performance."

"Kitty? Who's Kitty? And why did you ask me about that cute person?"

The op returned the holophoto to his pocket. "Kitty has been missing for several weeks. And I asked you because I'd received reports that a godlike woman no one had ever seen before had moved into this apartment. I figured it might be someone who had seen her in a mysterious byway, or that it might be her in disguise. It wasn't much of a lead, but none have been so far, so I figured it couldn't hurt."

"I'm sorry I couldn't help."

"Don't sweat it. It's not your fault."

"I know that. But for some reason my sorrow is more than perfunctory."

"That's nice of you." Neither the eighth-dimensional woman nor the eighth-dimensional man, looking on the scene from the higher plane, could tell if the universal op was sincere or sarcastic. He uncrossed and crossed his legs, turned his head in various directions, as if he was inspecting the sparsely furnished apartment out of idle curiosity, and rubbed his left elbow. "You know, miss, you really shouldn't have trusted me right off like you did. A godlike woman was killed last night, here in the East End."

The eighth-dimensional woman nodded blankly; the meaning of his words had not struck her. She smiled briefly. "Well, I can't say you've an honest face, but you do have an honest demeanor. It took me a few seconds to realize it, but I knew, somehow, I could trust you."

There was a lull in the conversation; they sat silent and uncomfortable for over a minute. Then the universal op asked, "Where did you come from? How did you wind up here?"

She smiled again, frowning before she spoke, evidently finding little humor in her story. "I existed with my husband on a higher mystical plane. We had become one with the universe. It was like . . . the oversoul had encompassed us; we saw everything like it really was, with no barriers to impede our perceptions. We were always around, but no one could actually see us. We felt sorry for everybody else when we weren't communing with the universe. I guess my husband still is."

"I don't take much stock in mystical experiences myself."

"They're not so bad. In fact, I was so happy, I can't imagine why I got tired of it. But something called me here. I don't know what . . . or why. I can't cope with any of it. I had forgotten all about the pain. I don't know how people can stand it, why they don't do something about it."

"They do what they can."

"Why was that woman killed?"

"We don't know. We won't find out until we catch him. I don't really think about it. I'm just doing what the consulting detective wants me to do. It's a lot easier that way."

"Who's the consulting detective?"

"You might say that as of the moment, he's the *de facto* leader of our little group. He's the only person really prepared to cope with this type of situation. He keeps on saying that he has the greatest deductive mind in history, and so far I've no reason to doubt him."

"What's he like?"

"He's got a real tight asshole, but outside of that, he's okay."

Again, they were silent. Finally, for no apparent reason, the eighth-dimensional woman said, "You know, nirvana was really swell. I'll never have such a good time again. But none of it is with me now; it's like I've just been born. Do you think all mystical experiences are that way?"

"How am I supposed to know?"

"You would think that I at least retain firm memories of what it was like, but I don't. They're all slipping away as if none of it had ever happened. It doesn't seem fair, to have known so much and to remember so little. I can't even remember what my husband looked like, not when he was corporeal, not as he is on the higher plane." She paused. "You know our sex lives were a lot different too. What is metaphor here was reality there. We merged and became one, and when we went apart, we carried something of each other with us. But now it's all gone. My husband isn't part of me anymore."

"Look, you don't have to go into these personal details."

"I want to. When I was part of the universe, I used to think mundane sex was icky and slippery, and I guess it still is icky and slippery, but it feels nice too, doesn't it?"

"I wouldn't know." Again, it was difficult to pinpoint the universal op's true sentiments.

"What are you doing tonight?" asked the eighth-dimensional woman.

"Uh, I'm working. Got a killer to catch. Real important stuff. Got no time for fooling around."

"I see. Are you free for, oh, the next few hours?"

"Er, ah, ahem, well, yes, I suppose."

As the universal op struggled to make his reply, she walked to the couch and sat beside him. She put her hand on his shoulder and stared at his smooth face. "I need some relief from the pain. I need to forget myself for a time. Already. I haven't known myself for so long and already I need to forget." Her arm slithered like a snake around his neck and she put her head on his shoulder.

After an indecisive moment the universal op put his left arm around her back, placing his hand on her shoulder; his right hand covered her tiny fingers.

The eighth-dimensional woman said, "It would greatly facilitate things if you created a mouth. You don't have to create a nose, ears, or anything else, just a mouth. And you can get rid of it after we're done. How about it?"

Well! thought the eighth-dimensional man, *if she's going to engage in petty bourgeois activities, I'm not going to have anything else to do with her. Humph. I am disappointed. Depressed too.*

But the eighth-dimensional man was not so depressed that he

lost his grip on the higher plane. However, he could not forget the woman who had been his wife; the glories of the universe gradually became meaningless to him. For several weeks he searched for a solution to his dilemma. Then it occurred to him that there might be even higher planes; once he elevated himself to the highest levels of reality, becoming a twentieth-dimensional man or perhaps a forty-second-dimensional man, he would forget her. He would not consider himself alone because the concept would be immaterial. He embarked upon a strenuous spiritual exercise course, in effect searching for those levels.

As of this writing, the eighth-dimensional man is still searching, but he holds every hope for success.

5. The mature eternal child awoke wrapped like an embryonic butterfly in the silk sheets and fur blankets on his circular water bed. He sensed that the noon sun was still too cold for his sensitive body, that his mansion on the outskirts of the golden city was not yet warm enough to allow him to ease into the waking world with the comfort to which he had grown accustomed. Beside him lay the sleeping body of a female eternal child which the colonel had convinced (through devious means) the shrink to age just enough to taste the delectable recipe of brain salad. The mature eternal child had lost count how many female eternal children (and, consequently, male eternal children to service them afterwards) had been so altered, but the aching of his strained muscles, his weary bones, his overtaxed pelvis informed him that the number was mind-staggering. As he rolled about, trying to summon energy and keep from becoming seasick, he tried to distinguish the night of pleasure from other, similar nights; he knew there had been something distinctive about it, but he lacked the strength to concentrate on finer details. He kicked the sheets and blankets away, braving the cool air of the master bedroom. He looked at the pubescent eternal child; she had long blonde hair, large dark nipples, a pretty nose, and (oh yes, this was what he had been trying to think of) a sex that raged like a vacuum cleaner, sucking up everything in the environs. His organs felt like they had been the instruments in a sonata played on a washboard. Flaccidity would be the order of the day.

Or maybe not. He had an appointment to keep.

He rolled from the water bed and stretched. He stood on his tiptoes; then he lowered himself and stretched his stomach forward, gently placing his pelvic muscles back in the swing of things; he scratched his balls for several moments, until the skin was red; it was an exquisite pleasure. His mouth felt like he had stuffed it full of cotton: too many cigarettes. He struck a match and lit a cigarette on his trek to the bathroom, twenty meters from the bed; he casually tossed the extinguished match in a marble ashtray strategically placed on a statue disguised as modern art, but which in reality was the collapsed structure of a realistic representation of an amoeba. He flicked ashes on the rug of otter fur.

Inside the bathroom, he placed the cigarette in a silver ashtray overflowing with butts and looked in the mirror. *I look like shit today*, he thought. *And greased shit at that*. His curly red hair stood out as if he had just suffered a devastating electrical shock. Stubble riddled his angular jaw and weak chin; his eyes resembled two moldy pools of sludge; dried mucous clung to nostril hair. Yet not even these humiliating evidences of humanity, dragging down his spirit into a morass of triviality, could disguise the alluring aspects of a face that made pubescent female eternal children go wild. He did not know exactly what it was about himself, but there was definitely *something* that lifted him beyond the realms of the ordinary, into regions that even the more fortunate, infinitely more powerful godlike men could not touch. He would have spent several seconds pondering that something, but the taste of cotton was rapidly becoming the taste of stale mothballs; so he concentrated on brushing his teeth. He was not quite prepared to grapple with the greater mysteries plaguing his existence. He spent an hour in a bathtub twelve by seven meters, basking in the luxury of bubblebath; and the chemicals added to the water softened his skin and soothed his aches. The bath enabled him to relax completely, and his mind flowed free; he was quite proud of himself. Life progressed on an even plane. All the comforts he could ever want were his. Finally, when he heard the stirrings of the pubescent eternal child, he forced himself from the drug of the bubblebath and combed his hair. Then he ran his hand over the stubble of his chin. He smiled. He did not have to shave. Instead, today, he had to play the blues.

As the throbbing chords of one of his most intense numbers resounded in his brain, the mature eternal child entered the bedroom and from a safe distance (lest the flames of passion caused his resolve to suffer a relapse) watched the pubescent eternal child drape her ivory skin in a flimsy green dress that provided his imagination with little inspiration. The new eternal children were a racy breed. As she combed her hair, she appeared oblivious to the carnal vibrations he could almost smell; the taste of her vaginal fluid surged in his memory, so powerfully that he became sorry he had brushed his teeth; some good items had been lost with the stale mothballs. But when she had completed the chore of perfecting her presence, she smiled and winked at him. She caressed her calf with the comb. The mature eternal child felt himself assaulted by an onslaught of unreality; the air tinged with cigarette smoke, the soft otter fur under his feet, the water dripping from his hair down his back—all sensation became dim, the stuff of dreams. And he asserted the stuff of reality with a burst of will; he would have succumbed to the most obvious cure to the dilemna, the cure of inserting his lizard into her nestegg, but he had no more time to fool around with this particular party doll. At least not today.

"Just make yourself right at home, toots," said the mature eternal child after he had put on his latest fab gear (a red-and-green plaid lumberjack shirt with snaps on the wrists and pockets, bleached pale bluejeans, green sneakers, yellow socks, and an assortment of bracelets and beads). "I've got a few trivial, yet time-consuming details to take care of. I'll see you tonight. Okay, toots?"

"Sure, babe," she answered in a voice that, once again, shredded the fabric of reality.

It certainly doesn't take much to shred the fabric of reality these days, thought the mature eternal child as he waved bye-bye with his twinkie, grabbed his acoustic guitar, and strutted from the master bedroom. *Maybe I'll write a song:* Got Dem Old Reality Blues. *But ... are the blues really the blues? What if I've been deluding myself all this time? I mean, if the blues are actually some other color, I'm gonna feel pretty foolish on the day of the final accounting. I just hope the blues aren't really the pinks. I ain't gonna play no frigging fag music.*

The mature eternal child suddenly became very confused. He had not been so introspective since the fine day the colonel had discovered him wandering about in the park. Since then life had progressed too rapidly; life had undergone change after change too quickly. His days had been a never-ending stream of information that caused him to feel simultaneously giddy and exuberant. He had never paused to wonder if there was a reason behind it, some hidden rationale which, if perceived, would illuminate his role in the scheme of the universe. Once he had been convinced he had a definite role; and he had always assumed he was following it; but now he wondered if perchance he had gone astray. However, though he might eventually become armed with the knowledge that he had lost the path, there was the distinct possibility that he might be able to do nothing about it; events seemed to sweep him up, to be totally beyond his control.

As he strummed his guitar, walking down a fifty-meter hallway, past holophotoes of his triumphant concerts and momentoes of his triumphant personal relationships, he reflected upon the days when he had been a slightly malfunctioning eternal child, one of the android pets of flesh and blood some godlike families kept to assuage their desire for true children. He once spent his days screaming at the lonely hawkman in the sky; to what purpose, he could not recall. Then, without prior warning, he became a pawn in a game of unnatural perimeters played by the demon, the lawyer, and the fat man. They, in their turn, convinced the shrink to pervert his superscience to the child's artificial maturation. And without the gradual comfort and disconcerting discomfort of adolescence, he became mature—at least in the literal sense. Something beautiful and wonderful had happened to him, despite the horrific overtones of the situation; and yet, when he visited his parents and asked them if they were proud of him, if they approved of him, if they were glad to see him an adult, they could not accept the new reality. They insisted upon treating him as if he was still the eternal child they had loved and chastised for eons. They wanted him to remain in his room until their reality became his, as if life could be manipulated so easily. He had no choice but to leave them with their delusions; he had no choice but to discover the purpose of his new existence without their support. But had he chosen the correct path after all? Would it not have been better if he had fought them until they had accepted him? By leaving the game, had he unknowingly lost it?

He felt that he had answered his questions with questions that pointed him to the night. Perhaps he had the colonel to thank for that.

One fine day the colonel heard him playing a few simple chords to a group of mesmerized eternal children. The mature eternal child was unaware of the effect he had upon his fellows; he had never thought of himself as a singer; and yet he sang with a voice uncorrupted by arbitrary standards of craft that distanced art from those it originally had been intended for. He stood under the shading branches of a drooping willow tree; and the very wind became silent as he sang of pain, of alienation from his parents, of a life without love. His words were simple and direct; yet in their lack of poetry was a poetry that eloquence could not touch. The eternal children could not understand the concepts behind his words, but they could hear his voice, they could hear his guitar, and those were effective enough.

They were more than effective as far as the colonel was concerned. The colonel conceived a grand design for the mature eternal child. Though the colonel inadvertently revealed time and time again that he had no conception, no true inkling of what was actually transpiring, the mature eternal child trusted him, because without him, without the impetus of a godlike man also caught in an incomprehensible game, nothing would have transpired; and there would have been no questions to ask.

The mature eternal child walked outside, toward a gazebo where, shaded from the stark sun floating inexorably like a mechanical disc across the clear sky, sat the colonel wearing an ice-cream suit and a black string tie. He drank mint julep through a straw. His white hair was slicked backward, held in place by a cream with an offensive odor; his thin brown moustache was darkened by a generous application of wax. Leftover fried chicken attracted flies to a plate on a glass table, and whenever it amused the colonel, he mentally ignited a fly, so that the flames had extinguished by the time the charred carcass struck the chicken bones.

Spying the mature eternal child, the colonel beamed and said, "Boy! I say there: boy! Come here, boy, and let me look at you. And stop wasting your talent, boy. Save it for the show!"

"Yassah, boss. Right away, boss. I is a'comin'. I'm gwan to git my ass right over der, right away!"

As the mature eternal child shuffled upon the gazebo, the

colonel frowned and said paternally, "Please, don't talk that way, boy. It reminds me too much of the good old days gone, done, and buried, when I used to hear the mellow voices of the darkies as they labored in the fields. You poke fun at those good old days, boy and you poke fun at certain aspects of our relationship—don't deny it, boy, you can't hide the truth from an old codger like me—but you don't know how much it tugs at my heartstrings to hear reminders of those lazy summers I spent at the plantation."

"But, boss, is you trying to tell me they had plantations and mint julep in Cleveland? It just don't seem possible to me, boss."

The colonel snickered softly to himself. He tapped his forefinger on his temple, leaning forward and scowling to emphasize the significance of the gesture. "Some places anything's possible, mi'boy, anything's possible."

"Shoot, you's pulling my leg."

"Nope. I'm flat out telling the truth; if I'm not you can cut out my heart with a rusty knife and stomp on it. And will you drop that ridiculous accent? I think I'm going to cry." He created a silk handkerchief and blew his nose; then he sent the handkerchief to the antimatter universe.

"Tell me, boss, how was dat old black stuff? Did you ever immerse yourself in darkie pussy?"

The colonel snorted and shook his head. "Me? Oh, no. My family was strictly the ritz. We didn't do such things."

"Too bad."

"I should say so."

"Well, friend colonel, I've got to be going before I'm tempted to ask a few direct, important, and entirely relevant questions concerning whatever happened to dem darkies after the rise of godlike man. You may have wondered yourself, seeing as how you're usually all-fired concerned about the internal logic in the social extrapolation of the Big Red Cheese's fast-paced sci-fi thrillers. See you around." Unheeding of the colonel's wishes, the mature eternal child strummed a few basic blues chords as he walked away. He received a thrill of satisfaction as he heard the colonel (doubtless holding his forefinger over his pursed lips) mumble, "I wonder: what *did* happen to those good and simple black folk? Internal logic? Logic? Humph. Who am I kidding?"

Because he did not have powers of teleportation, the mature

eternal child had to hoof it to his destination, a fifteen-minute walk from the outskirts of his mansion grounds. Somehow he could not summon up the misery to sing the blues properly; of course he always had that problem until he rehearsed with the band or played on stage, but he felt guilty at not feeling miserable because he had begun questioning reality. If one was to question reality properly, it had always seemed to him, then a prerequisite was misery. It was unnatural to be happy while doubting the natural order of things. But he doubted and nevertheless was happy. He could not shed the feeling something was wrong with him.

Actually, he thought, *deep down inside I don't give a fuck*.

He walked through fields of tall green grass and listened to the chirpings of birds gifted with incredible voices, singing in languages he had never heard.

He saw a flock of dancing toadstools concealed in shrubbery; he was positive they had no true minds of their own, yet they seemed to savor a particular joy as they jumped up and down, their disproportionate weight straining the fiber of their flimsy legs. The toadstools' routine reached several climaxes, several razzle-dazzle displays of their dancing virtuosity, but it never concluded. Though he heard no music (the songs of the birds did not correspond to this exotic dance), the mature eternal child could, with a tad of assistance from his fertile imagination, surmise the rhythms that drifted from another plane of existence to infect the mushrooms. They waved their hands in the air, beckoning him though they had no eyes to see him, no ears to hear him, as if they were imploring him to change his molecular structure and join them. The mature eternal child could not change his molecular structure, but this did not strike him as a tragedy. In fact, it somehow seemed right and proper that he could not join them; it was enough that he had become aware of their existence, of their dance, in a locale he had passed many times before, but had never investigated.

He caressed the smooth bark of a tree with red leaves and purple twigs that was the only one of its species on Earth; perhaps it could not even be said to have a classification. He plucked a berry from a descending branch and, when he ate it, felt a surge of juice between his teeth that tasted red; it could be described only with one word, with that color. He imagined the juice filling his throat, filling his stomach, filling his entire torso, and he experienced a warmth that radiated from a source beyond his body, beyond his spirit.

He caught a scent so pungent that he became dizzy, and he traced the scent to a flower with pedals that crossed the boundaries into other dimensions, remaining in his own universe all the while. And the pedals returned from those mysterious worlds with odors piled upon odors, each odor representing an object—a mineral, an ocean, or a city so alien, so foreign to anything he had ever conceived, that he failed to find pictures in his mind corresponding to any of them. And the flower itself appeared so fragile. It was amazing that the thin pedals could withstand the forces they challenged; he would have thought the power of winds hurling particles with ferocity would tear a pedal; and that another pedal would be dissolved in a sea of acid; and another would be eaten by a stray beast with no eye for the finer beauties of life. But the pedals always returned from their journeys unscathed.

He saw footprints—the paws of an invisible animal roughly the size of a tabby—pop into existence silently, one by one; and somehow his own senses were heightened, enabling him to perceive the general outlines of this animal prowling the golden city of godlike mankind, unbeknownst to all save him. For an instant that seemed to stretch into several minutes he feared the invisible animal would become angry at him; and he would be suddenly subjected to an attack of sharp fangs and claws; he would not be able to defend himself because he would not know when the animal was turning from his shoulder to his throat, when its claws were reaching toward his stomach or chest. The general outline he perceived did not provide him with sufficient information to guess the beast's weaponry. However, his fears proved unfounded. The animal did stop and look at him (or so he guessed); and the animal did make a noise, but not one which could be construed as preliminary to an attack. He did not know what the noise construed, but it did not matter, for the animal's tracks vanished into a clump of grass. Soon he could not see the grass part to make way for the invisible animal.

For a moment the mature eternal child felt sad. He realized that if he had only known how to see properly, he would have seen another wonder, another vision that would enrich him and his music. He was not resigned to sadness; perhaps next time he would see more than a general outline. Already he had learned much he had never thought he would learn. Perhaps he had played the game correctly after all.

His interests, which had been soaring, now plummeted. The shock of their collision with the earth of so-called reality was physically painful (or he believed it was, which amounted to the same thing). He leaned against a rubber tree, its rubber bark gently yielding an extra centimeter to accommodate his spine. He wiped beads of sweat from under his curly red bangs. He looked at the shrubbery where he had uncovered the dancing toadstools; he was afraid to inspect it again, for fear that he would not see them. If he did not, he would believe all he had seen and learned was a lie. He wondered what had happened to him. He had not been different, not in the least; instead, he had merely been *more* than he had ever been, although in theory the sum of his parts should have remained consistent.

He became aware that if he did not hurry, he would be late for his important appointment. This meeting took place once a week—though some weeks had to be skipped due to conflicting schedules—and virtually every meeting was memorable, regardless of the observation he had made countless times that the facts were always unchanged. The meeting was part of a project that (thankfully) never seemed to end; yet its successful conclusion would be the crowning touch to a career of loving and musicianship. He quickened his pace, not pausing to savor the breeze cooling the heat, the wind bending the grass, the snatches of birdsongs he caught when his mind wandered, until he reached the backyard of a cottage where dwelt the soprano.

Before climbing the white picket fence, he felt the wind drying the perspiration from his face; his eyes lingered over flowers swaying in the garden near the cottage; he became mildly interested in a birdsong. For a moment he felt shorn of his identity; all the pleasure and pain he had experienced was immaterial; whatever had happened to him on his journey here was about to happen again. He brought himself to "reality" with an effort that caused his spine to tingle. He did not have enough time for that sort of thing. Whenever he thought of the soprano, all other concerns were swept aside. Now, as an idealized version of her loveliness formed like a ghost in his brain, the stark sun was no longer responsible for the burning inside him. His skin wreathed across his frame like watery mucous. His identity slipped from his consciousness again, yet this time the process was not an advancement, but a primitive reversal. He felt vaguely disturbed. He felt vaguely dizzy, inordinately proud of himself for no apparent reason.

When the mature eternal child was in the backyard, even the wind stilled. He strummed his guitar. The quiet, simple music broke the silence like an explosion. After several bars, he stopped playing, raised an eyebrow, and smiled. His lungs felt as if he had inhaled a vapor congealing into a solid substance. The sensation of his lungs intensified when the soprano answered the call of his electrifying music.

Although her melodious statement overwhelmed him with its innate beauty, he thought sardonically, *Naturally she still won't talk like a normal godlike woman.* (He always maintained a sarcastic distance from the soprano and the emotions she stirred inside him lest he become smothered and lost forever.) Pretending annoyance, in case she was watching him from a window or via her powers, he sang a verse from one of his greatest hits:

> *I got them old daybreak blues.*
> *I got them all day long.*
> *I got them every day,*
> *Ever since I woke up without you.*
> *Oh, when am I gonna git rid of them daybreak blues?*

She answered him with a line from some sissy foreign language of mere man. He guessed the meaning and walked through the back door. In the kitchen he saw a plateful of steaming fried chicken. He thought—the words originating from a source he did not know—*I'm a back-door man. I can eat more fried chicken than any godlike man ever seen.* He bit a huge chunk from a breast; as he chewed it, grease slipped from between his lips, grease that he did not bother to wipe from his chin. He sang a verse from another smash hit, a fave rave among his more sophisticated fans:

> *Them old peach blues have got me again.*
> *Every day I think about your peaches,*
> *Waiting to be picked from your tree.*
> *Let me have a bite of your peaches, baby,*
> *Let me have a bite of you.*

The verse seemed to impress the soprano. She answered in an impassioned frenzy, her voice quivering so heavily that it would have been barely comprehensible even if it had been spoken in a language the mature eternal child could understand. Her reaction, in turn, inspired him to sing one of his most tortuous songs, a catchy little ditty that invariably brought tears to the eyes of his most sensitive pubescent fans. He did not feel miserable at all; in fact, he was a vessel of joy; nevertheless, his voice was the personification of anguish as he sang:

> Them railroads give me the blues,
> They give me the blues all day long.
> Them trains keep on a'rollin',
> They roll here and they roll there,
> But they never take me to you.
> And that's why them railroads give me the blues.

He walked from the kitchen. Strange words—another legacy from the unknown source—came to his mind, corresponding to his actions. *And he walked on down the hall. And he came to a room. And he looked inside.* And he saw the soprano in a huge bed, with white blankets and white sheets. The walls, the rugs, the fabric of the cushions and sofas and chairs—all were white. A mirror on the ceiling reflected the whiteness below. The wood cabinets and the wooden frames for the sofas and chairs were, of course, dark, but the only other colors in the room were the pale skin of the soprano and her ebony hair, an aura of blackness surrounding her triangular face and falling past her shoulders, covering her breasts. The mature eternal child did not require much imagination to realize that underneath those pure white sheets, she was completely naked. Utterly nude. Strictly in the buff. Draped only in her birthday suit. The certain knowledge caused him to reel. The primitive reversal gained full control of both his sense and his sensibilities, and already he could smell the sweet aroma of her love juice running over his lips as if he was guzzling a beer. He finally licked the chicken grease from his mouth, in anticipation of the tasty delights beckoning his arrival. He hurled his guitar onto a white sofa and fairly screamed (as he rushed toward her, in the meantime frantically attempting to divest himself of his clothing) a verse from his latest song, a sure-fire hit, guaranteed to silence the pubescent critics who claimed that the glories of his success had cost him

the cutting edge that had made his work unique in the first place.
He fairly screamed:

> *Them blues are destructive baby,*
> *They're destructive all day long.*
> *I don't know how much longer I can take them, baby,*
> *I can't stand them all day long.*
> *All I know for sure is that*
> *When I think of you, baby,*
> *I think of jelly-filled doughnuts with icing on top.*

The soprano's voice was more impassioned than he had ever
heard, and as he leaped naked into the bed, and kissed her neck,
shoulders, and breasts, he knew with finality that he had no
reason to doubt the power of his latest composition. Yet a part
of him was disappointed. As his mighty organ plunged into the
throne of Venus, becoming immersed in that soft substance that
yielded to his hardness forever, he wanted, more than he knew,
for the soprano to answer him in his own vernacular. Regardless
of how often their love-making made them one organism, he
could never forget that her thoughts were always distant from
his, that never had the opera singer gotten down to sing the
blues. On the day she did, a day he was positive was imminent,
then his project would be complete; and, as lovers, they could
watch the dancing toadstools and the invisible animals together.

However, the mature eternal child would have been
pleasantly surprised (and extremely confused) to know that he
had already accomplished more than he had ever dreamed. He
would have been irritated to know that the rewards of his grand
design were not his to enjoy; he would not have been able to
shrug and fatalistically say, "That's life, boss," because an
acceptance of the inevitable had always impressed him as
pathetically futile. He did not know that throughout the
afternoon he had been shadowed by the man in the yellow suit.

This extraordinary gentleman with a whim of iron set out in
the morning to interview the mature eternal child, disregarding
the instructions of the consulting detective to spend the day
interviewing pubescent eternal children wandering the East End
and to wait until just before the concert in the park to interview
their idol. He concealed himself in the mature eternal child's
mansion. Rather than searching for clues which would either

prove or disprove his suspect as the ripper, the man in the yellow suit became lost in his dreams. He examined various aspects of his personality and found himself so fragmented, so damned objective, that he could not say with certainty that he had a true personality at all. He did know with certainty, somewhere in the back of his mind, perhaps in a dusty little broom closet he had not gotten around to exploring yet, that if he did not arrive at the demon's castle with information that the consulting detective could use, if only to dismiss the mature eternal child from his list of suspects, then the legendary godlike shamus would be miffed. To say the least. It was vaguely comforting to know that there were some things you could realistically depend on, whether or not you were sure they were actually real.

Spurred by the possibility of social chastisement (one of the rare occasions when such a possibility stirred him into action), the man in the yellow suit turned invisible and floated behind the mature eternal child when that idol of the pubescent masses left the mansion and walked to the cottage of the soprano. Something unusual happened to the man in the yellow suit's mind as he followed his suspect; try as he might (though it must be admitted that he did not try very hard), he could not quite pinpoint the particulars of the mystical experience which, rather than overwhelming him, snuck up on him and gently picked him up by the back of the neck, shaking him as one would shake a naughty kitten. Inspired by the example of the mature eternal child, somehow able to deduce spiritual failings in his suspect and to correct them, the man in the yellow suit heard the music of the dancing toadstools. Somehow he had opened his spirit to a source of which he, with all his unique perceptions, had been previously unaware; and it seemed that the very oversoul had embraced him. The music was the composite of all music—all genres, with all chords and all arrangements playing simultaneously, the sum total of an urge that had existed eons before the wake of godlike mankind. The experience lasted but a few moments, but in those moments he understood all that was to be understood about the mature eternal child; and he knew, though the proper vocabulary for the explanation had not been conceived, that the mature eternal child could not be the ripper in any assortment of the scheme of things. The music passed from the man in the yellow suit's mind (and from his comprehension) when his suspect examined the flower with petals that probed into alternate dimensions, as if he required the assistance of others to maintain his experience. And when the invisible animal passed them, the man in the yellow suit saw its every detail, though once again, when the animal left his range of vision, the memory was erased, leaving behind only an undefined glimmer of knowledge gained and lost.

When the mature eternal child and the soprano began singing to one another their songs of love and devotion, the man in the yellow suit realized the sublime ridiculousness of his suspect's project—though the miracle that occurred in his mind possibly might not have happened were it not for that base motivation. For when the mature eternal child entered the soprano, causing their bodies to spasm in mutual ecstasy (the soprano, in particular, reacting like a Venusian flytrap upon receiving a succulent feast), the man in the yellow suit, seized by a voyeuristic impulse, disregarded all social conventions and entered their minds, partaking of their pleasure like a parasite. Yet the intentions and the results were not parasitic. The man in the yellow suit became immersed in a synthesis of thought that caused their metaphor to become reality in his brain. He was dazzled by music infinitely more powerful than the mere sum total of all music he had heard earlier. He writhed invisibly above the writhing bodies on the bed. He experienced both their pleasures and more. But most importantly, he realized that the mature eternal child's project had been completed upon the consummation of their urge to couple, and that it would be completed again and again. What they perceived as disparities was in reality indistinguishable; the essence of their music, despite external appearances, was the same. And the music of their souls sang to one another, each unable to hear its partner. For their souls, it was simply sufficient to sing; the fact that the singing was in vain was of no consequence and, in truth, was partially compensated for by the mundane (but by no means unsatisfactory) physical pleasure. The man in the yellow suit, however, was unshackled by mutual disabilities; and the songs, their mellowness and internal harmony contrasting with the pulsating rhythms of their shells, filled his entire soul with a vision—with a vision so perfect, so immense, so intense, that he realized his previous visions had been but glimpses into the center of the ultimate perception, the final insight which, once perceived for the first time, would provide him with a faith that conceivably would guide him through chaos. For the man in the yellow suit saw that everything was good; nothing in the universe was less than perfect; it was only godlike man's perception of the universe which was less than perfect. The man in the yellow suit realized that nothing—not even the ripper—was evil; not even the ripper was beyond salvation. Everything godlike mankind had struggled eons for was there, coolly glowing in the mind, waiting to explode into an inferno that would destroy all so that all would be reconstructed; godlike mankind would see things in their proper places; and then godlike mankind would be able to take the final step illuminating the whole of existence. The man in the yellow suit saw that his impulse was his only virtue, the only virtue he required; any impulse he followed would result in only good. And each impulse would inexorably, gloriously, lead to more life. Each impulse fulfilled would add an infinity of experience to infinities of experience. His vision, derived from the synthesis below, filled him with energy, energy he did not quite know how to apply, but energy which would somehow be utilized, energy which would effortlessly find a purpose. Everything would be accomplished, somehow, through some means. And all experience, the whole history of mere man and godlike man, was implanted in his personality. The mature eternal child erred in believing there was a difference between himself and the soprano; in truth, in a reality that superseded all realities of partial impressions and knowledges, there was no difference; they were one being, and it was destructive to make distinctions where there were no distinctions, to conceive of the synthesis as mere metaphor when the metaphor was the only truth.

Voices spoke to the man in the yellow suit writhing in his vision. Voices from the past, voices speaking in languages he did not know, but languages he could understand. Voices he could not hear, but voices he listened to with rapt attention. Voices urging him to break through to the other side, where day no longer destroyed the night, where the night no longer divided the day. Voices urging him to break through the doors of perception, into a universe where all life was immortal, where death was not an end nor a beginning, but an irrelevant fabrication. Into a universe where life was a series of moments that stretched into eternities.

Yet beneath this vision, the fulfillment of a secret, unvoiced wish, the man in the yellow suit felt fear. What if there was no outlet for the energies of the soul he had harnessed? Would the fault lie with the energies, or with himself, the vehicle they had chosen? Could he communicate what he had learned? And if so, would others be prepared to share his knowledge? These fears tainted the vision, but they were essential. And the man in the yellow suit knew when the vision had left him, when the first hot rush of energy had deserted him, inevitably leaving him tired and drained, there would be more, much more to ponder. Each impulse would be a challenge. But at least the impulses would no longer be vague whims. And he had found hope for himself, a hope which might provide salvation for those without hope.

6. He called himself the terrible. Once, he believed, the entire world had called him the terrible; and the populace had feared his wrath, sought his approval, and obeyed his laws. His word sustained life or brought death. Yet the days which had seen his rule had passed long ago, so long ago that he could not ascertain the date of their passing. Nor could he recall an instance of a peasant cowering before the piercing white light of his glaring eyes, of a fawning advisor requesting he sanction an advantageous marriage, or of a rebellious merchant succumbing to his will. Once, he did not care to think how recently, he wondered if those days had ever existed, if he had ever strode through the stone halls of his isolated castle like a giant, knowing that the earth revolved around his thoughts and deeds. But he had cast those doubts aside, as one would exile an incompetent fool to the wastelands; his enemies had created those doubts, to incapacitate him further, and therefore his doubts were both insignificant and false. His enemies always plagued him. At best they were a minor annoyance; his inherent greatness was such that they could never humble him; he could never consider their materialistic grappling for an iota of power a cause for true concern, requiring effort to circumvent.

But if that was so, how did his enemies manage to wrest all his power away? His enemies—called the boyars—wanted the earth divided into several countries, allowing each a nation to tyrannize ruthlessly, with the terrible retaining the power to rubber-stamp their rulings and little else. The terrible would not permit it; the people called upon him to protect them from the boyars. And he believed that he had succeeded. Nevertheless:

The boyars had also succeeded: in stealing the terrible's lovely wife, the one woman who could soothe and quiet the demons raging inside him that so often forced him to submit to the childish rantings of his spirit. Exactly how they had stolen her, he could not remember. Nor could he remember her face, or the color of her hair, or the warmth of her fingertips. They had loved each other long ago.

The terrible suspected that the boyars' petty intrigues had grown so frustrating after the loss of his wife that he had renounced his throne, thereby depriving the boyars of the pretense to legality essential to the consolidation of their rule. He had said that he would return to his throne only when the people cried for his rule; he could not continue without the certain knowledge of their support. Then, when the people did call, the boyars would know that his power, stemming as it did from the very soil of the planet, was mightier than theirs; the boyars would have no choice but to resign themselves to his centralized control.

If all this had indeed occurred, why did the people not call? What was preventing them now? It was impossible that the voice of the people of Earth, people so simple and noble in their poverty of materialistic possessions, could be stilled for eons. Inevitably the people would rise to cast off the yoke of their oppressors. It was the way of history. And yet they had not risen up. The boyars continued to oppress them, and their voice was eternally silent.

That is, if his scenario of his fall from power was correct in the first place. The boyars were uncommonly tricky for base, imperialistic pigs.

When he was not occupied performing the various biological obligations necessary for his tall, thin body to continue functioning at its socialistic peak, the terrible strode throughout his castle, attempting to harken back to the days of his power. The castle was furnished with bare, hard chairs, hard beds with animal-skin blankets, suits of armor, weapons, tapestries, and other items he deemed appropriate for one in his position, but there were no luxuries. Eternally burning torches spaced ten meters apart provided light and, not incidentally, an atmosphere of smoke rivaling the pollution of the East End. He wore coarse yellow robes and sandals. His thick black eyebrows were constantly scowled with concern and worry for the people surely suffering without his protection. Occasionally he tugged at his whiskers. He resembled a tottering scarecrow, but in reality his thin limbs were gifted with incredible natural strength. He walked and he walked; he brooded and brooded. His days were filled with emptiness and loneliness, but he was too preoccupied to notice it. He never saw any of the people whose welfare formed the purpose of his existence. In fact, he could not recall any person he had met (eons ago) as an individual; the person was but a part of the life organism, and never a complete entity in himself. Nothing ever happened to the terrible, save for the annoying persecution of the boyars.

The terrible was certainly unprepared for the unholy trauma that seized him when he turned a corner to enter the throne room and saw, before the seats of honor he had once shared with his wife, a 1955 Chevy convertible with whitewall tires, rabbit-fur seats and dashboard, air conditioning, a tapedeck, automatic transmission, four-wheel disc brakes, tinted glass in all windows, an adjustable steering column, a trip odometer, a locking gas cap, and an engine that hummed like a dream. The combination of the headlights, grill, and fender made the black Chevy resemble a huge mechanical cat ready to pounce on a helpless rat. The terrible did not fail to notice the pair of mirror sunglasses resting on the dashboard. He staggered backward until he rested at a forty-five-degree angle against the stone wall. He placed his right hand at his heart; closing his eyes, tilting his head toward the ceiling, he placed the back of his left hand over his forehead. The unholy trauma gave way to an unholy urge. He resisted it; with all the considerable emotional power at his command, he resisted the urge. But the power was insufficient to prevent him from mumbling, "Oh wow, man. What a *gorgeous* machine!"

Knowing that he was doomed if he looked at the Chevy again, he did so anyway, beads of perspiration rolling down his face as if he had just stepped from a hot shower. He winced as he noticed that his body odor had increased sevenfold; but his smell was the smell of the toiling people, trapped in the yoke of oppressors who forced them to slave for starvation wages; so he was not ashamed of his muskrat odor, bringing him as it did closer to the common soil. Yet visions of the hard-working, hard-playing people, laughing and drinking and fucking and trying to keep what joy there was in the world, were the farthest things from his mind for the first time in his memory as he wallowed in the pleasure of the urge. Yes, he could not deny it, the urge was pleasurable; he had never before known anything so gloriously filled with the promise of freedom without a past and without a future as that 1955 Chevy. He pushed himself from the wall, swaying slightly, dizzily, back and forth, as he stared at the vehicle. Already he could smell the sweet fumes of exhaust in the air as he gunned the powerful engine. He could feel the machine responding to his touch at the steering column, the wind slamming his face and blowing his hair in all directions at once, scenery speeding past him at a blur, with only the road ahead and behind him, the power flowing smoothly from his foot to the gas pedal as he pushed down, harder, and harder, until he thought his foot would break through the floor. He was in control. He had power, power he could feel throughout his body. His personality was shorn from his frail mortal shell; and the shell was now something more than frail and mortal—it was truly a part of the oversoul. All life was encompassed in his touch as he traveled without a destination, seeing everything, daring anything, driving forever. He had always driven this machine, and he would always drive the machine.

His fantasy abruptly ceased. He felt a crippling pain in his intestines as he adjusted to reality. It was unthinkable. All that he had been thinking of was . . . unthinkable, simply impossible, but its impossibility did not prevent it from being truth, the only genuine truth (as opposed to nebulous truth) he had experienced in eons. He just had to take this baby for a spin!

But . . .

What would the people say?

Surely they would see him; surely this menace had been planted by the boyars. Ah, what a marvelous stroke! He had not thought those capitalistic swine capable of such devious inspiration. He should have. Scum totally without redeeming social value had been known to rise to great heights, thanks to the potency of the dreaded capitalistic virus. He would not succumb. He would send the car to the antimatter universe. No, he could not do *that* to the gorgeous machine, but he could walk away. He could straighten to his imposing full stature, turn around, leave, and allow his thoughts to return to the welfare of the simple and noble people.

The terrible walked to the Chevy. He ran his fingers over the black hood, barely preventing the gesture from becoming a caress. For once, he was glad he lived alone. He could not take the car for a test drive; he would not. He found himself staring intently at his distorted image in the mirror sunglasses; he looked very forlorn. Doubtless the tapes were recorded by that musical peon, the mature eternal child. No, he could not succumb to his urge. His duty to the people came first; it always came first. Materialistic pleasures such as this were fit only for the evil boyars; the people invariably made the down-payment. Some men had to sacrifice pleasure and freedom for the general good. Men such as he had a single-minded purpose, and one moment of swerving (perhaps he should have selected another word) from their duty was the first step in an epic trek of defeat. Well, maybe just a quick spin around the castle. The people's faith in him would not suffer too much. They would forget in a little while.

When he pressed his thumb against the button of the door handle, his muscles quivered (though his hand remained steady) and he feared he would not be able to open the door. However, his thumb performed its appointed task admirably, and the creaking of the opening door filled the castle with sound and his heart with anticipation. He reached toward the mirror sunglasses, by this time his hand actually trembling, but before he could touch them, he was distracted by a disconcerting jingling. He turned around to see the demon standing with his elbow resting against his throne; the green visage of the intruder was distorted by a satanic smile as he dangled the car keys hypnotically before the terrible. "You might find these useful," said the demon.

The lawyer sat cross-legged on the throne the terrible's wife had once occupied (if she had ever occupied it at all). He pressed the button of his sword cane, fingered the blade, and said, in a voice as menacing as his piercing wail would allow, "We've come to ask you some questions, my friend."

The terrible's eyes widened until each muscle strained and throbbed with the effort. He felt a cold, remorseless rage take hold of his heart. "How dare you invade the sanctity of my privacy! Do you have any idea who I am?"

"No," said the demon tonelessly. "Isn't there anyone who can tell you?"

"I am called the terrible."

"Then what are you worried about?" asked the lawyer, confused by the sudden turn in the conversation.

"I am worried about nothing, absolutely nothing," said the terrible, "for I know that you are agents, lowly flunkies of my immortal enemies, the boyars. And there is nothing you can do to divert me from my righteous cause."

Having dropped the keys in a pocket, the demon applauded. "Bravo, bravo," he said with an effeminate intonation. "What is your cause?"

"That of the people—the toiling masses you, bound by your misguided ways, exploit and grind into the earth. I will struggle always to free them from your oppression. I have and will continue to devote my life to their ultimate liberation from your capitalistic webs, and nothing, including this magnificent set of wheels, will distract me."

Raising his eyebrows, the demon sauntered down the steps before the throne and to the Chevy. "Then your life will always belong to the common good, and never to yourself?"

"Yes."

The demon rubbed his chin. "The common good is an intellectual fantasy at best, as I well should know."

"What do you mean?" asked the terrible.

"Yeah," said the lawyer. "What do you mean? I thought we were supposed to devote ourselves to the common good, whatever that is."

"Friend lawyer, you've answered your own question."

"Oh. Well, that was extremely clever of me, wasn't it?" said the lawyer, smiling to himself for five seconds. Then his face assumed the blank expression of a man who had grasped all the implications of the Theory of Relativity for the first time, only to completely forget them a moment later. "I have?"

The demon placed his left foot on the fender, resting his forearm on his knee, ignoring the wince of the terrible (who was unduly concerned about the mark the shoe would leave on the shiny chrome). He stared down the hall before him, the flickering light of the torches gradually diminishing in size and effectiveness until they trailed into nothingness, as if the hallway continued forever, somehow becoming a metaphor of the paradoxes on his mind. "Everyone who ostensibly devotes his life to the common good has a different idea of what that good actually is. He wants the world to conform to his vision, and he doesn't care if the world wishes to conform. If this is true, and I've no reason to doubt it, then isn't everyone who professes to care about others above all else in reality working solely for his own good? Why should 'the people' screw up their lives for the sake of his spiritual well-being and his power fantasies?"

"Those asinine pontifications are immaterial in the wake of the poor's suffering," said the terrible, breathing a sigh of relief when the demon removed his foot from the fender and turned to lean against the car.

"I agree wholeheartedly," said the demon. "But it's easier for people to identify with someone who indulges in a few moments of self-doubt. I was just trying to expand my character a little bit in the eyes of my fans."

"Helium has no need for expanison," said the lawyer. "It's light enough already."

The demon's self-confidence visibly drained as if he had just cut himself shaving. "Yes. Well, we can't concern ourselves with that right now." His confidence buoyed with an effort as he faced the terrible. "Why are the people suffering?"

The terrible thought fast. "Because the boyars horde all the material wealth for themselves. The people have nothing; they have no abundance of food and ready cash. They don't even have credit cards."

"Due to the boyars' insistence upon a capitalistic economy?" asked the demon.

"Of course."

"Now, if the wealth was distributed more equally, what would the people have? How would they use their new-found wealth?"

"Why, for the good of their fellows."

"You answered that too intellectually. Let's get down to some serious practicality. After all, the common folk can't afford to spend their lives with their thoughts in the clouds like us more fortunate specimens of godlike humanity. If they did, they wouldn't be common anymore, and then where would our vaunted superiority be?"

"Well, the people, acting individually I suppose, would exchange a portion of wealth for the goods and services provided by others."

"Which is a characteristic of . . . ?" said the demon, grinning maliciously.

"No. You can't make me say it."

The lawyer, seeing his opening to make a point in the conversation, said, "Would the people donate goods and services for nothing?"

The terrible took three steps backward from the Chevy. He covered his eyes and turned his head. His free arm was held out stiff behind him, as if his atoms could ward concepts as well as objects. "Of course not," he said in a miserable voice. "That would be stupid. People require incentive of some sort."

"Then you realize you're living a lie, which isn't exactly uncommon," said the demon. "Rather than battling for your communism or socialism (I always get the two mixed up; definitions are so vague), in truth you're battling for the concept you consider the most grotesque in the universe."

The terrible whirled as if he was preparing to defend his ideals with an exhibition of kung fu. "No! It isn't so!"

"Tsk, tsk, how ineloquent of you," said the demon, shaking his head. "But I perceive that even you can't deny reality. You realize those who are at the forefront of a revolution eventually become what they despise. It's the way of history."

"The way of history is what I proclaim it to be," said the terrible. "Each revolution will be succeeded by another revolution, until all traces of capitalism are eradicated. And I will be true to my vision; I will always be at the vanguard."

During the moment of silence, the two friends recovered from the force of the terrible's impassioned, if dogmatic, defense. "Then what's stopping you now?" asked the lawyer.

"The boyars are preventing me from performing great deeds. They fear me. Wherever I turn, they are there, thwarting my actions for the sake of their materialistic purposes."

"Why are they so tenacious?" asked the demon.

"Because . . . just as men with vision seek to mold the scheme of things, men who lack vision, or who denounce vision, also seek to impose their personal order upon the universe. They struggle as mightily as men armed with the truth. The antithesis will forever battle the thesis, to the detriment of progress and social evolution. They would create a world without vision, a world as dreary and as insubstantial as their dreams."

"You're hardly the personification of a thesis," said the demon. "Immediately upon our arrival, the lawyer and I sensed your innate hypocrisy. We realized you were denying your true self for the facade you believe you prefer. To fortify the facade, you've sought to protect yourself from temptation." He rapped the hood of the Chevy. "Not an eternity of sacrifice was sufficient to prepare you for this—the realization of a secret dream I plucked from your mind."

"This . . . this monstrosity cannot hope to triumph over the purity of my spirit."

"Ah, but it already has," said the demon. "And more than that, it has exposed a multitude of weaknesses. Watch."

The demon snapped his fingers, and a tableau appeared on a stone wall. The terrible saw himself wearing a corduroy blue shirt, a large black-and-red striped tie, and a green shirt; the array of colors was in extraordinary bad taste, representing as it did not only a poor eye for complementary design, but the self-image of a bland individual. The terrible saw himself sitting on the front porch of a one-story, four-bedroom brick house; beside him was a briefcase; on his knee was a three-year-old girl with blonde hair. Watching him proudly was an elegant woman holding a baby boy. As he pretended to concentrate on his play with the child, the terrible found his attention wandering to the woman's face. She appeared familiar, but her features were, to his eyes, vague. He felt a hollow sensation in his stomach and breast; and he realized she was the wife he had lost, somehow, long ago. He saw himself as a man who was loved.

The terrible whispered, "Why? Why are you doing this to me?"

"We apologize for its social unacceptability," said the lawyer, twirling his sword cane, "but we had no choice."

"We're engaged in a great struggle against a foe who, if his PR is to be believed, has incredible personal defenses," said the demon. He snapped his fingers; the tableau, and all it represented, was gone. "We're not flunkies of your boyars; I suspect they exist only in your mind, though currently the matter is no concern of ours. We perceived that your defenses were of such a nature that we had to destroy them lest you trick us with a glib facade of sincerity. We're not as practiced at unraveling duplicity as the consulting detective, and we could not afford to experiment. Once we decided that you defined life in terms of the past—in narrow economic terms, at that, the lowest common denominator of man's spirit—as a critic judges books of the present by outmoded literary conventions and standards, the vanquishing of your defenses was ... simplicity itself."

"Indeed," said the lawyer. "A magnificent strategy. I'm glad I thought of it."

"Indeed," replied the demon with the cold of space in his voice. "It's remarkable that such a mind could conjure such a devious scheme all by its lonesome."

The lawyer cleared his throat. "Well, yes. But bygones must be bygones. Let's get down to brass ticks."

The demon smiled. "If they're brass, that would explain why the lye was ineffective."

"That's not what I meant!" exclaimed the lawyer, thumping the butt of his sword cane on the floor. "You know lye always kills my ticks."

Experiencing a weariness that allowed him no succor, that provided him with no energy to cope with the friends' jibes at one another, the terrible said, "Please, if you must ask me annoying questions, begin. I've no desire to remain in your company longer than necessary." Though he still stood at his full height, he appeared somehow diminished, as if his weariness affected not only his perception of things, but others' perception as well.

The lawyer leapt from the throne to the floor, almost falling onto the Chevy when he landed. After a precarious moment, he regained his balance and stalked toward the terrible. He pointed his sword cane at the suspect as if he was preparing to run him through. However, his forward progress ceased when it became clear that the terrible was not going to begin backward progress. "All right," said the lawyer, "where were you on the night of June fourth, 1996?"

Again, the terrible thought fast. The day was certainly putting a strain on his cranial dexterity. "I was in Cleveland, of course. Wasn't everybody?"

The lawyer pushed out his cheek with his tongue. Turning to the demon, he said, "Gee, I don't know. I don't think I was. Hey, where was I on the night of June fourth, 1996?"

"I think it's best for the survival of civilization as we know it that your origins remain enshrouded in mystery," said the demon.

"They certainly were a mystery to my mother," said the lawyer.

"Surely that was obvious," said the terrible. "Surely she was a victim of the class struggle, undoubtedly a maid forced to submit to the carnal desires of her employer lest she be evicted and thrown out to the streets, without the security of shelter and the promise of food."

"She probably wasn't forced," said the demon, pointing at the ceiling. "But the lawyer is correct in one respect, at least, and we must proceed. Friend terrible, I must inquire: since you consider yourself a godlike man apart from society, what morality determines the nature of your actions?"

"Morality? Can there be such a thing in this day and age?"

"Yes; though we might not know its perimeters, we know when its boundaries have been crossed, when rules have been broken."

"There are no rules, save those which will eventually end the relentless class struggle vanquishing the spirit of godlike mankind; my actions are determined by those standards I reason will bring us closer to the revolution which will liberate us all."

"Are those standards magical?" asked the lawyer, his back turned to the terrible, the demon, and the Chevy.

"Magic is more a spurious concept than morality," said the terrible.

"Precisely my point," said the lawyer.

"Allow me to phrase it differently," said the demon. "Suppose you're wandering about the castle late one night, perhaps in the wee hours of the morning. You're fully aware you possess all the powers of our species; more than that, your power seems to well up inside you, until the energy is threatening to tear open your chest and cascade in violent waves of tangible force. Unlike most godlike men, friend terrible, I think you're totally cognizant of your limitless power; you know you can accomplish anything, fulfill every urge and desire that might plague you, if only you knew exactly how to channel that power."

"This is true," said the terrible, his lack of direction, despite his lofty goals, suddenly smothering his spirit and causing his voice to crack regardless of its lower register. He walked to the trunk of the Chevy and placed his foot on the rear fender, his back to the demon.

The demon stood between the terrible and the lawyer, who continued to face away from the scene. The demon walked to the terrible until his green face nearly touched the suspect's bony shoulder. He spoke softly, weaving a spell of vast concepts and imprisoned emotions. "Perhaps you define good as that which will further your cause; and evil that which will thwart it. Your definitions are something apart from the norm, neither better nor less, but simply different. However, this night, for some unfathomable reason you do not seek to understand, you've become something apart from your normal self, and you perceive your current self as an entity alien from your past self. And your power *demands* to be used. It doesn't matter if it's used in a manner or for a purpose your past self would approve, because for all practical intents and purposes that godlike man is dead. He will be resurrected when this mood passes, but as of the moment, he is dead as surely as the power churns and festers like a disease you must be rid of before you'll ever experience peace again. Nothing can touch you, and though you might press your hand against the stone wall until the grains penetrate your skin, or you might slice your wrists and watch the blood flow down your upraised arms, you can touch nothing. All this power, this excess of energy, has nullified your feelings; and you believe yourself a ghost, tangible perhaps, but no less unreal. The stone wall, the blood, your cause—you wonder if they had ever existed. You might think back to the days you spent with your wife, to the love you once shared under the delusion that a kiss, a simultaneous orgasm, a tenderly expressed emotion had granted you the peace you so fervently seek. But you realize your love was also a delusion, and in any case that love has passed forever; you had loved so long ago that you might as well have never loved for all the good it does you now. You realize the sexual act is a transitory pleasure at best; in the morning the glow and satisfaction of love consummated, however beautiful, however warm, however fragile, is gone; only more sex can make it return. Sex is an endless circle, a worm ouroboros. What is the good of sex if only more sex can quell your excess energy and return the simple feelings of being alive you've lost? And what is the good of love if you've become so divorced from your own emotions that you cannot be sure you've actually loved? You ponder these things, and you pause to look out a window at the street below, and you see a lonely figure wandering below, as aimlessly as you wander above. And you suddenly feel utterly indifferent to the fate of this individual; even an intellectual compassion is repugnant to you. And the power inside you wants you to direct it at this individual. You realize that only with an act of unspeakable violence can you restore the sensation of life. You don't know why it seems logical that violence is the only answer; it *is* logical and that's sufficient justification. And you somehow perceive that this act of violence you're contemplating will solve more, much more than your current problem (which, after all, may be only a lack of self-esteem; but that seems too trivial, so you choose not to dwell upon it). You believe that only through violence can the entire fabric of society be changed. For society and nothing less is responsible for your problem. It's not your fault you cannot be sure you feel what you touch. Society has caused others to avoid you, to distrust you, to keep you imprisoned in the cell of your own emotions. For your problems to be solved, society itself must change. And that change will begin—as if by magic—with your act of violence against that lonely individual. All society will notice your wrath; it will wonder how it has brought you to this desperate state; and after it has heard your explanation, after it knows what you're fighting for, it will immediately rectify things. And it will begin on this night, with this act of violence. And if that doesn't work, then another act of violence will follow; and another; and another, until society is remolded into a construction which will give you purpose, sensation, meaning, permanence. However, at the moment you can't concern yourself with the thought of failure, because your power is intensifying, threatening to explode and to leave you forever unless you act, act quickly, act without thinking; unless you channel the miraculous energy and dissect his body into so many disparate particles. And you proceed, creating a hazy yellow glow of floating molecules and atoms, the sheer force and unexpectedness of your attack dissipating his mind with his body. And you experience his pain and his panic as if it were your own; simultaneously the part of your mind that is not merged with his, preventing him from regrouping, is experiencing a joy you've never known, reveling in a power you've never before indulged in. You've never felt so alive, so much a being apart from the trivial problems, the insignificant dilemmas, the petty considerations that had shackled your spirit. You've never been so free, because you've made the ultimate choice, that of life and or death. Tell me, friend terrible, have you ever experienced those feelings? Have you ever experienced a night such as that?"

The terrible turned and stared at the demon's mirthful grin and clear eyes. He took three steps backward and said, "Have you cracked your brain? I would never do such a thing."

The lawyer whirled and pointed at the terrible. "And why not? We know what kind of man you are, and we're learning what men such as you are capable of! So why not? Why should we believe you?"

"Why should I murder a poor, downtrodden soul when I could just as easily murder a capitalistic boyar instead? And if I did murder a boyar, he would only be replaced by another. No, the fabric of society must be swept aside like gossamer, but a single killing won't bring about a revolution. (Except possibly under special circumstances, which I haven't been able to arrange yet, mainly because I haven't figured out what they are.)"

The demon rubbed his chin; he looked away from the terrible. "Somehow I'm not surprised you said that. And somehow, for reasons I can't explain, I'm disappointed in you; your fate is a matter of indifference to me; and yet I'm disappointed. I must be getting soft in my old age."

"Good," said the lawyer. "A lot of women will be eternally grateful." He sighed. "Well, I suppose we might as well blow this joint. We've got other things to do today. Friend terrible, forgive us for putting you under such a strain. Think of the Chevy as a gift."

"Take it," said the terrible. "Or send it to the antimatter universe. I don't want it."

The demon raised an eyebrow, the gesture communicating his question.

"My first duty is to the revolution. If the boyars ever knew I had such a machine in my possession, they would score a major propaganda victory."

The lawyer threw his sword cane on the floor; it clattered then rolled, until it stopped against the left front wheel of the

Chevy. He too was inexplicably disappointed with the terrible. "Damn it, man, can't you see what we're offering you? There, right before your baleful eyes, is the instrument which will grant you freedom."

"My place is here, for here the revolution will begin."

"We've already informed you that your concept of revolution is severely dated," said the demon.

"It will become current again."

"How do you know?" asked the lawyer as he retrieved his sword cane with a thought and a gesture. "How do you know the revolution won't begin in the wide-open spaces? The people live there, not here. How can you hope to save the people from some vague academic notion screwing up their lives if you can't communicate with them, if you don't know what they know and experience what they experience?"

"It's been done before."

"Possibly," said the demon, "but I would venture to say that it wasn't done very well."

"'Fess up," said the lawyer. "I don't believe your song-and-dance for a minute. What's the real reason why you won't take this baby for a test drive?"

The terrible walked to his throne. He looked downward at the demon and the lawyer as he attempted to summon the majesty he had once possessed as a ruler of godlike men. The attempt was an ignoble failure, notable for its sentiment rather than for its effect; despite their lower positions, both figuratively and metaphorically (in terms of class distinctions), the demon and the lawyer dominated the scene. The terrible realized he could not escape their domination. When he sat on his throne, he possessed no majesty at all, nor did he attempt to summon a trace of pride from his heart to provide him with dignity. He looked through a window at the sun blazing in the sky, and his eyes glistened. "I cannot leave this place; I cannot forsake my home for the uncertainties of travel. Not because I'm afraid; I fear no godlike man. But to do so would negate everything I've done."

"What have you done?" asked the lawyer in an irritated tone.

"As far as I can determine, you've accomplished nothing," said the demon.

"Perhaps I've accomplished nothing, but I have sacrificed everything. I've spent eons in loneliness and pain. I wish with the fervor of a god that I could escape my loneliness; however, my escape must be made in a manner making my suffering worthwhile. If I simply left, yielding to impulses which have nothing to do with my cause, I would be in effect admitting that all my pain and all my lonely nights I've spent yearning for a woman I cannot remember have been meaningless. I don't want you to think I've grown complacent in my plight. But the fact remains: if I left, I would be admitting my wasted years. I prefer to hope for joy in the future."

"What an incredible turkey!" exclaimed the lawyer.

The demon snapped his fingers and the Chevy disappeared into the antimatter universe. "And with my friend's accurate summation of your character, we will take our leave. However, I will give you a souvenir. Think fast!" He tossed the car keys to the terrible.

As the terrible instinctively caught the keys, the demon and the lawyer teleported from the castle. The terrible was alone; he thought that he would greet his loneliness with a sense of relief, but he was too cold inside. He remained there at his throne, letting the keys dangle from his fingers, until dusk. Then he resumed his aimless wandering through the corridors; however, the keys never left his hand.

7. *An account from the good doctor's notebooks:*

The sunlight outside the demon's castle faded in a long, steady decline; a single cloud was burned bright red by the sun: a streak of blood that was the only color I could see, the only color I could not expunge from my mind. Soon the sky would be pitch-black, sparkled by the stars, and the moon now pale against the blue would be a shimmering source of silver light illuminating the amorphous emotions of the inhabitants of the East End. Standing at the drawbridge, being careful not to near the edge lest I fall in the moat and be bitten by one of the demon's gluttonous pets before my keen mental reflexes could protect me, I waited for the coming of the sense of purpose, of destiny, that had eluded me ever since I had inspected the remains of the woman without a nose. The time had come for action; the only thinking we required (or could afford) was a prelude to action, of the sort provided by the consulting detective; nevertheless, I was thinking about matters I could scarcely comprehend. It is perhaps indiscreet of me to say so, but my lover and I had had an argument an hour before. Our bliss had decayed; our personal relationship had reached an impasse; in short, our affair had come to its inevitable conclusion, as all affairs must. However, I could not free myself of the notion that my depression was caused by more than the realities of the romantic condition. There was the possibility that I was becoming a victim of the unfathomable urge which had led my godlike fellows to wallow in the depression and negativism of the East End. If that was the case, and if I succumbed to the heinous urge, then I would be of no use to anyone, least of all myself, and would be a liability to the consulting detective when he most required my assistance. But my will has been known to be indomitable upon occasion, and I resolved not to succumb. At least not until the ripper had been captured and I had the leisure to indulge in self-pity.

The universal op slowly walked toward the castle. In the drab light that inundated the earth (save for the colorful exhibition on the horizon), he resembled a hulking beast, some hitherto concealed manifestation of the godlike spirit whose very freedom had resulted in a hideous slavery from which there was no escape. As he drew closer, I noticed the peculiar manner in which his shoulders slumped, and the way in which his meaty hands were stuffed in his trouser pockets; the two particulars of his mien contrasted sharply with his usual air of utter indifference, which remained only in respect to the aggressive angle of his head jutting from his torso. The consulting detective would have been proud of me for noticing the trivialities and for deducing, too, that something had recently altered the composition of the universal op's inner self. However, my respect for his privacy and my own natural discretion prevented me from contemplating the derivation of my observations.

Exactly when the universal op noticed my presence upon the drawbridge I cannot ascertain with accuracy. As he neared the castle, though, he regained his legendary indifference, seemingly with a mighty spiritual effort, as if he did not want anyone, including this chronicler, to perceive even the faintest clues to the mysteries of his soul. Contemplation was an anathema to his nature; it was far better, he had expressed upon occasion, simply to act and to be, to perform one's tasks adequately, without undue reflection. When we exchanged banalities of greeting on the drawbridge, his meaty palm embraced my hand with a warmth I had not expected. We had never before shaken hands.

I realized that whatever the outcome of his spiritual metamorphosis, he would be a better godlike man for it; and a portion of the confidence and purpose I had lost was returned to me.

By the time we had entered the locker room, I was once again my own self, whoever he was; and with delight I observed that the consulting detective and the man in the yellow suit were in the midst of a heated, yet friendly, discussion on matters which must have been on the minds of us all, whether or not we were aware of it. Sipping from a glass of wine, the consulting detective acknowledged the arrival of the universal op and myself with a curt but hardly perfunctory nod before saying to the man in the yellow suit, "When you have eliminated the existential, whatever remains, however jejune, must be truth."

At once I was fascinated. I have no keener pleasure, intellectually speaking, than in following the consulting detective in his professional arguments, and in admiring the rapid pontifications, as swift as intuitions, and yet always founded on an appropriately vague basis, with which he unraveled the concepts which were submitted to him. The consulting detective was also pleased with the discussion; his eyes glinted like the sparks of attritive flint; and though his sips were dainty, as befitted a gentleman savoring the fruit of Bacchus, the sips were frequent and exuberant. The consulting detective sometimes drank because he approved how alcohol heightened his senses, just as he approved of discussions because they heightened his mental processes and gave him the opportunity to show off.

The man in the yellow suit was no less involved; I am certain he relished the opportunity to exhibit the virtuosity of his mental capabilities no less than did the consulting detective. But I noticed a shade of weariness and impatience in his manner, as if he expected everyone to believe as he did, as if he could not understand why others would hold opinions differing from his concerning the ethical structure of the universe. He said, "But you can't eliminate the existential. We're always trapped in the morass of some existential dilemna. It really gets on my nerves. You can't proclaim that we'll punish the ripper when he might be a victim as much as the woman without a nose." He bit his lower lip, realizing that he hadn't quite made his point.

"And you believe that instead of dispensing justice, we should help him?"

"Yes."

"It would seem that the two are contradictory, that one goal cannot be achieved without eliminating the possibility of achieving the other." Scowling, placing his foot on a bench, he sipped his wine. Then he set down the glass on a shelf in an open locker and withdrew his pipe from the cape-backed overcoat casually thrown over his shoulders.

"How do you propose to punish the ripper?" asked the man in the yellow suit, thrusting his hands into his trouser pockets and turning his back to the three of us. "Will you slay him, in effect committing a crime identical to his?"

At once the consulting detective replied, "If necessary."

The man in the yellow suit, apparently thinking he had scored a major victory, turned and clapped his hands. "Then you admit it! You admit that society, with its unwritten laws and unspoken conventions, is an illusion that doesn't affect your actions in the least. You're apart from the concepts of good and evil, otherwise you wouldn't contemplate the act of murder without the slightest trace of remorse in your voice."

"I admit it," said the consulting detective with an air of indifference paling that of the universal op, as he lit his pipe.

"Then you must also admit that the two of you are superior creations, as far removed from godlike man as our species is removed from mere man."

The consulting detective smiled. He suddenly lost his exuberance, replacing it with a peculiar combination of compassion and pity that was somehow not condescending. "My friend, the ripper and I are not alike. The ripper is unlike all of us. We represent the forces of good as a matter of principle; and he represents evil. There can never be a bond between us, regardless of the identical paths our souls have taken. We've arrived at different destinations, you see."

The man in the yellow suit sighed. "And you represent good for the sake of the people, I suppose."

"Exactly. And I might add that you too represent good. Our differences are in method, that's all."

"What, then, shall we give the people?" asked the man in the yellow suit.

"All that is ours."

"Why should we give it?"

"For the sake of the trust."

The man in the yellow suit silently nodded; clearly he had

nothing more to say; for the moment he would concede the argument.

The consulting detective walked to him and placed his hand on his shoulder. "My friend, I have a turn both for existentialism and deduction. The theories which I have expressed here, and which appear to you to be so chimerical, are really extremely practical—so practical that I depend upon them to justify my existence. However: I may be dogmatic, but I'm not inflexible. When we capture the ripper, we may see that he can be helped, and help him we shall. But we cannot say we understand all the ramifications of the situation until we are actually a part of it."

The nature of the man in the yellow suit's reply, or of his overall reaction to the discussion's conclusion, I shall never know, for at that fateful moment, who should enter the locker room, breaking the pregnant silence, but the lawyer. And what an entrance it was! Unbeknownst to the little man, the demon had installed controls in the intestines of the simulacrum, enabling it to move under the direction of his loathsome pet, the tapeworm. Apparently the bugger (forgive me) had been practicing a good deal during our absence, for as the lawyer took his first step through the doorway, the simulacrum stiffly rushed to the vicinity with a blind, surreal force; in other words, I could see it, but I couldn't believe it. The lawyer, as is his lot in life, failed to notice the disaster rushing headlong toward him; and as he took his second step and prepared to utter some lackluster phrase of greeting, he tripped over the outstretched leg of the simulacrum. It was not difficult to imagine the tapeworm contorting its triangular head into whatever contortions tapeworms indulge in when they are overjoyed. For the lawyer's momentum was such that he was sent flying across the locker room, fully a meter from the floor. The distance of his flight, over ten meters, appears at first glance to be an exaggeration upon my part; but may I remind the reader that the lawyer invariably proceeded with undue haste, regardless of the endeavor or the circumstances? Therefore he frequently found himself bolting toward the most unexpected destinations. Such was my curiosity that I rushed to the doorway through which he had flown, the doorway to the rarely used gymnasium, arriving just in time to see him bounce from the trampoline and into the swimming pool. The lawyer's body was lost in a tremendous roar, in a mammoth splash that reached six meters into the air before large, singular drops began their lazy descent to the pool.

The remaining members of the party did not need to see what was transpiring when they heard the splash. I was barely aware of their laughter, so great was my own. "That demon just breaks me up," I recall saying. "He's a real card."

"Indeed," said the lawyer, surfacing and spitting water. "A veritable ace of spades."

I helped the lawyer climb from the pool. He shivered like a dog attempting to shake the scent of a skunk from his fur. When we returned to the locker room, the lawyer had already sent the essence of his dampness to the antimatter universe, and the simulacrum had returned to its customary station. The tapeworm protruded from the anus. "Where's my lemon cookie?" it demanded in an insulting tone that well-nigh canceled my mirth with a dose of acidic irritation.

"I'll give you a frigging lemon cookie," said the lawyer, his piercing voice rivaling that of the tapeworm.

The consulting detective halted the lawyer's rapid advance, punctuated by flourishes of his sword cane, toward the tapeworm with a gesture. He created a lemon cookie which the tapeworm snapped from the air and consumed whole, absorbing it like an unholy phallus swallowing a rodent. "I've no objections to the violence you're contemplating heaping upon this monstrosity," said the consulting detective, smiling. "But the pleasures of rage released must wait until we've the leisure."

"That's easy for you to say," replied the lawyer. "But I've already had my weekly bath."

"We know," said the man in the yellow suit. "We were relieved."

The lawyer stared at him with wide eyes threatening to manufacture laser beams that would disintegrate the very atoms of our whimsical acquaintance. However, he pursed his lips and quieted his ire when the consulting detective utilized the technique that always worked to perfection when the lawyer was tenaciously pursuing a line of thought we had grown bored with. That is, the consulting detective abruptly changed the subject; since the lawyer rarely kept two subjects on his mind, he usually completely forgot about the first one. My friend asked, "Where's the demon? Did you run into trouble with your last suspect?"

The lawyer shook his head. "The terrible loves his prison too much to do violence to escape it. So long as he possesses his ideals, regardless of how they suffocate him, he will not commit murder."

"I surmised as much," said the consulting detective, returning to his wine. "If, for the moment, we let pass the unlikelihood that he bamboozled you, we can dismiss him."

"As we can dismiss all today's suspects," I said.

Sighing. the consulting detective nodded his agreement. "It was a slim hope that we would discover him today, in a guise with which we were familiar, but it was a hope we could not allow to remain unexamined. Perhaps we shall have greater luck tonight."

"The demon told me that he would meet us at nightfall in the park of the East End," said the lawyer. "He would bring with him the person he believes will increase our luck."

"It's not luck that counts," boomed the voice of the fat man. "It's skill!" He entered the locker room. Beneath his massive arms were two visions of loveliness that heated my blood and sent it surging through my poor harried bod and to that very special organ capable of expanding to unheard-of lengths and scaling Cyclopean heights. My saliva glands worked overtime, my heart thundered and roared, and I immediately sat down, discreetly crossing my legs. The universal op appeared as if he would create a mouth, thereby shattering his preconceived self-image, for the sole purpose of licking his lips. The lawyer leaned on his sword cane in a vain attempt to stay his swaying; I believe he was close to fainting, and I couldn't blame him. The man in the yellow suit appeared as if he was on the verge of a transcendental experience. Even the consulting detective, still mourning the loss of an unrequited love, gulped the remainder of his wine. The two visions were more than adequate testimony to the truth of the fat man's pronouncement.

I blushingly confess, the fact that the visions wore paper bags over their heads did not diminish my sudden passion in the least. For I became aware of a sexual fantasy that had lurked in the mire of my subconscious for many weeks, only to surface now, at the most unexpected moment, totally erasing my sorrow at my recently concluded affair with an ease that shamed me. The visions were examples of that recent, alluring phenomenon, pubescent eternal children. They were not naked, and I suspected the state of their clothing was like life itself, that is, a temporary arrangement. I blushingly confess that blushing was the farthest thing from my mind as I considered the ecstasy of divesting the pubescent eternal children of their flimsy clothing (which left little to my fertile imagination), as I imagined my roving lips and tongue exploring the mountainous realms of their mammary glands, as I staked a claim in the piedmont between their legs. Pubescent eternal children had not affected me so strongly before (at least while I was actually in their presence; my dreams, I know now, were of an entirely different order, I assure you); but then again, I had never before seen pubescent eternal children dressed as cheerleaders. They wore white blouses and little green skirts that appeared to be cotton verging on papier-mâché. I am positive I would have pinpointed the exact (if constantly changing) locations of their nipples had not the aforementioned mountainous realms been camouflaged by green capital letters ("T") sewn on the blouses. They wore white sneakers and green-and-white striped knee-socks; their legs were tan and smooth. They carried, between them, four pompoms, the color scheme matching their uniforms. As they walked into the locker room, guided by the vast embrace of the fat man, they appeared to bounce like life-sized balloons, despite the tremendous weights of the arms pressing them to the earth.

"You're totally in error," said the lawyer. "Only luck could have gained you those two precious beauties when they could have me." Perhaps his verbal thrust increased his self-esteem slightly, in his own eyes if not in ours, but his confidence in his magnetic masculine attributes was seriously deflated when the pubescent eternal children giggled as if the notion was the most ridiculous they had ever heard.

"Only a consummate skill in the arcane arts of sexism could have gained me such absolute power over these innocent babes," said the fat man, his smile threatening to rip asunder the smoldering pink volcanoes that were his cheeks. He removed his arms from the cheerleaders. "At my command, my pretties, demonstrate your compliance to my demands." He stepped away and snapped his fingers.

Immediately the capital letters on their blouses concealed masses bubbling as if the eternal children were boiling pots of water. We were treated with a dance that caused my cerebro-spinal liquid to evaporate; we were delighted with a cheer that aroused more, much more than our envy. The adorable darlings chanted:

Life is a high school,
Life is a high school,
The pride of every student here.

We won't graduate,
We just radiate,
Of what comes next,
We don't speculate.

Rack us up,
Stack us up,
Give us semen, fat man!
Ream, ream, ream!
Hey! Rah!

They concluded their dance with a series of splits that numbed me; I wished I was the floor. The fat man applauded and said, "Now wait for me in my bedroom, my pretties. I shall return upon our success, or, if the unthinkable should transpire and we're unsuccessful, I shall have, oh, twenty minutes or so before I have to be at the office."

My eyes were transfixed, as if my pupils had been crucified, to the cheerleaders' wiggly bottoms as they made their exit.

Breathing what I interpreted as a sigh of relief, the consulting detective said, "Friend fat man, did you receive any news items which might provide us with a clue to the identity or hideaway of the ripper?"

The fat man's anticipation of sexual ecstasy vanished; the glaze of his eyes returned to life; and he said wearily, "Alas, I did not."

Although the answer was one he had fully expected, the consulting detective said, "Damn!" and struck his open palm with his fist. "What the world's million lips are searching for must be substantial somewhere..."

"Of that I've no doubt," said the fat man, reaching into his jacket's interior pocket. He produced a slip of paper which he gave to the consulting detective. "You might find this item of interest. You'll be happy to know that I've suppressed the story, pending your instructions."

"Why, that's highly unethical!" said the lawyer. "What about your responsibility to the public?"

"Don't bore me with trivialities," said the fat man.

The consulting detective tenderly held the paper in both hands, as if the slightest pressure would cause it to dissipate and be erased from his formidable memory forever; however, the veins of his neck protruded as if an immense flow of electricity was pulsing through his body. His complexion, never healthy to begin with, became as pale as that of the woman without a nose upon our discovery of her mutilated corpse. Only his reverence for clues, the very factor required for his most spectacular successes in his chosen profession, prevented him from tearing the paper to shreds in an insane furor; I read this in his eyes. Although the dark shading of the back of the paper informed me that the note was not of an undue length, the consulting detective read it several times, while turned at an angle where no one could peer over his shoulder. He read it as if he was involuntarily skipping lines, with the resulting confusion prohibiting him from grasping the full essence of the message.

"Don't keep us in suspense!" demanded the man in the yellow suit with the impetuousness I had come to expect from him. "Tell us what it says!"

Nodding blankly, as if he was alone in the locker room, the consulting detective gave me the paper. I could well comprehend his reluctance to speak the words after I had read it. Indeed, I read it three times, thereby increasing the impatience of the man in the yellow suit severalfold, before I realized that I was actually seeing what the small, almost classically precise printing said. The message carried an aura of unreality that stunned my senses. Finally I read aloud:

> *Dear fats:*
> *I keep on hearing the consulting detective is looking for me, but he won't fix me just yet. I have laughed when he looks so clever and talks about being on the right track. The joke about his suspicions of the mature eternal child gave me real fits.*
> *I am down on manic depressives and I won't quit ripping them till I do get buckled. Grand work, the first job was. I gave the lady no time to squeal. How can he catch me now? I love my work and want to start again. You will soon hear more of me and my funny little games.*
> *I saved some of the proper red stuff in a ginger-beer*

bottle over the first job, to write with, but it went thick like glue and I can't use it. Red ink is fit enough, I hope! Ha! Ha!

The next job I do I shall rip out the lady's intestines, just for jolly, wouldn't you? Keep this letter back until I do a bit more work, then give it out straight. My antimatter knife's so nice and pragmatic, I want to get to work right away, if I have the chance. Good luck.

Yours truly,
the ripper

P.S. Don't mind you giving me the trade name. Never had a self-image this good before. I got all the red ink off my hands; curse it. No luck yet. They say I am an avatism now. Ha! Ha!

My arm dropped; the letter rested in my lap. My head was clear of thoughts, as if I had never had a mind to speak of throughout my existence.

The man in the yellow suit said, "I expected him to be more intelligent."

"Don't be disappointed in him yet," said the consulting detective briskly. "His calligraphy denotes a godlike man of remarkable intelligence. His *non sequiturs* and attempts at the vernacular of the uneducated are forced; they simply don't ring true."

"The fellow may be very clever," I said, "but he is certainly very conceited."

"Absolutely," said the consulting detective. "He's brash confidence personified; he believes he cannot be caught."

"That was apparent when he dared call me 'fats,'" said the fat man grimly. "He shall suffer for that indiscretion as well as for his greater crimes against godlike humanity."

Thereupon followed an intense discussion of possible characteristics of the ripper, a veritable encyclopedic list of malevolent particulars; each participant had a different rationalization for his case, each rationalization providing insight into the personality of the speaker as well as elucidating a possible component of our foe, each component as valuable as the next (for it was all, however valuable, speculation). Doubtless I would recount every word, every exact detail of that fascinating discussion, for it would have provided me with an excellent opportunity to dazzle the reader with the riveting realism of my prose and my virtuosity in the area of total recall, had not the fat man, sidetracked by a sudden inspiration, drawn me aside, next to the simulacrum, and spoken to me in low tones heavy with the importance and social significance of his new scheme. "Friend good doctor, I must confide in you," he said, his fingers resting on my shoulders like malleable fried sausages kept in the refrigerator for several days.

"Of course," I replied. "You can always depend on my silence."

"It's not your silence I require, but the eloquence of your nifty gift of gab."

No one can resist a compliment like that. At the moment I would have done anything he asked. "What's on your mind?"

"I've thrown myself into the task of editing with a vengeance that has surprised even me. I find myself caught up in the responsibility of it all, in the knowledge that the words I select and the words I reject can have a definite and, I trust, positive effect on our troubled times. I've been examining the paper carefully and, frankly, I can't understand why the consulting detective depends so greatly upon it. The writing's frightfully dull. If I hadn't consumed an incredible dosage of speed while examining yesterday's paper, I would still be snoring away."

"The consulting detective depends on the information, not the writing."

"I admire his intestinal fortitude. There's simply nothing to interest people in general. They read the paper from habit rather than from interest. As I see it, the cause of the problem is that there hasn't been a new addition to the staff in over six million years."

"That would go a long way toward explaining the stagnation."

"You got it. The most dreadful section is the book reviews." The fat man rolled his eyes. "Egads, there're no words to express its consummate dullness. It made me wish I could forget how to read."

"I agree. Most critics couldn't write their way out of a used contraceptive."

"Of course," said the fat man. "Otherwise they wouldn't be

critics, or they would be out somewhere using contraceptives like normal people."

"It's probably just as well. There's always the possibility that they might accidentally perpetuate their stupidity."

"Which brings us to you. The Big Red Cheese's latest novel has just been published. I looked through it today, and I think the subject matter might be of interest to you."

I raised my eyebrows; I was still wondering how the perpetuation of stupidity would bring the discussion to me.

The fat man smiled. "The novel concerns a series of murders similar to those of the ripper in the days of mere man. It's only fiction, of course, but it appears that the Big Red Cheese's inspiration and source of information was that racial memory we hear so much about these days."

"Sounds to me like a case of fiction portending life."

"It might be of some revelance to our present dilemma. Would you care to review it?"

"Of course."

"Good," he said, squeezing my arm and practically crushing my muscles. "I knew I could count on you. I expect everything from you that you expect from yourself: a series of penetrating insights into the godlike condition, wild and wacky metaphors, an attack aimed at perking the reader's interest if you approve of the Big Red Cheese's effort. And above all, a discussion of the book's texture—its essence, its ultimate meaning, its value as an experience in itself—rather than a plot synopsis. That's all the current book-review section is—plot synopsis after plot synopsis. It bores the crap out of me, and as you know, I've got a lot of storage room for that sort of thing."

Doubtless my reply would have been an enthusiastic affirmation, but again my attention was distracted: this time not by words, but by silence. I looked to the center of the locker room; all eyes, including the blank ones of the simulacrum, were upon the lawyer. He still stood leaning on his sword cane, his shoulders slumped and his gaze directed toward the floor. I detected an uneasiness in the atmosphere; the consulting detective and the man in the yellow suit appeared embarrassed. As I learned, they suspected the discussion was taking them in a direction they had hoped to avoid for the nonce.

The lawyer spoke. His voice was shorn of its facade of

self-confidence; its tone was bleak. I realized, in a flash of insight, that whatever forces in the lawyer's breast prevented him from succumbing to the negativism which had blighted our race, they were grim and powerful forces indeed. Simultaneously, I realized perhaps the lawyer continued to pursue his nameless grail from sheer habit alone, that secretly he wished he could blindly submit to defeatism. He said, "It's not the thought of another death *per se* that concerns me. Chances are I won't be personally acquainted with the victim. You might grieve, but you'll grieve only as a matter of principle, or because the additional death will contribute to your suspicion that you haven't done your jobs properly. What concerns me is . . . Kitty's out there. She might be the next victim. Of course I don't know for sure she's in the East End, but it's extremely likely. You see, my scruples are a different color than yours; right now, I'm searching for the ripper for my own sake. Not for her sake. I've been thinking about it, and now I know I love her for my good rather than for herself. If something should happen to her . . . I don't know what I would do. Regardless of all the pain she's caused me, my love for her has been the one common denominator of my immortal existence. Regardless of what has happened to me as I've tried to help this crazy, mixed-up world of ours, I know my love will always warm my heart. Perhaps I love her solely for the sake of loving; if so, that's as good a reason as any. However, I can't forget that each moment the ripper is free, the chances I'll lose her will increase. If I lost her . . . I don't know what I'll do. Maybe I'll just sit in a tree all day and learn to play the flute, or do something else equally absurd."

The man in the yellow suit stared at the wall to his right; he apparently was attempting to forget the lawyer's words; perhaps they had touched something close to his heart. His body language—the manner in which his shoulders slumped in a deliberate effort to decrease his mass, the way he hung his head, the positioning of his hands in his lap—informed me that he could not, ever, forget the words. The consulting detective stared frankly at the lawyer; although the finer emotions made my friend uncomfortable, he was no stranger to them, having grappled and lost with the unknown factors in the equation of life. I knew my friend so well that I did not require additional information to surmise that he was wondering what life for himself would be like without the certain security that a certain goddess in a parallel universe lived. For so long as they both lived, they could both hope. And my thoughts, too, were similar. Though I had not seen or spoken to Kitty for eons—she was definitely becoming more mysterious as time passed—though I knew the quality of her life could never be higher than the basic pits, I thought of her occasionally; and my thoughts of the naive innocence we had shared, long before the realities of my romantic condition had tinged me with a distasteful jaded fatalism, had invariably filled me with a yearning for that which could never be regained. Only the universal op appeared to be unaffected by the lawyer's speech (for even the fat man was sullen and uncomfortable, but for what reason I cannot guess); therefore it came as something of a minor surprise to me when the op was the first to try to comfort the lawyer. "I've been searching for her all day. So don't worry about it. There's nothing you can do in any event, so why cause yourself all this mess and fuss?"

The lawyer pursed his lips and turned toward the universal op. The little man's features were distorted with an anger that made me want to shy away from the proceedings. He quivered as if his dunking in the pool had suddenly given him a temperature and the resulting chills. I had never before seen a godlike man so weak, with so imminent a collapse in his near future; all his energy was channeled toward fueling his anger, and none was diverted for the more prosaic functions such as standing up straight; yet the forces in his breast enabled him to stand. Against all odds, his words were coherent; I would have guessed that his next sounds would be a series of muffled stutterings spraying the locker room with an onslaught of saliva. He said, "And it's you who offend me the most, you with your smug indifference. Just once I would like to see you exhibit a genuine emotion; just once I would like to see you display a human foible."

Not unpredictably, the universal op shrugged.

This reaction, if I may call it that, increased the lawyer's irrationalism. He ground his teeth so heavily I feared my medical skills would momentarily be called to use. He said, "What sort of godlike man are you? Even the consulting detective occasionally displays signs of weakness." (This remark caused my friend to raise his eyebrows in surprise; the unvoiced question amused me.) "I haven't seen a shred of evidence to support the thesis that you care about anything. It would comfort me a bit, an insignificant tad but comfort nonetheless, if I thought you cared a little about Kitty. Just what is your attitude toward her disappearance, if you can be said to have an attitude at all?"

Not unpredictably, but this time shockingly, as if he was truly untouched by the lawyer's accusations, the universal op shrugged again. He said flatly in his dim, stifled voice, "It's my job to find her, and that's what I'm trying to do."

Whatever vehement expletives were about to explode from the lawyer and to assault my bleeding ears will fortunately remain lost, for the fat man silenced the lawyer by placing those formidable sausages as gently as possible on his shoulder and turning him away from the op. "My friend," said the fat man softly, "though perhaps there's room for improvement in the op's bedside manner, he's correct in all the essentials. You cannot search for Kitty precisely because you care too much."

"Possibly," said the lawyer. "But that's not all my beef. Just because a godlike man is defined by his limitations doesn't mean he can't transcend them."

"No one is under a social obligation to transcend his limitations," said the consulting detective, the cold tone of his words clearly stating that the time for discussion had passed. "It's night, and doubtlessly the ripper's beginning his search for another victim. We must teleport to the East End."

My friend blinked out of sight, but my mind registered the phrase "out of existence," and for a dreadful moment I was seized by an uncanny insecurity; and I questioned every assumption I had ever made about ... everything. I wondered if my dear, noble friend would actually materialize in the East End, if some unknown force, possibly manipulated by the ripper, had plucked his unprotected atoms from the atmosphere and cast them into the antimatter universe. There, in that hostile environment, his indomitable will, disrupted by the sudden shock, might prove insufficient to reform him, and his soul would languish and eventually die. I must admit, I was shocked at myself; never before had I been such an unwitting and fertile victim of paranoia. I concentrated, not only on teleporting myself to the East End, but on suppressing my fears. I was the last member of our party to teleport from the locker room. And in that brief instant of lightning transportation, a small part of me feared I would be a victim of unknown forces on my journey. What if I was a fool who could break up his body but not re-form? Would my lack of confidence result in a self-fulfilling prophecy? I did not know, but the time for reflection had passed long ago, and I regretted all the opportunities for meaningful reflection I had disregarded throughout the eons.

I sensed, though I could not feel, the stinging cold of the wind currents as I made my journey. I re-formed beside the consulting detective, and though the tart breeze was not by itself unpleasant, when combined with my morbid thoughts, it caused me to undergo the sensation of manning the barricades; I felt that the bulwark of my existence had been totally devastated; however, I had no choice but to continue. And I resolved to do this; the knowledge that once again I was by the side of the consulting detective filled me with strength and hope, as it had upon previous occasions. The tart breeze no longer distressed me; instead, it invigorated me. I inhaled deeply, suddenly seized by excitement. The starry blackness pressing above the dim lamps by the cracked sidewalk leading through the center of the park, the tangy smell of green grass dampened with fog, the quiet whisper of the ominous silence as it crept like an invisible, barely tangible beast through the slum for wasted souls—all seemed more intense, more complete than I could ever have imagined. The moon had never before seemed such a monstrous entity; the trees hidden by the darkness, far from the flimsy webs of the lamps, had never before been such malevolent ghosts stalking the fearful; the rustling noise of a purple squirrel dashing through the bushes and climbing up the coarse bark of an elm had never before been so loud, so whole, so complete an experience in itself. My every sense functioned at a peak. Not even the impassioned love of a woman could compare with *this*: the sensation of *aliveness* that magnified my entire being. I apologize if I seem vague, if that nifty gift of gab appears to be failing me, but the most precise and ingenious nuances of the language are insufficient to communicate the zest that permeated my being. I actually became thankful for the ripper, for if he had not slain the woman without a nose, if he had not railed so violently against his personal prison, I never would have had the opportunity of feeling the sheer thrill of daring all, risking all against the uncaring plot-twists of a sadistic universe. In that instant, though I can hardly say it was thrill-packed, I discovered the interior unity only danger can now provide for me. I learned, as I presume the consulting detective learned, that my life had meaning only as I challenged death, as I at least had the potential to earn the right others accept as natural, without a second thought.

We stood facing the demon. His face was a mask of stoicism, but his eyes had the appearance of glass, as if he had been beset upon by a mad taxidermist. My heightened senses enabled me to pierce the barrier of the demon's mask, without the aid of tedious observations and deductions; the demon was filled with a tense anticipation, his heart beating like thunder until it was the one sound he could truly hear. And I realized he had succumbed to the emotion to which he had believed himself immune. He looked to the starry blackness; he said, unnecessarily, "She'll arrive momentarily."

The consulting detective nodded grimly; though I would stake my life that his sensations in the park were similar to my own, his mask of stoicism was much more effective than the demon's. I could not pierce it; which isn't exactly unusual, since the consulting detective is a professional. The universal op was so indifferent that stoicism is too weak a word for his attitude, though I believe I detected a slight impatience for the night's work to begin. The lawyer nervously twirled his sword cane, nearly dropping it twice. The fat man seemed to look upon the proceedings of anticipation with amusement, as if he was somehow apart from traditional godlike weaknesses. The man in the yellow suit was an enigma to me; I suspected his thoughts still revolved about his discussion with the consulting detective.

A rustling of wings caused us to look as one to the neck of the streetlamp. On it alighted a male Batelur eagle, as if it had just materialized in the vacuum of night. After the bird had positioned itself, it ignored us totally, its head ticking this way and that, searching for something in the darkness. We were silent, speechless; even the swaying of the branches, causing the leaves to caress one another like timid lovers, was stilled. And the Batelur searched. Its skin about the dark yellow beak (tipped with black strokes that might have been made with a tiny paintbrush) was red and bare. Its crest of feathers was black. The skin folded fairly expressively at the end of the beak and mouth, turning upward slightly like a smile; that, and the fold of skin under the brown eyes, gave the Batelur the demeanor of a mirthful existential (and stuffed) force. (The eyes of birds lend them an air of unreality; it is difficult to conceive that any intelligence, regardless of how small, could lurk behind such glassy fluids and films.) Its wings were entirely black, though the secondary feathers were of a lighter shade, and the underwing coverts were white. The shoulder feathers were ochre-brown; the back, chestnut, fading to cinnamon-brown on the concealed part of its ridiculously short tail. The powerful red-orange claws gripped the neck of the streetlamp unsteadily, and I remembered that Batelurs were almost invariably on the wing. It must have been almost as uncomfortable as we.

Suddenly the silence was broken by the melodious call of a shrike, or to be scientifically accurate, of a black-headed gonolek. It sped like a projectile from the darkness directly toward the demon's face; I feared its beak, wielded with the assured adroitness of the most predatory of the perching birds, would rip out both his eyes in an instant and drop them to the ground. Shrikes have been known to do such things for the sheer heck of it. However, the shrike flapped its wings at a greater speed, tipping its rear as if it had spun on an axel, thereby diminishing its velocity. It landed on the demon's shoulder. The demon smiled as it nuzzled against his green ear like an overly affectionate cat. The shrike resembled a tiny zeppelin with a knitting needle in its bow. The black feathers on its head descended until they reached the line of the beak, giving the impression of an executioner's hood. The feathers of the chin and underbelly were blood red; the remaining feathers were a washed-out yellow. Its legs and claws were black. Although the creature was just over twenty-two centimeters, its aura of sadism was inversely proportionate to its size. Never before had I seen such a spiteful creature disguised in such a cute little body. For this reason, no doubt, the demon was attracted to it.

I scarcely had time to ponder the significance of the harbingers before a third demanded all my attention. As I stared at the demon caressing the shrike, I became aware of a warm glow descending from the sky. The very drops of the fog became illuminated, and I perceived the night much as a ghost must perceive the whole of existence. For all my awareness, I felt I had suddenly became an alien spectator in the expressionist drama of my life. The glow illuminated everything; there were no shadows; it seemed there was nothing I could not see as I tasted

its warmth. Even the titillation of danger was dwarfed by the
cool peace that blunted my insufferable streak of curiosity to
such an extent that I was the last of our select group to look to
the sky. To see that the glow was a bird with a wingspan of three
meters, a bird with black eyes reflecting the intelligence of
eternity, a bird composed solely of white light. I felt like a savage
whose god had returned. The white bird's warmth soothed my
every fear, comforted my every insecurity, and answered my
every question. I believed its eyes were directed only at me,
though I suspect each of us, including the universal op, believed
the same. Although it slowly flapped its wings in a vaguely
hypnotic rhythm, it did not require muscular action to achieve
flight; for when it was fifteen meters above the ground, and its
warm glow illuminated the park for a circle with a diameter of a
hundred meters, it ceased to move or descend. It hung there, its
light resembling that of a multitude of soft spotlights. And it too
waited.

The consulting detective was the first to hear the near
inaudible sound of flesh grazing timber and leaves. His
eyebrows arched and his grimly set mouth twitched nanosec-
onds before the heads of the Batelur and the shrike snapped
toward the individual they awaited. Though his demeanor
betrayed but an iota of trepidation, he had no way of knowing if
the originator of the noise was the individual the demon had
summoned (for surely he had guessed her identity, though he has
never mentioned the matter to me) or if it was the ripper, playing
an unfathomable game. The consulting detective touched my
elbow, diplomatically turning me to the correct direction, and
the others followed suit. Soon I heard the rustling of leaves, but
my auditory powers were strained to their utmost; it did not
require an effort on behalf of my olfactory powers, however, to
detect that magnificent scent, so clean, so natural, a spontaneous perfume derived from eons of contact with the sweetest
and most beautiful flowers of Africa, once I regulated my
abilities properly. And where the glow from the white bird
gradually tapered into the darkness of the depressing park, a
branch shivered ever so slightly, under the weight of one who
traveled with the substance of a phantom. And for an instant I
espied the ivory whiteness of a limb my lifelong experience with
women enabled me to deduce as a thigh; already I was becoming
victimized by a spell unintentionally cast. The thigh disap-

peared, and try as I might, I saw no more of her, as if she had teleported herself to an environment more appropriate to one of her sensibilities, until she desired to be seen. Until she slipped from the branches of a willow and alighted on the ground, barely causing the grass to bend under her feet. For several moments she stood before us, examining us with all the frankness of our examination of her, but with considerably more innocence. For the first time I saw a creature I had heard men discuss only in hushed whispers, a creature feared and loved by all males who had seen her (because they feared the love she inspired), a creature with white hair and dark eyes and a face like an omniscient child, a creature clad only in a bodice spun from spiderwebs; in short, I saw the bird woman. I saw a woman who personified all the naive dreams and yearnings I had ever entertained toward godlike womanhood.

No one was affected to a greater or lesser degree than I; we were all victimized. The contrast between the stark lust we had felt for the fat man's cheerleaders and the overwhelming passion for the bird woman was startling. We could claim no innocence, no purity of purpose, when we clearly considered whipping the old reptile on the cheerleaders; our one desire was summed up in the phrase, "Man on top, hurry up, and get it over with." Concerning the bird woman, I would never want it over with; having seen her once, I wanted her forever. I tore myself from the vision of her so I might fulfill my social obligation as chronicler of the consulting detective's exploits; never before had the obligation seemed so superfluous to life.

Upon the fat man's corpulent face was an expression that I would have expected to see on a father tenderly gazing at his loving (and I do mean *loving*) daughter; his eyes benoted a flurry of mental activity, an indication that he was already considering and rejecting schemes to win her love. But I detected an enormous reluctance to proceed, perhaps due to the fact that as a godlike man used to wielding the charm of power (enticing women to submit more than their bodies to his attentions), the fat man was wary of a godlike woman who negated the force of his personality so effortlessly. If he won her love, he would be the one to submit, and he would not submit at so great a cost.

The universal op put his hands into his trouser pockets; then into his jacket pockets; then behind his back; then at his sides, the fingers of the right hand mindlessly drumming his thigh. His air of indifference had been superseded by an air of annoyance, as if any female who aroused the gentler emotions in his heart was a bother instead of a blessing. The man in the yellow suit, however, accepted the blessing with a gusto; again, he was on the verge of a transcendental experience, of a slightly different nature to be sure, but apparently any excuse would do. The consulting detective smiled slightly, a shade weakly; only the blazing fire in his eyes truly indicated the depths of his passion, for it equalled that blaze his eyes assumed when the game was afoot. This heartened me, at least where my good friend's spirit was concerned; twice in one night he had demonstrated evidence of carnal desire. He had been asleep to love for so many eons, and his awakening had been tragic and tortuous. But he had actually considered making love to other women twice in an hour; perhaps he was nearly prepared to make the necessary compromises with life that would enable him to find the comfort he required in the future, though I knew he would continue to hope for the love of a goddess equal, in her own way, to the bird woman.

My attitude toward the vision of the bird woman slowly advancing toward us was strongly influenced by the adoration plainly written on the demon's face, as if an eternal child had scrawled nasty words of devotion. I was seized by a horrendous jealousy; I was aghast at the thought of that coy satanist entering the most private highways and byways of her body. For some reason, perhaps due to certain inescapable prerequisites of my *persona*, I believed it obscene that the demon should possess the bird woman; the act of love, between her and anyone, tainted her forever. Of course, if I spilled my protein inside a certain damp orifice, then she wouldn't be tainted at all. I suspect that my hypocritical attitude stemmed from the ancient notion that it was perfectly acceptable for men to nail all the women they desired, and unacceptable for women to be nailed, because men could wash it off. (Of course, nowadays women could teleport it out if they wanted to, but sometimes the old ways are the best.) For once, my emotions disgusted me. I wondered what such a vision could perceive in a godlike man such as the demon who, although basically a pleasant person and dandy conversationist I wished all the luck in the world, was undeniably shallow; that is, I wondered until it occurred to me that even the personification of purity must feel the need to lubricate for a man every once and awhile, and there was no accounting for taste.

And then there was the lawyer. Ah, the lawyer. I would have expected him to throw down his sword cane, stamp his feet, and howl like a lonely wolf attempting meaningful communication with the moon. But of us all, his reaction provoked the vast majority of my admiration, though his attempt was foredoomed to failure, though his disgusting little scheme was carried out with his customary, if endearing, incompetence. His eyes twinkled like those of an eternal child seeing his favorite candy; he danced up and down on his toes a few times, as if his body shivered with a delightful tingle; he shook his head back and forth, as if accepting a compliment not too graciously; and he placed his sword cane on his shoulder, obviously intending some sort of symbolic statement. Inhaling deeply, he sauntered toward the bird woman; his hips swung, his feet bounced, his shoulders swooped, rose, and drooped in rhythm to his steps, though the choreography was a bit vague. I imagined an acoustic bass being plucked somewhere in the background. When the lawyer reached the side of the bird woman, he deftly spun on his heel, a maneuver requiring a great deal of practice, and gestured at her elbow, half expecting her to allow him to take it. He was doing pretty good until he handed her his line, which was execrable in the extreme. He said, "Hi there, toots. Glad you could make it. How's about you and me splitting this scene and breezing to my pad? I've got some vintage apple wine and a few heavy jays. I've got a water bed and a chandelier you won't believe until you swing from it. How about it? Huh? Huh?"

The bird woman ceased walking and presented us with a smile that melted me. She asked the lawyer a simple question; the first words I heard her speak in that memorable voice proved to be the only words I heard her speak. She said, "Is that a paper clip in your pants, or are you just glad to see me?"

The lawyer's face turned a number of colors, each successive shade brighter than previous shades. He opened his mouth, a base retort obviously ready to fly from his lips, but the glare of the demon, whose intent could not be mistaken, prevented him. He stepped away from the bird woman, twirled his sword cane, and said, "When thou goest to woman, take a whip." Advice he had not the nerve to heed.

The consulting detective, his passion completely shuttled to its usual hiding place deep in his subconscious, nodded curtly; he said, "I thank you for arriving so promptly, bird woman. Doubtless the demon has informed you of the nature of the beast we seek and of the neighborhood he prowls. Already I see my fears concerning your ability to withstand the hideous onslaught of negativism were unjustified, and though I did not express them to you personally, I apologize." There were times when I wished my friend the consulting detective wasn't so blasted polite, for he was rewarded with a smile I would have sold my soul for. There were times when I wished I wasn't so blasted romantic.

My friend then turned where he could look at us as a group. The bird woman walked to the demon; she smiled demurely as they hesitantly took one another's hand. The mere act of their touching seemed unduly private; the soft glow of the white bird hovering overhead was inappropriate. I thought it improper that the bird woman engage in P.D.A. of any sort. (Or perhaps my prejudices are influencing my value judgments. So great was my desire for that perfect creature that I would have gladly carried her child.) The shrike leapt to her free wrist and the demon reached to caress it. The purity and innocence of his gesture of love toward the reprehensible beast disturbed me.

As near as I can determine, the remaining members of our group became oblivious to the demon and the bird woman. The consulting detective, his formidable charisma oozing at its utmost, was once again the center of attention as he casually filled the bowl of his pipe; for a moment he seemed oblivious to everything, and he might as well have been standing in our apartment, wearing his smoking jacket, lost in his private speculations, for all the evidence he displayed of true awareness. However, I knew, as did the others, that he had but cast an illusion. Every iota of his energy was concentrated on the task at hand. Even the Batelur and the white bird looked at him, rather than at their mistress. The preparation for the satisfaction of his oral fixation concluded, the consulting detective stared at us for a few moments; evidently he was amused at our tense anticipation of his words, for he smiled slightly, and a warm feeling of a totally different order than my passion for the bird woman surfaced in my breast. He said, "My instructions for tonight's work are few and simple; doubtless you've ascertained their nature. We'll separate, some into parties of two, and others singly. I've qualms about the possibilities of one of us facing the ripper alone, but I've decided that we must take the chance. We'll patrol this slum, warning women to return to their homes and searching for evidence of the ripper's passing. Should the ripper be sighted, either alone or at the scene of a crime, we should be notified telepathically immediately, and then we'll pounce upon the ripper's person." He pursed his lips. "I guess that's about it." Not an uplifting conclusion to a pep talk, by any means, but the consulting detective never was at his best during social functions.

The white bird then lifted its wings and ascended; it floated from the park and over the golden buildings which, though they reflected the silk moonlight and the sharp radiations from the streetlamps, were nevertheless immersed in darkness. The bird woman slipped her fingers from the demon's hand; the demon was understandably reticent to release her, and he leaned forward, in a half-hearted attempt to retain her, until they were no longer touching. He watched her as she vanished in the blackened park, followed by the Batelur and the shrike. He turned to the lawyer; he appeared ready to say something, but instead he shrugged and walked in the opposite direction of the bird woman's flight. The lawyer, in his turn, stared at the demon vanishing in the night; then he too shrugged, and he followed his friend. Their disappearance was so eerie, so final, their passing so silent, that I imagined they were gone forever, that I would never see them or their like again.

The fat man drummed his mighty fingers on his stomach, as if to the rhythm of a savage rite. He smiled; clearly he was quite enjoying himself. Throughout the eons he had engaged in many games of wit, pitting his abilities against those of a worthy adversary; but he had never before, I would wager, played a game such as this. He whistled to the gunsel. "My friend, are you there?" His smile metamorphosed into a grin when he received a whistle in reply. "Then I shall join you," boomed the fat man before he too disappeared.

The universal op's exit from the scene was notable for its lack of noteworthy details. He simply walked away as if he was going to create a six-pack of beer. The man in the yellow suit stood transfixed for a few moments, as if listening to music we could not hear. Then he shook his head like a man dazed upon awakening too early in the morning. He smiled mischievously, said "Toodle-loo," and fairly skipped away. I do not know the exact nature of my expression as I watched him depart, but whatever it was, it caused the consulting detective to snicker. My friend placed his hand on my shoulder and we began the night's work. We patrolled the East End in an easy, comfortable silence, totally relaxed in one another's company. The night proceeded without significant incident, but the consulting detective's concentration never flagged; his mind did not stray. Most of the time his eyebrows nearly touched at the top of his hawklike nose; his lips were pressed together like two lines in a clumsy drawing; I sensed that he was continuously holding himself back, that his muscles were winding like those of a snake in anticipation of the moment when he would spring forward into action and bring into play his full capabilities for the first time in history. The idealistic glories of love paled before the ecstasy, the total sense of life that he experienced now. Not only did his eyes and ears search for the ripper, but also his mind, as he emitted telepathic feelers in the hope that he would touch a mind permeated with blackness and evil. As for my gray matter, it was considerably less active; there was no reason for me to do the hard work since he excelled at it anyway; as always, I fulfilled a supportive capacity, but this, in its own way, was more than satisfactory, and I had the advantage of the freedom to examine the night and its meaning with the pretense of objectivity. Sometimes I felt as if I was a character in a dream or a charade, but before I began to become lost in such impractical musings, I noticed the startling contrast of a broken window in a golden building, and I saw an ugly, misplaced vine digging its roots into a wall, and I felt my shoes crunch glass, and I inhaled the whiff of the East End's inefficient sewer system, and I remembered that dream or no dream, this was not a charade; what we did or did not accomplish would affect the lives of our fellow godlike men and women, and my personal feelings regarding the situation were immaterial when I considered what hung in the balance. I was not living for myself, or solely for the sake of aiding the consulting detective; nor was I taking part in this adventure merely to have something thrilling to write about during a leisurely evening. I was more altruistic than a mere man of medicine ever could be.

I can still picture us there, walking through the East End

smothered by night; we appeared as if we were casually strolling, though the unsuspecting onlooker might have perceived the possibility of a grim purpose behind our constitutional; we cut through the layers of fog like racers cutting through the ribbon at the finish line. And I can imagine our faces as we walked under a streetlamp; I can see the shadows of our eyes and the shadows under our noses and cheekbones as if I had been an unsuspecting onlooker myself. And if the entire experience had indeed been but a dream, then I wish the meandering chaos of my life could be as vivid and as meaningful as that dream. Each step, each gesture, each glance hinged with the potential of drama; it was impossible to be bored even for a moment (though I confess that occasionally I was impatient), because each smell, each sound, each sight hinged with the potential of significance. Even the buzzing of a moth striking the glass plate covering the bulb of a lamp was somehow larger and more important than it had ever been before.

And it is not merely the gifts of an overzealous narrator constantly striving for verisimilitude that enable me to picture the rest of my comrades stalking the ripper as, conceivably, he stalked his next victim. No, something else, something more than a sense of camaraderie enables my mind's eye to picture the universal op turning a corner, his hands deep in his pockets; and though he has no eyes, he sees that the street before him is deserted and lonely, and this makes him feel at home on this street, and so he walks down it, his faceless presence now appropriate to his surroundings. And I picture the fat man saunter as much as his elephantine frame allows, the bulbous layers beneath his white suit shaking like jelly in an earthquake; perhaps he leers too blatantly at those he is protecting, but perhaps his naked lust puts the women at ease in this dark situation. He is shadowed by his mysterious gunsel, who has become, for me, a concept more than an individual. Perhaps they communicate, discussing trivial matters like old friends, but I cannot speculate. It is enough for me to know that the gunsel is there, serving the fat man as the fat man serves his fellows. And I can picture the demon and the lawyer; they insult one another; they play practical jokes; perhaps the lawyer makes too much noise as he throws a temper tantrum and stumbles into a garbage can, the clattering of its falling seeming to last forever and threatening to shatter the silence all over the world. But

underneath their shenanigans, there is purpose too, for the
demon's old lady is likewise engaged in the search and he would
like to discover the ripper first, laboring as he is under the
misguided notion that she is somehow less equipped to protect
herself than he. For the lawyer still pines for Kitty, which is an
emotional state I can certainly relate to, and he knows that as
long as the ripper is free and her whereabouts are unknown, she
might be slain and her corpse never discovered; he will continue
to worry over her disappearance after the ripper's capture, but
he will not have to worry about her life, and he will be secure in
the satisfaction that he has been as faithful to her as possible
under the circumstances. This is not an attitude born of residual
sexism on his part, for Kitty is as famous for her lack of caution
as for her lack of taste. For some reason I picture the man in the
yellow suit experiencing joy as he prowls the East End. But his
joy is not derived from himself, as is the fat man's; it is of a more
profound nature. His joy is that of a man who sees what little
good can come of this slum. He walks like a man meeting for the
first time in years a long lost love, and his smile is bittersweet.
Only a part of his mind is concentrated on his actual task, but
that part is sufficient, for without his joy, which may alter to
despondency without provocation, he would not be able to
continue at all. And traveling on the rooftops, accompanied by a
Batelur, a shrike, and a bird of light, a wish watches over us. And
it is the picture of this wish that is somehow the center of my
vision. And though my lust to possess this wish has faded like a
dream long ago, the thought of it is the whole, the goal I aspire
to; and perhaps even the consulting detective thinks of this wish
in some secluded corner of his mind, and perhaps he is warmed
in his heart, as I.

CHAPTER FOUR

1. *An account from the good doctor's notebook:*

At dawn my eyelids bore down with the weight of a dwarf star, and my muscles had reached such a state of weariness that I feared my fibers, accompanied by my precious bodily fluids, would slip from my rickety skeleton. I had not known that living at the peak of awareness would be so exhausting. We had patrolled the East End all night; we had not discovered a trace of the ripper, but thankfully we had not discovered a victim. For the next few hours I could rest, satisfied we had done well; there was a definite possibility that one of us had neared the ripper during the night and that his proximity had prevented the ripper from fulfilling his foul desires.

We stood near an apartment crowded with a wealth of inhabitants; some rooms had an overabundance of sleepers; these people were so lost, so downtrodden by the wasted feelings of their collective spirit, that they had mastered the art of being alone in a crowd; thus they had not the need for privacy as we knew it. A filthy stream of water gushing from a sewer pipe near a building up the street flowed past us, at the curb; the nasty odor did not penetrate the veil of my exhaustion. The sun was

stark and lonely; I yearned for a cloud to shield me from its
resilient light. The only sounds were those of the water gurgling
past us and the laughter of distant eternal children who had
awoken early to play in the East End park. The universal op's
shoulders hung like he held an anvil in each hand; I deduced the
man in the yellow suit had inadvertently fallen during the night,
for his trousers were grass-stained at the left knee; the lawyer
and the fat man conversed in low tones, but I did not desire to
increase my hearing to learn what they were saying. The demon
and the bird woman absently held hands; though the demon, in
his fatigue, did not look away from the bird woman's upturned
face, she kept her eyes to the sky and the rooftops. Her birds
were not with her; where they had gone, or why, I cannot say,
but she clearly missed them and was awaiting their return; the
comfort provided by the demon was evidently insufficient, I
decided with more than a trace of self-satisfaction. Of us all, only
the consulting detective possessed vast quantities of ergs. His
mind was replaying every sight and sound it had registered
during the night; and he was searching for an insignificant clue
to disaster that he might have overlooked. When he was not
smoking his pipe, he sucked his lower lip into his mouth,
pressing down slightly when it was between his teeth, generally
acting like a nervous child. The night's vigil had been
anticlimactic as far as he was concerned; he had hoped to engage
in mortal combat, and he might as well have slept at home. His
anxiety and his inability to discern the connections between
apparently unrelated objects and noises prevented us from
teleporting to our respective quarters. We milled about like
cattle while the consulting detective stood apart like an
apparition from an altogether separate existence. Normally I
would not have approached him; normally I would have
believed that given but a few more moments, his singular mind
would perceive what no other mind could perceive, and that the
path to the revelation would be, in retrospect, so obvious that
only a genius of the highest order would have pinpointed it. But
this morning I was not my usual self. My jealousy of the demon,
acting in accord with my impoverished residue of ergs, dulled me
to my responsibilities; all I cared about was myself, which
seemed to be a lot less than upon previous occasions. So, with
the firm resolve of the self-indulgent, I took the bull by the tail

and faced the situation. I walked to the consulting detective and said, "My friend, I think the time has long since passed for us to vacate the neighborhood. As the pubescent eternal children might say, 'There ain't nothing going down.'"

Fully ten seconds passed before the consulting detective realized I was speaking to him. Then he blinked, shook his head, and looked at me as if he was seeing me for the first time. "Yes, I suppose you're correct, friend good doctor. There is no logical reason for us to remain. But as loathe as I am to admit it, I have this premonition that the night's endeavors haven't been as successful as we would like to think."

I'm afraid that my reply, which probably wasn't exactly deathless, has been lost to my memory, for as I spoke, the sentence was drowned by the lovely (but unusually sinister) call of the shrike, broadcast at such a volume that it canceled all competing vibrations. The bird woman's head snapped to the source of the call—the rear of the overcrowded apartment building. She yanked her hand free from the demon's—again, he was reluctant to release her—and she gracefully leapt over the barbed-wire fence which served as a pathetic line of defense between the apartments and the desolate world it belonged to. The consulting detective followed her while we watched them turn down the side of the apartments; we were momentarily stunned, both by the call of the shrike and their quiet response. The demon was the first to recover, and he too leapt the fence, though not quite as gracefully as his predecessors, for he placed one hand on a post and swung over rather than merely relying on his *gastrovenia* and *tendo calcanea*. The rest of us, save for the lawyer, ran through the open gateway. The lawyer, following his predictable impulses, decided that if the demon could leap the fence, so could he. And he leapt the fence quite well; that is, his entire body, with the exception of one item, cleared the barbed-wire without incident. That exception was the trouser cuff of his left leg; it tore on the barbed-wire, upsetting the lawyer's delicate sense of balance just enough to prevent him from straightening before he hit the ground. As it was, he most assuredly hit the ground, but there was nothing remotely graceful about it. We did not have time to share his misery at his failure, or even to observe his reaction, for more important matters were on our group mind. Realizing that if he ignored his pratfall, we would also, the lawyer clammered to a standing position, teleporting the soil on his clothes to the antimatter universe, and attempted to catch up.

When I arrived at the rear of the apartments, the first thing that caught my eye was the shrike crucifying a grasshopper on a barb. Though it could have easily broken the creature in its hard beak, it held it almost delicately. Then it jerked downward, and I imagined (more than I actually heard) the barb loudly piercing the grasshopper's soft underbelly. Resting on the wire, the shrike released the grasshopper and stared at it as it vainly struggled to push itself from the shaft, though it could touch only air. In fact, the grasshopper's struggles served to thrust the barb deeper and deeper; and soon the barb was coated with yellowish fluid. When the grasshopper was motionless (fortunately, after but a few moments), the shrike turned away, now totally disinterested in its handiwork. I had half expected the bird to eat the grasshopper, thus perpetuating the give-and-take of the balance of life, but apparently it had killed solely for the sheer enjoyment of it.

If my comrades noticed the shrike's conduct, they gave no evidence of it. Their attention was focused on the bloody heap between the consulting detective and the bird woman. We silently stood about it for a few moments; and I was assailed by a tremendously remorseless sense of desolation, as if my entire existence had amounted to nothing, as if I had not even brought a moment of happiness to one godlike human. The fact that I had shared an infinite number of such moments did nothing to alleviate the intensity of my feeling; the truth is surprisingly ineffectual in combating the sensation of failure and depression. I imagined that my body temperature had approached absolute zero, so great was my numbness. I had forgotten my weariness in the excitement while I had raced to this site, but now my weariness returned, accompanied by nausea, and I feared I would be weary forever.

The consulting detective nodded. Kneeling, I began my examination. The corpse was that of the dark-haired woman carrying a rusty sword, the same godlike woman who had chastised us yesterday for not caring what happened to the denizens of the East End. I wished, oh how I wished, with all my heart, that I could now do something to dissuade her.

The ripper had left her body in the open, without

camouflage. She lay parallel to the fence. The knees of her drawn-up legs were turned outward; and seven pieces of gold (which, I understand, mere man attached value to) had been thrown at her feet. One thought in particular occurs to a man when he sees a woman in a position like that, especially if she is alive; apparently the ripper nurtured that thought when women were dead, though I detected no evidence that he had carried out the fantasy. She had not been disemboweled with the precision of the earlier victim; the ripper was becoming, if anything, more violent. His antimatter knife had cut so deeply into her throat that only a small strand of muscle and skin and vertebra held the head to the torso; the ripper had tied a silk handerchief, now caked with dry blood, about her neck, partially concealing the wound. Skin from the lower abdomen had been placed on her right shoulder. The swollen tongue protruded between the front teeth but not beyond the bruised lips. Needless to say, when the ripper had disemboweled her, he had removed the uterus and its appendages.

My examination complete, I stood and faced the consulting detective; I did not believe I could face anyone else. His eyes glowed like white coals as I said, "The ripper suffocated her by placing his hand over her nose and mouth. This also prevented her from crying out. He probably deadened her mind so she could not create her own air. The murder accomplished, the ripper then proceeded to perform his subsequent deeds. You can plainly see the results. If you don't mind, I'll give you the details later."

The consulting detective nodded. "That will be fine. Thank you, my friend." When the fat man pointed a finger to the sky, his manner of signaling he desired attention, the consulting detective raised his eyebrows and said, "Yes?"

"The gunsel has already questioned a sampling of the inhabitants of this block." The fat man gestured at all the apartment buildings containing windows facing the site of the murder. "Apparently several individuals espied this unfortunate many minutes before the shrike called us, but they are so lethargic, so lost in their depression, that they could not conceive that a multilated corpse would be of interest to anyone. In short, they did not care that she was dead."

"And I thank you and the gunsel," said the consulting detective. "I suggest we dispose of the body. We should sleep for a few hours and then return to work. Obviously, there is more, much more to be done."

2. *Most men lead lives of humorous desperation,* observed the thinking machine as he contemplated godlike humanity from his vantage point on a solitary peak overlooking the golden city twenty kilometers away. He had contemplated godlike humanity for eons. He had contemplated the entirety of existence—not only of humanity, but of the flowers growing in the soil outside his cave, of the trees touching the clouds in the early morning, of the brightness of day, of the peaceful silverness of night when the moon and stars illuminated the earth with soft, consoling strokes of cool pastel. And of the blue jays that nested in the tree nearest to his cave, of the beasts of prey that sometimes wandered from the forests and the fields below in search of subsistence, and of their timid victims, and of the plants those victims grazed upon. He contemplated how a blade of grass screamed its silent scream when a deer casually nibbled at it. And he contemplated what he perceived with irony were the higher planes of existence; he contemplated the music emitting from all things that lived and that had never lived. He sensed, more than he heard, that music everywhere. Often he had seen, as clearly as he saw a sapling grow into a solid oak, the eighth-dimensional man and woman making love in the sky, and he was aware that he saw much more than they saw, heard more than they heard, knew more than they could ever know. They saw only colors, and he saw the frequencies that created colors; they heard only a series of notes, and he heard a symphony; they knew only themselves, and one day he would know... everything.

Of course, there were those who considered it a serious drawback in the thinking machine's near-consummate knowledge that while he understood the music of life as a mathematician understands an intricate equation, he could feel nothing. He could not feel love or loathing, just as he could not feel the damp soil when it rained and the brisk summer evening breeze. The thinking machine did not consider this characteristic of his unique physique a shortcoming; instead, he considered it essential if he was to achieve his ultimate goal of unqualified omniscience. He had distanced himself from the particulars of life so he would be free from coping with them; he was never concerned with the trivial; his contemplation of the sublime was never interrupted, not even for a moment, by such dull realities as having to take a leak. Of his entire race, of which he could be considered a part only by an extreme stretch of logic, he was ideally suited for his self-appointed task.

There had been a time when the thinking machine had been a part of life, when he was possessed by the desire to utilize his intellect to its utmost capacity, but was prevented from doing so by his involvement in the chaotic stream of godlike entanglements. Even then he called himself the thinking machine; he was well known as a gentleman with a personality that was the logical result of a supremely logical mind. His affairs with women, which were his only affairs when he was not putting his mind to the particulars of the sublime, took up vast amounts of his energy. He was vaguely upset, even while enthralled in the ecstasy of the moment, that he was drawn, by hidden forces within him beyond his control, to couple with an individual whose mind could never equal his. He was disturbed that logic had nothing to do with his choices, and that his choices would not allow logic to have anything to do with their selection of him. Perhaps he would not have been so concerned with this one inescapable fact of reality if he could have found a permanent mate. But his heart was profoundly fickle (that is, if the writer may be permitted an illogical description, for hearts in and of themselves can be neither fickle nor faithful; they can merely pump blood until their host expires); and he found himself attracted to a succession of beautiful women who thought his gray eyes, black hair, stark features, and compact frame gorgeous. He convinced himself (several times) that he would settle down with one certain female, putting aside the problem of love by focusing his emotions in a single direction until the situation became one of the constants of his existence; then, so securely in love with one woman that his personal life was no longer a distraction, he could pursue his true goals. Perhaps this strategy would have worked, but he could not convince himself that the female in question, whatever her unique qualities, was sufficiently different from all others. It did not matter with whom he was infatuated, so long as he was infatuated. It did not matter with whom he shared himself, so long as he shared. And it did not matter who he fucked, so long as he was fucking

somebody and wasn't distracted by the *extremely* overwhelming
problem of his recurring horniness. He was cursed with one of
the grandest (and most grandiose) sex drives on the planet, and
he required at least four discharges of protein into a warm,
damp, undulating orifice a day if he was to function at the
efficiency he deemed minimal. Most women found this tiring
after a while; not without reason, they believed he had but one
thing on his mind; after all, the other things on his mind were
essentially incommunicable. Consequently, the thinking machine's search for a woman with an incurable protein deficiency
was hampered by their view of him as ripe fodder for a one- or
two-year fling, but nothing more. He was good for pure, raw,
naked sex with no redeeming spiritual value, but for fulfilling
romance—well, they dropped him at a moment's notice if
someone promising came along. In other words, his quest for
that very special someone was always thwarted by the
indifference of the universe at large. For hundreds of years at a
time, he would seek to circumvent this problem by holding his
sex drive in abeyance and by treating women coldly, treating
their sex drives contemptuously, as if the opportunity to explore
wayward vaginas was basically an unrewarding opportunity;
however, he discovered that he derived an utterly unholy sense
of power from this aloofness; this reinforced certain opinions he
held regarding himself, but the entire matter of treating women
with the high-hat was distasteful, too contrary to his natural
inclinations. In addition, his aloofness attracted still more
women to him; it was a greater strain to avoid their tempting
advances than it was to give in. So the thinking machine gave in,
again and again, until it seemed he had explored every orifice on
the planet (which was definitely not the case; there were a lot of
orifices to go around), but he could not discover a romance
differing from all preceeding ones. Eventually he conceived of
any affair he was involved in as a romance of mud; and soon this
metaphor applied to all other affairs as well. He still maintained
enough objectivity about himself to realize that what had
become a deeply ingrained attitude was only the result of
rampant cynicism. He had truly loved many times, but he
realized it in retrospect. And the result of all those loves, all that
painful loss which he had concealed from himself as well as
others, was the belief that there was no such thing as love, that all
of life was indeed a romance of mud, that godlike humanity

resembled nothing so much as a morass of copulating cockroaches; and this belief was the result of self-fulfilling prophecy. As long as the thinking machine was cynical regarding love, then he would experience no genuine love; he would experience only pure, raw, naked sex, which was all very well, but the pounding meat of two pairs of hips could never be anything more than pounding meat. Rather than retracing his steps to discover how he had lost his vestigial idealism, the thinking machine found that he had experienced too much pain already in his immortal existence; he would hear forever the identical series of notes and he would never grow into the being he so fervently desired to become; if he retraced his steps, the danger of remaining in the hideous circle of his life would nevertheless be too great. No, radical steps had to be taken. He had to remove himself from the never-ending stream of women and pain once and for all, with one drastic action. His decision was irrevocable; consequently, his deeds also must be irrevocable. So, one dark and stormy night when the summer winds were raging, causing the raindrops to plummet like tiny metal projectiles, the thinking machine found himself standing in the study of the shrink.

"What are you doing here?" asked the annoyed shrink, never a master of clever conversation.

"I want to become a thinking machine in fact as well as name."

"Then why don't you change yourself into one? It'll only take a moment."

"But this gorgeous compact frame will still be mine. I want to lose it forever."

"Might I inquire why?" asked the shrink, removing a pen and pad from his desk.

"No."

The shrink returned the pen and pad to the drawer and closed it. "Well, I suppose we might as well begin immediately. I could use a little distraction right now. However, I'm under a social obligation to inform you that it might be impossible."

"Nothing is impossible; the mind is master of all things."

"And the heart?"

"The heart is master of none."

Indeed, nothing is impossible; what can be imagined can be accomplished. The thinking machine became a complex conglomeration of wires, electrical currents, screws, nuts and bolts, thin metal slabs, colorful lights, springs, transistors, generators, batteries, glass, plastic, oil, lenses, transmitters, superchargers, step-down transformers, rheometers, and thousands of other parts too numerous to mention. He stood two meters high, three meters wide; the majority of his new body was a rectangular metal box the color of rust; at the section vaguely analogous to shoulders were two series of coils forming new arms and fingers which bent at any point between the coils; he could shape his arm into a circle if he chose. At the tips of each leg (which was four centimeters of coils) were thirty tiny wheels which enabled him to maneuver with a semblance of limberness. He had a head, or something which can be called a head unless you're a purist where the English language is concerned, for the head was a huge circular concoction of wires and transmitters and flashing lights and a grill through which he spoke and antenna and relaying systems, but his brain, the last remaining item of his legendary compact frame, was where his stomach should have been; and his brain, the wires piercing it, and its life-sustaining liquid, were visible through unbreakable glass. The thinking machine never asked the shrink about the fate of his human body; he was totally apathetic toward his mortal remains, now that he was no longer human.

This new arrangement suited the thinking machine wonderfully. The apparatus in his head transmitted all the necessary information to his brain, but without the emotional involvement, the personal touch that had been so disconcerting before. He could see the dew on grass and leaves glistening in the early morning sun; he could hear the howls of lonely wolves; he could smell the fragrance of a red rose; but he regarded all these things intellectually; they aroused no sentimental response. If he could be said to be happy or satisfied, it was due to the loss of loneliness and pain. He no longer felt the desire to share his existence, even temporarily, with a woman. He had become sexless, an entity in and of himself, a self-perpetuating machine. Finally, after years of struggle, he could examine life and the universe with the proper objectivity, so that he might understand the natural order of things. At last, he was free.

In fact, he had not imagined while weighing the pros and cons of his scheme that he would be free of so much. He had known, of course, that unless he took on human form by applying his power to alter his shape (which he did not expect to do under any circumstances), that all impulses toward sexual intercourse would be null and void forever; but he had not thought that the need for social intercourse would be totally negated. He had imagined himself pontificating upon his discoveries to those select godlike men and women who were interested; after all, an ego such as his would always require bolstering. However, his ego became self-sufficient; it was enough to know he had progressed along certain lines further than anyone in history, and it was immaterial if others should know. it too.

So he had spent several million years in seclusion, in and near the cave on the solitary mountain. He required no sleep in his new form, only fifteen minutes daily with his input systems closed down; and the millions of years stretched endlessly in a languid ballad of peace and discovery. If he learned nothing new about the universe in any given period, he learned something new about himself, or at the very least discovered a nuance of his freedom from triviality he had not previously noticed. He could conceive of no logical reason why he should travel far from his cave; an understanding of the universe was derived from an understanding of the tiniest particulars, and all knowledge came to his territorial boundaries once he knew where and how to look. If he contemplated a rock, and contemplated it not only in relation to itself, but to its immediate surroundings—a passing insect, a weed, dust, neighboring rocks—then he contemplated all rocks, and he could learn nothing from rocks on the other side of the world, or on another planet, or in the vacuum of space, that he could not learn from this rock. And if he returned to that rock in a million years, there was so much more to learn from it. Sometimes he believed he could never learn everything, but such was his peace that he never became frustrated and impatient. All time waited before him. He imagined the race of godlike man finally expiring as the guiding life-forces of the universe faded, and still he would be there on his mountain on a cold, darkening world, and still he would be learning. By removing himself from history, he had placed himself in a position to comprehend it as no other being could.

He discovered that winter suited him most aptly. Although Earth had been blessed with an eternal summer since the dawn of godlike man, a tenacious eternal summer that remained regardless of the tilt of the Earth's axis, or its proximity to the sun (springing as it did from the subconscious desires of godlike men, who wished it to be warm and pleasant, with life in full flower, no matter where they were), the thinking machine could call on his vast resources and create a winter on his mountain that lasted years at a time. In a world of eternal life, he was the only inhabitant fascinated by the birth-rebirth cycle. He enjoyed (in his detached, inhuman manner) watching the leaves turn red and golden, and then fluttering in the air, and then covering the ground with fragile loveliness. And of the entire race, he was the only one capable of viewing the budding of flowers and leaves without sentimentality; thus he was alone in appreciating its true meaning. He contemplated best, however, in the cold air and white snow that embraced only his mountain, when his environment was as singular as he. It was during winter that life had the true consistency the thinking machine craved. During winter the chaos, the turbulent flow of life, was minimal. The animals strayed from the sudden cold of his mountain and he was able to contemplate the lonely starkness of bare limbs outlined against a blue-gray sky without distraction. Though the trees lived, he found a harmony in their dormancy that complemented his own nature. It was wonderful to live without illustrating evidence of life, without the pain of struggle. And when it snowed, the tiny flakes smothering the drab brown of the landscape, the thinking machine stood exposed and allowed himself to be smothered until he too was nearly concealed by the whiteness; then he could pretend to be actually part of the universe he studied with such devotion; though alive, he could pretend to possess none of the attributes of life, and thus be closer to the mysterious cosmic forces that had forced him to embrace what he called his radical peace.

It was during the thinking machine's longest, coldest winter, when he had stood in the snow for several weeks, his spare mental energies protecting him from the dampness that inevitability seeped through his cracks, that his peace came to an abrupt conclusion.

Only the lower portion of the thinking machine's metal body was visible through the snow; his wheels were also concealed. He did not know how long he had stood there; something in his nature, or perhaps something in the aforementioned cosmic forces, had dictated he withdraw from life more completely than usual; he was possessed by the necessity to achieve ultimate objectivity, to progress beyond his new boundaries, being essentially unaware that his rapport with the universe had become so profound that he could sense approaching disaster more accurately than mundane individuals with mere paranormal tendencies. Nothing in the thinking machine's rapport with the universe, however, could have prepared him for the owner of the lusty, passionate voice singing the tale of a soldier mourning for his lost love to the accompaniment of a twelve-string guitar.

At first he could not pinpoint the location of the voice, despite the fact that his electronic devices picked up frequencies with an accuracy that paled the abilities of godlike men at their best. The voice came from everywhere; it seemed the entire universe was encompassed in that one alien (and unexpected) sound. For several minutes the thinking machine remained absolutely still as he listened to that eloquent voice sing of loftly passions with an underlying attitude that was definitely (without being too blunt about it) bawdy. The thinking machine attempted to be inhumanly annoyed that his solitude had been disrupted, but as those minutes passed, he became afraid he would radiate a heat from within that would melt the snow from his metal body. Even as he denied it to himself, denied it with all the singular sense of purpose that had brought him to the pinnacle of a successful existence, the thinking machine was deeply affected by the voice. Thoughts which had been lost to him for so long that he could not recall having possessed them, however peripherally, now surged forward with an intensity all the more debilitating because he was not used to that sort of thing. He realized the voice originated directly in front of him, that it had always originated there; the possessor of the wonderful organic instrument had teleported silently before him and without so much as inhaling (creating a sound he surely would have detected) had begun playing and singing.

The thinking machine felt more than heat in his internal construction. Gears, wires, and instruments were becoming overtaxed with sensory input; his parts were being torn askew. But he did not feel as if his engineering excellence was on the wane; to the contrary, he felt that he was once again on the verge of experiencing some peak of existence. If only the peak did not feel so familiar, despite his mechanical body which, logically, should have prevented him from experiencing any sensation as if he was merely human.

The thinking machine teleported the snow covering him and the snow immediately surrounding his wheels to the antimatter universe. The sheer violence of the impulsive gesture astounded him; normally he would have created a spring so the snow would gradually melt. But he had little opportunity to be astounded, for he immediately contemplated the vision before him, a vision such as he never could have conceived, trapped as he was in his inorganic state. He had seen beautiful women before while an actual thinking machine; he had even seen women in the buff; but he had seen them while watching particulars in the golden city from the vantage point of his mountain, and he had viewed their nakedness, or their sexuality, or their availability as dispassionately as he viewed the sexuality of a she-wolf in heat. But he had never seen a woman such as this. She casually sat on a boulder, her dainty feet seven centimeters from the crust of the snow. At least, he imagined her feet to be dainty; he could not be sure as his visual systems lingered upon her black leather boots. She wore a red sleeveless dress that clung to her strictly enticing body as if a mad painter had dipped her in a bucket of oils. She had removed her black gloves so her fingers could strum the guitar with greater sensitivity, and for a few moments the thinking machine's visual systems lingered on the nearly instinctive movements of her fingers as they played a passionate series of chords that brought still more seething concepts to the forefront of his brain. She shook strands of long brown hair from her big brown eyes and smiled at the thinking machine. Her smile caused a few discordant noises to emit from the thinking machine's mechanism.

Her smile also provided the impetus behind the thinking machine's insight into exactly what was happening to him. He was in dire danger of losing all he had gained in a matter of moments. Already dark, perverted, disgusting, nasty, and indescribably wonderful emotions were roaring in his brain; their impact was increased by the fact that his body had no nerves to tingle with warmth, no heart to pound, no lungs to breathe irregularly, no dong to reach toward the sky and throb in anticipation. All sensation boiled in his brain. The thinking machine resisted. Sex, while not exactly abhorrent, was certainly out of the question. Nevertheless, quite illogically, he recalled the incident of when he was performing the act of cunnilingus with a superiority that was exceptional even for him due to a few discrete revisions he had made on the construction of his tongue; he brought his partner to such ecstasy that she lost control of her other bodily functions during an especially spasmodic orgasm and pissed all over his face; but he was not called the thinking machine for nothing, and he changed the urine into lemonade as it poured upon him; the incident had absolutely nothing to do with current events, except perhaps to illustrate how much he had lost, but he recalled it completely, nearly reliving the sensations as if he still possessed his old body. He was so lost in experience that he could not fully understand it; he did not desire to wait until another time to regain his accustomed detachment; he took steps to distance himself from his metallic passion. He imagined her groin infested with crabs. He imagined her lying on silk sheets, picking and scratching at her pubes with desperate ferocity. He succeeded in grossing himself out, which had been his intention, but his success intensified his passion. What he wanted, what he had possessed for so many millions of years, vanished like a creature without substance as he contemplated what he now wanted. He imagined himself human again, human and piercing her submissive, willing, and enticing bod, and he could not imagine the wonderfulness of the sensation, though he had a good idea of what it would be. His desire erased all other thoughts, resistance, and ambitions from his brain; and he pictured wild and wacky visions of babies dancing in a midnight sun and old men crying at their own gravesides. He was reimmersed in the birth-rebirth cycle, and the time had arrived for some serious loving.

The woman ceased playing and singing. She set her guitar aside, gently placing it in the snow on top of the boulder. She slowly, oh so slowly and sensuously, put on her long black gloves. This task accomplished, she smiled.

The smile moved the thinking machine to action, but to action absolutely without premeditation. He juggled back and forth, to his right and left, as if the ground beneath was shaking him; and smoke jetted from his openings. Anyone watching him (with the exception of the woman, who evidently knew what she was doing) would have thought he was falling apart, in danger of exploding; but in truth his mechanical body had never given him so much pleasure. He felt his interior parts rattling as if they had broken from their support, and the liquid surrounding his brain seemed to bubble as if he had been deposited in a raging fire. He had not communicated with anyone for so long, though he had always possessed the appropriate apparatus, and his speakers crackled with static caused from underuse when he said, in a voice sounding as if it was transmitted from a hundred kilometers away, "I'm so dirty; you're so clean. All I need is a spin in your washing machine."

The woman turned slightly to her left, no longer looking directly at the thinking machine. She arched her back and totally ignored him.

"Listen to me," said the thinking machine. "I want you. I need you. I require a dip in your vaginal fluid. I can't get much more diplomatic than that."

The woman then turned and said coldly, remorselessly, placing the fingers of her right hand at her cleavage, "You talking to me?"

The thinking machine was stunned silent and immobile. Of all her possible reactions, he had considered this one the most unlikely.

"You talking to me?" she said. "You're talking to *me*? Well, I'm the only one here. Who the fuck do you think you're talking to?"

Suddenly, utterly without volition, the thinking machine leapt up and down so rapidly he feared he actually would break apart. The smoke jetting from his openings was now accompanied by hissing steam. His speakers crackled incoherently until he begged, "Oh, please, talk dirty to me some more. It's been so long since someone's talked dirty to me. I love it. I need it. I fervently desire your verbal abuse."

The woman regarded him with a condescending smile. "What do you want me to say?"

"Tell me all about shit and vomit and piss and bile and all about how you lubricate and how much you want me to eat you and *vice versa* and maybe even simultaneously and how much your nipples harden when I kiss them and how you want me to stick my finger up your asshole or even how you want me to stick my mighty dong up your asshole and how much you want to give me a hum job and I understand, though I've never experienced it personally, that the low notes are the best, though of course it doesn't matter what you hum, but *how*, and maybe you can explain something that used to be on my mind—a sleeve job—because no one could tell me what it was though it sounds fascinating and please don't tell me how much you love me and I won't tell you how much I love you because nobler sentiments have nothing to do with what I desire from you and please, please, talk dirty! Won't you? Pretty please?"

The woman patted her brown hair as if she was inspecting her image in a mirror, though in reality she stared at the thinking machine, her blank eyes vaguely resembling those of a bovine. But beneath the dullness of those eyes gleamed a sadistic light illuminating the whole of thinking machine's existence. "And why should I talk dirty to you?" she said. "What pleasure could possibly be derived from it?"

"I will have to make a few adjustments in my construction."

"What kind of adjustments? A steel rod hooked up to your brain?"

The thinking machine pondered the matter. "That seems a little radical, but I think it's our best bet."

Placing her palms at her side in the snow, the woman, grinning malevolently, leaned over, providing the thinking machine a delicious view of her ripe melons. "Really now? Are you sure you want me?"

"Indubitably! I...I want you now and forever. I can't explain it. I know what's happening to me, but I don't know either. I can't feel hot, but I feel hot. I can't feel emotions, but I'm utterly irrational. I...I take back what I said about love...because I love you. I want you to manipulate me like a pawn, a toy; I want you to torture me forever; I will take no end of punishment from you, spiritually or physically or both simultaneously; I want you to be a sexual vampire, sucking away my intellectual creativity. Only...please reward me occasionally. Let me possess you occasionally. Grant me the privilege of plummeting inside you; grant me release from these passions that drive me. Allow me to be a..."

"To be a man?"

The thinking machine hesitated. "Yes."

"Do you want me regardless of what sort of person I ultimately prove to be?"

This time the thinking machine did not hesitate. "Yes. May I have you?"

"I don't know. I truly never considered it before," said the woman in a playful tone whose implications totally escaped the thinking machine. "I believe that whether or not you will want me in the future depends on how liberal you are." The woman was engulfed in a blinding yellow light radiating from within her system, and when the light faded, she was changed.

The thinking machine crackled incoherently once again, but from shock rather than from passion. "Why, I know you! You're the consulting detective!"

"And I know you. You're the creature I might have become if I hadn't a moral direction, a firm purpose in life."

"I wouldn't say that; I've always known where I was headed and where I was coming from."

The consulting detective slipped from the boulder and brushed the snow from his cape-backed overcoat. He regarded the thinking machine with an enviable objectivity (though there was an unfortunate trace of moral outrage in his smoldering eyes). He nodded as if his words were purely instinctive, in reality very far from the matters truly on his mind. "Your efforts have invariably centered upon yourself, and the godlike man who is supremely interested only in himself gradually succumbs to a suffocating sickness. Perhaps you might have been more fortunate—or at least have selected a more appealing *persona*— if you had pursued knowledge for its own sake, but instead you pursued knowledge for the sake of your ego."

"I pursued truth; I could not have pursued it had it not been for my ego."

The consulting detective's eyes lingered on his wisps of breath as he absent-mindedly filled his pipe. Recently he had been disciplining himself, cutting down on cocaine, and the substance in his pipe, when lit, would have a distinctly sweet aroma. "I don't doubt it. But it's patently obvious that your distance from the texture of life has taught you little; and it too is obvious that your distance, however great, was easily crossed." He returned the plastic baggie containing the substance to his pocket.

The thinking machine had once believed he was immune to indignation; after all, what did the opinions of others matter to him? Nevertheless, his sensory input systems were burdened with an unpleasant overflow of nomadic electrons as he said, "Don't be so smug, you conceited bastard. I know the truth. I've known it for eons, only I hadn't expected my theories to be confirmed so indisputably upon my own person."

Without exhaling smoke, the consulting detective asked, "And the truth is?"

"Life is a joke. If my distance from its texture had been great enough so that I would understand the meaning of a flower in bloom or of two insects battling for the honor of *shtupping* their queen without the hamperment of my metal shell, that is, if I could experience life as a spirit must experience it and retain my emotions, I would be too busy laughing to take time out to study. It has been said, without truth, that life is a series of moments which, though connected, bear no relation to one another; an individual should not allow the occurrences of a previous moment to affect the savoring of the present moment. That attitude is analogous to a pastrami and mayonnaise sandwich." (The consulting detective winced at the thinking machine's imagery.) "Life is a series of moments of suffering; all pleasure is merely a relief from otherwise continuous loneliness and pain; godlike mankind searches for that relief desperately. What is commonly referred to as the urge to give life meaning is a euphemism; the urge is merely an aspect of the search. However, the urge also provides the humor, the dramatic irony, the intellectual slapstick of emotional fools thinking with their reproductive organs—even when they don't have any, as my case proves quite conclusively. Life is a joke because people muddle through their moments like a crowd of cripples attempting to scale a cliff. As soon as an individual comes (prematurely) to the conclusion that he's accomplished something worthwhile, one of the factors that led him to believe in the inherent worthiness of his deeds alters and renders the struggle of previous moments meaningless. For example, the individual might be an artist who becomes noted among our race just after his lover, the source of his inspiration, leaves him forever. Or, in the case of myself, he might travel along a spiritual path only to find his existence shattered by an emotional weakness he believed to have rid himself of eons ago. The love I experienced for you while you were a woman, under the guise of providing me pleasure, in actuality caused me more pain than I have ever undergone as a man. I can take consolation in that my life-failure—for the incident has convinced me that my life has amounted to nothing less—is not unique. All men and women can say the same about their lives. Life is a comedy, and we are all the butt of the jokes."

"Comedy isn't pretty," said the consulting detective after mulling over the thinking machine's words for a few moments.

Though his mind had begun to grapple with the matters on hand, his eyes were dreamy and glazed, as if he had difficulty concentrating. In truth, sometimes he realized the meaning of a phrase only several seconds after it had been spoken.

"And now you've shattered my illusions," continued the thinking machine. "I suppose you had your reasons for what you did . . ."

"I had them."

"But they're unimportant. They were only an excuse the cosmic forces fostered upon you so they could get a laugh. It would have been nice, however, if you were actually a woman. To love an illusion causes the greatest pain of all and love between ourselves is impossible, due to my true form and yours."

The consulting detective blinked, then raised his eyebrows. "Let's pass the subject of your form for a moment. What's wrong with mine?"

"Hey, I ain't no queer," said the thinking machine. "I don't swing that way."

"Nor I. But you discounted the possibility before you even considered it. As I well know, the physical frame is of no importance when the spirit of love enters your heart. Rather than regaining your distance from life, you should instead seek to expand your definition of yourself, that is, to draw more of life into your being."

"How can I draw life into this metal construct?" asked the thinking machine, an eerie forlornness crackling through his speakers. "Who would love a creature such as I?"

His pipe dangling precariously between his lips, the consulting detective held his hands behind his back and stalked in a circle about the thinking machine as if he was hot on the trail of a despicable foe. Ostensibly inspecting the metal case of the mind he was debating philosophy with, he was actually savoring the sensation of snow caking and falling from his shoes as he scraped his feet through the white superimposition. "You're not listening. You've the power to alter your form into the design of your choosing."

"And, if I should find a love, would she still love me when she learned the truth?"

"You're talking to a godlike man who has loved a giant clam."

The remark, delivered with the utmost seriousness, convinced the thinking machine that he should change the subject. However, to his surprise, his words did not stray far from the thoughts uppermost on his mind. "Would you love me?"

"In some respects I am as trapped as you, though I admit that logically, if two minds were ever meant to love one another..." The consulting detective turned from the thinking machine and inhaled the sweet smoke deeply, with unadorned gusto. He stared at the golden city in the distance, at the warm sun bathing it in bright light.

"I see," said the thinking machine. "I also see that you believe everything I've said. You believe that there is no point in continuing, because regardless of what you do or who you love, the immortality of yourself and our race insures no permanence to your deeds. Our days stretch into eternity, but the days of eternity are infinitely more numerous, and there will come a time when godlike mankind is dust. Personally, I had hoped to avoid the fate, but now there is no avoidance. And you know as well as I, as if each cell of your being burned with the knowledge, that ultimately your perseverance will come to naught."

The consulting detective nodded. "And yet I persevere, as you must. Godlike men such as we realize that mere living is insufficient, that there must be more to life than even love can provide. For the majority of our species, the act of living is satisfactory; they've no need to question it. But there must be levels we haven't imagined, reasons we haven't conceived, and until we discover them, we must play the game as best we can. There is something inside us we cannot deny, something that keeps us going despite our yearning for death and peace and an ending, despite our utter conviction in the futility of it. Friend thinking machine, you must cultivate the element inside you that maintains your grip on life. I wish I could tell you exactly what to do, just as I wish I could love you (though, unfortunately, a part of me is morally outraged at the notion). But each unique being must proceed in his unique way, and your decisions must be your own." The consulting detective turned to the thinking machine; he had a summation to add. But he suddenly staggered in dizziness. He silently stared at his pipe for several moments. "Oh wow. I must go home and lie down. The good doctor outdid himself this time." He looked up to the thinking machine. "Farewell. I trust our paths will once again cross." And he blinked out of existence, his atoms speeding to his apartment.

The thinking machine stood alone in the snow; surrounding the mountain was summer beckoning him, a call that had been inside him for eons, a call he had not noticed, for all his examination of life, until now. Of what happened to the thinking machine after he had re-entered the turbulent stream of life, we may not recount here. It is only important to add that there came a spring to the lonely mountain that lasted over a hundred years.

3. The sign painted in bold black letters on the glass door of the editor's office read:

ENTER LUBE ROOM AT YOUR OWN RISK
—the chief

Usually, when godlike women found themselves manipulated by fate and had no choice but to pass beyond the gaping portals, they rapped timidly on the glass, the rattling drowning the flurry of typewriters and chattering like an ominous sonic boom. For beyond the portal was the tremendous conglomeration of perverted molecules known as the fat man; and upon occasion his mind strayed from the particulars of making trivial decisions and he leered at the particulars of a firm breast or a shapely buttock, and there could be no mistaking what new decision he was on the verge of making. Thus far his resolutions had not been met with success; there was a point of persistence he would not pass. Nevertheless, he was a force to be reckoned with, and women did not choose to ignore his emotional dependence on the outrageous prodings of his gonads.

The staff of the newspaper had learned this in less than a day; the women, since their acquisition of knowledge was of necessity gained under fire, adjusted more rapidly than those of the masculine persuasion. One thing was learned above all else, and that was that social protocol must be observed; the fat man would not allow familiarity to enter into his relationship with any member of his staff. Everyone wondered why he insisted on distancing himself, since to all appearances he was attempting to become familiar in the most personal sense of the word with the more delectable beauties in the office (with the exception of the ace reporter, whose icy glare embarrassed him; however, this was not common knowledge). The truth of the matter was that the fat man was not entirely serious in his romantic overtures; he was simply attempting to make life more interesting and to keep himself amused in the process. When the fat man made serious romantic overtures, he possessed a masculine intuition that was never wrong.

The afternoon following the discovery of the death of the dark-haired woman carrying a rusty sword, the staff was stunned into silence, their hands hovering in the nether regions above their work, when the shrew pushed open a door with such force that it cracked the plaster from the wall and caused two holophotos to fall to the floor. She had altered her appearance again, but no one had difficulty recognizing her due to the remarkable consistency of her disposition. She had rejected physical beauty altogether (once she had possessed such a magnetic attraction that her disposition frustrated males cursed with drumming heartbeats). She had discarded her pale smooth skin, preferring ruddy pigmentation; her hair was still red and silky, but somehow it seemed wilder, more frenzied; her breasts were too large for her short, stocky body, and the common denominator of her physical design was sloppiness. She wore an unflattering pair of baggy slacks that created an illusion of unduly massive, round legs; her yellow cotton sweater was too large; everyone knew at a glance she was not wearing a bra. Her face, though the features were slightly altered to match her new composition, possessed the same boyish elements contorted into insane anger; nevertheless, there would have been something appealing about the flattened nose, large nostrils, fat cheeks, and pointed chin if she chose to allow her expression to soften into one indicating normalcy. Occasionally her expression was relatively normal, but the glare of her green eyes invariably belied it. Recently she had come to the conclusion that her physical beauty had been a prison of her spiritual self; she had become unattractive so that her spirit might burst from its cell and permeate her being with its innate wonderfulness. However, if her present mood was any indication, godlike mankind had been better off when her spirit was shackled. She radiated rage, rage which was all the more terrible because it was reinforced by the charisma she never lost, could never lose due to the power her spirit retained even while shackled. Holding a crumpled copy of the latest story concerning the ripper (which she had taken from a typesetter with a minimum of verbal violence), she sped across the office like a wayward projectile; typewriters ceased clattering and reporters ceased talking as she passed, and all eyes were upon her as she approached the fat man's office. She glared at the sign on the door, and the reporters considered themselves fortunate that they were unable to see the fire burning in her green eyes. They were shocked, immobile, stunned for an infinite moment, as the shrew violated all social protocol with reckless indifference. She confidently entered without knocking.

The fat man was no less surprised at the appearance of the shrew than his staff; unlike them, however, he made a moderately successful attempt to conceal his surprise. His jacket and Borsalino hung on a rack with antlers in a corner. His vest was unceremoniously draped on the arm of his swivel chair. The three top buttons of his white shirt were undone, exposing a vast portion of his pink chest; and his sleeves were rolled up to his elbows. He had been examining the copy of the ace reporter (who was regaining her legendary touch) upon reactions to the ripper's killings. He had not expected to meet a reaction face-to-face while perusing the copy; and once he recognized the shrew through the disguise of her new appearance, his surprise doubled. He felt a strange stirring throughout his being. His first reaction to her new appearance was adequately summed up as *"Ugly!"*; but he nevertheless felt the stirring. It was more than his masculine intuition working overtime (which it frequently did; it often passed the point of diminishing returns); it was more than the unexpected dramatic moment rushing upon him; it was tied up in the notion of destiny, for he quite inexplicably felt that the chaos and disorder of the random events and vague ambitions of his life had somehow inexorably led to this meeting. The fat man had rarely turned to introspection; his mind was so active, so searching, that he had never had a great opportunity, much less the inclination, to ponder the mysteries he believed he could solve through examining the personalities and deeds of others, as an anthropologist would examine the society of the cigar-smoking frogs. He felt that if he was going to indulge in some serious introspection, he had better do it quick. But it was already too late. The shrew was inside his office, slamming the door behind her, waving the copy in the air and glaring at him as if he had wantonly murdered her favorite eternal child. "Ah, what may I do for you?"

"Don't try to sweet-talk me," said the shrew, her lip curling like that of a growling dog. "You don't care what you can do for me; you're probably wondering how you can get me to do something for you."

The fat man realized her remark was close to the truth. Uncomfortably close, considering the thoughts coming unbidden to his mind.

"And if you're wondering why your gunsel didn't stop me, you might be interested to know that he's afraid of me," continued the shrew. "Nothing could ever convince him to bother me again."

The fat man raised an eyebrow; he wondered what the shrew had done and said to the gunsel to diminish the effectiveness of his notoriously fearless servant. He gestured to the William Morris chair, asking the shrew to sit without actually being polite about it.

The shrew casually tossed the copy about the second murder on the desk, taking care to see that the pages became mixed up in the flight. "I'm here to protest the creeping sexism in your paper. The ripper has killed twice, and both times your filthy sexist rag has presented the victims as pathetic losers."

"That's because the ripper has only murdered pathetic losers," said the fat man.

"That's no excuse. Just because the news is true doesn't mean it's okay. The news is saturated with that sort of thing. Society is obsessed with anything and everything that demeans women, in no small part thanks to you. People are brainwashed by what they read in the paper."

"What prevented you from being brainwashed?" The fat man smiled, but maintaining the smile required an effort. He was uncommonly and uncharacteristically disturbed by the intensified glare of the shrew's eyes. She leaned forward, her entire body tensing until the muscles of her neck threatened to burst through her skin. Her nostrils reddened and flared; her breathing was loud, so loud that in the fat man's ears it drowned the resumed typing and talking outside the office. In fact, it seemed his senses were inordinately obsessed with her; all he saw was related to her, all he heard were sounds of her making, all he smelled was her odor—a vague scent he feared existed only in his mind. The fat man attempted to quiet his emotions. His lust for the shrew went against everything he had ever stood for, both in the philosophical and sexual meanings of the phrase. Yet the reversal appealed to him. This woman was a challenge. She was more than a challenge. He recalled the weaknesses that had led to his first marriage; perhaps they had not been weaknesses; perhaps they had been strengths. Perhaps none of it mattered.

"I'm not brainwashed because, unlike my sisters, I'm totally attuned to the essence of my womanhood. It offends men who perceive themselves as reasonable, but a woman's spirit differs from a man's spirit. The essence of her godlike humanity is more closely attuned with the essence of love and life. Nurtured by her greater rapport with the oversoul, a woman is inherently more intelligent than a man; her thoughts and deeds are more informed. Unfortunately, because she is readily prepared to accept the truth that an individual is incomplete when alone, she is readily deluded by insidious masculine propaganda."

"I have always believed women were smarter than men because they have always possessed what we have been seeking."

The shrew's exasperated sigh pleased the fat man. "I'm trying to stick to the subject," she said.

"That is precisely my intention," said the fat man, "if only you would provide me with the opportunity."

When the shrew's face flushed red, he experienced a curious satisfaction, though he was simultaneously frightened and chastised by her anger. She glanced about the office as if imagining how it must have looked before its last remodeling (three million years ago); the silent seconds enabled her to ponder how she might best control the conversation. "Of all things living, a man's the worst. I've never before met a man who obviously hates women to such a degree. If you've no power over them, you fear them; that's why you embrace your ludicrous sexism with tenacity."

"There are all too frequent moments when I hate male and female alike, with equal passion." The fat man believed that a little confession or two might provide her view of him with sorely needed depth.

"I know," said the shrew offhandedly, as if he had told her the sun was shining. "You aren't an altruist; you care nothing for those you profess to care for. Your power, and your insistence upon possessing it in all social situations, is indicative of your true self."

The fat man pursed his lips. Under the desk, his hands tightened on his knees until he feared the caps would pop out. He was in danger of losing what minuscule control he had; and the hard tone of his voice, sounding as if it was compressed in a vise, astounded him as he attempted to express himself as coherently as possible. "What you say about me may be true, my dear, but since you obviously detest men as much as I am supposed to detest women under the guise of being deeply moved by all their nice round and fuzzy places, I hardly consider you an adequate judge of my character." He paused, but when the shrew opened her mouth to speak, he ceased examining phrases in his mind and spoke rapidly. "It might very well be true that the victims of the ripper had redeeming positive qualities, but if so, no one has come forward to speak of them. I doubt if you knew the victims personally; they are martyrs in your mind, and you seek to graft your cause upon others' memories of them. Though news of necessity requires artifice, I am not about to distort it to benefit your petty concerns. You succumb to the common error of judging a social climate or movement by its least attractive elements rather than its most attractive. Your vision has been blinded by hate for so long that you have forgotten what life on this planet was like before the advent of depression and sexism. Life was...boring. Each godlike man and godlike woman possessed great power and intelligence, and to what end? The answer is: to no end. The injection of sexism into our society, as abhorrent as it may be to you, is not an injection of evil, but simply of the texture of life. My exploration of sexism, though it might be tied to my psychological profile in ways I do not wish to know, is simply my way of playing the game."

"To what end?" asked the shrew.

The fat man could not fail to notice that she was now quiet, though certainly not subdued; the glare of her green eyes was subtly different, perhaps reflecting the light of reappraisal. However, her question had confounded him. "To what end?" he said, as if to convince himself of the reality of her words. "I do not know. I simply play the game. I simply take each step of the journey, and I hope that one day I will take the step that illuminates all others. I do know that while we conventional godlike men were wasting our time on education, agitation, and organization, some independent genius has taken the matter in hand, and by simply murdering and disemboweling two godlike women, converted the consulting detective into an inept sort of crusader. Perhaps he will soon take that illuminating step and will guide us on our collective journey."

"Has society degenerated to the point that such crimes should be condoned as serving a higher purpose?"

"Society has not degenerated; it just has not progressed. Too many individuals have succumbed to the ravages of stagnation." He drummed his fingers on the desk. The shrew, though calmer, less volatile, did not appear to have reconsidered her perception of the universe in general. The fat man and the shrew were not four meters apart, and they were sitting as if they were having a casual conversation in a restaurant, and yet he could not be sure she was in the room at all. His respiratory system was smothered by the scent of her shampoo, he had not looked away from her for so long that the muscles of his eyes throbbed, he had not stopped thinking of personal matters, not even once, while pretending to be preoccupied with the sublime, and still he suspected she was actually a million kilometers away, or that she was a figment, the manifestation of his masculine intuition gone wild. It had gone wild in any case. Though he could not frankly contemplate her sexual potential, he could be aloof about it, and there was nothing, absolutely *nothing* about her short, dumpy body that appealed to him. But he knew, though he could not tell her, that as of the moment, she was the reason he played the game. The singular steps had taken him to this office, to her. He felt positively mushy.

"I think you're mad," said the shrew. "I think the whole race is mad."

The fat man leaned back; he imagined her sexual history; she had loved many men, and the fat man doubted he would respect most of them as godlike beings. Doubtlessly he had encountered many of her lovers, those brave enough to endure the attacks of her shrewness, and thought of them with disdain, if he thought of them at all. He had hoped his judgment might sway the proddings of his ferocious gonads, but his gonads remained firm. He was lost. If his enterprises were successful, he would not respect himself in the morning. "If godlike mankind was sane, we would have gone mad long ago."

The shrew nodded, making some observation to herself. The distance between her and the fat man was more pronounced, and the fat man felt the barrier between them was somehow smothering him. He knew he would continue all his nefarious activities if he did not win her, but they would lose their nebulous meaning while he was doing them, though they might regain it in retrospect. For the first time in many months the fat man wanted to submit to defeat; some force deep inside him, perhaps the force identical to that which had driven so many of his fellows to reside in the East End, urged him to yield, to give up, to pack it in, and he actually believed that vanquishment would be the easiest course. However, his masculine intuition whispered, *Keep coming on strong.*

The fat man turned on the charm. "My dear, sanity and reason are the very essence of boredom, insanity and chaos are the very essence of life, and if life makes you happy, nothing else can. Only those who love can fully understand how unreasonable the emotion can be, and though it grates on my nerves, though I resist the impulse and refuse to commit myself totally to chaos (despite my advice to others), I must proclaim that I love you with all my sexist heart."

He mentally prepared himself for her reaction, but no amount of preparation could have been adequate defense against the sheer violence of her response. The shrew screwed her mouth into a series of unbelievable contortions, and her reddened skin most resembled the red sky of a particularly emblazened sunset. She gripped the armrests of the William Morris chair and trembled as if vainly holding back a geyser of vomit. "Well, I never...! You men! You think you all have a magnetic attraction to women! I could never think of anything more terrible than loving a fat pink toad such as you! Why, even something as ordinary as sex would be unbearable. You neo-sexists think only of yourselves, twisting women into this position and that, changing things around at a moment's notice, never caring that we might think things are perfectly all right as they are, and then when you finally shoot your wad, after pounding us until our quims are as sensitive as a wound, you figure everything's all over and you quit, just like that, regardless of whether or not your partner might find it satisfactory if we just lay there, with a man inside. No, I would never, never love you."

The fat man thought about it. "I suppose even women have a right to sexual gratification."

"Which you're remarkably unqualified to provide," said the shrew, turning toward the wall, away from the fat man, and crossing her legs.

"My dear, in the minds of some women, I have replaced bread as the staff of life."

"Yet you are withered."

"'Tis from overuse," replied the fat man, smiling.

"You're an ass, and asses are made to bear, and so are you."

"My dear, you are a woman," said the fat man tenderly, "and women are made to bear, and so are you."

The shrew snorted. Despite her anger, her utter rejection of him, the fat man felt warm inside as he looked at her. He could think of nothing about her body or her spirit or her mind which could create that feeling, but it was there, it actually existed, irregardless of the distance between them, and so he savored it.

"How can I love you?" asked the shrew, suddenly shedding her anger as if divesting herself of an odorous coat. "You represent all I detest about life. It is my destiny to oppose you; I was born to fight you. How can I love you when the oversoul is watching us, sitting in judgment?"

"Possibly it is, but it is the oversoul and we are but a part; consequently we must live as best we can."

The shrew covered her mouth and stared at the floor; the fire in her green eyes had extinguished itself. The silence was long and awkward, but not entirely uncomfortable. The fat man was about to speak when a yellow glow appeared on his desk. His eyes widened. He had no logical reason for knowing who was creating the glow; nevertheless he knew: it was the ripper! The glow faded, and in its place was a letter in an envelope. The shrew's expression radiated nervousness; she too sensed the envelope's sinister origin.

The fat man opened the envelope and read aloud:

> *Beware, I shall be at work tonight in the East End at twelve midnight and I give the consulting detective a good chance, but he is never near when I am at work.*

The fat man pursed his lips and placed the letter on the desk, resisting the urge to crumple it and set it afire. All thoughts of the shrew were momentarily erased from his mind, though the vision of her still filled his sight. She stared at him, clearly waiting for him to speak. After what he deemed an appropriate pause, he said, "My dear, the game is nigh afoot, as the consulting detective would say. Tonight, if we are not successful, someone may die. A spirit with the potential to live a life which would brighten our dark days may be snuffed out forever, and we will never know what we have lost. We do not have time for other games. I must take this letter forthwith to the consulting detective at the demon's castle; and I would consider it an honor if afterwards we got naked together in my quarters."

The shrew bit her lower lip; the fat man thought he detected a trace of moisture in her eyes. She said, "Then we must put away our masks. We must cease living our preconceived roles, if only for a few hours. We must be our true selves."

"And what shall we discover, what shall we learn?"

"Perhaps we shall then know who we truly are."

"Perhaps, but all this talk is depriving me of the tenderness of your lips. Kiss me, dear shrew, kiss me."

4. *A report from the universal op:*

Life is a bowl of shit. When the dinner bell sounds, you'd better smile and dig in, otherwise things will go a lot tougher on you. I've worked out a compromise, myself.

The Old Man had recently moved the offices to the East End. He said we should be located where the work is. It didn't make any difference to me. He had gentle eyes behind gold spectacles and a mild smile, hiding the fact that a million eons of sleuthing over nothing in particular had left him without any feelings at all on any subject.

He got older every year. He just didn't feel like eradicating or even retarding the aging process, I suppose. He said, "There's a haunt of some kind over at a theater here in the East End." He gave me directions. "Go over there and check it out. It might give us a clue to the whereabouts of either Kitty or the ripper." He smiled mildly, drooling white saliva from the left side of his mouth. He was a senile old goat. I didn't like to think about him too much.

On my way to the theater, I noticed that I wasn't as objective about things as I used to be. I saw the East End as if I was watching a holomovie out of focus, but it had never seemed as clear to me. I couldn't pretend to be unaffected by the dank humidity, the glare of the sun (occasionally obscured by clouds), and the sharp odor of the filth on the streets. I saw people staring at me, staring at where my face should have been; them I didn't have to pretend to ignore.

I arrived at *The Eibon* before I had become aware I was approaching it. Momentarily confounded, I realized that my mind hadn't been on the job. I had been thinking about other things.

The Eibon would have been a living legend if only it had had an opportunity to live. Nearly a hundred meters tall, its stone walls were studded with jewels which had been intended to reflect the sunlight, but instead merely threatened to. The jewels were crusted with dirt and grime. The trees alongside the walls needed trimming, and the weeds had choked the plants in the dull silver pots. The wind hissed, and the front page of today's paper, with a picture of the fat man announcing his new editorship, crackled against a wall. A lizard nibbled at a mid-morning snack; he stuck his tongue out at me.

I pushed open the swinging glass door, avoiding a little round pile of dog shit in my path. The glass was so dirty that when I touched it, a generous sampling of dust adhered like paste to my fingers. Inside, I wiped my hand on my trousers and looked around.

The lobby was big and spacious; it could have been populated with a thousand people and still felt empty. Now it felt lonely, an observation I wouldn't have been able to make before I started on this little caper. There were a lot of circular lights on the white enamel ceiling twenty meters above my head, but only one in five was switched on. The dirt on the red rug was so thick I left my footprints behind me as I walked around. There were other sets of footprints scattered about, so I kept cool, my mind on my job, as I walked past plants that had died from lack of water long ago (except for a huge plastic fern concoction, which nevertheless looked a little under the weather to me). A lot of gaudy decorations signifying nothing were strewn on the walls. I couldn't rid myself of the notion that someone or something was hiding behind the columns and giving me the once-over. Every time I neared a column, the premonition strengthened as if it derived from someplace other than my body. I had never before experienced an outside force fucking around with my insides; I had always been my own godlike man, and now that I wasn't entirely my own, I didn't like the sensation a bit.

I heard someone move behind a column. All I knew for sure was that whoever he was, he hadn't been watching me for as long as I had sensed myself being watched. I figured this bozo (who had probably communicated telepathically with the Old Man) was pretty scared, because he should have known who had sent me. Not that I could blame him for not trusting anyone; he was just a little stupid, was all.

"Hold it right there!" I said. "You can turn invisible on me, or you can teleport into a closet if you want to, but either way I'll be able to detect your mental energy as sure as if I was seeing you." I began slowly circling the column, though I was still too far away to see him. "Come on out and talk. I won't hurt you."

"Who is youse?" the someone wailed pitifully.

"I'm the universal op," I said impatiently, stopping.

"How's can I be sure?"

"Damned if I know. You'll just have to take the chance, I suppose, because if you don't, I'm turning around and walking out. I'm the only person who can help you resolve the dilemma which has so obviously driven you to this desperate state. But, unfortunately for you, I ain't got no time to fuck around today."

"All...all right. Don't go. I'll come out." The someone whined, on the verge of tears, presumably to add a touch of pathos to the proceedings. He should have strived for dignity instead. He was a short little runt, with thin arms and legs and a gut like he had swallowed a basketball. I've no idea what his hair and face really looked like, because he wore a wig of wiry black hair and blackface smeared by the tears he had shed while awaiting my arrival. His baggy yellow trousers, held up by yellow suspenders, had square red-and-green polka-dot patches at the knees, and a blue-and-purple-striped patch on the right thigh. He wore white gloves with four fingers; I figured his hands must have made a perfect fit. His black shirt was so large that I couldn't have made an accurate guess at his weight without utilizing my mental powers, which wasn't worth the effort. As he walked toward me, waving his arms like a rabid windmill, he did a little instinctive (and terrible) softshoe. "Oh, mastah universah op, youse must help me. I is in serious difficulty, and my ass is definitely grass, no matter how youse slice it."

"I've no intention of slicing it. What's the poop?"

"It is da stage manager. He has gone nuts. He has gone nuts a long time ago. He has been sucking the blood of the illustrious actors of our repertory company, turning them into zombies one by one."

This sounded interesting. Kitty had never been known to turn anybody into a zombie (she was supposed to be good in the sack, but not *that* good), but there was a decent possibility the ripper was involved. "How long has the stage manager been killing people?"

"I didn't say he was killing them, suh, begging your pardon for contradicting youse. I said he was turning them into zombies. There's a distinct but subtuh difference."

I felt like going home to bed. "Okay, how long has he been turning people into zombies?"

"Nots long. Just ever since we moved da theater to da East End here. I don't know what has happened to da stage manager. He used to be a sweet old joe, he did, he did, you gotta believe me."

"I believe you already. Why haven't you just left the theater?"

"Because da theater is my only home, mastah universah op. I's got nowhere else to go. Da theater is my life, it really is. There ain't no audience, 'tis true, but I's sometimes find myself lost in a song, and I's gotta get up on dat stage and sing and dance. Though there ain't no audience, I can experience a vicarious thrill."

I wished, for the first time, that I could make a face. "Where is this stage manager?"

The minstrel (for that's what he was, despite the fact he probably wasn't any good at it) looked to the right and left with his wide eyes. His pupils rolled about like sentient marbles. "I's doesn't know! I surely wish I did, I do, I do!"

"Well, he sounds like a stay-at-home, just as you are, so he should be around here somewhere. Let's go."

As I turned and took a step, the minstrel grabbed my wrist. His grip felt like that of a drained, but tenacious leech. "Go? Go? Mastuh universah op, go where?"

I removed his hand with my free forefinger and middle finger. "Go looking for the stage manager, of course."

"But I's can't do dat. If he sees me, he's gonna go drain my soul, and youse knows my kinda people can't sing and dance if we ain't got soul."

"If you don't come with me, you're going to be all by your lonesome."

"Oh no, not dat! Anything but dat!"

"Then come along. Don't worry; I won't let anything happen to you, much as I would like to."

So of course something did happen to the little runt. Powerful rays of mental energy, beyond the range of my ultraviolet vision, inundated the lobby and embraced the minstrel. Just as he screamed, I tried to contradict the power, but it was too late, I had been taken too much by surprise. And in the space of a nanosecond, the minstrel was gone, without even leaving a residue of atoms speeding to his destination so I could follow him. The mind that had taken him had been very thorough; it had concealed its vibrations from me until the last possible second, and though I sent out telepathic emittances, hoping something would relay back to me that would help me pinpoint the mind's location, I could pick up nothing. Not a ping.

For several minutes I stood there in the lobby. I felt like a sap. I was positive of only one thing, and that was that the presence I felt hovering in *The Eibon* was separate from the mind (undoubtedly the stage manager's) which had taken the minstrel. I didn't have any words to describe the presence, since the subjective esoteria of existence doesn't concern me much. But it was there, attempting to influence me, trying to make me give up, go home, and fake a report to the Old Man. It might as well have saved the effort. The consulting detective couldn't make me fake a report to the Old Man, even if he was a senile old goat.

I walked to the snack bar. Mostly for the benefit of the invisible presence, I prepared some hot buttered popcorn in less than a minute. Absorbing it a kernel at a time, I looked around. I could search for the minstrel telepathically, but then the stage manager would always know where I was. If I searched physically, it would take longer, therefore increasing whatever danger the minstrel was in, but then I would be able to conceal my presence by maintaining vibratory shields which would make it impossible for the stage manager to pinpoint me telepathically. It was a calculated risk, but the minstrel had survived this long. Chances were the stage manager, being an arrogant sort, still wasn't in a hurry to drain his soul. Probably the little runt's soul wasn't all that appetizing anyway, since he had been saved for last.

The men's room, where the men sent their wastes to the antimatter universe in the privacy of their own sex, was to my right, on the far side of the lobby; I went there first. Two paths on the stairs had worn through the red rug, exposing the rotting wood underneath. Winged termites scurried about the wood on the bottom stairs. I stayed in the middle. The air in the lounge still stank of cigarette and cigar smoke, though it looked like no one had been escaping a performance for years. The plants on either side of the couch covered by the frayed black blanket were also dead from lack of water; dried leaves rested in the dirt below the tan stems and on the floor. Three crumpled paper cups were in the square glass ashtray on the table in front of the couch. A broken ashtray, in seven pieces, was underneath the table. The solitary lamp cast dull radiation, making the lounge appear even tackier. Inside the men's room, I took some paper towels and stuffed them in my hind trousers pocket; the popcorn was making my fingers greasy.

I approached the ladies' room more cautiously. Not that I expected the stage manager to be there; it was simply force of a habit I had picked up after an embarrassing incident while working on a case. I stood in the ladies' lounge, listening for sounds of activity in the bathroom. The lounge was exactly identical to the first, save for the addition of a desk with a big round mirror so the ladies could apply appealing little touches to their makeup. Around the mirror were tiny light bulbs, all of which needed replacing. I hesitated before the door to the bathroom, steeled myself, and pushed it open with my greasy fingers. I don't have any fingerprints, so I left greasy round and smooth smudges on the brass plate. I was pretty relieved when I looked at the stalls and couldn't see any feet. I still got out of there quick; never did know what to expect from women, since they always fooled me just when I thought I had 'em pegged.

Back in the lobby, I saw there were two staircases leading to the next level (and presumably the entrance to the auditorium) on either side. At the end of both rails were naked cherubs with dicks the size of midget maggots blowing long horns and plucking harps. Really offensive. I walked up the staircase nearest the ladies' room, casually looking for doors or halls leading to the area behind the snack bar wall which might be revealed to me by benefit of my higher vantage point. There weren't any, but now the lobby seemed to be smothered by the presence, as if it was a round black monster sitting in plain sight and staring up at me. I hesitated a moment, as if I could actually see that black monster squatting below a light, near a column, as if I could barely keep my mug turned to the gaze of its hollow red eyes. During that moment I didn't fear the monster as much as I feared myself, every aspect of my job, my personality, my existence. I had always liked myself, for some reason I could never figure out (probably because I was me and was therefore prejudiced in my favor); but now I hated myself and everything that came along with me. I had never before felt such intense hatred of anything. I shrugged off the hate and continued up the stairs. I didn't have time for such thoughts, not when there was work to do.

Upstairs there were a few more battered couches (one had a spring protruding through the cushion), dead plants (one pot had been tipped over, and the dirt in the rug had never been sent to the antimatter universe), ashtrays (all filled with butts), and another flight leading to the rear auditorium entrances. Three sets of double swinging doors on a green wall twenty meters away led to the middle auditorium. The house sat approximately ten gross. The darkened aisles were filled with trash; as most of the trash consisted of white paper bags and yellow Styrofoam boxes for double cheeseburgers, I figured it belonged to the actors in residence. I walked down the sharp angle of the center aisle; each step caused my gut to jiggle; I could imagine my intestines bouncing up and down. Many of the seats were broken, either the backs or bottoms resting at uncanny angles. The metal frames were rusty; the upholstery was a mess. A gaudy red curtain with the cherubs stitched in concealed the stage from me. The cherubs were also painted on the ceiling. A huge chandelier hung from the center of the ceiling; it would have been perfect to swing from, if there had been anything near it so you could grab it and land somewhere other than at the beginning of a sixty-meter fall.

A flexible apron, the lift raised to a height equal with the stage, was before the curtain. I figured the stage manager was probably in the scenery shop, which I guessed was below. If not there, he would be in the offices, which were most likely on a floor above the auditorium. I walked up the stairs on the left outermost thrust of the proscenium. I ducked through the curtain and arrived at downstage right. The downstage area was pretty much bare, though the boards didn't look too good. The backstage area was pretty much of a mess, with a surfeit of brushes, a twenty-meter snap line, a spray gun, a flogger, cans of shellac and flat varnish and turpentine, a stepped-level platform on casters, a moving paint frame, costumes, props, various grains and lengths of wood, burlap rocks, stock doors and windows, a white fireplace, backdrops, hardware, pipes, sheet metal, and all kinds of other stuff, most of which should have been neatly stacked in storage. Or in the scenery shop. However, at the moment, I was pondering a far more significant observation.

On the motor-driven spot-line system, normally used to place and hold backdrops in their proper positions, were hundreds of glowing golden cocoons, each the size of my substantial fist. There were no electrical lights backstage; that would have been redundant. The cocoons burned a cold, bright light that repelled my nervous system; I wanted to shield my unprotected mug despite the fact that it was impossible for the light to pain me, except maybe to freeze me to death. Most of the cocoons were stacked like abstract pyramids on the trimming and loading galleries, but many also hung below the galleries and on the apparatus. As I stared at the cocoons, I couldn't imagine a sound anywhere in the world. Everything had stopped, including my absorption of oxygen, as I tried to accept the glowing cocoons, as I tried to shrug off the numbing effect they had on me.

I don't know how long I would have stood there trying to accept them as the most natural thing in the universe. They hadn't seemed like living objects. They seemed to have been a staple feature of *The Eibon* since the dawn of godlike man. But the cracking noise that suddenly resounded throughout the theater, that startled me as surely as if the ripper had stuck his antimatter knife in my back, proved that the illusion wasn't close to the truth. The noise was followed by the lesser sounds of the creature in the cocoon making tinier cracks, and then by the louder sound of another creature making the first crack in its cocoon. In less than a minute the cracking resembled the fire of a hundred gatling guns simultaneously spitting bullets. I felt like the target, and as cocoon chips (still radiating eerie cold light) fell about me, it wasn't too hard to imagine the bullets tearing the boards at my feet. There was something vaguely musical about the canopy of sounds, as if I was the theme in the symphony of my death. I was nearing the bottom of my bowl of popcorn as the first creature, hanging from the loading gallery, protruded its head through the cocoon.

It was a moth. When it freed itself from its embryonic prison, when it was uncurled and could flex its wings, it would be three times larger than its cocoon. Its entire prothorax burst through the cocoon as if someone had created it instantaneously. Its color was a glowing combination of gold and gray, created by its scales and hair. The moth should have appeared alive; instead it resembled a primitive automation burning with a force beyond my comprehension. There seemed to be nothing alive about it. Though its black compound eyes were on either side of its head, I knew it was staring at me, its blank slate of a mind appraising me, because its red proboscis rolled and unrolled. The menacing air about the gesture wasn't deliberate; I was reading things into it, but I knew when the Old Man read my report, he wouldn't blame me a bit. The antennae quivered, bent toward my direction.

The moth crawled from the cocoon and awkwardly walked on it and the gallery until it could hang upside down. My first estimate of its size had been a little conservative; it was one of those fat moths with round thoraxes; the metathorax was especially round, looking like a witch's idea of a pot pie. The moth contracted its abdomen, pumping blood into the small wing pads; and the pads expanded into full-fledged wings. It would have been beautiful if I had been watching it on a holodocumentary. The wings stiffened in less than a minute, and now the moth was prepared for flight.

By this time the entire spot-line system was covered with moths. They looked like the mutated offspring of a mating between an owl and a sloth. And I had the distinct sensation they were all, each and every one, looking at me.

The mandibles differed from those of similar insects. At first I could not believe my perceptions, and I was tempted to create a pair of eyes on my face to confirm my data. But my perceptions of the mandibles at least gave substance to my uneasiness, and at least I now knew why they looked at me. For the mandibles were sharp, pointed ivory fangs; the proboscis was a kind of tongue in the vaguely mammalian mouths of these moths. For they were vampire moths. The nourishment of their cocoons had been sufficient, but it wasn't the nourishment they craved.

The first moth to break free of its cocoon fluttered its wings. The sound was metallic, as if someone beneath the stage was rattling a pencil over a washboard. I knew I was in for it. At the same time, I was glad. I needed a little action, an opportunity to show my stuff, not only for the benefit of the invisible presence watching me, but for my own benefit. I absorbed the last kernel of popcorn, casually threw the bowl onto the pile of paraphernalia backstage, wiped my hands on the paper towels, and then threw the towels at my feet, amid glowing cocoon chips. I was ready.

A moth—I couldn't tell which one, not that it made any difference—flew erratically toward me. They would all be unused to flight for a brief time, and that was in my favor, while it lasted. The cocoon chips on the floor and those still hanging from the spot-line system washed out all the shadows, save for those in the corners. I felt like the light was piercing me. The moth's wings created a low-pitched rattling, as if the air itself had turned into iron filings. The sound made me imagine the moth was flying toward me faster than it actually was. Suddenly I panicked; I wasn't so sure of myself anymore. I didn't (and don't) know if it was me or the invisible presence responsible for the change, but it didn't matter. I tried to send the vampire moth to the antimatter universe, to get this thing over with as quickly as possible. I almost shit in my pants when the moth's mental vibrations, supplementing its compound eyes (which weren't so hot when it came to resolving clear images), deflected my mental waves of energy. A lower frequency sent the moth hurtling backward into the paraphernalia, where it chipped a wing, but I would still have to deal with it. That is, after I dealt with three other moths who, ravaged by their cravings, felt enough confidence in their power of flight to speed toward me. I hated to do it, but I dropped my mental shields; the stage manager would now know exactly where I was, if he didn't already. However, I had no choice. I had no energy to spare.

I tried burning the three moths. This frequency they absorbed; I knew at once I had made them stronger; they nourished on more than blood. One moth collided into me before I could move away or formulate another defense. (The trouble with being able to do practically anything is selecting from the wide range of possibilities; it always slows you down a bit, and I'm better at selection than most.) I hit the boards hard. My back and head hit particularly hard, though my butt wasn't exactly overjoyed about the experience. It was a good thing I didn't breathe through a nose; otherwise the wind would have been knocked out of me and I would have been cold meat. As it was, with a cocoon chip tearing through my jacket and cutting my arm, and one moth holding down my legs and preparing to stick its ivory fangs into my neck, I wasn't exactly in the pink. I thrust my left arm upwards and, increasing my strength, broke off one fang; I was strong enough to keep the moth from lunging forward and succeeding in biting me. The moth's proboscis, however, was razor sharp; it wrapped itself about my arm, as if it operated independently of the moth, slicing through my jacket and shirt. It was like receiving fifty paper cuts all over. I almost fainted. The tip of the proboscis was as sharp and as thick as one of the good doctor's needles; it pierced my arm. I felt the blood ebbing from my body. I could manufacture blood to maintain a consistent level, which I did, but I knew I wouldn't be able to keep it up indefinitely. In seconds the vampire moths were swarming about me. I avoided being bitten in my right arm by waving it about frantically. Only the mass of the moth on top of me protected my chest. Nothing, however, protected the rest of me from the moths, particularly from the quick insertion of the proboscae, and it wasn't long before at least twenty moths had cut through my clothing and were sucking out my precious bodily fluids. Occasionally a proboscis was torn from me as if the good doctor was tearing an arrow or knife from me without much regard for my subsequent treatment or survival; I deduced that the moths about me were fighting one another for a chance at the magnificent treat (me) and that sometimes a moth succeeded in replacing a weaker fellow. The pain of a proboscis ripping from me was much greater, much sharper, than its insertion. Each time it happened I wanted to give up. But each time I resolved to hang it up, I realized I couldn't, however much I wanted to. The mere though was an anathema. Though I didn't particularly care about my demise (I wouldn't be around to mourn about it), I still had a job to do. The minstrel, jerk that he was, depended on me. The Old Man depended on me; he couldn't do this kind of work anymore. And for totally different reasons, the eighth-dimensional woman depended on me. But I couldn't think about them; I had to concentrate on my survival. I was thinking about so many things, none of them related to the job at hand. I experienced self-reproach, for some reason, not quite loathing myself for the things I had done and the things I hadn't done, but wallowing in a sense of regret over nothing in particular. It didn't seem logical to me. I didn't understand how I could have ever been different from the way I was. I couldn't understand why I was deliberately clouding my mind, until it occurred to me that the invisible presence had the power to cloud men's minds. It wasn't me at all. And that thought, that sudden remembrance of a fact the presence had caused me to overlook, gave me the strength, the will to continue. I thought about moths. Somehow, while I still possessed the energy, I had to send them to the antimatter universe.

Since I wasn't able to do it directly, more devious methods were called for. I possessed those in abundance.

I tried to forget my fear and my pain. I tried to think clearly. I maintained my blood level. I had thought that some of the moths would be satiated, that some would leave me, opening the way for others but providing me with a little relief, but none of the moths showed any intention of leaving. As soon as I created blood, they sucked it out. Death, if it did come, would be more than a relief.

But I would not die. I began sending the cocoon chips to the antimatter universe. I could only send a few at a time. I got rid of the ones on the floor first, and even that was quite a strain. But I couldn't consider resting, though the hardest part of the job was yet to come. I just didn't have the time. When I finished getting rid of the ones on the spot-line system, I scanned the paraphernalia, in case a chip had fallen into concealment. All I found was the chip from a moth's wing, and I sent that into the antimatter universe too. Now the only light in the auditorium was caused by the glow of the vampire moths, and that glow illuminated nothing, as if the moths were the only bright creatures in the universe, and all else was forever darkness. Now the moths could see only in the ultraviolet range.

And I created a huge ball in the air at the center of the auditorium. The ball, approximately ten meters in diameter, attracted the moths. They perceived its ultraviolet radiation, as did I. The moths who were unable to partake of my precious bodily fluids flew to the ball immediately. The first moth to reach it fluttered about it with an aura of caution, but after a moment the moth alighted on it; the siren call of the ultraviolet light had ensnared the creature. The ball, which was really a gateway with a few sophisticated suction devices, pulled the moth into the antimatter universe. The moth's disappearance didn't stop its fellows from yielding to the call, and in five minutes the only moths remaining were the twenty or so trying to suck my bones through my skin.

I had hoped that the moths would forget their hunger and would fly directly toward the ball with the rest. Summoning all the strength I could without drawing from the energy necessary to maintain my blood level and the existence of the ball, I grabbed the moth on top of me with both my hands and crushed its head. The chitin cracked at once; glowing yellow blood and green brains oozed between my fingers and down my arms. I felt tremendous satisfaction. (I would have tried to kill them all physically, right at the start; but there had been too many; they would have beaten me down. Things were different now, though I was becoming weaker by the second.) I pushed the dead moth aside and savored the sensation of the blood and brains sticking to my hands. I liked that too. I tore the moth's proboscis from my arm (it had been a tenacious proboscis) and punched a moth as if it was an opponent in a boxing match. I liked that more. In a matter of minutes I had shaken the moths from me and had pulled their proboscae out of me. Those I hadn't killed warily inspected me as I rolled over and climbed to my knees. Each of them seriously considered renewing the attack, especially since their acute sense of smell was still being overwhelmed by the blood soaking my clothes and running from my wounds. (I hadn't thought to repair myself yet.) But one by one they perceived the ultraviolet radiations, and one by one they disappeared into the antimatter universe, taking approximately twelve hundred liters of my blood with them. The disappearance of the last moth was almost anticlimactic, though my relief, when it came, left me washed out. I closed the gateway and my wounds and lay in the dark for twenty minutes. I felt the earth turning. I liked that sensation too.

I think I slept for a bit, though I hadn't intended to. The twenty minutes didn't seem like that long a time and I can't recall feeling the earth turning during my entire rest. At any rate, when I stood up and cleaned my suit, I was refreshed and the fears that had crippled me while I fought the vampire moths had been put totally out of my mind, as if everything had been only a vivid nightmare, to be forgotten as soon as I went about my daily business.

A staircase in a corner backstage led to the scenery shop below the boards. When I turned my hearing up to maximum intensity at the top of the stairs, I could barely detect the humming of machinery. My instincts, generally a tad overcautious (especially since they don't hold me back that much), told me the humming probably didn't indicate a trap; instead it indicated life as usual. That made sense. The vampire moths would have sucked practically anybody else dry. The stage manager probably figured I had bit the big one. I floated above the stairs to the door; I still didn't want to take more than my fair share of chances. At the door the humming wasn't too much louder, but I could hear the patter of someone wearing half-moon taps walking about. There didn't seem much point in allowing the someone to continue his overconfident delusions any longer, so I just opened the door and walked in.

"Hi there," I said, waving.

The stage manager, who already looked like his skin had absorbed all the whitewash from all the fences in the city, paled considerably more: the slightly pink hue on his large cheekbones disappeared. A single bead of sweat rolled down his hawkish nose. He was a big man, with more muscle than fat except where his gut rolled over his belt. He had quite red, thin lips; and his canine teeth were pronounced. His eyeballs were black and his irises were white. His flowing black cape, which appeared to have a perverse relationship with his arms, obscured his clothing, save for his ruffled shirt and his hushpuppy loafers. When I had opened the door, he had stopped cold, providing me with an excellent, if narcissistic, view of his charismatic profile; I especially liked how his black hair curled just over his ears. Now, wrapping his cape an extra layer about both his arms, making the gesture appropriately dramatic and menacing, he slowly turned face forward, bending his head back slightly so he had to lower his eyes to look at me directly. He inhaled magnificently, implying that he was preparing to burst into calculated rage at my impertinence for merely existing in his space-time continuum. Then he was startled. He exhaled; his eyes widened in surprise; he almost smiled before he remembered he was supposed to be upset. "You!" he said in a deep, robust voice which made the syllable eloquent when it was really uninspired. "I didn't know this was your world!"

"Good morning, Bernie."

"Don't call me that. You know it isn't my real name."

"Neither is 'the stage manager.'"

He nodded gravely, turning from me, his taps on his loafers creating a few sparks. "True, how true. The truth can never hide from one such as you."

"That's what I'd like the Old Man to believe. Why don't you change to your real form, Bernie, and then you can explain to me the meaning of all this." I waved at "this." "This" represented quite an accomplishment. Except for some tools around the metal-working area, some comfortable easy chairs and other homey fixtures in a corner, "this" consisted of a huge mass of apparatus. I had no idea of the exact functions of the computer, the glass tubes with bubbling colorful liquids, the batteries, the pistons, the wires, and the pipes, because scientific details never impressed me as having much to do with the more important results. One entire wall was a bank of machinery, and at the other wall were the pipes and tubes of mingling chemicals. A few power generators were scattered throughout the room, creating a fancy little maze. At the wall before me, beyond the two steel columns holding up the pneumatic stage lift, the minstrel and seven others just like him (of all sizes and sexes—with a few it was difficult to tell) were hooked up in giant glass tubes; they appeared to be in a state of suspended animation, which would explain all the apparatus. Without it, Bernie would have had to keep some small portion of his mind concentrated on maintaining their life forces, and I knew from experience that his attention span wasn't that notable. From clear plastic tubes inserted in the actors' and actresses' left wrists flowed a slow, steady stream of blood, which mingled and dripped into a single glass container on a folding kitchen table equipped with napkins, pepper, salt, cheese, and an open loaf of rye bread.

"Yes, I suppose I should change back," Bernie said. From somewhere deep in his cape (I didn't want to know exactly where), he produced a mirror. He studied his face. "This form no longer suits me." He disappeared in a bright yellow flash and reappeared on the kitchen table. That was the Bernie I remembered. Of course he had been speaking the truth when he said Bernie wasn't his real name; it's just that he had always seemed like a Bernie to me. On other worlds, in other dimensions, he was known as the Armadillo of Destruction. He looked just like your average armadillo, except that the bony plates of his armor were yellow on his body and pink on his tail and the hair on his tummy was green. The shield at his head was pink; his face was black and his eyes were green. Yep, he was your regular old armadillo all right, but his green eyes burned with an energy that was about to go nova at any moment. And when he turned on the old magic and pulled up the corners of the mouth on that long snoozer of his, you prayed to the oversoul that the mean little mother would be on your side. Naturally, when I met him, on a case that had taken me to a parallel universe, we had exchanged a few harsh words and some significant energy blasts to back them up.

"Okay, Bernie, let's take it from the top," I said, sitting at the kitchen table, crossing my legs, and creating a cigar.

The armadillo created a cigar of his own, rolling it about in his long pink tongue. He lit both cigars simultaneously. He waddled about, thumping his tail, until he was comfortable. "I guess it started when a friend of mine died. I had never had a friend before, at least not one who could be called a companion, and he died, thinking it better to have experienced a moment of love than to live for eternity without love. He was a romantic jerk, but he started me thinking. Since then I've gone through some pretty heavy changes. You know how it is."

"Probably not."

The armadillo's mouth curved upward, but into a smile; there was nothing malevolent about it, at least to me. But then I was an experienced observer. "Hey, bro', don't hand me that bull. When I met you, you had a face that drove the women wild. And when you smiled . . . they knew what was on your mind."

"Which was where it stayed." I paused. "Yeah, that case started me thinking too. Sometimes you can't help but think, no matter how much you try to stop it. And now my mug has been smooth for so many eons that no one remembers I ever had a face. And the women I smiled at . . ."

"They were all mortals. They've been dead for so long that even the histories of their worlds has faded from the memories of the scholars."

"And now nothing of them remains. Their smiles, their

laughter, all the love they bestowed—it's all gone. And for what? What's the purpose of love if its ultimate fate is either the negation of death . . . or abnegation?"

"Don't ask me. I used to work from the other side of the fence. It's one of those confounded eternal dilemmas. Perhaps it will be resolved someday, if only in the heart of a single individual, but until then we must accept it. You seem to have adjusted to the situation pretty well."

"Oh? In what way?"

"The casual ease in which you channel the cigar smoke to your smooth mug, where you absorb it like a sponge. And the nonchalance with which you force the smoke from your facial pores when you tire, momentarily, of the sensation. You live without a face as if you had never possessed one."

"Practice, Bernie, practice."

"Acceptance, my friend, acceptance." The armadillo looked away from me, toward the minstrel and his comrades in the glass tubes. He rolled his cigar about on his protruding tongue, then retracted the tongue and cigar into his mouth. The smoldering nova in his eyes was just barely smoldering. "After my friend died, extinguishing his life force in an explosion of the hatred of all the frustrating common denominators of existence, a hatred he had to rid himself of before he could truly love, I accepted my lonely fate. You know how it was with me in the old days. I spread death and destruction through a familiar with whom I had a symbiotic relationship. The blind existentialism of our victims' demises and tragedies appealed to me. But after a few thousand eons my fate wasn't so easy to accept. I continued raising all the havoc I could in my universe, but my heart just wasn't in it. I tried to think back, to remember how I had initially embarked on my destructive path. Well, my remembrances were in vain. When I quit thinking back, I had no more inkling of my origins than I did before I started. I don't know how I became a god, why I embraced my philosophy, why it was necessary for me to live at the expense of others. However, it eventually dawned on me that destruction *per se* didn't really nourish me. For what is destruction but a primitive form of creativity? Admittedly, in my case it was a vicarious destruction, but that only meant my subsistence depended upon vicarious creativity. The time had arrived for me to take a step, not necessarily a spiritual step upwards or backwards or sideways or in any other

direction implying a self-righteous value judgment, but merely a
step. I had traveled the same path for too long, and the time had
arrived for the next segment of my journey. The subsequent
identity crisis and the breaking of all prejudices, preconceptions,
and habits was definitely a pain, but it was exhilarating too. I
had never thought so much. I had never questioned so much. I
had never dared to experience so much. And I knew that if I did
not succeed, I might die, and that knowledge, the notion that I
might experience the final ending of mortals, somehow
intensified the sensations of my spiritual odyssey in a way I'll
probably never understand. I only understood that I would
never, never regret my decision, and that I would likewise never
regret my death if it came. I tried many things in many bodies in
many times in my own universe, and my search for a vicarious
creativity eventually led me to many universes. The history of
my journey, even if I just touched the high points and a few
marvelous sexual exploits, would put a tremendous strain on
your bladder; suffice it to say that several months ago I felt a
calling. Some far-out cosmic force broadcast itself across the
vibratory patterns to tell me my place was here. That force was
the soul of godlike man. The various crises of your race paled my
own, and I couldn't help but pity your kind, whereas before I
would have delighted in my hatred and destruction of you (for
your race is ripe for plunder; its cancer must be cut out before it
blights all the existences in all the vibratory patterns).
Simultaneously, the warmth of your race's potential fired my
spirit in ways unique to my experience. I cannot specify the exact
nature of the potential; I don't know where your collective path
will lead you, if you're allowed to explore it without interference
from the darker side of your nature which has resulted in such
ludicrous creations as the East End. But I wanted to be a part,
however small, of that advancement. Rather than destroying the
cancer of your souls, I wanted to take part in its soothing and
healing. For once, I wanted to belong to something my keen
intellect couldn't comprehend, and believe me, it takes
something pretty confusing to baffle my keen intellect."

"Yes, I know how you feel."

"I figured you would say that. You're not as confusing as you
like to think you are. During our little encounter, you treated the
women like ice, but I got the feeling you would have preferred to
succumb to . . . whatever was on your mind. You just had a slight

case of arrested development."

"More like it was thrown into solitary confinement."

"That's what you would like to believe." The armadillo dangled the cigar from his mouth and winked at me. "Anyway, it didn't take me too long to discover *The Eibon*; something about the name, I don't know what, appealed to the repressed malevolent nature inside me. And the location, here in the heart of your race's plaintive cry, was the very place to be, the site of the struggle, the calm center of the maelstrom. Soon I became the stage manager. In those early days, the joint was packed with rubes every night. Strictly S.R.O. I didn't care much for the show; frankly, I thought it sucked. However, the rewards of my lowly work—seeing that the props were always in place, the lights set at the proper level, the instruments properly out of tune for the calculated plebian touch—were considerable, especially when I heard the thundering applause, the love and appreciation being showered with regularity upon those no-talents over there. Your race may have potential, but its entertainment could use a dose of class."

"I've always thought so."

"Humph. An intellectual. How quaint. The next part of my story is the most confusing, even for me. Because I don't know exactly what happened to my mind. I don't know if it was my former self manifesting itself at an inopportune moment, or an outsider subverting me for his own obscure purposes."

"Let me be the judge of that."

"Sure. It's okay with me." I had never known that an armadillo could shrug so naturally, but this one did, continuing, "I hadn't really been jealous of the no-talents, certainly not beyond the norm of technical people who feel their work isn't appreciated enough by both the public and the actors. Sure, occasionally I felt jealous, and I took my part in the trivial backstage politics of *The Eibon*. It kept life interesting, especially since the show was always the same old boring bullshit. When I think of the number of times I've sat through "We'll Meet Again," arranged by the Big Red Cheese for black-faced tap-dancers singing in dialect, I practically get the runs. However, eventually my jealousy became overpowering. As the show lost its hold on the denizens of the East End (which wasn't exactly surprising; the only time it was different was when someone went onstage with his fly unzipped), the politics intensified, draining my energy, taking my mind off my work. The calm center of the maelstrom had become the very source of the plaintive cry, and no one received temporary succor from entertainment. Hell, it wasn't worth the effort. The actors blamed the management, and I, secretly the most powerful and ruthless of all, blamed the actors for robbing me of the sense of purpose I had lost. The feeling wasn't entirely natural; there was something wrong with it I couldn't quite put my finger on; but I didn't care. I felt that somehow I had triumphed over my altruistic impulses; unlike other knee-jerk liberals who discovered their souls weren't all that lily-white, I discovered I enjoyed the darkness, the hatred, the loathing of my spirit as I contemplated the banality of those worthless piss-ants. I experienced a freedom greater than any I had ever known, as if I had broken the remaining shackles of my spirit. For this time there was nothing vicarious about my hatred; I required no familiar for my emotions to assume a direction. My hatred was universal, all-encompassing, but most important, it was mine, no one's but mine. I felt like I could do anything without fear of paying the consequences. And I would do anything. But first I would treat the actors in the same manner they had treated me. The management had split for parts unknown (businessmen have no loyalty to the arts if they can't garner a little fame and glory from them), so that left me, the rest of the crew, and the actors. The crew split for the most decrepit sections of this district; they never did have any self-respect, otherwise they wouldn't have worked for this dime-a-dance joint in the first place. That left me and the actors, who had no place to go. And when I wandered the aisles and hallways late at night, cloaked in the darkness only the despicable can summon, I laughed at the frightened actors even as I hated them. I had assumed the qualities of an elemental force, and they feared me as they feared the depression sucking the life from their souls. I haunted the theater, even as some peculiar force haunted me. But I didn't think about that. After the obligatory melodramatic preliminaries, I succumbed to the vampirous urges that nigh overwhelmed me. As the actors had preyed upon my services, I would prey upon that substance which perpetuated their lives and humanity; I would prey upon the very essence of the human body. You guessed it. Approximately every four weeks, I drank minstrel blood."

I thought I was going to die.

"Soon I succumbed frequently. Now I require wrapping my lips around a tall cool glass of minstrel blood spiced with two drops of lemon extract three times a day. As it became too wearying to chase these fools up and down *The Eibon* at feeding time, I rigged up this apparatus from old props in storage and kidnapped them one by one. Little did I suspect the star of the show would call in the fuzz."

"It's a good thing he did," I said, doing whatever it is I do to the rich aromatic cigar that corresponds to inhaling (I didn't want to think I was sucking something in, not during this conversation). "Otherwise you would have degenerated into the being you once were, and then where would you be?"

"Well, fecally speaking..."

"Don't say it."

This time the armadillo's shrug was faintly contemptuous, not that it mattered to me.

"What are you going to do now?" I asked.

"I don't know. While I was talking to you, a great burden was eased from my mind. My thoughts are much lighter now. And the thought of chugging a glass of minstrel blood, frankly, makes me nauseous. I guess I can't stay in this world. My feelings toward it have gone slightly sour."

"Don't worry about where you're going. I've seen a lot of vicarious artists in my day; they're all over the place, infecting the oversoul with their insincerity and vicarious creativity. You'll find another home and another direction sooner or later."

"You mean you're not going to try and stop me? What kind of fuzz are you?"

"I've got a dose of class. What happened here wasn't your fault. I'll see that whoever is responsible will suffer for it."

"Okay. See you around."

And the Armadillo of Destruction blinked out of sight, just like that. Something inside me, of my own derivation, made me wish I could call him a nice guy.

I put my cigar out in the bread, stood up, and stretched. My buttocks felt like they had turned yellow; the armadillo's taste in decor could have used a little class too. I rubbed my smooth chin as I turned my mug toward the actors in the tubes. I didn't know exactly how to free them scientifically, and I didn't feel like spending twenty or thirty minutes on the job anyway, since there

were more important things to do. So I caused all the apparatus
to disappear. The actors awoke in mid-air, too stunned by their
sudden recovery to prevent the law of gravity from determining
their fate. I created some pillows, and they all landed
comfortably, except for one poor bozo to the far left who
struggled so much that he managed to twist and turn until he
avoided the pillows altogether.

"Mastuh universah op! Mastuh universah op!" exclaimed
the minstrel I had met in the lobby, who must have been the star
of the show. He ran toward me like a crippled Ping-Pong ball.
"You saved us, suh, you saved us! How cans we ever repay you?"

A tall minstrel with a deep voice said, "Do you mean to tell
me we was saved by the universah up?"

"That's op," said a skinny actress with kinky hair that could
have put out your eyes when you snuggled close to her if you
weren't careful. She sauntered to me, her long legs enabling her
to pass the star minstrel without effort; and she reached me first,
placing her charcoal-black hand on my shoulder and bending
her body like a deformed spoon around my belly. She blinked
her eyes at me. I was surprised that her huge false eyelashes
didn't cause her to topple over. "I knows how we can repay him,
and I would be only too, too happy to do de honors."

I put my hand somewhere above her melons and pushed her
back. "The only way you dear folks can repay me," I said to them
all, taking care that she wouldn't think she was an exception, "is
to vacate the premises for a little while. I've got work to do.
When I'm done, the show can resume."

The skinny actress snorted, managing to maintain her
artificial accent, and sauntered off. The star minstrel said,
"Yassah, mastuh universah op. We shalls do dat right 'way, isn't
dat right, you all?"

The folks chorused their approval, and in a few minutes I was
alone in the theater. I greeted my loneliness with an immense
relief. Though I wasn't alone in reality, I could pretend for a bit,
and I did, sitting at the kitchen table as if I had experienced
nothing but leisure throughout my days. When I grew tired of
idly drumming my fingers on the table, I left the scenery shop,
mentally turning off the lights.

The auditorium was pitch-black. When I lit another cigar,
the glowing ember was solitary, alone, as if it was the initial light
in the universe; and if I had had eyes, I wouldn't have been able

to tell if it was near me or was in reality much larger, far away from me. By carefully listening to the ruptures in my sonic vibrations, I navigated through the blackness easily, avoiding the paraphernalia backstage, missing the edge of the apron by three meters, and walking unerringly down the steps and into the second row of chairs. I propped my feet on the back of a chair and savored the sensation of smoke in my throat and lungs. "Okay, bub, you can manifest yourself now. It's just you and me."

A voice that wasn't part of *The Eibon*, but which seemed to emit from every column, wall, chair, and prop, a voice that was devoid of every human or suprahuman attribute, a voice whose tone didn't register the indignation I would have ascribed to its words if I hadn't been such an objective detective, said, "I am not a bub."

"All right. Toots."

"Nor am I a toots."

"Both, either one at a time or simultaneously?"

"I am devoid of sex."

If anything, the voice was part of the blackness itself. It came from in front of me, behind me, above me, below me. It hinted at tremendous power barely held in control, but that didn't cut any ice with me.

"Then who—or what—are you?" I asked.

"I call myself the invisible individual."

Wonderful, I thought. "And you are also the presence which warped the mind of the Armadillo of Destruction (which sounds like an instance of overkill to me), which presumably inspired him to create the vampire moths, and which has been attempting to subtly influence my thoughts and deeds throughout this little caper?"

"I am the one."

"Why don't you tell me about it?"

"Why should I?"

"Because entities such as yourself, being basically cowardly little creatures, are too chickenshit to stand their ground when they can't hide anymore. Your abilities may be equal to mine, but I know how to use them and you clearly don't, otherwise I would have been long gone by this time. You have the word 'amateur' stamped all over your dainty invisible self. You might as well have used a neon sign to announce your comings and goings. Now talk. I'm listening."

The voice was silent for nearly a minute. Then it said, "All right, I'll talk, but understand that I'm talking not because I'm afraid of you, but because I can't bear the inherent social obligations of sharing the same territory, however briefly, with another. The sooner I tell my story, the sooner you will depart."

"Get on with it."

"My story begins long ago, so long ago."

"Just hit the high spots, will you?"

"Be patient, please. When mere man became godlike man, I do not know what identity I first selected. All I recall is the hideous social pressure the survivors of our race put upon their fellows to impress some order into a world which had embraced chaos with only the vague meanderings of a few puny philosophers and confused existentialists as forewarnings. I recall that every time I expressed a thought, I was upset because I did not know if the thought was mine and mine alone, or if I was merely mouthing the thoughts people expected of me, whether or not they agreed with my observations. When I acted, I did not know if my actions were my own, or if they were merely the extensions of the wishes of society as a whole. At first I was concerned only with environmental pressures, but soon my concern extended itself to hereditary pressures as well. I began to realize how much time and energy I had spent eating, or merely deciding what to eat, or deciding what to do, or deciding who to do it with. I realized how much time and effort I spent fulfilling all the tasks that you might say are the axioms of the human body. Not even the convenience of godlike manhood was an adequate defense of my bodily duties. Sleeping, laughing, talking, crying, shitting, fucking—I had an overpowering urge to do all these things, as does all godlike mankind. Yet I believed I was the only person aware of how most people were swept into the tide of life, to be plummeted about without the slightest realization of what was happening to them. How often I saw men looking about for a woman to love, and *vice versa* (and homosexuals looking for homosexuals), without pausing for an instant to wonder why he should search for love in the first place. The mere act of loving does not alter you; any problem or shortcoming that you have while you are not loving will still be with you while you love. What is it about the human that insists he has not lived unless he has loved? Some people are not equipped for life, regardless of how much they love, regardless of how successfully, for they have not the slightest conceptions of the dilemmas of life, of how to spend what hours they have, of the nature of the spark that sends them searching until they have traveled so far from the mysteries of their soul, the mysteries which had resided in the heart forever, that they could not look inside themselves for the answers they desire, even if they did, finally, perceive that simple truth. And yet... when I looked inside myself, I perceived nothing unique, nothing that could not be explained away as the manifestation of environmental or hereditary forces. I had always tried to believe I was my own person; I had always clung tenaciously to the belief despite the overwhelming evidence against it. Yet when I thought, it was not of my own free will, but because images and phrases burst from my subconscious and forced me to think. When I spoke, it was either to myself, to soothe my loneliness, or to others who would have been uncomfortable if no one spoke and we just sat around looking dumbfounded at each other. When I shitted, it was not because I said to myself, 'Ah, I surely would love to take a dump right now,' but because the pressures of my shit inside my intestines was demanding release so that it might fertilize the earth, feed the plants, provide flies with homes for larvae, and in general continue a cycle of life I did not wish to be a part of. And when I made love... that was the worst, most humiliating happenstance. I do not recall my actual sex, only vague animalistic urges overwhelming me. I wanted to experience an orgasm at all costs, and masturbation was insufficient (but if it was insufficient through some biological factor or due to beliefs of society I had blindly accepted as a youth, I do not know). And I did experience orgasms, orgasm after orgasm, at a frightful price, though now I recall only the price and not the sensation. And the price was terrifying in its simplicity. Making love is supposed to be the greatest act two people (or even more, if you are so inclined) can perform. Its reputation, perpetuated by society, is that its spiritual rewards are fully equal to its physical rewards. It is not even the act itself which is of supreme importance, but the act of being close, touching, comforting, which, when combined with the pleasure derived from exploring all those sensitive and extraordinarily interesting portions and crevices of the body, makes it one of life's prime ingredients. Or so they say. But one day I discovered that it was not me *per se*

that demanded I take part in that activity which has sparked so
much controversy and discussion throughout the eons, but my
animalistic urges, pure and simple. Nothing else was involved;
my spiritual urges were but a series of delusions like gossamer
curtains which, once I pushed them aside and viewed the
unadorned truth, could never be reconstructed. And I therefore
became aware of the truth in others; I know what my partners
were really thinking, what they really wanted, unbeknownst to
themselves. Once that high ideal of existence became shattered, I
perceived making love as no better or no worst than taking an
extremely gorgeous dump. Why not? Why should I have
allowed the banal poop of the greatest poets of history singing of
'the greatest joy in life' to distract me from believing the truth?
There was no reason why I should live succoring the inane
delusions of others. Yet, it cannot be denied, my new perception
robbed me of much, if not all, joy. I still pursued orgasms; oh,
how I pursued, vaguely searching for someone who would help
me delude myself. But let's face it, being great in the sack isn't
exactly a difficult accomplishment. I could have derived
comfort from the lecherous memory that I had made love to
many, many delectable creatures, but a talking dog could make
the identical boast. Is that why I was alive, so I could accomplish
the same thing as a dog? I can think, I have a mind, and
presumably I have a soul, I am part of the great oversoul that
encompasses all the universes in all the vibratory patterns. Was I
placed into the universe so I could merely eat, shit, fuck, nurture
an eternal child, and, eventually, in a dim future I can barely
comprehend, die? Something deep inside me, but only the
manifestation of chemicals running amuck, forced me to screw
around, as other forces preyed upon me, preventing me from
realizing my full potential. For I felt I was a being with potential.
With more than mere potential. I was destined for a greatness
that would change forever godlike mankind's perception of
existence ... if only I was allowed to grow and mature and
change myself without the hinderment of biological urges and
social duties. I had to change my perception of myself, strip
myself of all self-expectations; I could not discover my true
potential if I was bound by prejudices so deeply ingrained in my
thinking that I was unaware of them. The task was most easily
accomplished, though as you may have guessed, I do not
remember the details because as I successfully stripped myself of

the particulars of my identity, I deliberately forgot them, erased the convolutions from my brain, so not even their memory would subtly influence me. The next steps were the most difficult, but not nearly as difficult as I had expected. I had not realized that despite their undeniable power, the biological drives were intertwined with the environmental pressures. Thus, as I divested myself of the social need to fuck, I simultaneously divested myself of much of the instinct to fuck; for instinct is negligible without knowledge; and recalling my purpose, which by now had become almost an instinct itself, I completely eradicated the vague yearnings in my breast. Yet the pressure derived from average everyday social intercourse increased as I failed to live up to my acquaintances' expectations. Former sexual partners were distraught because I failed to hop into the sack with them. I no longer attended parties, told jokes, altered the landscape in amusing ways, or argued academic philosophical points. However, this pressure too passed, more quickly than I would have imagined, as my acquaintances gave up in disgust and left me to my own devices. Their seething hatred at what I had become was in itself torturous, but eventually they forgot me, as if I had never existed, and their hatred no longer disturbed me. All that remained for me to do was divest myself of my corporeal body, which I did a few eons ago. I still had no idea of the potential I would reach, of the goals I would attain; in that respect I am still as ignorant as the Armadillo of Destruction. But not long ago, as I wandered about the planet, I came upon this theater and decided that it would be the proper location for me to realize myself. I had long since learned the value of inaction, of how the one who does the least accomplishes the most, and this was my strategy for taking *The Eibon* for myself. I hung around until the show inevitably failed, and then I influenced the stage manager (learning his true identity only when you recognized him), until his mind was totally at my command. And then I ordered him to draw nourishment from others and to protect himself in a fashion thematically related to the manner society itself once drew nourishment from me, draining my energies and life-essences to prevent me from becoming a superior creature, the invisible individual on the threshold of greatness that you sense today."

I flicked my cigar onto the stage. As it spun in the air, I extinguished the ember. "You fill me with inertia," I said.

The invisible individual was genuinely shocked and indignant, the first true evidence of feelings, as he said, "What do you mean?"

"I mean, simply, that you think your story is unique. Maybe no one before you has gone to such ludicrous lengths to solve your problems, but I've seen people go through the same traumas a hundred thousand times. Well, I don't care about that anyway, not really. If I was the consulting detective or the fat man I would make a speech of some sort, just to even the score. But I'm not them, so I'll just tell you to get out."

"What?"

"Get out. Leave. Shake the dust from your metaphorical feet."

"On your say-so? Surely you are pulling my metaphorical leg. I cannot leave under any circumstances. Too much remains to be done."

"So?"

"You would have me leave my sanctuary just as I have nearly completed the preliminaries to realizing my full potential. I would not have thought you such a lowbrow. Have you not directed your enviable abilities to an investigation of the plight of godlike mankind? Have you not felt the pain of the helpless souls of the East End? I assure you, I have, for divesting myself of my personality and instincts has already granted me a vision keener than that of anyone I have previously encountered. Did you not listen to your friend the armadillo? Did you not hear him express his concerns over our race's destiny? Do you not realize that once I have concluded ridding myself of the illusions about what I am, I accomplish the same end regarding what I am not? It is not merely a remote possibility that I will be more in accord with the secret rhythms of life than anyone before me, and that I will have accomplished this by rejecting life. I have an opportunity to provide our race with the solutions to some of our most pressing dilemmas, but I can do nothing, I will have to begin anew, if you thrust me outside, away from the confines of this safe theater."

I perceived my muffled voice as I would have a stranger's as I said, "Listen, bub or toots or whatever you are, all that amounts to nothing more than a huge mound of donkey shit. I was given the job of exorcising *The Eibon* and that's what I intend to do. The only thing that matters to me is doing my job. The helpless souls of the East End will take care of themselves without the two of us running around like fag chickens giving them spiritual advice. I'm going to count to an unspecified number which I'm going to conceal from your mind probes. You won't know what it is, but when I reach it, you'd better be out of here and headed for parts unknown. Otherwise..." I started counting.

Actually, I hadn't specified a number. I had only made myself a private bet that the invisible individual would be gone by the time I reached ten. I was right. As usual.

Mercifully, I was able to fulfill my, ah, social obligations to the minstrels waiting outside the theater in record time. When I told them *The Eibon* was now safe for both matinees and evening performances, they were so overcome with happiness that they commenced the most awkward group soft-shoe I had ever seen. They didn't notice my exit, which was fine with me.

For some obscure reason I wanted to think. I didn't feel like writing out this report and giving it to the Old Man. I felt this report could wait. So it waited. I walked to the East End park and sat on a bench. I just sat there, not doing anything in particular and not thinking about anything in particular either. I felt pretty good, even if I was supposed to be thinking. Listening to the invisible individual whine with that self-pity characteristic of some kinds of people had left me drained and numbed inside. But energy and a strange sort of peace stirred as I perceived an old depressed couple walking hand in hand past me. Two eternal children played tag. A pubescent eternal child practiced playing the guitar, and though she needed more practice than anyone in his right mind could conceive, it sounded okay to me. The kid had potential, I realized, as I listened closely to that kind of music for the first time. The East End didn't seem like the East End I had come to know these past months. It was almost normal. I was surprised to notice that the sun shone with unsullied might, as the good doctor would say. I perceived with greater intensity and sensation the green grass, the white clouds, the blue sky. Yep, I felt pretty good, but I knew that one day the sun wouldn't shine my blues away.

I heard the wind howl.

I visited the eighth-dimensional woman. I don't know why; I hadn't even considered it all day. But there I was, and her smile lighted up her drab apartment. The lines on her face shouldn't have been beautiful when she smiled, but I couldn't convince myself they weren't. She said as she took my elbow to usher me inside, "So you decided to give me the afternoon with you despite all the work you had to do."

"Have I ever denied you anything?"

She frowned. "Yes."

"Don't hold it against me."

She didn't. She fixed us lunch. Hot dogs a third of a meter long. Before she ate her second hot dog, she removed it from the bun and put it in her mouth, not biting it, but drawing it in and out, staring right at me. I didn't have to be a Rosicrucian to figure out what was on her mind.

5. I am so alone, thought the wanderer. I have been alone forever. I recall the death of a loved one long ago, and I recall the grief which shattered the vestiges of my forlorn soul. I recall the love I felt for her. My love for her provided me with my sole succor from the hideous existential forces assailing my being; my love provided me with comfort and warmth; my love filled my thoughts and hours, and my life was worthwhile as long as I had the exquisite privilege of caressing her pale skin. My love was really quite intense.

And now . . . Look at me now. A pathetic excuse for a godlike man. If only I had not been born with such a romantic soul. If only I had not been born quite so sensitive. My sensitivity astounds me. I have never met another as tender and as susceptible as I. How can the poets dare call themselves sensitive when my very existence attests to the paucity of their sensitivity?

Ah, life. That's what the people say. But who are they? What do they know? I perceive instantly I do not have to answer that, not even to myself. I have no reason to demean my mind with such obvious observations.

If only I expressed myself as the poets do. Perhaps then I would not be so alone. But I have not the motivation. And why should I? Why should I secret myself in a lonely room with inadequate lighting, sort out my most private thoughts, and struggle to put them down in the proper order until I have practically collapsed from mental fatigue, a calamity of our time which has reached near-epidemic proportions? And for what? So an individual I do not know, I do not care to know, can receive some small delight and entertainment which, in effect, is derived from a vampirious communication? And I do not care for the poets' fame and adulation, for they have not yet seen the truth—that all society, including fame and adulation, is a delusion, a shallow game played by cretins afraid of the true reality beneath their monstrous surfaces. All they care about is what they have and who they know and who they have fucked. What they have is no different than what another can have. And they care to know the famous and exalted and unique only for the sense of importance it provides them. And they recall their delight at sucking the cock or finger-fucking the physically or intellectually gifted not through a sincere desire to give pleasure to their partner, but for a more ludicrous sense of importance, operating under the delusion that being a good fuck somehow gives them social status or justifies their worthless existences. How wonderful it must be to take joy in being no better than a cow. It is all a game they play, a game I do not care to play.

And so I stand here in the East End park.

Alone.

I have a lot of problems.

Most, if not all, of my problems are basically existential in nature, but a few are more concrete than that.

I can no longer abide the winter surrounding me. Though the sun is bright, and the crabgrass is basking in its life-giving rays, I stand clothed in black, my shoulders slumped, my arms folded across my chest and my hands pressing hard against my sides, drawing my black cloak more closely about me to protect my natural radiations of warmth from the cold that has never left me since the departure of the one I have grieved for lo these many eons. My coldness forms a sheath of approximately two centimeters; it automatically embraces everything I touch. My coldness is, in part, responsible for my loneliness. For how can I grasp the hand of an old acquaintance (assuming I could remember having met him in the first place) if my expression of purely masculine, strictly nonsexual affection creates instant frigidity permeating his being? And how can I engage in a close encounter of the hetero kind if my mere touch causes my partner's lubrication to turn to ice? Even if I desired social contact, the extent of my activities would be severely limited.

Perhaps I could live with this crippling attribute (for my loneliness has been so long a part of me that I fear I could accept no other condition) if it did not affect my perceptions with such unrelenting tenacity. I know the brightness of the sun provides even this shabby district with the clear luster of summer, when even the odious debris packed in out-of-the-way corners possesses an appealing starkness to those unafraid to explore life in all its aspects, but I perceive everything—including the beautiful blue sky which awes me with its sheer vastness—with the gray tinge of winter. To me, the sky is covered with dark gray clouds forever promising snow. But the snow never falls, lightening the cityscape with its pure whiteness. The sun is forever denied me, though years of practice piercing my veils inform me that it is doubtlessly there, providing godlike mankind with a warmth I can never feel. The tragedy of it stuns me; it always has stunned me; and now I feel my soul has been numbed forever. Should the winter suddenly disappear, and should I suddenly see the sun and feel the heat in the soil, I might not take joy in the experience. For joy has been denied me for so long that I fear I would not know how to accept it. My every instinct would deny it. I would no longer be crippled physically, but . . . that would be of no concern to me. I would flee from life, as I have fled since the death of the one who was the source of my soul. Often I have wondered, recklessly wandering through the pathways and highways and byways of my subconscious as I have aimlessly wandered this forlorn planet, searching for the cause of my winter. My portable winter, as I called it during a period when I attempted to deal with my problems through humor. I know (I can feel the certain knowledge resounding in every fiber of my being) that I can accomplish whatever I wish, that I can divest myself of the peculiar irrational weather pattern surrounding my attractive body. (I used to admire my body while standing naked before a mirror, but now the stimulating pleasure, which often caused my penis to reach toward the ceiling, is lost to me because I get too cold and my buttocks turn an embarrassingly hideous pink.) There must be some psychological reason preventing me from curing myself, but I will never know (and this knowledge too is certain) what it is.

Perhaps I would be able to accept the winter (and I have been cold for so long I fear true warmth would be an anathema to me) if it were not for my other major problem. As I stand here, though my perceptions allow me only the vaguest hints of the long shadows cast by the objects and people in the park, I readily perceive that I cast no shadow. I have not cast a shadow for eons.

That, in and of itself, would not be quite so bad (it would only be vaguely disconcerting) if my shadow was not trying to kill me.

I suspect, though I can hardly be sure, that the trouble began with the death of my loved one (a subject I find myself turning to more frequently of late, though I cannot imagine why). Perhaps her unfortunate demise (the exact nature of which I could never ascertain) caused a schism in my soul. How this affected the laws of the universe, which could be altered only by my godlike powers, I shall never know. But if light travels in straight lines, how could it or why should it then curve about my body, which definitely has not lost any mass throughout the eons? Yet the waves pass through my molecules as if I do not exist. When I hold an object to the light, the object casts a shadow as if it were floating in the air. All my powers cannot create a shadow, nor can I cause light to reflect from me, despite whatever alterations I might make in my body's composition. (However, I still reflect an image in a mirror, for all the good that does me.)

Just why this phenomenon would cause what is essentially the absence of light to become whole and take on a life of its own, I do not know. I only know that the morning following the death of my loved one, I awoke in my cockroach-ridden apartment to find that a lifelong friend had deserted me. I did not have to perform a series of tests to know my shadow had fled. What grievous sin I had committed, I could not imagine. But it must have tortured my shadow indeed! Whatever I had done must have filled my shadow with such intense self-loathing that it felt its only hope of survival lay in cutting itself forever from the very source of its existence. Surely it must have taken into consideration the fact that without me, it would cease to be. It would die, leaving me a fraction of my former self, and all for no good reason; for its demise would have accomplished nothing. But it had not died. By deserting what the both of us had foolishly believed was the very foundation of its life, it had discovered reservoirs of strength neither of us could have conceived. It had always possessed a life separate from mine, as many seemingly intertwined and dependent objects or people possess uniqueness and independence; and now it presumed to take revenge upon me for the ignorance we had possessed.

I also knew I would never defeat my shadow. Men as sensitive as I can never summon the viciousness required for life-and-death combat. In addition, I am a coward. I angrily imagined myself grappling with my shadow in a public square of one of the three golden cities of godlike mankind, while a crowd surrounded us and watched with uncomprehending faces (the blankness characteristic of those incapable of understanding the eternal struggles they have lost due to their abysmal ignorance and unwillingness to see the truth); and the crowd applauded as I stood triumphant, my chest swelled, my belly sucked in, over the submissive substance of my shadow and pointed at my feet, where it dutifully assumed its proper position in the scientific structure of the universe. But a more realistic fantasy assured me that my black shadow would stand triumphantly over my broken and bloody body, and that my shadow would ensure much suffering and pain on my part before it would finally allow my soul to flee my wretched shell and embrace the beckoning infinite. No doubt about it, for once my *angst* was justified. I strained my spirit to allow me to face my doom bravely and fatalistically; I did not want to face the desolate life awaiting me. But one form of cowardice defeated another; I dressed and then casually held my cloak in the crook of my right elbow as I walked from my apartment, into the lonely winter that has plagued my tormented soul.

I could not teleport from one destination to another; something, probably of the shadow's origin, prevented me, otherwise I would have teleported myself to a distant planet in the hopes that it would be able to trace me. It was and is a game, a wearying game we play. And so I wandered this tedious planet, carrying my winter with me, until my *gastrocnemia* and *tendo calcanae* developed spectacularly. That was all of me to develop spectacularly; as I stand in the park I realize, with an overwhelming intensity that threatens to cripple me, what a wasted specimen I am. I have seen every secluded location on this world a hundred times; I have walked through fields and forests containing the most dazzling visions, and it has seemed as if I have been the only godlike man ever to have witnessed them, so great is my loneliness; and yet I cannot say I recall the sensation of having experienced either the beauty or the ugliness; I cannot truly say their memory remains with me. I have been seen, I am sure, by every individual and eternal child and pubescent eternal child on this planet; yet they have not attempted to engage me in conversation, nor have I attempted to engage them; no one has even uttered a perfunctory "Hi there," nor I to another. No one has the vaguest glimmer of my torment, my sensitivity, my plight; and what is more, if someone did know, he would shrug his shadow and forget, for the matter would not be his concern. Throughout these eons, I have seen my shadow only a few times, always in the distance; and upon each occasion I had the distinct impression that it could have easily overtaken me, if only it had possessed the inclination. My most vivid memory of the chase consists of myself and my winter trodding across a vast desert; the yellow of the sun was painful to my sensitive eyes, and my winter suffocated me as it protected me from the heat. And on the horizon I saw my black shadow, a mere speck, following me, the distance between us remaining constant regardless of my speed. Whenever I saw my shoulder I resolved never to allow it to catch me, though simultaneously I wondered how long I would be able to maintain this pathetic charade.

Perhaps that is why I have appeared to have surrendered to my third problem, my eternal *angst*, and am now standing here, mulling over all that I would have become had it not been for the evil manipulations of fate and the callous nature of the universe in general. In Africa I felt a peculiar siren call; it reached through my loneliness and pain and cold, somehow informing me as definitely as if the oversoul had sent me a mundane telegram that my place was in the East End. Why my place is here I have no idea; and though I should feel as if my journey has concluded and that I have, at long last, arrived at a home where I can hang up my cloak, I feel as lost as ever. I fervently desire to continue my eternal trek, for my shadow is closing in on me (I know it; I feel it). But there is a bond between this place and me, a bond forged entirely without my permission, as most bonds are forged. I sense that nearly all who reside in this decrepit golden neighborhood are as lonely as I; but they have not the courage to struggle as valiantly as I have in my own cowardly, sensitive fashion; I cannot imagine any of them fleeing their demons for thousands of eons—rather they would submit and die and end it. So, though I feel this bond, I am still comforted, in a small way, by my incredible superiority over every worthless being on this despicable planet. I am the king of the cockroaches.

Yet my vaunted superiority cannot conceal from me that I would gladly give up everything to become a part of the spirit of this place. I do not know how or why, but an indefinable *something* is permeating the atmosphere as concretely as if I was whiffing the frigid fumes of lemon extract. A struggle I cannot take part in is occurring; games more significant than mine are being played to their inevitable conclusions. Through my veils, I can see the evidence everywhere. The faceless man wearing a tacky suit over there on the bench is a participant. He is not as wise or as perceptive as I; one would think (I certainly do) that a godlike man such as he would be singularly inappropriate for a tumultuous series of philosophical constructs manifesting themselves in words, actions, deeds—or more precisely, in the game of life itself—but the forces swirl about his pudgy frame like black ghosts. He displays no outward evidence of his concern; he might as well be feeding nuts to the red-and-blue pigeons at his big feet for all the internal anxiety he exposes. But the truth cannot be hidden from a sensitive man weighed down with ponderous, unanswerable inquiries into the oversoul, and it is in the hearts of godlike men and women such as he, assailed by forces they possess not the capacity to understand, that the game will ultimately be resolved. He deludes himself into thinking he is mysterious, but I know, though he believes no one knows, that he is listening with interest to the pubescent eternal child playing a discordant, pathetically simplistic tune on a guitar. She is not playing well. She will never play well, especially if she continues shamelessly exhibiting such poor taste. The faceless man is not the only participant in the game. Those two godlike men over there, speaking softly and nodding in his direction, also have landed starring roles. One has a phenomenally ugly green visage; the other wears the expertly tailored black clothes of the aristocrat; but like the pubescent eternal child playing the guitar, he does not meet his aspirations well. I, the faceless man, and those two are three points in a straight line, with the faceless man in the center, his back to the pair. The sense of importance pervading this trio, whether or not with their knowledge, offends me to the very marrow of my frigid bones; and I turn away, bored beyond words by the mediocrity of the park, the inhabitants, and the games they play. I have only the assurances of the black ghosts that the games are of universal significance, and frankly, I choose not to believe them. Existential forces are the most untrustworthy of...of...Not only am I beyond words, but in a different category entirely.

My winter seems to be increasing its intensity as I walk from the park, as if some foreign element is invading my territorial boundaries. Eternal children, blissfully unaware of the East End's sinister atmosphere, rush by me. A child pauses in my path; he has bushy red hair and wide blue eyes and his mouth is open; from my vantage point I can see silver fillings in his teeth which were not placed there because he had cavities, but to add to the illusion that he is a growing boy (though he will never change unless he mysteriously becomes pubescent). I brush by him and, propelled by a curiosity he does not understand and I do not care to, he reaches out and touches my cloak. And I do not have to look behind me to know that he holds his suddenly frost-bitten fingers before his wide-eyed face for a moment before he opens that abyss he calls a mouth and wails, the tears streaming from those tightly closed lids. I hear the rapid tapping of his light footsteps diminishing as he runs away from me, either toward the park or toward his parents. Now all the eternal children on the sidewalk keep their distance from me, as if they had communicated through some mysterious means of which we, the race that created them, are unaware. But most likely it is nothing as ominous as that, merely some communal instinct to avoid pain.

Perhaps it is that same instinct which instructed me to turn around before I walked to the left at the intersection. Previously, I had paid no attention to the screams and the running of the eternal children; I had, true to the nature of my superiority, assumed I was the cause of their fear and I had decided to ignore it disdainfully in a manner befitting my role in the universe. So I am disappointed for more than one reason when I see that the children are not fleeing because of me, but because my shadow is boldly strolling down the center of the street; it does not even have the good taste or the subtlety to cower on the sidewalk near the walls of the tall, dull golden buildings. I never would have thought that my shadow would be so dramatic. It possesses the appearance of a black haze, somehow with mass and substance equal to my own. It possesses no features, no depth; when its hand passes over its torso or thigh, I cannot discern the two separate parts. I have never before seen my shadow so closely, and so I am ashamed that it does not wear appropriate shadow clothing; it does not even conceal itself with a cloak. Already I sense its perverted racy personality, and I hate it for flaunting its freedom of choice so recklessly. Perhaps I would not be ashamed if it had a pecker vaguely resembling my magnificent specimen. Its groin is perfectly smooth. I know I have not been laid for thousands of eons, but I find my shadow's implied insult entirely gratuitous.

Perhaps it is that insult, more than any other factor, which causes me to stand here. I feel like I am standing next to myself; and I perceive the twitching of the left side of my grimly set mouth as if I was idly watching a drama without verisimilitude. I wonder why I am suddenly facing my ever-approaching, eternally silent and mysterious shadow with such foolish stubbornness. Surely one who has not savored the luscious fluids of a quivering quim in a tremendous span of time cannot be so stricken by the notion that his dork has withered up and dried away. Of what concern is my dork to me, if it has not fulfilled its primary function for so long? Ah, well, there is no explaining it; even one as sensitive and as perceptive as I cannot know all the facets of his hidden primal motivations, otherwise I would have tidied my performance upon the initial absence of my shadow. But now I view myself as usual, inside myself, and I see a bead of sweat turning into ice as it rolls down my nose. My shadow approaches me like a dream given reality. It is not twenty meters from me, and it reaches toward me, its arms outstretched as if it had lifted and was choking an annoying eternal child. It is a frightening thing, to see part of myself advancing so remorsefully, its intentions so plain; and still I do not flee. I feel ridiculous; there is no reason for me to have finally submitted to this confrontation at this time: it could have been delayed indefinitely, without making a difference one way or the other; there is not even an audience to applaud my victory, which is probably just as well since I have been struck by the powerful, numbing intuition that I am going to lose. I will be a bloody heap on the street, wallowing in defeat and self-pity, which is a much worse way to wallow than the way I have been all these years; and my shadow will kick me to see if I am actually dead and not just pretending. I see this vision as clearly as I suddenly see the pale face of my loved one before me, obscuring the smooth, seemingly two-dimensional face of my shadow. But the time has passed for such musings. It is a sorry state of affairs when a godlike man such as I cannot muse, when he is forced to deal with his considerable problems by direct action. But this is definitely the time for action. No doubt about it, for the black hands of the shadow have pierced my winter...

...and they are choking me. The winter has not rendered the shadow's hands frigid; instead the hands burn with a fire unlike any I have ever experienced. The fire burns my brains; it burns every nerve ending in my body; and I stand like a limp doll, supported only by the baffling muscular power of my shadow, power of a magnitude I never could have guessed, but power I can only revere and awe since it is supporting my entire weight without a trace of strain. I attempt to counteract the heat with the power of my winter; I feel secure that only the utter desolation of my spirit can defeat this part of myself which, I suddenly know, represents my own perverted self-anger. Some inner part of me has yearned for this confrontation for eons, and now that circumstances have forced it upon me, I relish it. Of what good is suffering, what meaning can be derived from it, if it does not end eventually? Even death, that most final ending which has become a concrete concept rather than an abstract one in my immortal mind, will provide a good reason, if only my death leads to a plane without spiritual torture. Why do I continue to muse, my mind leisurely following its own murky impulses, when I should be concentrating on the situation at hand? Is it my way of ordaining my demise? Why do I muse upon my musing?

I realize, with startling finality, that I do not want to die. I cause my winter to radiate from my body. During each instant I think a thousand thoughts; I cannot categorize or comprehend a single one, they fly by so quickly and disappear into an imaginary haze somewhere in my mind. My winter has become a visible blue sheath, cracking in long jagged lines where my shadow's hands have pierced it. My winter is cooling my shadow's fire. I sense its moral outrage weakening into a kind of subdued tenacity, a hatred born of reason rather than of passion. I smile, wondering why I smile, but not really feeling like taking the time out to reflect on it. For the first time I feel my spiritual desolation has a purpose, that of my survival; and I revel in it. It has been so long since I have experienced joy that I almost forget the gravity of my predicament, but I do not forget to reach toward the shadow and, driven by some impulse which forces me to treat my foe as if it were human, jam my thumbs where its eyes should be. I am vaguely surprised that it does not spurt blood as my fingers immerse themselves into blackness with all the force I can muster. At once winter spreading from all ten fingers contaminates the shadow's head, and I feel the winter exploring the infinite blackness inside as if the icy waves possessed nerve endings to communicate information to my tortured brain. And the shadow communicates its pain to me, for despite our years of separation we are still attached in an unfathomable fashion. And as it releases its terrible grip on my throat, and as I suck in the cold air that pricks my lungs, I sense its utter hatred, its complete disagreement with my way of life. Fuck my shadow! Who does it think it is, anyway? I am the host; what I decree, it fulfills, and there can be no other arrangement, not if the universe is to have any meaning.

Of course, my shadow's attitude toward me and toward the meaning of the universe is eloquently summarized by its rather blatant and brutal conduct upon my person, as it plummets its fists radiating fire upon my chest and stomach. My hands are frozen in its face, and I am dizzy, staggering backwards, trying to yank myself from its black visage. And still it continues to pummel me with barbaric uppercuts, especially since it is able to connect occasionally with my jaw. It wants to live—it furiously wants to live! It wants to destroy my desolation forever, and since we have long since passed the point where we can settle any differences like a reasonable man and his overwrought shadow, I cannot communicate that life is nothing but desolation. Not loving is pain, but so is loving. Not thinking is pain, but so is thinking. Not doing is pain, but so is doing. Everything leads to ennui; and there is no stimulation. Why my shadow refuses to accept this rather obvious, basic fact of life, I have no idea; all I know is that I want to survive, perhaps because I have come to enjoy my pain and ennui because they are the only true experience to savor and everything else is false. So it is with a vague sense of hypocrisy that I throw away my inhibitions, and I flow free with the desolation I have nurtured inside, the desolation I have previously refused to admit to myself; the entire universe is desolation, the entire universe is journeying toward only its inevitable death and nothing more; and I experience a curious triumph: a vindication.

The fire of my shadow diminishes. Rapidly. A part of me is appalled by its quick and unexpected dying, but the greater part of me is overjoyed—overjoyed that soon I will be able to embrace my desolation without obstacles. The shadow's blows upon my stomach have now lost their force; I feel like I am being smitten by cantankerous feathers. The shadow's legs are bending, and soon I will be standing triumphantly. My fingers are gradually emerging from its face. And now they are free, with only scraps of blackness limply clinging to them. And without effort, with only a slight wince at the warmness, I pick the clinging shadow pieces from my fingers and let them drop beside the body of my fallen nemesis, which is now flat and motionless. All pretenses of mass and form are gone. I glance about, wondering if my exciting struggle has enticed an audience in this district of such excruciating boredom, and I see only two godlike men, the one with the green visage and the would-be aristocrat. I realize, belatedly, that they had not been nodding at the faceless man, but at me. I fling my cape across my chest and over my right shoulder; and I inhale deeply, drawing myself to my full height and looking as noble as it is possible for me to look considering the trials and tribulations I have just undergone.

The aristocrat applauds; it approximates the sound of one hand clapping as nearly as anything I can imagine. He says, "Bravo! Bravo! How about an encore, sweetie?"

"I am not your sweetie."

They stride toward me. The aristocrat twirls his sword cane and smiles obnoxiously. I try not to show it, but the leer of the green one causes a frigidity of quite a different nature to permeate my bones, a frigidity not even my shadow could cause.

"I must say you passed our test with a graceful aplomb," says the green one. "I thought we had finally found our man."

"Your man? You two do not care what people think of your sexual proclivities, do you?"

The green one laughs. "I don't mean that; please refrain from inflicting your insecurities upon our conversation. It won't take long, in any case."

"What?" inquires the aristocrat. "You mean we're not going to explain to him how we suspected him of being the ripper, how we easily deduced his greatest sorrows and fears, and how we devised this little test to see if he would react like a seasoned murderer?"

"No," says the green one. "It wouldn't do any good."

The aristocrat frowns and rubs his chin; somehow the gesture is not as indicative of deep thinking as he would prefer it, but I cannot help but be dismayed at the brutalness of his frank appraisal; for he is regarding me as coldly as he would regard a wayward hermit crab. "I suppose you're right. He will continue upon his path despite what we say to him. Fortunately for our race, though, it appears that no one will listen to him, nor will he attempt to make them listen. However, I do think we should warn him."

"Yes, we should," says the green one.

"What could you buffoons possibly warn me about? I have just vanquished my greatest foe. For the first time in recent memory, I am free. I am vindicated."

"We told you this was a test," says the aristocrat. "This shadow at your feet is a sham, something the demon created." He snaps his fingers, and the shadow disappears. "Your true shadow is on the outskirts of the city. It should be arriving here soon."

I am hideously aware of my jaw slackening. As the aristocrat speaks, I perceive his message as if the words are being distantly spoken to me in a nightmare. I am not free after all! My vindication is only an illusion! "Help me," I say. "You must help me."

"We can't," says the green one. "Our friend the consulting detective summed it up, according to the good doctor, when he said, simply, that some souls can't be saved. I wish we could help you, but let's face it, there are too many other important matters for us to attend to. Though we're immortals, I don't believe that in the future we shall ever have time ... to waste."

"Go see the shrink," says the aristocrat. "He wastes a lot of time. In fact, that's all he ever does."

"But hold, you do not understand," I say. "My shadow has been trailing me for eons. He desires my death; nothing else will satiate him." They cannot hear, they have teleported away, and my powers of teleportation are so atrophied that I cannot even perceive the residue of slow atoms traveling to their destination. "Help me." I look at the empty streets, at the tall buildings, at the sky, at the shadowless space at my feet; I look everywhere and nowhere, fearing I will see my shadow approaching me. "Hey, guys, listen ... Fellows ... Help me. Please, help me."

6. *A lot of peculiar callings have been going around lately*, thought the man in the yellow suit. The calling which had affected him the most deeply, the calling which had touched emotions he thought withered eons ago, had been from a more mundane source than the mystical realms of the tortured oversoul; it had emanated from the lonely heart of the woman in the black veil, and though the man in the yellow suit was tempted to learn if she still thrived on rejection, a vague characteristic existing on the perimeters of the call caused him to cease his search for the ripper and to heed her wishes. Having once witnessed the wholeness of the universe, and having grappled with the notion that he might have only *thought* he witnessed it, the man in the yellow suit was, understandably enough, reluctant to descend to more prosaic matters—such as those of the godlike heart, his or anyone else's. But the siren call had been simple and direct, the sadness and the yearning and the grief and the hopelessness being only an undercurrent; and it was the undercurrent which had caused him to respond. Filled as he was with the vision and strength of true reality, he had forgotten that something as simple as a lonely heart could distract him so completely, could arouse such compassion, and could reduce the whole of the universe to an insignificant mote of dust. He had followed the dictates of the call, and consequently he now stood alone on the top of the highest peak of a planet far away from Earth, a planet known as the Land of Melodious Comets.

And in this eternally dark sky dotted with tiny white stars, there passed comets with a white fire so great that the entire surface within his range of vision seemed to glow as if the barren, brown landscape of jagged rocks and deep crevices had somehow burst into spontaneous illumination. And though the comets did not pass through the atmosphere of this planet, they might as well have; for in their wake came eerie songs that hummed in the marrow, that soothed the nerves even as they anguished the heart. As the man in the yellow suit waited for the woman in the black veil, he heard the songs four times, and upon each occasion he saw the vast barrenness below, devoid of life and the promise of life, light up like a painting in a dream. And he wondered if the world and its black sky, suddenly burning, would be any different to his eyes if he stood on the plateau below, or in the lands beyond the plateau, lands which appeared to have been forever scorched and devastated by a long-ago catastrophe. He wondered what the planet would look like, what the songs would sound like, if he stood at the bottom of a crevice, burying himself, hiding himself from all but a few perceptions, renouncing the entirety of life. Would the songs sound the same, or would they sound lovelier, more beautiful, more alluring? Would his starved senses drink their sound; would he perceive the songs with greater intensity, undistracted as he would be by the other properties of the comets? Or was he, metaphorically speaking, standing in a crevice now? Were there other properties of which he was unaware? If so, could he take the steps necessary to shatter his barriers and to achieve the actuality of his delusions? What new songs would he hear? What new sights would he see?

And would the air be so cold if he rose to a new level? The comets warmed the atmosphere instantaneously, but they passed by so quickly, flying by so close to this world, and they left behind only the memory of them and the rapid decline in temperature. The man in the yellow suit warmed himself internally, but this Land of Melodious Comets was so stark and the music aroused such tenderness in his soul that his method of keeping warm was somehow unsatisfactory; and he wished he could rely on the less efficient method of embracing a warm body, preferably that of a woman. It irritated him that the songs were responsible, that he was not responsible for this curious tenderness directed toward (he was slightly surprised when he realized it) the woman in the black veil. And it was not only the songs with their lovely notes and hums defying all traditional descriptions and breakdowns of musical patterns, but the realization of all the pain and suffering the woman in the black veil had undergone as she had tried to secure his love. For all his insight (which was decidedly not a delusion on his part), he could not comprehend why an individual would undergo such torture for something as fragile as love. He knew that for all the spiritual advancements he might make in the succeeding eons, he would never understand it, certainly not if he continued exploring his current directions to the exclusion of all others.

He wondered where the woman in the black veil was. It was extremely impolite of her to call him so far away from Earth and then be late for their appointment. *When all is said and done,* he thought, *she's just a typical broad. If only I had been born without a dick, then I wouldn't have been subjected to this aggravation.*

"If you had been born without a dick, I would have made you one," said a feminine voice in a sarcastic tone behind him.

He did not have to turn to know the speaker. "Is it absolutely necessary for you to parade your spiritual weaknesses so shamelessly?" Nor did he have to exert his formidable powers to know she blushed beneath her veil. Why was it that the most forward godlike women were the most susceptible to false modesty? "And I must have told you a thousand times to stop reading my mind. It's impolite!"

"Reading your mind is the only way I can discover what you're really thinking. If I relied solely upon your words and actions, I wouldn't have a glimmer. Besides, doesn't it strike you as odd that someone who fancies himself so above plebian concepts of good and evil would be annoyed that a certain deed is 'impolite?'"

"When it's done to me, it's impolite!" said the man in the yellow suit, spinning about like a top with a crumpled base, staggering slightly when he faced her. He had been fully prepared to glare at her until her demeanor shrank before the force of his rage, thus providing himself with the sense of power necessary to consider her emotional fate beneath his concern; but the sight of her rendered the stratagem futile. She did not meet his rage with rage, as he had expected, but with disappointment. He did not have to pierce the veil to know her brown eyes gleamed with compassion, that the nostrils of her flattened nose flared, that the dark lips of her wide mouth were set in a grim, pitying smile. She wore, as usual, shades of black, with an ankle-length, long-sleeved tight dress, stockings, gloves, and a hat that was gaudy in spite of its understated design and quiet black coloring. The low cut of her dress provided him with an excellent view of the upper rises of her breasts, and of the only expanse of skin visible—an expanse of a dark tan; he could never truly be sure if the tan was the result of long hours bathing in the sun or of natural hereditary causes. His supreme confidence, as well as his tremendous rage, was also severely taken aback by her pose, which he had expected to be either indicative of outrageous ire or demure caution; she should have been sitting in a classic pose on a rock, whatever her disposition. Instead she lay on her stomach, with her legs turned sideways, with her chin resting on her cupped hands beneath her veil; she resembled nothing so much as she did a cat. Her desperation had provoked her to desperate measures, and her body language indicated an awareness of her sexuality and her attraction toward him that the particulars of their relationship had always required her to disguise, though the pretense of manners and sophistication had fooled neither of them, had hidden nothing. The man in the yellow suit did not care to admit it (because she might pluck his thoughts), but he, in his turn, was attracted to her. And though the thought filled him with fear, he wondered what it would be like to boldly strut into unknown territory he had never had the courage or the opportunity to explore, to renounce his complete preoccupation with the spiritual—to embrace her, to kiss her, to declare his immortal love for her though he loved her not, to swear he wanted her for her mind even as he casually ripped her dress from her incredibly desirable body and slipped one hand over a breast vainly protected by a black bra as the other hand cupped her juicy crotch. His thoughts swirled in a maelstrom, if he could be said to have thoughts at all; he was reduced to a canopy of discordant, conflicting emotions; because he wanted her—his spiritual odyssey was meaningless without her—yet he knew the possession of her would forever impede his progress. And it was the sincerity of her desire which had capitvated him. He had been so stupid; he had to be hit over the head with the sledgehammer of love before he could acknowledge the fact that he too had been born for love; he too felt the need to love someone and to be loved; he too could not bear the inevitability of one day waking up cold and lonely. It did not matter if he had only deluded himself into thinking he loved her; the need had become part of his personality. It had lain dormant for so long that when it awoke, it had staggered him. It had altered everything. In the future, when he brooded, he would not waste his thoughts solely on the imponderable; he would also brood about himself. He decided he was a lot to brood about. He could never backtrack. Henceforth, life would not only be an elevated journey, but the tormented driftings of enterprising glands. In the symphony of the spheres, there was now room for a hamburger concerto. And as he loved the woman in the black veil, he hated her—hated her with equal passion for causing him to admit that, in many respects, he was just like everyone else.

"Why did you decide we should meet here?" asked the man in the yellow suit. The question was deliberately pedestrian; he wanted to hold off the discussion of the actual matters on their minds as long as possible. As he spoke a single comet rose in the horizon, whitening the sky with its superimposition of fire and song. And it seemed this song touched him with more force than the previous songs. And he was aware of an indiscreet quivering in his voice, a clue to his tenderness and concern.

The body language of the woman in the black veil altered considerably, and the playfulness was replaced, in the span of a nanosecond, by the manner of a stricken child, as if her heart had suddenly fallen in on itself and left her soul barren. She pushed herself to an upright position and lowered her chin, looking at the fiery land in the distance, avoiding meeting the eyes of the man in the yellow suit. For a lingering moment she clearly concentrated on the song of the comet to the exclusion of all else; and as the comet approached, the man in the yellow suit wondered that the gravity did not ensnare it and cause it to come crashing into the surface, demolishing the world; for the comet appeared to be larger than the moon of Earth as it hurtled through the sky; yet it also appeared to be moving from the world as it sang its eerie song. And when its light was so great that the man in the yellow suit was forced to create a pair of sunglasses, the woman in the black veil said, "Simply because this place suits me. I know you don't appreciate what you call the primitive poetics of my manner of expression, but I must tell you that for longer than I care to remember this place has been my home; and when a comet sings, I think of my love for you. We've been apart for so long—what am I talking about; we've never been together—that my love for you would eventually die if it weren't for the comets. I wouldn't want to live if I couldn't love you."

"My dear, we are immortals. Even if I declared I loved you—which I don't intend to do—there will come a time when you will no longer love me. You cannot love a man for the remainder of your life if your life never ends."

"Nor can you speak for me. I've already loved you for so long that the inevitable disillusionment due to an eternity of close proximity to you will not end my love. I can't conceive of myself without loving you."

"It's not part of your self-image." ·

"If you want to be objective about it—yes. But why do you have to be objective all the frigging time? Can't you be romantic, even for an instant? Just once I would like to hear a word from you that sounded like a human being said it."

"And what good would that do? It would only give you hope, when there is no hope."

"What difference would hope make? Hope wouldn't keep my love for you alive. I've kept the flame warm without hope for eons."

In the sky, the comet dived into the horizon, and its song became silent. Once again they stood alone beneath the stars and the eternal night.

"There are a thousand reasons why I shouldn't love you," said the man in the yellow suit, turning his back to the woman in the black veil and putting his hands in his trouser pockets. His shoulders were slumped. "But I suppose the most important one is the very nature of my mystical quest. It is my purpose in life to see through the illusions we create and to perceive the actuality of . . . reality. And it is my firm belief that love—even a love which is apparently as sincere and as enduring as yours—is part of our illusions. If I tried—which isn't to say I would succeed—to open up to you, I would be embracing another illusion. I would never, could never be sincere because I would always be aware of other forces operating, manipulating us, guiding us without our knowledge."

"I don't believe you when you say that you would be insincere. I've never met anyone as sure of himself. Or as stubborn."

He did not want to look at her. Even the sound of her voice upset and tempted him. Though he was positive not a muscle moved, his insides quaked; his stomach throbbed and ached; his intestines were hardened; and he saw the barren landscape of the Land of Melodious Comets in a watery blur. "I cannot say I was not born to love; but there are different degrees of love, and each degree has its own purpose. And the purpose of the kind of love you feel for me is to distract me, to blind me to the truth, to prevent me from doing what I must do."

"And what must you do?" asked the woman in the black veil, her voice hoarse, low, and defeated.

"I don't know."

"And what do you see?"

"I can't explain."

"And what do you feel?"

"I can't explain that either."

"Well, I can see that you've certainly been thinking things through. What would you like to do?"

The man in the yellow suit hesitated before answering. "I want to make people aware of my beliefs. I want to tell them, to *convince* them that they can divest themselves of all their pathetically preconceived notions and dilemmas; they will no longer be bound by the shackles of their personalities; if they have the will, they can perceive the true continuity of the universe; if they have the courage, they can be free. Godlike mankind is a race of slaves; just beyond the perimeters of their stunted perceptions lurk more truth, more lies, more pleasure, more pain than they can possibly imagine. And I've experienced it! I've realized it! I've known more sensation and more passion than any of them. Even the fat man, while drilling one of those damn fine cheerleaders, can't know what I know, otherwise he wouldn't be wasting his time on such trifles, alluring as they may be; he would at the very least let one or two fool around with somebody else for awhile. And yet, what I've accomplished isn't beyond the abilities of the average *schlemiel*. He too can understand the true beauty of a green field on a hot day, and can smell the sweet fragrance of the grass and flowers, and hear the sharp buzzing of the insects, and feel the breeze caressing his cheeks; and he will know more, experience more than ever before, because, if he would only listen to me, he will not be merely an observer on a sabbatical from the confining golden city, but he will truly be a part of all that transpires beneath the deceptive tranquility of nature."

"And what happens to the *schlemiel* who hasn't the courage and the will?"

The man in the yellow suit shrugged. "Unfortunately, the true continuity of the universe dictates that some people get the shaft."

The woman in the black veil smiled; she snorted, indicating that she was amused. "And just how do you propose to communicate this message?"

"That's the hard part; I haven't quite figured it out yet. I would paint, but I can't draw a decent stick figure. I would play music, but I haven't the talent or the patience to learn. I would write novels, but I haven't the discipline. I would write poetry, but I haven't the heart. I would preach, but..."

"You haven't the knack."

The man in the yellow suit sneered. He felt that she had struck an unkind blow at the base of his spine. He turned away from her because anger rose like a torrent inside him, smothering the warmth and compassion he had felt earlier; he could think of nothing more satisfactory than answering her verbal sally with a physical one. "And just what do you mean by that?"

"When you spoke of the fields, I could not see them; I could not imagine the tall grass stretching into the horizon and submitting to the gentle pressure of the breeze. When you mentioned the buzzing of the bees, I heard only silence. When you mentioned the fragrance of the flowers, I smelled only the dust on this barren world. I apologize for speaking so boldly; perhaps it isn't my place to do so; but while you may have a message, while you may have experienced a vision, while there may be something inside you urging you onward and onward, further and further away from me, until even the grim specter of eternal loneliness causes you no trepidation, you can't communicate any of it. You haven't the talent. I suppose your situation is hardly unique; the Big Red Cheese is filled with message after message, but the one message he can successfully communicate is restricted to a few spurts of protein. I don't know what to do or what to say that would convince you that the part of you which reaches out to others is the very part that no one you love or who loves you can touch; it is always fated to be so. And the part of your spirit which can touch and be touched is the part you withdraw from life. You believe that for one part to live, the other must die, but I'm afraid there will come a time when both parts will be dead; and I'll go on loving a shell of a godlike man, loving him not for what he is, but for what he once was or could have been."

When the woman in the black veil concluded, the man in the yellow suit closed his eyes; he felt dizzy, as if he had suddenly gazed down a universal chasm of blackness. His anger had faded like the voice of a lover whispering in his ear, until the emotion was only a dimly remembered entity. His soul had suddenly become a ghost ship, with frayed sails and rotting timbers, silhouetted by hazy moonbeams penetrating a silver fog. He did not want to believe a word of her speech, but he could not deny that she had finally reached him; and he wanted to embrace her, he wanted to love her; but though he could take her right here and now, making wild, passionate love on the hard rocks and lifeless soil of this desolate peak on a desolate world, he could not love her as she wished to be loved. He could pretend, but the pretense would not fool her; she would eventually pierce the deception. And how could he pursue the truth if he willingly fostered lies, for the sake of brief moments of tenderness, sexual release, and spiritual escape? No, he could not love her; he simply was not capable of the emotion. But one thing, above all other things, was suddenly on his mind. "What's this about the Big Red Cheese and his spurts of protein?"

"Oh, I did a one-night stand with him a few years ago. He was quite nice, but nothing like his reputation."

"What did you do that for?"

The man in the yellow suit was painfully aware of a condescending smile on her dark face (a smile he could not see, but which he was aware of, nevertheless) as she touched his elbow. "My dear, I love you with all my heart and soul, but I've needs too. Besides, I enjoy sex."

"I thought you enjoy suffering more," he said coldly.

"I endure my suffering in the hope that it will end."

The man in the yellow suit stood in front of her and stared at her uplifted, concealed face. "I too wish with all my heart and soul that it will end, but I am not the one."

"Let me be the judge of that."

"I'm the judge of whether or not you will have the opportunity. And I must say no, you do not have the opportunity. You've touched me deeper than anyone has touched me throughout my existence. I am but a dreamer; and you're just a dream. Never before has an immortal man conceived of such a dream. But I simply cannot imagine myself loving someone in the manner in which you wish to be loved. Of all my possible futures, that is the very one which is least likely to come to pass."

The woman in the black veil nodded solemnly. "And that's it, huh?"

"That's it. It won't work, for two faces have I. You must continue suffering; you must go on; but if you wear your love like heaven, you discover that the beat goes on with you."

"I might, but personally I think all I have to look forward to is a manic depression in a purple haze." She turned away from him, with her head bent and her shoulders slumped. "You've bitten off a piece of my heart."

The man in the yellow suit helplessly looked at his palms; they had turned a whiter shade of pale.

"You could have made me so very happy," continued the woman in the black veil, staring at a melodious comet hurtling across the horizon; it would not pass near them, and the music was eerie and vague. "And for all this time, I've loved you eight days a week. For all these years, I've wanted to awake with you whispering in my ear, and now all I've to look forward to is the sounds of silence."

"You must keep hanging on."

"No. I'll return to my apartment in the East End and paint it black. I'll never experience any satisfaction. This could be the last time I'll ever speak to you. I know now that my love-life is doomed to be a beggar's banquet. When I die, people will throw dead flowers on my grave. And as my soul walks that last moonlight mile, with no expectations, my heart still broken like a jigsaw puzzle because I could obtain no connection, the sky blue will turn to gray, and still I will sing of you. If only I could have found a song in life..."

"It's the singer, not the song."

For several moments they were silent. It seemed that a thousand comets blazed in the horizon; and not a one moved in their direction. The horizon was a shimmering orchestration of color; and above them each of the cold white stars seemed alone, unreachable, incapable of receiving one another's light or of touching the souls of the man in the yellow suit and the woman in the black veil. The man in the yellow suit had never been so indifferent to the stars before.

Finally he said, "Please go home; I'm out of time. You've loved in vain; and my obsession has made me too complicated."

"I've opened my heart to you, and you're just going to let it bleed?"

The man in the yellow suit shrugged. "You can't always get what you want." He looked away from the display of comets in the horizon, only to discover that she was not there. He whispered to himself, "But, baby, I hope you get what you need."

7. *An account from the good doctor's notebooks:*

As dusk fell over the drab environs of the East End park, I stood apart from my comrades, even apart from the consulting detective. Despite the grisly murders of the previous two nights, which surely should have been sufficient to set my nerves on edge, this was the first night I can honestly say I greeted with intense forebodings vague feelings of fear and discontent that seemed much more natural, of a greater profundity, than the moment of insecurity assailing me while teleporting to the park the night before. The forebodings might be best called a feeling of dreadful anticipation; I was not afraid for myself (for I was positive I was perfectly safe, so long as I remained by the consulting detective's side), but I feared for my comrades and the denizens of the East End. The fat man's riveting editorials—verbose calls for action and mundane pleas for people to insure their own safety—which had been scattered throughout the paper appeared to have had minimal effect upon the populace. Two godlike women had died, and life proceeded as normal. It was most disconcerting; somehow the deaths should have ultimately been more significant.

My subjective distance was enhanced by the darkness surrounding me; my friends all stood beneath the pale glow of an ineffectual streetlamp; and the darkness shielded me from the pains of life and participation like a cloak of death. I watched my friends as if I was watching the actors in a dreary drama. The consulting detective's pipe had extinguished itself many minutes ago, yet he continued to puff at it occasionally, his hands remaining in his pockets as if his skin had been stitched to the lining (an action I had often suggested to the landlady, so that she might keep him away from the kitchen until dinner was fully prepared). The universal op was his usual inscrutable self; despite my considerable compassion toward him, he was beginning to bore me. And as for my remaining friends—they all appeared to be suffering from similiar problems; their minds clearly were not on the forthcoming tasks. The eyes of the fat man radiated a haze completely identical to that in the lawyer's eyes; and the lawyer was pining for Kitty, a fact that had become rather obvious since he had pointedly alluded to the matter of her disappearance four times to the consulting detective in the locker room. As the man in the yellow suit was gazing at the stars above the foggy halo the streetlamps created for our fair city, so was the demon; and the demon was clearly pining for the bird woman, though she was due to arrive at any moment.

And when the bird woman arrived, preceded by the shrike, the Batelur, and the bird of light which set afire my cloak of darkness, I too pined for her. She encouraged feelings in my breast that I had always been too obtuse to express, though I cannot quite recall their exact nature, nor their general perimeters, save that they seemed to be directed not toward the bird woman in particular, but to godlike womanhood as an entity in itself, an entity I have been privileged to know as a series of individuals, but never to the extent that I could be confident I knew what I was really dealing with. This yearning in my breast to reach out and engage in a symbiotic relationship with Womankind shuddered and died with a frightening promptness when the bird woman kissed the demon on his hideous green cheek. The shrike flew in large circles about us, like an annoying gigantic bee. The Batelur picked vernom from the ground. And the bird of light floated above us all, like a celestial creature approving their disgusting display of affection. My misanthropy (though but a mood, it was no less intense for that) reached infinite proportions.

Readers who have followed my narrative thus far will doubtlessly breathe a hearty sigh of relief when I proclaim that our interaction was negligible, that our words before and after the consulting detective's instructions were few. In truth, I paid little attention to my duties as a chronicler of the consulting detective's deductive exploits, for so great was the sudden chasm in my heart that I simply did not have the attention span to dwell on anything but myself.

So it was that when the full moon had finally revealed itself and the pitch-blackness of the tentacles of the night had woven its way through the halo to settle upon little-frequented alleys and long-lonely streets, I found myself silently walking in step with the consulting detective. Both our pairs of hands were snug in our respective coat pockets, but my hands were balled in fists and my shoulders were slumped, whereas the shoulders of the consulting detective were thrown back in a manner befitting a detached professional man, confident that he would get the job done regardless of the circumstances. His extinguished pipe, which had not been refilled since we had teleported from the locker room, was still in his mouth, like some gnarled protuberance that had grown from his tongue and had shoved its way through the teeth and lips. A slight smile, which he occasionally resisted, caused the lines of his face to wrinkle and then to flatten, depending on how hard he was resisting. Finally he said, "Well, my friend, we've a long night ahead and have nothing else to do unless the ripper manifests himself, so why don't you tell me what the matter is?"

I grumbled something.

"What?"

"Nothing's the matter. Everything's cool."

The consulting detective chuckled. "Friend good doctor, surely you did not think you could fool me. I know when you are depressed, and usually I know exactly what the matter is."

"Then why did you ask me?" I inquired, though my tone was not quite as snappish as the words, printed nakedly on the page, imply.

"Simply to confirm my suspicions," said the consulting detective.

We walked in silence for several more minutes. I saw the bird of light flying above a tall building three blocks away, and at the rear edge of its expanse of light was the bird woman, effortlessly keeping pace with that wonderful creature as she raced across the rooftops, leaping from building to building. I heard the distinctive lovely call of the shrike, and for a moment I prayed the bird woman and her companions would come our way; but the bird of light suddenly turned and descended, and I could not see it for the buildings. For a moment I saw the tiny lithe figure of the bird woman silhouetted against the sky before it merged with the night. And suddenly I became afraid that a dream had ended, that some part of my soul had fled my being forever. When I tried to imagine the substance of the part of my soul in question, so that I might regain it, I discovered I had no inkling. Then it occurred to me that perhaps I had spent my entire existence without the part, for everything I had ever done or wanted to do seemed drab, dingy, unimaginitive; and it seemed that just beyond my perceptions was a world where everything was wonderful and glittering, and if I could only take those few important steps, I would enter that world and be eternally fulfilled. *What malarky*, I thought.

The consulting detective startled me out of my despondency by lightly tapping his pipe on a lamppost. The ashes floated through the fog to the cracked sidewalk. He tapped his pipe an unnecessary number of times, long after all the ashes had fled to escape that dreadful clammering; and he did it solely to annoy me, I am positive.

"Will you stop it?" I asked. "If the ripper is in the vicinity he will surely be alerted!"

"Will you lighten up?" asked the consulting detective. His tone was mock-scolding, given away by the mirthful grin on his stark features. I feared he would descend into zaniness at any moment. I have never discovered just what it is about my melancholy moods that invariably drives him to levity; as if the race did not have enough comedians.

Perhaps my mood would have been more befitting that of a fighting man of justice had not, before we had embarked upon this night's search, the gathering in the locker room been especially wearying upon my harried nerves. While mulling over the prospect of another horrendous inspection of a victim's corpse (which, I had to admit despite my faith in the consulting detective's abilities, was a distinct possibility), that damned tapeworm demanded, over and over again, its daily ration of lemon cookies. It's whine soured my very existence. And for some reason I will never fathom, the demon was of the opinion that the slender vermin was putting on a few excess pounds. "All he ever does is eat," said the demon. "It's getting so I'll have to reconstruct the entire simulacrum so he'll be able to move around." And the demon refused to feed the tapeworm, and the tapeworm refused to be quiet, despite my rather blunt demands that it accede to my wishes, and I thought I would go bonkers. When the tapeworm finally tired of demanding lemon cookies, we all mulled about in silence, contemplating the nature of the game to come, until the demon tired of the silence, as if it was somehow a personal affront, and said to the lawyer, "You know, I can understand your concern over Kitty, but I don't understand why you enjoy drilling her so much. She always tried to insert her finger up my asshole. I hate that. How can fags stand it?" He grinned maliciously and put his green hand on the lawyer's shoulder, thus insuring that the little man would not mistake his meaning.

Nevertheless, the little man mistook it. "How am I supposed to know?" he asked, his eyes bright with curiosity and confusion. "I always assumed they just gritted their teeth a lot and I've thought nothing else about it."

This exchange perturbed me due to its indiscreet content, all the more so since my sentimental feelings toward Kitty have continued unabated throughout the eons. And if the reader thinks I am going to answer any question concerning the particulars of my sexual relationship with Kitty, namely if she ever explored my anal orifice, then he should not only feel acute disappointment, but shame. I am most assuredly a gentleman.

However, my examination of the reasons for my irritability convinced me that I was inadvertently taking it out on my best friend. And dear reader, I was disappointed and ashamed of my personal shortcomings. I attempted to convey this to the consulting detective, but I succeeded only in shrugging, wringing my hands, and mumbling incoherently.

"I understand, friend good doctor," said the consulting detective softly, "but I fear it is I who must apologize."

"No, no; that's ridiculous."

"It is appropriate. I knew fully well the sincere depths of your disturbance, and I knew your foul mood was but an outgrowth of the more compassionate qualities of your nature. However, perhaps you will want to know that I spoke to Kitty this afternoon."

"Why, that's impossible!" I am quite certain that the sudden paleness of my complexion exceeded all the sudden palenesses of complexions visited upon me during a lifetime of unexpected shocks. My heart beat wildly, as if I had been struck by the mythical thunderbolt, the selfsame thunderbolt that had struck me when I first espied Kitty. The smothering blackness of the night, the enveloping fog, the mood of dankness and darkness permeating the lonely, forlorn East End—all receded into the background and became the vague flickerings of a long-ago dream as I basked in the blinding light which cascaded throughout my consciousness, seemingly setting aglow every pore, every internal vein and organ, every intangible substance of my spirit at the consulting detective's mention of her name. My passion for the perfect femininity of the bird woman, and for every woman I had loved since Kitty—an unholy number— became insignificant, incredibly insignificant; and all my eloquence, my every talent for putting together a glib series of words into a coherent narrative, became inadequate to communicate how very much, oh how so very much of my former love for this mysterious (if slightly mentally lame) woman returned. I wanted to see her. I wanted to touch her. My every emotion reached toward her, a spiritual figment before my eyes, though she was nowhere to be seen, though she had left my life eons ago.

The consulting detective smiled compassionately; he deduced, if he did not sense, my thoughts, but I believe his compassion was directed more toward himself than toward me, for no doubt he occasionally experienced identical sensations directed at a goddess in a parallel universe. "Friend good doctor, I am surprised at you. It is not impossible that I conversed with Kitty; it is quite the opposite."

"For one such as you, perhaps. But tell me, what remarkable deductions led you to her location? What trivial detail, what minor observation, overlooked by both myself and the universal op all these weeks, which when extrapolated upon by your keen logical facilities, led you to this extraordinary development in our adventure?"

Now it was time for the complexion of the consulting detective to alter its shading; instead of paling, it blushed a fine and endearing red. (Sometimes the consulting detective is as cute as a precocious eternal child.) "Alas, my rather unique abilities and my crystal-clear thinking in all manner of situations had absolutely nothing to do with my discovery of Kitty."

"Then you are saying...?"

"After my confrontation with the thinking machine, I decided to take a walk through the East End and ponder a few matters which, though unrelated to the case, were weighing heavily on my mind. Besides, I hadn't counted on your dope being so strong, and I was stoned out of my gourd. She boldly walked up to me and said in a sultry tone, 'Hello, sailor, new in town?'"

"That's Kitty, all right."

"Exactly. Never had I seen her so radiant. I tried to pry information from her, and all I could learn was that she had spent these past weeks in the East End, where not even the tenacity of the universal op could uncover her. I could not learn who she had been seeing, what she had been doing, or even if she had assumed a wholly different identity, which I suspected. She was too clever for me, and she parried my questions with a surfeit of double entendres. I impressed upon her the need for information, but to no avail. Something about her life in the East End has made her a happy godlike woman, despite all the pain and degradation running rampant around her."

I must confess, my joy was diluted by surprise; rarely have I heard the consulting detective speak so glowingly of womanhood, and to hear him speak glowingly of Kitty—who had never been held in high esteem by our cronies—was totally unexpected.

The consulting detective sighed. "There must be a million women like her, but I can't think of one."

"Where is she now?" I blurted.

He shook his head. "Alas, I do not know. I impressed upon her the need for caution and safety; I rattled on at great length about the ripper, but she pooh-poohed me. She laughed and entreated me not to be concerned on her behalf. Whatever happened, she believed, she would be alive and well."

"You don't know how happy I am that you're telling me this, but why don't you tell the lawyer? He's half out of his half-witted mind with worry."

"She asked me not to tell him. I'm afraid I wasn't supposed to tell you either. Whatever she is doing, apparently, requires continued privacy. And while she is happy, very, very happy, she believes that if we should possess any knowledge of her activities, she would be hindered. I can trust you to be discreet, but the lawyer is another matter. She admitted she is being cruel to him, but she assured me she would allay his fears and concern when the time was right."

I rubbed my chin and nodded thoughtfully. "The last thing the lawyer would grant her, whatever his state of mind, would be privacy."

"Exactly."

"Don't you fear for her?"

"Of course I do, friend good doctor," replied the consulting detective a trifly impatiently. "And I will continue to fear for her every second while the blasted ripper is roaming free. But what was I to do? I could have tried to force her to remain away from the East End; I could have sent her to a distant world or to a black room, but she is as powerful as I; anything I accomplished, she would undo, and my efforts would be for naught. In addition, and you might find this motive to be slightly suspect, I also thought it best that any interference in her life would ultimately be counter-productive. Not only for her, but for our entire race."

"Oh?"

"Think on it, my friend. Of all the wretched souls in this environ, of all the downtrodden spirits I've encountered while this disgusting district has been in existence, there has been only one truly happy individual. Our entire race is diseased; were but one or two particulars of our personalities altered, we would be as desolate as those we're trying to save. Only Kitty has found an answer. What that answer may be, whether or not it might prove to be applicable to our entire race—I cannot say. Nevertheless, she is happy. After all these eons of desperately searching, of disappointments, real and imagined, that we can barely conceive, she has found fulfillment. It may be something as simple as loving, as rejuvenating a pessimistic soul; it may be something as complicated as living a philosophy to its fullest, or as mere resignation and acceptance; whatever the case, it may be an answer which can help us lead people out of this emotional slum. Kitty has learned to live without hope; and what's more, she has learned how to set hopelessness aside so that she might live a rewarding life. Perhaps it is cruel of me to allow the lawyer to suffer needless pain, but after all, my decisions, like it or not, will affect many more people than the lawyer, at least for the foreseeable future."

I smiled. "We crusaders must think of the common good."

The consulting detective grimaced. "I think I liked you better when you were upset; you weren't so facetious."

We walked in silence for quite some time. We were each occupied with our private musings. Eventually I was seized by a glorious zest. I did not perceive the droplets of fog clinging to my sideburns, the hazy lonely streets in the distance (like the brightly illuminated exits to fanciful shimmering tunnels), or the regular tapping of our footsteps violating the silence with any particular intensity, as I perceived all these things and more during thrilling moments of danger and excitement; but everything seemed quite right, in its proper place, and my irritable mood had become an abstract. I could not imagine myself ever again becoming so dissatisfied with life, though some intellectual portion of myself that I chose to ignore knew full well that I was as human as anyone else and was therefore subject to moments of bad feelings and behavior. But how far away those moments seemed! Surely they would happen to someone masquerading in my flesh and spirit! Those moments were not part of my true character.

Perhaps now is the proper time to set down a few words concerning our patrol of the East End, as this information might be of some value to the reader as he sits enthralled by my upcoming telling of events. The demon and the lawyer patrolled the northeast sector; the man in the yellow suit, the northwest sector; the fat man and the gunsel, the southeast sector; and the universal op, the southwest sector. The bird woman and her companions were free agents, patrolling where they wished, as did the consulting detective and I. According to the consulting detective, this arrangement served two functions: a)each section of the East End would be guarded constantly, equally distributing whatever safety we could provide and b)the ripper could never be quite sure where the free agents would be at any given moment, though he might learn to avoid those assigned to a certain sector. Of course, so far this arrangement had not seemed to hinder the ripper's activities, but for all we knew, he could have planned on slaying more than one woman the night before and refrained from fear he would be apprehended. I personally did not see the wisdom in assigning the man in the yellow suit a task of importance, but the consulting detective assured me that the dreamer was capable of discovering the ripper, due to some peculiar affinity of their minds I did not particularly wish to understand; consequently I dropped the matter almost as soon as I brought it to the consulting detective's attention.

During the early hours of our patrol we did not see the demon, the lawyer, or the man in the yellow suit. Acting on a hunch (which was uncharacteristic of him), the consulting detective preferred exploring the southern portions of the East End, and whenever we ventured north, we soon returned south, occasionally blatantly backtracking.

Though I have written that the streets were lonely, I do not mean to say they were deserted. Usually there was at least one other individual somewhere in view, and in a few squares the streets were positively teeming. In the crowded squares the people reveled; our presence did not deter their revelry in the least, though they undoubtedly were aware of our mission. They jealously clung to their laughter, drink, love-making, and noise, as if the coming dawn was but a figment; and upon the few occasions we tried to question someone concerning a mysterious godlike man, we were rebuffed or ignored for our troubles. We found it much easier simply to send out vibrations in search of a mentally disturbed person, in the hopes that we would detect a flaw in the ripper's shields which would allow us to pinpoint the evil aura we were positive surrounded him. We utilized the same technique when we sighted an individual on a lonely street. These individuals did not choose to disguise their negativism; for what is the good of reveling, if it is beneficial for only a few hours? What is the use of drinking problems away, if the problems return in the morning accompanied by a massive hangover? And why cure a hangover when it distracts you from more depressing affairs? No, for these sullen individuals it was better to mope in private, to walk about alone and afraid, in the certain knowledge that no godlike man and godlike woman was safe so long as the ripper prowled. The lonely individuals would not allow us to come close to them, either speeding or slowing their pace, depending on what the situation called for, unless they were sitting or leaning against a wall (and then they fixed their eyes to the sidewalk until we passed). It was as if our very existence was an invasion of their privacy. Like all godlike men and women, these pathetic creatures had distinct identities, accentuated by gaudy or outrageous dress, or by uncommon beauty or ugliness, or by some object carried about, or by some combination of these factors. But I cannot recall seeing any particular individual, they have blended so much in my mind. They all possessed the same darkness and bleakness of soul, and this was the first thing I noticed about them. After awhile I ceased to think of them as individuals, as I would cease to think of a stream of patients as individuals, regardless of my bedside manner, during a plague.

Consequently, when the consulting detective and I saw the fat man lumbering down the street, his ice-cream suit nearly glowing with its pristineness, I was overjoyed. Even if the fat man had not been instantly recognizable, of such a distinct appearance, I would have known that he was not a typical resident of the East End from the bounciness of his gait, which thanks to his considerable poundage resembled the personification of an earthquake rejoicing in its rumbling and shaking. His belly thudded in all directions like a jell caught in the spell of rock music. He jerked his massive arms back and forth, up and down, in a rhythm as close to his gait as his mass would allow; and I feared he would rub the fabric of his suit to shreds. As we neared him, I noticed his lips were pursed; I detected his whistling only after making adjustments to my hearing, which I promptly returned to normal. If his broad grin was an accurate indication, he was as overjoyed as I. "My friends," he whispered with a hearty tone, "how fares the search?"

"We've discovered no indication of the ripper," said the consulting detective. "Have you?"

"Alas, no. My gunsel, who is lurking about in the shadows surrounding us, has frightened near to death twenty godlike men and twelve godlike women, and they too have provided no clues. I've spent my spare time browbeating a person here and there, trying to convince them to abandon their heinous negativism, but unfortunately I've not the time nor the opportunity to give the task my undivided attention. The people like it here. That's all they like, the poor fools!" He smiled grimly, inhaled until he was in danger of sucking in all the air in the district, and glanced about, his hands resting on his mountainous chest. "But by gad, it's a marvelous night for a stroll! The air, as dank as it is, invigorates these old bones. The city, as lost as it is, excites me anew with every observation. There's something in the air. Don't you feel it?"

This time the consulting detective's smile was of an entirely different order. "There's something in your breast. And *that* I feel."

"Then you too?" asked the fat man with an incredulous expression manifesting itself upon his bulbous features.

"Not I. But the study of godlike nature is every bit as important as the study of the prosaic clues of crimes. I know what you are feeling, just by looking at you; and I say without hesitation I envy you."

"Wait a minute, fellas!" I said. "What are you talking about?"

It was my turn to be the recipient of an enigmatic smile of the consulting detective. "Friend good doctor, I'm surprised at you. I would have thought that you, of all people, would have been the first to guess exactly what is on the fat man's mind."

"The same thing's always on his mind. I want to know what's in his breast."

"You old romantic simpleton," said the fat man without

rancor as he put his hand on my shoulder, "I'm in love!"

"What? You?" I exclaimed.

"Yes, me. And I tell you, I had completely forgotten how it felt. It's wonderful, absolutely wonderful, though at times I feel I've gone mad. It happened without warning; and I fought it from the beginning. But I was aware all my struggles would be in vain—and I can struggle mightily—so I decided to accept it. That woman made me love her despite my better judgment; she shattered the cold barriers of my heart. For all those eons I believed I was above—or beyond—such emotions; and now, to love, to finally love! I'm positively inarticulate. I'm positively flabbergasted."

I grinned maliciously; I do not know why; perhaps I too envied him. "I trust she has stamina."

"She will require it," replied the fat man, as if he did not notice my bad intentions. "I've sent the cheerleaders to their old boy friends and their glossies of the mature eternal child. My lady will henceforth be the sole object of my lust until our inevitable mutual tragedy. I fear, as I've never feared before, the pain I will suffer when we ultimately go our separate ways. But the pain is the price you pay, and even then it is a bargain. For unlike the souls in the East End, I will always know I'm alive. We must convince these people; I will never require convincing."

Before we could continue our conversation (I confess my curiosity to know just what kind of woman had aroused such blessed irrational fervor in the fat man was well nigh overwhelming), the consulting detective espied the warm glow of the bird of light descending from untold heights in the atmosphere. His smile too descended—into an ugly grimace that caused him to appear haggard and lost. The peculiar shadows created by the dim streetlamps and the bird of light and the positioning of his deerstalker cap made the wrinkles of his face appear like huge crevices, wounds of blackness that not all the light of a fiery sun could heal. His grip on his pipestem tightened until his knuckles were as pale as his complexion. The consulting detective sent out vibrations meant to relay to him the outline of every object in the immediate vicinity. Such was their intensity that just standing near them weakened and dizzied me. Only the analytical and disciplined mind of the consulting detective could have sorted out so much information at once. I knew that he was immediately discarding all information concerning innocents in the environs, the decor of shabby apartments, the trash in the streets; he was searching for the ripper. However, he could not keep up the pace for long. Despite our race's immense powers, our brains can operate at maximum efficiency for a limited length of time. The consulting detective staggered as I held his arm to support him. He cursed. "Nothing, nothing! Friend fat man, tell the gunsel to be on his guard and redouble his efforts."

"It is already done," said the fat man.

"Good. Then follow me!" And though he was still weakened by the mental exertion, the consulting detective ran at top natural speed, utilizing only a fraction of his powers, so that the ripper might not detect him. The bird of light was now hidden by the buildings, the tops of which glowed as if endangered by a mystical fire from another plane; and the dim streetlamps became totally ineffective; comparatively speaking, the fat man and I had been plunged into darkness. We complied with the consulting detective's instructions as soon as our eyes adjusted; the fat man's pace, for obvious reasons, was considerably slower than mine. I, myself, was propelled as if by unseen forces; and though I despaired of catching up with my friend, I did so quickly; my heart and lungs were frantically overworked, and I felt the heated redness of my face like a rag soaked in boiling water adhering to my skin, yet I was very satisfied with myself, the satisfaction nearly assuaging my anxiety over what we would discover. I say "my anxiety," I imply uncertitude, but I felt the truth in my marrow long before we made that fateful turn; I knew what we would find. I was only one step behind the consulting detective when we turned and stopped as one.

And we saw the bird of light paused above the neck of a singular streetlamp in a courtyard. The buildings to either side, though not quite thirty meters each from the streetlamp, seemed like dim creatures with many black eyes stoically watching from another world, or, less poetically, as if their actual distance could be measured only in kilometers. I felt like I had just emerged from a long, harrowing journey in a tunnel, only to learn that the expanse I had eagerly sought had greeted me with a nauseating horror.

For at the base of the streetlamp lay yet another victim.

I stood stunned as the consulting detective slowly walked, as stiff as a zombie, toward the victim. Though he was attired in his cape-backed overcoat, as always, I did not have to see his naked back to know that the muscles about his shoulders and surrounding his spine were screwed tight as a result of his attempts to remain calm. Fully half a second lapsed between his steps, though as the reader might have expected, the periods seemed much longer. His footsteps were like the footsteps of death itself. Soon I followed, walking more quickly. Halfway across the courtyard, I was able to enumerate the particulars of the scene.

The victim lay in a heap, her tattered, foul black clothes resting on her corpse like a blanket. Red-and-white flowers were pinned in her black coat; and flowers, beautiful flowers of a species I had never before seen (not unlike roses) lay strewn about her, some immersed in coagulated blood from the terrible gash in her throat. Blood had flowed throughout the cobbles of the courtyard in her general vicinity. From what I could see of it, she had an altogether pleasant face, which had not been contorted in the least by the strictures of death. I could not recall having seen her before; I surely would have remembered the golden curly locks of her blonde hair and the dimple in her chin. The greater portion of her face, however, was concealed by the shrike, perched on her nose and tearing away an eyelid with its beak.

The shrike had wallowed in her blood; its black head was capped with a shining red under the glistening of light of the remarkable creature above it. It paused in its task to sound a loud call, and before the consulting detective or I could prevent it, jerked its head at the woman's face in a spastic motion and tore the eyelid away, taking with it a portion of skin surrounding the eye. The consulting detective barked something as we approached, though I think he was much less indignant over the matter than I; but it was the snapping of delicate fingers, once, that arrested the shrike's attention.

To our right stood the bird woman with the Batelur resting on her forearm. She seemed to sneer, not in contempt but in annoyance, and the shrike flew rapidly in the air, taking the eyelid with it, until alighting on the dull golden gutter at the roof of one of those dim buildings.

My stomach rumbled in all manner of ways as I stared at the victim's torn and punctured eye. Still her face did not seem disturbed by death. As I knelt, I saw the legs of the consulting detective from the corner of my right eye, then the bare legs of the bird woman before me, beside the base of the streetlamp; and I heard the wheezing approach of the fat man.

The victim's right hand lay on her ample chest; her left arm was bent under her torso, the hand at the lower spine. She wore a silk scarf about her neck, and the incision was just below it; the initial incision had been made on the left, six centimeters below the angle of the jaw. The antimatter knife had irrevocably cut the vessels on the left side, completely severed the windpipe (thus preventing her from calling out for aid), and terminated approximately three centimeters below the angle of the right jaw, without severing the vessels on that side. She had probably bled to death just as the bird of light had discovered her; most of the blood had spurted through the partial severance of the left carotid artery. Except for one significant item, there were no noteworthy bruises or cuts or anything out of the ordinary, other than those on the neck, which could be attributed to the ripper.

I stood and reported to the consulting detective, deliberately omitting the significant item. The consulting detective had by this time regained his resolute calm, and he listened to my report in the general manner of a godlike man daring me to arouse his interest (though precisely the opposite was true). "Very good, friend good doctor," he said briskly.

"Where are the others?" I asked. "Surely they must be informed."

"They have been, but I instructed them to remain on the job, in the hopes they might sight the odious villain." He lit his pipe with a thought, put his free hand behind his back, and turned away from the victim, still facing the three of us, as if he too did not want to be reminded of the unfortunate, unknown woman we had failed so miserably. "In my opinion, there was no struggle, which would account for the lack of bruises. Also, she had been slain while on her knees or lying on her stomach. The position of her left arm clearly indicates that."

"Then the ripper somehow induced her," said the fat man.

"Exactly," said the consulting detective.

I cleared my throat.

The consulting detective, the fat man, and the bird woman all raised their eyebrows at once. Even the Batelur perched on her wrist seemed to perk up.

"There is one more thing," I said. "I withheld it due to the presence of . . ." I pointed to the bird woman. "It's unseemly to speak of such matters in the company of ladies." I stammered a few incoherent phrases.

The consulting detective was a mite peeved. "Out with it, man! This is no time for mere social protocol."

I cleared my throat again. "Well, while sending out vibrations in search of bruises and the like, I noticed that beneath her skirt, the victim's black panties were folded halfway down the buttocks, in a manner which seemed to me would be most uncomfortable." I feared I was blushing mightily. "And so I inspected further and consequently discovered . . ." For the third time I cleared my throat. "I discovered an inordinate amount of semen in the rectum."

The consulting detective exhaled and removed his pipe from his mouth; he appeared in danger of deflating. The bird woman looked at me in a puzzled fashion, as if she had difficulty understanding my reluctance to speak forthrightly. The fat man frowned a curious frown of approval; he nodded, saying, "He fucked her in the ass, right?"

"Uh, right."

"That would certainly explain it," said the consulting detective.

"My educated guess is that he ejaculated during or immediately after he cut her throat. He pulled her head up by yanking on her scarf."

The fat man said, "He probably let her pee in his face so he could see where it was coming from."

"Somehow he doesn't impress me as the type," said the consulting detective.

Before we could elucidate further upon our speculations, we received a telepathic communication from the universal op. He was engaged in mortal combat with the ripper himself!

The consulting detective immediately informed the fat man to remain behind to guard the body of the victim, even as his atoms were beginning to break up. Then, his orders delivered, his atoms sped to the site indicated by the universal op, followed by those of myself and the bird woman. Doubtless the shrike and the Batelur and the bird of light followed by their own means. I never discovered the means of the bird of light, though I have often wondered, now that I have had the leisure to reflect upon the matter. But at the time, caught up in the flurry of events, I did not pause to wonder how it could have arrived upon the site before my atoms collected themselves. Yet there it was, hovering neutrally over the square, as I formed three steps behind and slightly to the left of the consulting detective. There was too much other meaningful information to assimilate at once.

I wondered, crazily, why the consulting detective did not spring into action at once; it was certainly uncharacteristic of him to stand amazed. So close had I been to him throughout the eons that I knew immediately he was shocked immobile, shocked to the core of his righteous being, by the tableau before him. I confess to an impertinent amount of impatience with him, and with the bird woman beside me; I depended upon him (and would have depended upon her) for guidance in all melodramatic situations, and I felt vaguely betrayed that I had not been greeted with orders upon my formation. Then I too began to assimilate the horrible tableau, and not in my thousand most frightening nightmares could I have imagined such an array of images guaranteed to rip asunder the carefully sewn fabric of my existence.

The square, so much like the one we had just exited, save that instead of apartment buildings it was bordered by warehouses storing materials of some importance to the denizens of the East End, was an unlikely location for such a tableau. It had three entrances; it was frequented regularly, as evidenced by the debris (candy wrappers, cigarette butts, and empty beer cans) strewn about the cobblestones. I heard the distant bass tones of a recorded song by the mature eternal child emanating from a club on an adjacent block. Yet, except for the two bodies lying in the center of the square, it was deserted.

One body belonged to the universal op. Some inner sixth sense originating in my subconscious, perhaps born of the need for self-protection from grief and pain, prevented me from recognizing the second body immediately, though in retrospect it is amazing that my entire range of perception did not swirl about the horrific corpse. At first I feared the universal op was dead, as I vaguely perceived the second body to be deceased, but a muffled groan allayed my fears—fears which arose unbidden, fully grown, paralyzing my very soul, when the consulting detective, finally stalking toward the tableau, uttered an expletive of such cruel foulness that I refuse to record it, knowing that even the demon and the fat man would be stunned to read it memorialized in print. And only then did I belatedly recognize the corpse. I felt myself pale and stagger; and a rush of heat, wholly out of place considering the circumstances, pervaded my system as the bird woman held my arm and placed her other palm in the small of my back to support me. The shrike, singing joyfully, sped past the consulting detective as that worthy neared the site; it landed near the universal op, its intentions rather plain, and remained until my friend loomed above it and frightened it away. It alighted next to the Batelur on the roof of a warehouse.

My legs moved me to the corpse as the consulting detective knelt and stared at the smooth mug of the universal op. I did not feel as if I, myself, was responsible for the progression; and I resented the bird woman, momentarily kicking her altar from beneath her, for guiding me so surely to the corpse. For this fourth victim was none other than the woman who has been highly and lowly alluded to in this chronicle, though circumstances had prevented her from taking the stage herself, the woman who had been the light of my life even when she had not been a part of it for eons, even when I had not thought of her, had put her out of my mind as if she had not existed. It was none other than Kitty lying in a bloody heap on the cobblestones—none other than Kitty! It was unthinkable, hideously unthinkable, and yet as I stared at her mutilated face, searching for a nose I did not recognize, eyes of another color, breasts shaped differently, a facial structure I had not previously encountered—in short, searching for an indication that I was mistaken—the reality of it gripped me and would not set me free.

A part of my mind seemed displaced from itself, though by far the greater part of me was numbed by the sentimental emotions I have learned invariably arise in such instances. I stared at those lovely, open red lips, I felt remorse that they would never touch another again, I prayed to whatever gods godlike man prays to that some portion of my soul would touch the warm light fleeing her mortal shell forever, I was indignant, consumed by hatred, that the mind of a man could conceive of heaping such atrocities upon her person, I was wasted, erased, devoid of true feeling and personality, as if I had been born to experience only the overwhelming numbness and nothing else; and yet my instincts would not permit me to savor totally my grief, for I watched from the corner of my eye as the consulting detective touched the area where the forehead of the universal op should have been. This was purely a perfunctory gesture, so that the recovering universal op would be aware the consulting detective was reading his mind. There simply was insufficient time for social niceties to run their course.

As soon as the universal op was able to support himself on a palm and a forearm—he was recovering rapidly, I must say—the consulting detective stood and unleased a chorus of vibrations of such staggering intensity that even in my grief-stricken stupor I was stunned. When he had cast out similar vibrations earlier in the evening's proceedings, he had actually been holding back! Perhaps he had been concealing his true power from the ripper, but since the ripper seemed quite capable of disguising himself in any eventuality, I suspect that it was the consulting detective's anger and indignation which were responsible for his unadulterated power. The vibrations lasted briefly, less than a few seconds, but apparently they were more than adequate, the ripper perhaps being caught off guard, for the consulting detective suddenly spun on his heel and ran toward an exit to the square which would take him through several alleys between the warehouses. I barely caught a telepathic direction to the bird woman to retain both the universal op and myself, since we were in no condition to aid him. The bird woman nodded; perhaps she too was reluctant to remain behind, but this was not the proper time to argue. I strenuously composed myself, shaking free of the bird woman's warm grasp, and took a few dizzy steps toward the universal op, who was struggling to stand, perhaps a bit prematurely. He shook his head as he rubbed the back of his neck. I was grateful that, for the moment, I would have something to do which would preoccupy a portion of my mind, so I would not have to look at my beloved Kitty.

I felt very peculiar as I grasped the universal op's face between my thumb and forefinger and turned it to my eyes. I wondered anew at how he was able to see and hear, and it strained my numbed brain to keep in mind that he definitely could see me despite all the evidence to the contrary. "Don't speak." (Somehow I knew he wanted to speak.) "Let me look at you."

But he would have none of it. Like a beast of prey, he preferred to nurse whatever wounds he had taken in privacy. He pulled himself away and turned his smooth mug toward the corpse of the woman the consulting detective had enlisted him to uncover and protect. He put his hands in his trouser pockets and, with that eerie muffled voice, which echoed from the warehouses until I could not be sure that it originated from his person, said, "I walked through this square every fifteen minutes. When the consulting detective informed me that a third victim had been discovered, I didn't see the need for continuing the patrol, taking as I did the ripper's *modus operandi* into consideration. But the consulting detective insisted, and I wish he hadn't been so damn right."

"Yes, it sometimes annoys me too," I said in a hoarse voice.

"Because now I feel I haven't done my job properly, though I know I've done everything I could do. Anyway, I continued my patrol, thinking I would take a rest and smoke a cigar when I came to this square. I immediately sensed something was wrong—the square was totally dark; I detected no light anywhere. Well, you don't last long in the shamus biz unless you keep your cool, so I pretended to be unaware. I created a cigar and shuffled toward the center of the square. I had this chilly feeling around my spine; I knew the ripper was somewhere. Then I detected a slippery liquid under my shoes when my right toes slid over a cobblestone; I didn't have to inspect the ground to know that, say within the last ten minutes, the ripper had discovered, manipulated, killed, and mutilated another victim. I *felt* his presence, but I couldn't detect him. Well, though I was near the corpse, as far as he was concerned I was only in imminent danger of discovering it; perhaps I hadn't actually done so. I decided to pretend everything was copasetic and I created a thick match half a meter long to light my cigar and to provide me with an extra edge to detect the ripper. A match had to be that big if I was going to take a good look around, but I guess the ripper was too smart for that. As soon as I lit the match, he materialized from *somewhere*, which accomplished my ultimate goal anyway. Only I think things would have gone a lot better for me if he had hit me from the front where I might have defended myself rather than from the behind. We struggled, but I was at a disadvantage. I was lucky to inform the consulting detective before I passed out. I want to thank you, though, for your promptness."

We left unsaid what we all knew: the ripper would have gladly violated his *modus operandi* for the sake of escape. I asked, "Did you get an indication of his general appearance?"

"That and that only. The ripper is approximately one and one half meters tall, of a middle-aged persona, with brown hair and a small dark moustache, with black clothing and a black cutaway coat. He carries with him a parcel twenty centimeters long and ten centimeters wide. He reeks not of evil, but of amorality; I wouldn't tell the man in the yellow suit that because he's the kind of guy who thinks one similarity to his theories would automatically prove the rest of them."

"You might find the ripper amoral, but to me he's hideously evil," I said as I watched the bird woman conjure a blanket with which she covered Kitty. I cannot bear to record here the particulars of the wounds on her body, especially those on the face; if I should do so, then I would forever think of Kitty as a maimed corpse, and not as a whole living person who once loved me. Usually victims of murders are mere excuses to furnish motivations for the chase, but upon occasion the victims are far more important than that, for permutations of life are invariably lost; and I cannot help but think what might have happened if I had met Kitty, oh, a hundred years hence. We might have shared only a dinner and a few drinks, but now in my heart of hearts I pray we might have shared something more, that I might have finally formed the union I have always been searching for, the union which would have rendered previous ones immaterial— you know, the union romantics always dream of, but which the realities of the godlike condition and the nagging thoughts that valuable experience is being denied preclude. I will state for the record, and for my peace of mind, that there was no trace of semen lodged in her myriad orifices. At least the ripper had granted me that small favor, perhaps to make amends for slicing off a portion of her right ear.

My inspection had not been concluded for three minutes when the silence which now seemed organic with the surreal glow of the bird of light hovering overhead was broken by the sound of loud footsteps echoing throughout the warehouses, with a rhythm I immediately recognized as that of the consulting detective. I had been so lost in my grief that I had not given a thought to his danger! At once I mentally chastised myself for my self-absorption, but I fear it was derived from my desire to inflict pain upon my spirit rather than a genuine concern for my friend the consulting detective.

We turned to face the entrance to the square as the volume of his footsteps heralded his imminent attendance. Upon his emergence he seemed remarkably solitary and alone, though if that aspect of his demeanor was the result of his failure at the chase or of Kitty's demise, I do not know; in respect to matters such as these, he is far less blunt than the universal op. His hands were stuffed in his cape-backed overcoat, and as he walked toward us with a purposeful stride (for no apparent reason), I detected the twitching of muscles of both arms, manifesting itself with involuntary jerking of said arms, as if his hands remained in the pockets only through a supreme effort of will. His pipe was nowhere to be seen; I guessed (correctly) that upon the commencement of the chase he teleported it to our apartment so it would not sustain damage. He stopped short of Kitty's corpse, and he stared at the blanket shielding her from the elements, and he nodded, making some private philosophical observation. He looked at the universal op, whose featureless face seemed to return his stare just as boldly. He said, "Thank you for providing me with the information I required so freely."

"Think nothing of it."

The consulting detective then returned his gaze to Kitty. I think he would have stared at her until dawn if I hadn't said, "Well, man, tell us! What happened?"

The consulting detective spoke slowly, in a voice that could accurately be described as that of a dead godlike man. "You know my methods, friend good doctor: I put myself in the godlike man's place, and having first gauged his intelligence, I try to imagine how I should myself have proceeded under the same circumstances. In this case the matter was simplified by the ripper's intelligence being quite first-rate, so that it was unnecessary to make any allowance for the personal equation, as the astronomers have dubbed it. Since I had detected no breakdown in the ripper's shields, I had only to pinpoint which of the three exits from the square he would have taken. Since the other two led to busy streets and establishments, since the ripper flaunts his singularity and therefore wouldn't conceal himself in a crowd, he took the exit leading to the alleyways. The ripper's record thus far has demonstrated his uncanny familiarity with the East End, so I took those routes which would demonstrate such a familiarity. It all sounds like guesswork, but when faced with a certain number of directions to take, after weighing the advantages and disadvantages of each, usually one presents itself as an obvious route, and the others seem like ridiculous choices in retrospect. I knew I was on the right track when I heard a faucet pouring water, and arrived just in time to see the blood-stained fluid swirling about the drain. The sink was well set back from the street, in a tiny close, thus confirming my appraisal of the ripper's geographic skills. Unfortunately, from there I lost all trace of him, and now I have returned here, angered and defeated."

"What of the lawyer? Surely someone should inform him, though I sincerely hope it will not be I."

"He will arrive in a moment," said the consulting detective.

And he did, followed by the demon, the fat man, and the man in the yellow suit. They had teleported to the site. I stared at them as they stared at the corpse under the blanket, and as I saw their faces mask their grief and shock, I felt anew the hideous upheaval in my life. I felt like an invisible creature was crushing my chest in an unbreakable vise, and I felt the beginnings of hot tears sting my eyes. The man in the yellow suit had not known Kitty; but he saw and knew our grief, and he could grieve for our loss. He wisely kept his silence, standing awkwardly away from the body of our group; his eyes betrayed confusion and pity. The demon was like a mask; his green complexion paled only slightly. I think he wanted the bird woman to comfort him, but as she did not move toward him, keeping her eyes on the lawyer, he stood alone, breathing heavily, attempting to accept the evidence of the foul deed. The fat man too felt awkwardness; he only glanced at the corpse before allowing his eyelids to shield him from the sight. His face was devoid of all expression, as if the event had numbed his sensory apparatus. More so than the rest of us (with the exception of the universal op, who was a law unto himself), he was the type to conceal all sorrow, as if to convince the universe that he could not experience it.

The lawyer tottered toward the corpse and fell to his knees near its head as if some heartless soul had knocked him over. He looked at the consulting detective and me with plaintive, tearful eyes, his expression seeming to ask if what appeared to be undoubtedly true was really transpiring. I nodded, the consulting detective looked away from him, and he lifted the blanket. I fear that not all my descriptive abilities would suffice to communicate to the reader the contortions of the succession of shock, love, grief, and pain manifesting themselves on his face. He let fall the blanket and covered his face with his hands, sobbing convulsively.

At last I found the personal strength to feel pity for one other than myself. I wished with all my crippled spirit that I could do something to comfort the lawyer there, beneath the dark sky and the bird of light, surrounded by the stoic warehouses in the East End. But it was the task of another to comfort the lawyer. The bird woman walked like silence and knelt beside him. Her strong hands gripped his shoulders and pulled him toward her, his wet face eventually resting in the cradle of her shoulder. She caressed his hair with her right hand. At first he resisted her embrace, as if he was belatedly attempting to contain his emotions; however, after approximately a minute he gave in, returned her embrace, and wailed like a mournful ghost.

I wanted to look away, to find something else to occupy my attention, it finally having occurred to me that his grief (and that of the others) was no less deep and personal than mine. Relief was not forthcoming until the fat man felt the time had arrived to get back to business, and he took the consulting detective aside and whispered, "I sent the body of the third victim to limbo, where it will remain undisturbed until we can perform a more complete inspection."

The consulting detective nodded. I discovered that, save for the lawyer and the bird woman, we had formed a circle, possibly the result of a subconscious urge to afford the lawyer a semblance of privacy. The consulting detective said, "Our current situation is rather dubious, to say the least. This hurts my pride, my friends. It is a petty feeling, no doubt, but it hurts my pride. It becomes a personal matter now."

"Do you mean it wasn't personal before?" asked the man in the yellow suit, still lost in his eternal state of confusion.

"When we lost Kitty, we lost more than someone who was a friend to some of us. We lost the potentiality for a solution. An answer had been arrived at here in the East End, but the cosmic forces have, in their mirth, seen fit to play another prank on us." He paused. "I fear that I have lost the one individual I might have needed most in the years to come."

My eyebrows rose; I felt a twinge of jealousy. I knew Kitty had impressed the consulting detective, but I had not realized the depth of the impression. As the years passed, he became healthier and healthier, regardless of his personal tragedies.

"What are we going to do now?" asked the demon.

"We will take Kitty to your castle, mourn her properly, and then go home."

"Wait, what about the ripper?" demanded the universal op. For the first time I saw him register something like genuine indignation. "He could be prowling the streets right now, killing someone else."

The consulting detective looked above our heads, at the warehouses and through the warehouses, as if the East End and its people had suddenly arisen in plain view before him. His lower lip curled like that of a rabid dog as he considered the possibility. "Let him," he said at last. "Let him kill them all!"

8. *An account from the good doctor's notebooks:*

Somehow it was singularly appropriate that we mourned Kitty in the demon's locker room where she had been the object of so many raunchous discussions (though I hasten to add, without my participation). Even the lawyer nodded his assent at the demon's suggestion, perhaps due to the fact that he had spent an infinitely greater amount of time in the locker room discussing her finer qualities than he did actually plummeting them. So it transpired that at dawn, when the yellow sun was peeking over the horizon, in its hesitancy to ascertain any radical alterations on the landscape which might have occurred in the darkness, we had already sat in the locker room, lost in our collective despondent silence, for several hours. We had repaired the external damage to Kitty's body; there was not even a scar on her face, nor a missing portion of her right ear. We had clothed her in the gaudiest red dress in her ex-apartment, restored the color to her face via the liberal application of makeup, and encased her in a glass casket resting on a bench. The lawyer had placed a lily in her hands folded beneath her bosoms. The bird woman illustrated quite plainly to me, if to no one else, that if she should ever become domesticated, she would be extraordinary in fulfilling her homemaking obligations, particularly those in relation to the general decor. For she created an astounding array of exotic flowers, many with petals and stems of colors I had never before seen, and she placed them at strategic points about the locker room, stifling the primitive masculine atmosphere in a manner conducive to the more serious matters on hand.

On the whole, we mourned in silence, each of us with memories of Kitty replaying them in our mind, perhaps vainly trying to convince ourselves that so long as she lived in our memories, she would be alive, in some small way, forever. In retrospect, the futility of such a way of thinking depresses me. What is past is gone for all eternity, regardless of how nobly the mind deludes itself. Time is a crook; it steals the good with the bad, and soon there will come an evening when I will peruse these memoirs and discover that all which remains of Kitty is what is written here. She will have left merely a legacy of words. True, I have my memories, but a godlike man is the sum and total of what he is now, not of what he has done or who he has touched. There, in the locker room, for a long while, my sole thought was that once I had touched and felt the life of a person I could never touch again. She almost looked alive in her glass casket, surrounded by the flowers of the bird woman, with a single lily stuck between the stiff fingers of her overlapped hands. Sometimes I stared at her with such intensity that I expected her to twitch, but of course, I was deluding myself with memories again.

The only emotion the universal op gave slight indications of was boredom. Even if he had known Kitty, or had felt any sort of compassion for her predicament prior to her disappearance, it would have been of the most intellectual sort, of a man fulfilling his obligation to his client and little more. Perhaps, even now, I am being too harsh on him, because he did have his problems; but I cannot help but think that those who did not know Kitty had faced a greater loss than mine, a loss of which they were unaware. Once having found the bench most suitable to his buttocks, the universal op did not move; he leaned forward, his legs spread apart, his elbows resting on his knees and his hands clasped, his smooth mug staring straight ahead, at and through Kitty's casket. He resembled a terrible mannequin in a department store; and if I had been in the mood, I might have put a dirty red wig and plastic features on his head just for the sheer yoks of it.

The man in the yellow suit studied us as if he could not understand why we were dwelling on our pity with such tenacity. Perhaps some quirk in his temperament prevented him from taking disasters to heart. But that is only the crudest speculation; the fact remains he studied each of us, eyeing us quizically, while upon his face a curious expression of innocence provided us with the only cue to his innermost thoughts. Once he scowled at the consulting detective, who stood with his back to the casket and his hand supporting him as he leaned beside a table, where he could watch the coming sun; and when the consulting detective felt the quizzical vibrations emanating from a mysterious source behind his back, he turned in annoyance, whereupon the man in the yellow suit looked to the floor and pretended there lay his only interest. Similar incidents, with each one having a different object, occurred throughout the mourning period. However, the man in the yellow suit did not stare at the simulacrum, containing the demon's tapeworm, but he could hardly be blamed for overlooking that particular object.

The sun had been in the sky for two hours when we received a package, teleported from a location we could not ascertain, upon Kitty's casket. My eyes widened in shock and surprise, for I knew, as we all knew, who had sent that little cardboard box wrapped in black paper and a red ribbon. At once I sprang from my bench and hastened toward the package; but the consulting detective was there first, and his lanky outstretched arm, with its fingertips at my chest, prevented me from grabbing it.

"Wait!" he demanded. "I'll open it mentally."

I backed up, unknowingly beside the demon's simulacrum, and watched as the ribbon untied itself and the black paper folded away. Upon the box was a note. The consulting detective scowled and commanded it to float in front of his face. He read aloud:

> *I was not coddling, fellows, when I gave you the tip. Double event this time. Do you think I'll become a star? Here's a present which might help you complete your ritual.*
>
> *the ripper*

The consulting detective obviously had not wanted us to touch the package for fear that a valuable clue might be damaged. I suspect that his extraordinary mind had deduced what awaited us upon the opening of the box, for all accepted procedure was violated when he caused the note to burn into ashes. The fat man paled, even the universal op displayed signs of trepidation; I suspect they too knew what I should have guessed. For when the consulting detective caused the box to disintegrate, without harming the contents, I saw lying upon Kitty's casket the portion of her right ear that the ripper had sliced off after he had slain her.

For several moments we stood in silence. Then I said, "Egads! What kind of barbarian would perpetuate such mindless violence?"

Perhaps I would have received an answer to my query from an acceptable source, but of course I already knew the answer. And my knowledge was made quite plain to me when the tapeworm emerged from the simulacrum's anus, looked around, crawled up the construction, and said in my ear, "Where's my lemon cookie?"

Without the slightest reflection of the matter, I created a ball peen hammer and smashed the tapeworm's head against the simulacrum. Green guts seemed to spray the locker room, but most of them merely sprayed my clothing. The tapeworm dropped to the floor, still hanging from the anus, and landed with a splat.

"Aw, come on," said the demon, "was that really necessary?"

The lawyer, who had been so lost in grief that I feared nothing could elicit a response from him, snickered, turned his face away from the proceedings, and covered his mouth.

I did not have the opportunity to learn the reaction of the others to my mindless display of violence, for I staggered to a bench where I sat, staring at the green guts dripping from the ball peen hammer I had created, until the consulting detective put his hand on my shoulder and informed me it was time for us to go home.

CHAPTER FIVE

1. *An account from the good doctor's notebooks:*

At our apartment, I was quickly between the sheets, for I was weary and depressed after my night of adventure. The consulting detective was a man, however, who, when he had an unsolved problem on his mind, would go for days, and even for a week, without rest, turning it over, rearranging the facts, looking at it from every point of view until he had either fathomed it or convinced himself that his data were insufficient. Though we were not to interview suspects today, so that we might rest, it was soon evident to me that he was now preparing for an all-day sitting. He took off his coat and waistcoat, put on a large blue dressing-gown, and then wandered about the apartment collecting pillows from his bed and cushions from the sofa and armchairs. With these he constructed a sort of divan, upon which he perched himself cross-legged, with an ounce of shag tobacco and a box of matches laid out in front of him. In the dim light peeking through the shades I saw him sitting there, an old briar pipe between his lips, his eyes fixed vacantly upon the corner of the ceiling, the blue smoke curling up from him, silent, motionless, with the light shining on his strong-set aquiline features. So he sat as I dropped off to sleep, and so he sat when a sudden cry from my lips caused me to wake up several hours later. The pipe was still between his lips, the smoke still curled upward, and the living room was full of a dense tobacco haze, but nothing remained of the heap of shag.

I put on my bathrobe and stumbled into the living room. The consulting detective did not look at me as he said, "Did you have a nightmare, my good friend?"

I sat down. "Yes. Obviously, I dreamed of Kitty. Her spirit was wandering the East End. I followed her and tried to touch her, and when she turned to face me, I saw the damage the ripper had done to her face. She had been so beautiful, so beautiful."

The consulting detective closed his eyes. "Of all ghosts, the ghosts of our old lovers are the worst."

I nodded silently in reply. Outside, the equinoctial gales had set in with exceptional violence. All afternoon the wind screamed and the rain beat against the windows, so that even here in the heart of the great city we were forced to raise our minds for the instant from the routine of life, and to recognize the presence of those great elemental forces which shriek at godlike mankind through the bars of his civilization, like untamed beasts in a cage. As evening drew in, the storm grew higher and louder, and the wind cried and sobbed like an eternal child in the chimney. By that time, the consulting detective sat moodily at one side of the fireplace cross-indexing his records, while I at the other side was deep into the new novel by the Big Red Cheese. It was called *No Orchids for Miss Bummerkeh*; it was subtitled "Extravagant Fiction Today—Cold Fact Tomorrow." Though I secretly wished the Big Red Cheese had presented us with another thrilling installment of his *Platypus of Dune* series instead, I could not help but admit that his novel was extremely interesting.

The Big Red Cheese's foreward states that recently he had been converted to a new psuedo-philosophy (of which the race has become plagued of late) called dietology, concocted by a fellow artisan called the hermit. By following a strenuous diet of asparagus, squash, beets, grits, pastrami, and ketchup, the devotee is soon able to alter his delicate chemical balance so that he can put himself in a trance which connects his conscious mind (or what is left of it after that diet) with his racial memory. He will relieve himself of a series of false impressions which have prevented him from recalling not only his true identity in the past before the coming of godlike mankind, but the entire history of mere man. The purpose to all this culinary deprivation and mystical revelation is the ultimate restoration of our race's self-image, a purpose of which I heartily approve, but frankly, I do not believe the method will achieve the results the devotees of dietology claim. I cannot understand how having beets and ketchup for breakfast every morning will help a man view beyond the boundaries of his limited perceptions, just as I cannot understand why people yearn for knowledge of the first thirty or so years of their lives, when so many millions have passed. True, I too felt an uncanny sense of loss when Carter Hall, containing artifacts of our past, mysteriously disappeared, but it was no big deal. Perhaps I am so secure in my role as the good doctor that I do not require the past; others have not led a life as rewarding, for all its tragedies, as mine.

But I digress (as usual); on to *No Orchids for Miss Bummerkeh*!

According to the Big Red Cheese, he has only reached the first step in his spiritual development and temporal regression; he can only glimpse unrelated images, whereas he hopes to reach eventually the point where he can live completely in the past, without having to waste his life dealing with the present or the future. This novel is based on his glimpses, and I must admit that I was extraordinarily grateful to the fat man for allowing me to review it, though certain aspects of our conversation on the matter still confound me. The plot is very simple, really, and it bears a striking resemblance to what I have been recounting in my memoirs. Cleveland is menaced by a murderer and raper of women, and the novel records the effort of a brilliant detective and his dim-witted accomplices to capture the murderer. In sure hands, this could have been a rousing good story, but for some reason (perhaps the overdose of pretentiousness all writers succumb to when they believe, rightly or wrongly, that they have something *Important* to say) the Big Red Cheese chose to delegate those aspects of his tale to the background, in the favor of making allegorical observations of the ethical structure of the universe and the more perplexing dilemmas of the godlike condition, while utilizing his own peculiar interpretations of the conceits of the past. This was all very interesting in its banal way, but I could not but help wishing the story would inch forward occasionally. While reading a book of this length, surely the reader is not being unreasonable in requesting that something happen every once and awhile. Characterization is of course of paramount importance, but I wondered why the Big Red Cheese felt it necessary to go on and on about the rather pathetic case histories of his characters, when I wanted to read about what the murderer was up to, who he was planning to snuff next, and how he was managing to stay one step ahead of the detective. I got the distinct impression that the Big Red Cheese did not know himself, that he was hoping to somehow avoid the issue, and that he had constructed the novel in such a way so that when (and if) he arrived at the answers he was searching for in his personal life, then he could set them down without fear of rewriting much that had gone on before. (Everybody knows how the Big Red Cheese hates to rewrite; his loathing of the boring task borders on legend.) During other sections of the novel I received the impression that the Big Red Cheese feared he would arrive at no answers, that he was fully aware of a sneaking banality behind his eloquence; and it was at these points that he appeared to make a concerted, if slightly doomed, effort to propel his novel onward to its ultimate conclusion. Unfortunately his technical virtuosity failed him, and I was subjected to the irritating experience of reading sentences such as these: "And then, all of a sudden, before anybody knew what was happening, seven more murders occurred, one right after the other. Then nothing happened for a few days, save that Detective Bumpkin got drunk a lot." Perhaps the low point of the novel occurs when the detective (who, in my opinion, fully lives up to his name) gets so drunk that he decides only a sabbatical to his home town in an amusing little community located in the Appalachian Mountains will clear up the vague existenial questions on his mind (if the character was concerned over more practical matters, such as capturing the murderer before he killed again, I could not see it). There, cozily sitting beside a roaring fireplace, served hot tea by his mother, he reads a mystery novel with a plot vaguely similar to the events his own life had rather peripherally been caught up in. From the curious parallels he draws absolutely no answers, this section being merely a device by which the Big Red Cheese can have a lot of fun with his readers and see exactly how much ludicrousness they can stomach before the suspension of disbelief disintegrates. Them writers; ain't they something?

These were the observations I made when I sat at my typewriter and banged out a review of *No Orchids for Miss Bummerkeh* before the consulting detective and I resumed our hunt for the nefarious ripper.

2. The man in the yellow suit did not have a home; residing in the universe in general was not conducive to settling down in a particular abode, with or without a warm acquaintance with whom he could share a bed. Consequently, when the consulting detective informed him that the time had arrived for him to rest, he did not know where to go. He could have teleported to one of the many guest rooms in the demon's castle, and in truth, he pretended the intention of doing so while in the presence of his comrades. But he could not bear to remain at a site of great sadness and sorrow, particularly when he too carried a weight of woe within his spirit.

He teleported to the river where he had met the lawyer. He stood on the rusty iron bridge striding that mighty polluted waterway and watched the sun, unusually timid that dawn, toss tiny sparks of whiteness in the rippling river. The black silhouette of the golden city was an alien force somehow superimposed over the soft blue, the stark yellow semicircle, and the fiery red—a hard black force which seemed to have little to do with the universe which beckoned the man in the yellow suit even as he attempted to deal with a profound sorrow that crippled him, a sorrow of such intensity that he knew its origins were more basic, more deeply rooted in his soul than the logical causes would indicate. It had not occurred to him that when he had opened up his heart to the transcendental joys of existence, he had sown the savoring of great tragedies as well. He had believed that as he progressed mystically, he would grow as a godlike individual as well and, consequently, would be able to place into proper perspective the rejection of love and the inevitability of death, whatever the cause. However, not in his most pessimistic dreams or his most realistic rationalizations had he considered the possibility that his mystical progression (and, for that matter, his pragmatic growth) would seem so irrelevant upon the onslaught of despair. And he sensed this was but the initial onslaught, a mild excursion, a tentative prodding from a bureaucracy of pain and madness and despair existing just beyond the boundaries of his ever-expanding perceptions. If anything which transpired was ultimately good, so that everything in the universe was good, then what good could possibly be derived from the death of Kitty? His mourning at her demise, true, had been more intellectual than emotional, because he had realized that oftentimes the general comforts of philosophy have little to do with certain particulars of reality. Perhaps he would have been more resilient if he had not just rejected love, and the hope of love, so that he might remain faithful to his beliefs. Yet—and he had realized this at the time, being fully cognizant of its ramifications—the very foundation of his beliefs was love. He wanted to love everything and everyone, and he had subconsciously embarked upon a mystical course which would enable him to love such vermin as the ripper, along with a whole bunch of more deserving individuals. For only in infinite acceptance and an endless search for the truth could he adequately express his love. Or so he had believed. Now he found it difficult to love the ripper, and he could not in all honesty say that he had loved Kitty because he had never met the lady, and he could not say he had expressed his sorrow for the lawyer's loss because he had not thought of an appropriately memorable sentence. He did not love those he had hoped to love, and he could not love those he wanted to love because he had not the means. All his considerable compassion would reside within him forever, strangling him. And he had rejected love so that he might remain faithful to his self-imposed prison.

All his hopes for his future were suddenly dashed, and when he contemplated the inevitable change the future brings, each alteration seemed bleaker and bleaker, until the pattern of his life reached such an intense desolation that he made no effort to conceive its full magnitude, lest he accidentally crush himself before he was prepared.

And yet—what mattered preparation? After he died, he would not be able to regret his lack of preparation; he would feel no shame, no embarrassment. He felt that the hot onrushing stream of his life had smacked into a frigid, impassable wall, and that his warm life essences were slowly dripping down a tremendous precipice, facing a limitless plain a thousand kilometers below. Why should he have reached for the sky? It had been the same for ages.

Life ultimately came to nothing; it was full of pain. There was no goodness, only evil and pain.

Then I reject life! he thought, much to his surprise.

And as the man in the yellow suit stared at the rippling polluted water, he was amazed that he was inexplicably gripped by a curious peace, a peace much more relaxing than any he had previously experienced. The gurgling of the river, which had been present throughout his contemplations, suddenly canceled what he had thought was silence. The static scene was suddenly brimming with sounds. In the fields across the river a lonely godlike woman played a soaring melancholy melody on a flute. The breeze whispered a chant. Even the pedals of grass caressing their neighbors created a comforting, near-inaudible drone. And then there was the river, always the river, its babbling urging him onward and onward, to a secret destination. And those sounds all beckoned him forward, urging him to cast his soul from his body. Those sounds whispered the tranquility of death.

And as soon as the man in the yellow suit accepted the fact of his forthcoming exit from life (which he did with a readiness he found disconcerting), he felt an anticipation on an order different from previous anticipations. He realized that his journey was not nearing its ending; he was merely taking another step. He had not noticed how much his eternal life had burdened him, how desperately he had sought to relieve himself of meaningless experience. This could be accomplished only in death. The entirety of existence was eternal; each droplet of the oversoul that had spilled into the plane of godlike mankind had actually spilled before and would again. What he had feared—so secretly that he had been unaware of the anxiety—would be the conclusion was but a pit stop for the soul, a refreshment in the soothing waters of the oversoul, as his life forces would be renewed before they took the next step. And death also promised the release of his love, of the smothering emotion which should have granted him salvation, but which in truth had robbed his soul of the opportunity to discover its true potential—at least this time around.

The man in the yellow suit floated over the polluted river; he encased his feet in concrete and ceased manipulating the forces of gravity. He willed himself into unconsciousness as the concrete struck the water.

3. The lawyer discovered, much to his dismay, that as he lay in the circular bed in the center of his quarters, as he communed with his inner darkness, the silk sheets still caressed his bare body with the same sensuality, the feathery pillow remained much like a cushion of air, and the fur blankets continued invigorating his throbbing passions with a healthy zest. Kitty was dead, the consulting detective had just sent him to his bedroom, he had been trying to sleep, the curtains protecting him from the flourishing light bombarding the castle walls, and still he considered searching the city streets, or loafing in her old apartment, or spying on her old lovers, in the hope that he might but catch a glance of her or, if he was really fortunate, gain an opportunity to explore the chasm which was his fondest godlike memory. Kitty was dead, the passions which had driven him to untold and innumberable humiliations should have been destroyed, or at least severely diminished, and yet he was still the pawn of unseen forces originating somewhere in the vicinity of his pelvis. He lay on his back, his eyes closed (darkness shielding him from more darkness), his right forearm resting across his eyes; his left knee was drawn up, his right leg was flat, and he was aware that a spying woman would find the angle separating his legs beneath the blanket intriguing; before he could control himself, he imagined that the spying woman was Kitty, and from there it was a logical progression to imagine her standing beside the bed, smiling at him because he lay in repose and unaware of her presence, slipping her sleazy black nightgown from her ivory shoulders, deliberately causing throes of anticipation to cascade through his body. The lawyer felt utterly ghoulish, positively delighted, singularly nonplused. But in his mind's eye (where the darkness was of no consequence) the sleazy nightgown glided to the floor as if it had been cloaked about an apparition. And as he lay there, unmoving (save for a steady stream of blood rushing toward a particular destination), he imagined her placing her knee and palms on the bed as she leaned forward, with her own destination quite clear. The thought of her had always thrilled him as much as the fact of her, which partially explained why he had been able to endure her frequent and prolonged absences. But this time she would not return, and now the thought of her filled him with a despair the equal of his desire, for his desire was heretofore to be unfulfilled, the thought of her fated never again to be a reality. He thought he had convinced himself of that inescapable fact; he could have created a body, or asked a lady friend to take on her image, but the soul was gone forever, that he had convinced himself of, and it was the soul which was important. Yet . . . he imagined lips of a fine redness and a stirring warmth pressing against his with a tenderness and compassion and—most importantly—lust that was utterly impossible in real life; and, in a blinding heated moment, he imagined the series of events and the inescapable conclusion following that remarkable kiss, throwing in a few variations and paradoxes for good measure. The lawyer had not known that death could change everything so irrevocably and yet allow him to remain the same. He sat up and shook his head, causing the fantasy to disintegrate in a showering display of silent electrical sparks. Kitty had never entered this room—not even when she had had her affair with the demon—but the lawyer knew that if she had come here, she would have immediately given in to the near-overwhelming passion he was certain lurked beneath her casual acceptance of him whenever he jumped upon her bones. The decor had been especially calculated to have such an effect. In the darkness he imagined her walking through the doorway, holding onto his arm as he proudly gestured, feigning humbleness, at his dwelling place, and he imagined her smiling in delight. Round, fluffy white pillows were haphazardly tossed on the red oval couch. He had created green fur for the rug, the fur of an animal that had never existed. The wood paneling was shaded to resemble an oak (though its species, too, had never existed), importing a masculine overtone to counterbalance any unfortunate effeminate effects of the comfortable furniture. The lamps in two of the corners and behind three of the chairs all had a base of medium width, which narrowed and narrowed, expanding quickly at the top; the design of the lamps, and of many similarly structured artifacts scattered about and on the shelves, was intended to have a subliminal effect upon Kitty, who was pretty open to suggestion anyway. At various places along the walls were the stuffed heads of a golden lion, purple-and-green striped alien beasts with fangs and deer-like antlers, yellow rams, and a slimy monstrosity which constantly dripped goo into an aluminum pot the lawyer had liberated from the kitchen; these quaint specimens were intended to impress upon Kitty (or anyone) the lawyer's hunting prowess, thus indicating that he possessed a comparable amount of prowess in other fields of endeavor, but in truth he had borrowed them from the collection of the Big Red Cheese (who had created them rather than slaying animals); and since the lawyer had been unable to persuade a lady, even one of the fat man's cheerleaders, into visiting him while he was in a susceptible mood, he wondered why he had tolerated the infuriating drip drip drip of that icky goo. And the glass eyes of the golden lion seemed to burn with life itself, particularly now, since they glowed in the dark. It was too eerie, and the lawyer was unprepared and unwilling to cope with the minor pranks of reality. He created a black cloth draped over the lion's eyes, but he could not erase the glowing stare from his memory, the notion that a soul from another plane was housed in the stuffed head, housed and staring at him when he should have been alone to sleep and to grieve.

The lawyer was too self-centered to hate the ripper for what he had done to Kitty; the lawyer did not even fantasize venting his anger upon the culprit, though he reserved the right to do so at some future date. He was not concerned with the cause so much as with the results. Kitty was gone. Kitty was gone. He had stared at her corpse in the locker room for an untenable length of time and still he could not reconcile himself to the fact. He felt the urge to sleep hold him with a thousand intangible fingers that slipped through his skin and gripped his muscles, robbing him of energy; and yet when he wearily placed his head on the pillow, snuggled himself into the blankets, lying on his side and holding the sheet at his chin as if it was in danger of slipping away, and closed his eyes, the intangible fingers slithered about, releasing his muscles and returning his energy; the fingers dangled over him, seeming to brush his hair and caress his chest. The reality of it was clear: the lawyer was exhausted, he wished for nothing more than an opportunity to escape from life for a few hours, but he would be unable to sleep. He lay still, once again, but instead of concentrating upon what he wished, he pondered what had been. Upon reflection, he realized that his relationship with Kitty, logically, was nothing to grieve over; in fact, many would say that he was now better off. They had never known quite what to say to one another, though they occasionally made some effort to open up avenues of verbal communication. As for physical communication, well, the lawyer had never had any complaints, he had been thoroughly satisfied, and he had considered a bout with Kitty the quintessence of the sexual experience. Kitty, however, had had other opinions on the matter, and though she had approved of the lawyer's loyalty and devotion upon her inevitable return, she had approved it because she thought she deserved it, not because it was an unexpected pleasure; in fact, she had often inferred rather blatantly that his loyalty and devotion would be well-becoming were he a dog. Although the lawyer had understood intellectually that a person such as Kitty would always be searching for that indefinable *something* he had heard so much about, he had not accepted it emotionally because she was one of those godlike women who, on the surface of things at least, did their searching with their quims; and the lawyer was a creature whose emotional well-being required a regular dosage of the fluids manufactured by her quim. Consequently, when she was away from him, he did not suffer the pain of a lost love as much as he did withdrawal symptons. Her death had intensified his loss, but he still suffered withdrawal. Despite the innumerable reasons why they should have been irrevocably separated throughout the eons, they had nevertheless been drawn together, regardless of the steps Kitty had taken to ensure that she would not have to settle for "Old Unreliable" again. It had seemed a new understanding, a successful attempt at obtaining the much-heralded *something* would come about as a result of their couplings upon their reunitement, which, it must be admitted, Kitty had carried out with considerably less zest than had the lawyer. Yet the feeling had been there, despite her reluctance to admit it, despite the urge to continue her search for a satisfaction and fulfillment that was probably unobtainable due to the very nature of her personality. And the feeling remained with the lawyer; he could not imagine himself living without it. He believed that he could face the coming days if he knew the feeling would recede into the background, and he believed that he would despise himself forever if he allowed the feeling to recede. If only this affair had not reached a conclusion without a resolution, then perhaps he would not be continuing to love her so remorselessly, with so little mercy for himself.

Though nothing had changed, the lawyer suddenly could not imagine living any longer. The soul of Kitty, whatever or wherever it might be, seemed to be calling out to him. For once, Kitty wanted him to be joining her. The lawyer was not concerned if he was deluding himself, for once having accepted the inevitability of his own demise, there remained only the act of carrying it out. He felt the calling stirring in his breast, washing away all the grief and exhaustion, and for the first time in hours the lawyer approached a measure of contentment. He mentally turned on the lights of the bedroom, dressed, and teleported to a site he considered appropriate to his demise.

His atoms coagulated on the rusty bridge across the polluted river. He lowered his derby so that its rim would protect his eyes from the sunlight, noting it was a curious thing to do when personal comfort would soon be so immaterial; and he was mildly amazed at how far the sun had risen; he had not known that he had grieved in darkness for so long. The light was disquieting; it seemed to touch more than the bridge, the fields, and the golden city; it touched his spirit as if he had reached into his heart and withdrawn it, for where there had been frigidity there was now warmth. The lawyer was not much of a philosopher, though he often pretended to be while in the company of the demon and the fat man, lest they think his mental deficiencies more acute than they actually were. Consequently he did not know, nor did he care, what was happening to him as he smiled at the sound of a godlike woman playing a flute in the fields. The beautiful music partially compensated for an element which had been missing from his spirit; simultaneously it opened vistas beyond his current range of thinking, far removed from his current preoccupations; for a few moments the lawyer could not truthfully be described as self-centered, seeing as he did the universe from many angles at once, viewing events and emotions in ways that previously had not occurred to him. He was not so dense as to think that Kitty had died for a reason—no reason was sufficient justification, and, what is more, the tragedy had obviously been blind happenstance—but he sensed that he had grown in some indescribable fashion; the growth would not manifest itself for quite some time, but he definitely felt it as he listened to the flute fade away in the distance, as the woman walked beyond the normal range of his hearing forever. And when there should have been silence, there was the sound of the river rippling past him, and the sight of sunlight sparkling on the waters. The lawyer watched the river for a long time, contemplating its eternal journey without an ultimate destination, before he sighed and walked across the bridge, to the golden city of godlike man, where he too would continue a journey, unaware that he had stood over the corpse of the man in the yellow suit, that he had been the sole mourner for a dreamer.

4. The seller of speculations inhaled, her lungs so numb due to the emotion of the moment that she could not be sure she breathed at all; for she certainly did not feel the cool night air tickling her nostrils, nor did she feel the coolness seep downward into her chest; all she was aware of was the tremendous beating of her heart, which manifested itself not in her chest, but at her right temple. The pounding in her brain threatened to obscure all other sensations as she stood facing *him* in the rain-swept streets, but so long as she could see him, so long as they continued their approach toward one another, the seller of speculations could carefully govern her emotions and perceptions. Her nervousness, her awkwardness, her trepidations, and her fears of inadequacy were concealed with a mask of utter aloofness and total control, with the facade of self-assurance that inevitably derives from having been in similar situations innumerable times.

However, *this* time the situation was, in her opinion, far more significant than previous ones; and she believed she was experiencing anew emotions she had thought would lie dormant forever; and she pondered, in this briefest of eternal moments, how her entire existence had inexorably led her to this fulfillment, this anticipation which, if not soon satisfied, would surely crush her. In fact, it now seemed her life had been part of some cosmic plan; beneath the series of apparently unrelated moments was a pattern she had just discerned. It seemed that the past had suddenly merged with the present, and as she approached *him*, she reflected on her destiny.

The moment during which she became the seller of speculations embraced her and became real. She did not know what she had called herself before that moment, nor did she know how long she had been godlike. She did know that she had once possessed another, definite identity, for her lean body, with her long limbs and her small breasts originated from the earlier period. At any rate, whatever she had been was negated forever during this moment, for as she sat on a park bench and brushed her blonde curls, she overheard a statement by the doughnut-mix specialist which aroused her interest; as very little could arouse her interest, she regarded his statement as significant. The doughnut-mix specialist—wearing his white apron and white hat—was amusing a gang of eternal children sitting in a circle around him; he was telling them a story, a fiction, an outrageous lie. Most fictions, she had noticed, could be accurately described as observations on the trials and tribulations of life, and these always bored her, as did almost everything else about her existence; but this fiction hypnotized her. The doughnut-mix specialist could not be called a great storyteller by any stretch of the critical faculties; he stuttered and backtracked and neglected important details and gave only a perfunctory nod to verisimilitude, but his joy was infectious, and what was more, his tale could hardly be described as an observation. Both implicit and explicit in his words was the notion that, in the world he weaved, life was different from what she had experienced. What few scientific laws were still immutable had altered slightly, in a manner totally of the doughnut-mix specialist's choosing, and the consequential variations in people's lives, customs, and spiritual ambitions were explored. His story was an absurdly simple one—he was, after all, telling it to a group of eternal children—but that only enhanced the qualities which fascinated her. The doughnut-mix specialist was totally unaware of what he had accomplished; while seeking but to entertain, he had accidentally created a new art form, a new kind of story which set free the imagination. The few remaining boundaries were surpassed; the few remaining chains, broken; and a childhood which had been forgotten was mysteriously returned. In addition, the doughnut-mix specialist had earned himself a reward the likes of which he, for all his imagination, had never dreamed; for when the godlike woman who had overheard his tale conceived of her plan to become a seller of speculations, she had decided that he was the very godlike man who should have the privilege of fucking her like mad for the next few weeks. She wanted to lie down, spread her legs, and let him plunge into her; never before had she wanted to have a man impart his essence to her with such fervor. Her immediate plans were carried out forthwith, and with the usual ease, for her apparatus was especially suited to such activities. She was aided by the fact that the doughnut-mix specialist was supremely unattractive, for his own reasons, and therefore was rarely a participant in a romantic encounter. For several days and nights they indulged themselves, the doughnut-mix specialist being particularly pleased at having finally found someone who would allow him to play "motorboat." The seller of speculations, meanwhile, implemented her plans by convincing her partner, in between orgasms, that he should set down the story he had told the eternal children. "What?" said the doughnut-mix specialist. "Compete with such undisputed literary giants as the Big Red Cheese? Why, the very knowledge of the classic heights attained before me would cause me to paralyze myself; I would succumb to the literary bends!" To which the seller of speculations replied: "Who said anything about literature, you lout? I'm talking about entertainment. First, everybody knows literature and entertainment are mutually exclusive and second... well, face it, buster, you couldn't ponder the mysteries of the universe if your erection depended on it; you haven't the brains for it. But you've got something else. I don't know what it is, exactly, but I believe you're eaten up with wonder and the joy of life and you would like to create a few thoughts yourself. If you became a speculator, you'll rise from the ranks of the amateur thinker to the professional—by definition! And besides, writing will give you something to do while I sit around and create a few experimental scents for your amusement and sexual edification at night." This proved to be the very inducement the doughnut-mix specialist required. He did not care much for writing or for speculating, but he did care for a certain tunnel of delight, and while he was routinely inspecting her plumbing, he felt that life had finally yielded to him its greatest reward. The doughnut-mix specialist loved the seller of speculations; at first he loved her body; then his love grew into the love which, circumstances permitting, has lasted for eons. And in the months to come he created his most remarkable speculations, his most thrilling fictions, all for the seller of speculations, so that he might experience her love in return. The doughnut-mix specialist had no illusions about his relationship with her; she did not care for his body or his personality or his technical adroitness in the sack as much as she cared for his speculative mind, and she hoped that what she pictured as his unique understanding of the universe would be communicated to her in such a way that it would actually become a part of her, so that she might not feel alone, or alienated, or lost, or confused when facing the curious manipulations of life transpiring about her. There had to exist someone, somewhere, who could alleviate her boredom, or teach her what she needed to know, or love her adequately, for now that she had actively begun searching, she would always search; and once having reached a particular goal, she would wonder if it was enough, if she was correct in feeling satisfied. And her own self-doubts would be sufficient cause for dissatisfaction in the object, be it a material thing, a man, or a work of art; and she knew this, and yet she did not force herself to cease searching because it simply could not be done. However, during this liaison with the doughnut-mix specialist, she experienced some measure of satisfaction, for she believed his speculations contained the proper balance of adult reasoning with stupidly or nastily adolescent anger at the universe. She sighed with hope, and allowed him to fuck her to his heart's content even when she was bored, for with her assistance he would soon be a commercial success.

And the first books of the doughnut-mix specialist were indeed commercial successes, though not in the way the seller of speculations had initially envisioned. The manner of their success, however, afforded her with greater opportunity to search. Speculations appealed only to a certain type of mind; at least that was true of the first wave of speculations over a period of approximately five hundred years. This type of mind was not exactly the highest quality the race had to offer, but what it lacked in intellectual sophistication and finesse it compensated with enthusiasm. Of the random sampling of godlike men and women who read the doughnut-mix specialist's early books, only the loneliest, most socially alienated individuals (usually suffering feelings of sexual inadequacy) who could find nothing else to excite them continued reading his books; they even read the previous ones; and when all his books had been exhausted, they reread them, fervently awaiting the next. At first they felt vaguely ashamed for enjoying the speculations of the doughnut-mix specialist; however, they eventually began to take on a perverse pleasure in their enjoyment; and gradually all feelings of shame vanished. At first each reader felt curiously alone, his alienation from society somehow accentuated by his pleasure in the poorly written, totally absurd books that had captivated his imagination; and, in truth, each reader was indeed more alone, for those who sampled a passage of the doughnut-mix specialist's scintillating prose, whose mind was not of the peculiar type which required this sort of alternative thought patterns, were violently indignant and intolerant toward the "mindless doggerel" and immediately began spreading unkind rumors concerning the art of speculation in general and the doughnut-mix specialist in particular. However, the admirers of the speculations continued their reading, reasonably undeterred by social chastisement; and soon they could accept no other type of literature; not even the greatest works of the Big Red Cheese were satisfactory. And, within a decade, the admirers were meeting and talking, at first in small gatherings at public places throughout the planet, then in slightly larger gatherings at private apartments. Some of the gatherings became extremely private, the number having been reduced to two; and feelings of sexual inadequacy were soothed, largely due to the writings of the doughnut-mix specialist, writings which had brought the happy couples together. Eventually the admirers finally banded into formal clubs; there were rival clubs, splinter clubs, back-stabbings, and nasty arguments, but simultaneously there was deep friendship. Most importantly, there were pleasant arguments over the merits and faults of the doughnut-mix specialist's speculations. Soon the admirers tossed all sense of aloofness to the prevailing winds and called themselves "fans," a phrase complementing their childish enthusiasm. Their "fandom" became the mainstay of their existence, whatever the particulars of their identities. For the first time they could truly say to have friends and antagonists, all of whom were comrades; the love and affection they felt for the doughnut-mix specialist's speculations spilled into affection for one another, and the fact that the majority of godlike mankind was virtually unaware of their activities increased their pleasure.

After nursing a bout with disappointment that made everyone in close proximity to her miserable, the seller of speculations (who after a time had opened a small shop which insinuated it was the sole source of speculations) realized that, while she might never enjoy the esteem of the world at large, she had the potentiality to be a social success in one small circle. Already she felt that her liaison with the doughnut-mix specialist was nearing its ignoble conclusion. In addition to boredom, a quality which had always been prevelant in her world-view, she felt depressed and wasted; she no longer derived a sense of personal importance from allowing the doughnut-mix specialist to fuck her. The questions which had been plaguing her, the arcane notion that beneath all the glitter and laughter and pleasure and glib phrases, life ultimately had no meaning, either in the personal or the metaphysical senses—these questions still had not been resolved. Each morning when she awoke (usually to the sensation of the doughnut-mix specialist manhandling her clitoris), she wondered why she did not will herself to die, why she persisted in living; just what did she expect from each new day that would make it different from the preceeding one? And would she ever experience a day completely unique, a day which in the ensuing eons she would remember distinctly, as opposed to the dreary blur which currently oppressed her? She surely would not experience such a day in the company of the doughnut-mix specialist, who by this time caused her a boredom greater than any she had ever known; if there had ever been the hope that she would receive a significant communication from his uniquely speculative mind, it had withered and died long before the day she told him their affair was over. "I did everything I could for you," she told him. "And what have I received in return? A feeling of emptiness, that's what. We can still be friends; after all, what you did to me wasn't your fault, it was simply due to your blind, unthinking, stupid preoccupation with yourself. Now your speculations belong to the world, or at least to fandom; I'm privy to nothing special any more. Maybe there's someone else who can give me what I'm looking for; it certainly isn't you." Then she left, walking out of the apartment, taking care that her ass swayed enticingly. The doughnut-mix specialist stared at her with alarm, and then returned to work. By this time his work had assumed a vast amount of importance in his life, especially since he had grown accustomed to fucking the seller of speculations; and though he sometimes felt that he was going to suffer brain damage as a result of thinking so absurdly with such regularity, he persevered, cranking out speculation after speculation on a rickety manual typewriter. In fact, he worked harder than he had ever worked before, to forget the image of the seller of speculations, an image that would not leave his brain, an image which, through a devious means he could never fathom, created a vast vacuum in his torso. He was haunted by a dream which had escaped him. And over a period of a hundred years fans began noticing a serious decline in the quality of his work. During the next hundred years the doughnut-mix specialist noticed it too; he wanted to do something about it, to somehow renew his inspiration, but he could think of nothing which had a remote possibility of success. He became so self-conscious of his decline that he visited fan clubs less and less frequently, and then saw his friends less and less frequently, until he became a virtual recluse. His decline as a speculator became complete; his new books were like poor parodies of the early ones; the quantity of his output declined also, until his occasional volume was received as a curiosity and little more. The doughnut-mix specialist passed not only from our story, but from the world of godlike man as well; not an inkling has been uncovered pointing to his current whereabouts, and no one has cared enough to search. In fact, his decline had not reached its final stages when he had been virtually forgotten by fandom (save for a few specialists who now regarded him as historically valuable and with sentimental interest); he had been replaced in fandom's esteem by others.

Needless to say, the seller of speculations had been one of the prime factors leading to the doughnut-mix specialist's slump in the eyes of fandom. But aside from confidentially telling thirty-five people that he was a lousy fuck, her manipulations were not motivated by malice; indeed, the fate of her former lover aroused supreme indifference, when she did not wonder how and why she had tolerated such a bore for so long. Her first concern was to ensure that her store had some sort of product to offer in exchange for the fame and glory she desired. She did the only thing she could under the circumstances: she encouraged others, in her own inimitable fashion, to become speculators. This proved to be remarkably easy; several fans had already secretly wished to do so; they simply had not wanted to tread in the footsteps of the great. Now that the doughnut-mix specialist was falling from his altar—well, that happenstance opened up the field. Soon the new writers did not even require a roll in the hay with the seller of speculations to announce their intentions of capturing their friends with a net of words. This unforeseen development caused the seller of speculations some trepidation—for some reason she had envisioned herself as constantly

at the center of activities (of one form or another) in the
speculative field—but after a time she shrugged, accepting the
inevitable, for she could do nothing else. It took several years for
her to realize that the inevitable had been for the best; the more
speculators there were, the more product her store had to offer,
and the more handsome godlike men would wander inside. She
could not expect to bed all the speculators anymore; she now
had the advantage of being able to concentrate on the more
attractive ones. Eventually she bedded an extraordinary
number, but she was unable to exert any degree of influence over
them. The field of speculation was now attracting extremely
independent minds (usually those possessing some feelings of
sexual inadequacy) which were not susceptible to feminine
wiles, at least those belonging to her. To her surprise, she greeted
this masculine independence with relief; despite her pleasure in
the prestige of responsibility, she loathed to discharge the duties
associated with it, and now she was not burdened with the
(admittedly unrealistic) notion that the fate of the field somehow
depended upon her guidance. In this respect she was finally free;
she could sit back, be entertained, and try to fuck all the pretty
speculators she could.

And the developments in the field were as fast and as furious
as in any arena of the arts, perhaps faster and more furious due
to the fact that an ever-expanding number were discovering
speculation and were treating it as if it filled a hitherto
unsuspected void in their lives. At first the new writers
unabashedly imitated their favorite work by the doughnut-mix
specialist, invariably an early work; many of these imitators
were greeted with well-deserved scorn by those who considered
themselves the radical left *intelligentsia* of fandom, but the
plebian members were overjoyed; the quality of the speculations
did not matter, just so long as there were many speculations to
choose from. After five or six years of this, after many neophytes
were added and subtracted, even the *intelligentsia* noticed that
some very interesting apprentice work was being written. After
another five or six years, fandom was in a perpetual state of
excitement. It seemed that at least one undisputed classic per
year was being written, and, what was more interesting, several
disputed classics. Now the fans really had something to argue
about. And as their number continued to increase, society as a
whole began to take notice. The ace reporter wrote: "The

best-known speculators are the reverse of anonymous or interchangeable; they are more likely to be annoyingly idiosyncratic. Moreover, fans often show a genuinely critical attitude, however crude their bases and arguments. The fans are addicts, but they are active addicts, positive enthusiasts who are conscious, often all too conscious, of being a specialized minority." The Big Red Cheese, who read regularly in the field, believed that at least a dozen current practitioners had attained the status of the minor "observer" whose example brings into existence the figure of real standing. Eventually scholars were even able to apologize for the humble origins of speculation, a true sign of status; one scholar wrote: "It must have been a painful experience to speculate in the beginning; one had to conform to the formula or get out. There was no sort of cultural tradition or precedent to appeal to. Low amounts of recognition engendered much hack-work." The fans attempted to ignore the world's notice of them as much as possible, particularly since the writings concerning their activities, while accurate, were subtly phrased with the intent to condescend; they pretended that the interaction between themselves and the rest of the world was negligible. The folly of this pretense was demonstrated when the hermit deserted the ranks of the speculators and created dietology. Most fans, however, continued pretending; too much was occurring within their own sphere of interest for them to be distracted by world events. Many schools of speculation had grown, roughly dividing themselves into two major categories— the logical and the illogical, the fans supporting each category pointing to "reality" in order to justify their speculative tastes. In addition, the history of the development of literary technique was conveniently divided into "waves." The "Old Wave" had been superceded by the "New Wave," but when a third wave of literary change washed over the field, implied value systems had to be replaced by neutral numbers; eventually there were fifty waves, each and every one affecting both the logical and illogical categories. And, if the process of defining the boundaries of any given speculation was not already complicated enough, there were the themes, the set of literary conventions, which had to be identified before a serious discussion on the work could be commenced; sometimes it was quite difficult to pinpoint exactly which theme, or which combination of themes, the work dealt with. Many fans could not agree on the distinct differences between logical positivism and dialectical materialism, or between radical subjectivism and historical consciousness. The fan of speculation had to learn to deal with phenomenology, alteration of natural theses, metaphysical skepticism, positive science, pragmatism, instrumentalism, absolute ideas, logical analysis, scholasticism, uncompounded appearances, empirical methods, the contiguity of time, genetic psychology, complicated definitions of "simplicity" and "common sense," and the philosophical implications of various forms of sexual inadequacy, a problem obsessing many speculators years after they claimed to have solved it. The conventions confused many of the fans, though upon this matter too they pretended to understand all, vacuously nodding at someone's pontification whenever the occasion warranted it. They might have eventually succeeded in understanding all, if only the speculators themselves had cooperated; whenever the field seemed to settle down into a chaotic mess the average fan could deal with, along would come a new writer whose new techniques regarding certain conventions would dazzle everyone, and off the speculators would be; experimenting, reworking old ideas the fans had thought exhausted, or switching from the logical category to the illogical one for no apparent reason other than to confuse (and delight) the fans. Nothing remained the same, and though it was exasperating, at least it helped prevent several fans from succumbing to the mysterious depression which had sent many of their less spiritually hearty fellows to the East End.

Needless to say, the seller of speculations was utterly lost in a field which had grown too complex (perhaps due to the gross over-familiarity of everyone involved). She discovered that as time passed, she steadily lost interest in this form of literature, as it still had not answered the questions she had once believed it could answer, and as it now failed to relieve the tremendous ennui that haunted her every thought. She did not understand one iota of what was happening about her. She had given up reading speculations when it had become too difficult to get the writers to sleep with her (they had all grown weary of her, both physically and platonically). Oh, occasionally she met a writer of speculation with whom she had had few dealings in the past, and who did not therefore object to a quick banging in the storeroom in the back, but in the main, most of her social prestige was a result of the fans' respect for her, and even that was diminishing rapidly. She had difficulty relating to the peculiar group of fans who belonged to no official organization and who looked down on those who did; these fans read the entire spectrum of speculative literature and acted in every respect like the fans of old, save for the unfortunate snobbish streak which made them proud of being outsiders. The seller of speculations did discover one advantage to becoming friends with this type of fan: when her social reputation inevitably declined thanks to an emotional outburst of some sort, it declined in a smaller circle, and she was not ostracized from so many people at once. The rate of decline was never the same; she had mastered the art of being entertaining and bright in the eyes of others, and her skills rarely failed her until an individual knew her well; and then not all her skills could save her. But when a group of fans heard her say, "The doughnut-mix specialist was the first great progenitor of modern speculation—in their logical aspects his speculations were, of course, of poor quality, a feature certainly reproduced with great fidelity by most of his successors," everyone nodded, thinking from her manner that she knew what she was talking about. She took such pleasure in her abilities that she never tired of her performance; she must have said (about whatever writer happened to be under discussion), "The most noticable quality about his work is that the speculations are used to arouse wonder, terror, and excitement, rather than for any rational or enlightening end" a thousand times, yet upon each occasion she said it with such a freshness and obvious delight that all who heard were convinced she had just conceived the sentence; they never would have thought they were watching a performance rehearsed just as carefully as the minstrel show at *The Eibon*. But, for reasons the seller of speculations never could quite figure out, her friendships with these people were never satisfactory, even when she made allowances for the patterns of her existence; so she was almost relieved when the friendships reached their conclusions. She was forced to emigrate to social circles which had absolutely nothing to do with speculation; but after people were impressed by her identity, they had difficulty engaging her in meaningful conversation, because speculation was all she knew (however dimly), and they knew nothing about it. She finally realized, with a numbing certainty threatening to shatter her ennui with its implications, that if for some reason she should become unable to fuck, she would have relinquished all her social functions and, therefore, would have absolutely nothing to live for. Even so, sex was losing much of its attraction; it was becoming as boring as any other aspect of her existence; and only a succession of new partners with no interest in her as a human being could provide her life with meaning. For only when she was fucking was her mind free of the questions; only when she was fucking were her thoughts attuned to one particular matter to the exclusion of all others; she did not have to worry about what she was doing, or what she would be doing, because while she was fucking time was suspended, and whatever plans she was making were concerned solely with fucking and it was unlikely that her partner would object to any of them. But as soon as it was over and her partner was in the shower (she always wondered why men had this irresistible urge to wash her fluids from their members as soon as possible), she started thinking again, and the moments stretched together, endlessly, reaching into a dim future she was afraid she would not be able to face, because she knew it was not her essential dimwittedness that invariably drove her friends away, but her fears instead, for her fears caused her to become rude and angry and demanding because no one was helping her soothe her anxieties, no one was protecting her, no was doing anything for her, she who had midwifed the art of speculation, she had done something important and it was not her fault that people disliked her, but each rejection only increased the fear, the fear she forgot while fucking which was the only thing she could do well, the only good thing people said about her anymore was that she was attractive and that she was a good fuck, and she knew that as long as somebody was fucking her she would receive attention from somebody, it did not matter who so long as he was pretty, but it was becoming more and more difficult to find someone new to fuck, it had to be someone new because her fears were warping her personality to such a degree that even she was noticing it and so no one would fuck her for long. Which was why she had traveled to *this* moment, when she walked to *him* and *he* took her hand, and she felt that her long journey was over. She felt the fears die that night in the East End. She felt the answers arrive to the questions, and she learned the questions were immaterial as long as this moment lasted. As long as he held her hand, the moment would last forever.

5. *Assholes! I'm surrounded by legions of assholes!* thought the ripper as he stood at the window of his apartment on the seventh floor and watched several lonely and depressed people exit their buildings to begin their long day wandering the East End. He stuffed both his hands down his white pair of long underwear and scratched his balls until the sac turned red, as if he had suddenly been afflicted with a rash; his mouth felt like he had swallowed an inordinate amount of cotton; and his eyesight was blurry, rendering him incapable of clearly interpreting the images transmitted to his brain. The ripper had not slept for a week; he did not have the power to imbue himself with artificial energy, yet his strength derived from unsuspected sources deep within his soul; nevertheless, he felt as if he had awakened from a long sleep, an arduous sleep which had exhausted all his energy for all time, but which somehow allowed him to continue. When he removed his hands from his balls, he still itched, but he ignored the annoying sensation as he wiped an imaginary film from his eyes and stretched, pretending he could feel his red corpuscles surge throughout his tired muscles and bring him life. *Legions of assholes! Yes, that's what they are. The sorry state I'm in... it's their fault, it's their fault. The sorry state I'm in... it's my fault. What am I going to do?* he asked himself suddenly as he thought of the events of the previous night. He staggered backward to his single bed and sat when he felt the mattress touch his lower thighs. He rubbed his left eye as hard as he dared, still attempting to peel away the film. He stared at the dust caked in the corner, where the purple carpet was not quite able to reach the green wall; a meter above the dust the plaster was cracked and the ripper followed the trails of the white streaks until he saw the top row of the bracket where rested several dirty glasses and a stack of grimy white plates; on the bottom row was a surfeit of instant coffee, macaroni, salt, pepper, stale bread, and dehydrated peanut butter ("Just add water!"). Below the bracket was the table where the ripper had eaten his peanut butter sandwiches until a week ago, when he had suddenly, for no apparent reason, lost interest in his favorite repast. Now the most delicate dishes he could conjure, or could have others conjure in public diners, failed to entice him, though he stuffed himself with regularity in the hopes that he would acquire a liking for the new tastes. Regardless of what he consumed, his taste buds failed to transmit a delightful sensation; he felt as if he had eaten merely an extra serving of the aforementioned cotton. He hated having to eat; somehow it was the fault of his system, for surely, if it had wanted to, it could have arranged matters so he would not have had to suffer so much, with the only discernable purpose being a continuation of a life which, in the main, offered little enough joy; and that joy invariably fled, forcing him to seek more joy. *What am I going to do?* he asked himself again and again before he noted *The joy is becoming more and more elusive. Perhaps I should go down to the Joy Mission and listen to those immature scum. Those fuckers really piss me off but maybe they'll show me something, for a change.* The word *change* in his thoughts sparked a notion and he stood and walked with plodding, almost timid steps to the mirror next to the tiny bathroom. Below the mirror was a sink and a mantel, upon which lay a comb with dusty strands of brown hair matted between the teeth and a solar razor; save for the bar of soap, there were no more articles of personal hygiene and cosmetics (he had sent his toothbursh and an empty tube of toothpaste to the antimatter universe five days ago, but he had not summoned sufficient will to create replacements). The ripper stared at his reflection in the mirror. *I wasn't always the ripper.* No, he certainly had not been; he had not been much of anything. Among the most timid and shy of godlike mankind, the abruptness of his metamorphosis in Cleveland, so many eons ago, had intensified his already unnatural self-effacement and debasement. The dreariness of unrelieved spontaneity repelled him, and even the social structure which eventually evolved was too frightening for a mind which required as much order as his. He might have created some sort of personal order which protected him, as had the thinking machine for example, but he lacked the courage, the faith in himself, to assert himself even that unique amount, believing as he did that uniqueness was, if not alien, then certainly undesirable in the human (or godlike) condition. He had forgotten these beliefs and motivations eons ago, but his lapse of memory had not prevented him from renouncing all godlike customs; throughout the eons, he had possessed no identity, he had taken part in no activities, he had loved no woman or man. He was of the opinion that godlike mankind would eventually destroy itself, and he did not want to be destroyed with it. Occasionally (or more presicely, four times during all his history), he wondered if his opinion was logically derived from valid assumptions or if he was merely justifying his own misanthropy. Granted, he was shy and awkward in the company of others, but even before he had become the ripper, his hatred began to manifest itself in ways that surprised him, and his unkind words which he was unprepared to back up with more unkind words often placed him in embarrassing situations. Why could not people understand that his hatred of them and all they represented, his hatred which he usually suppressed admirably, was entirely deserved? People deserved his loathing because they were responsible, in some fashion he could not fathom, for the shyness which made him so uncomfortable, so withdrawn; people made him feel that they were doing him a favor regardless of how casually they treated him. And they never treated him with respect, though they did not have to deal with him often, he kept to himself most of the time, surely asking for a little respect now and then was not asking for too much. But as he stared at his reflection, at his thin brown hair combed over the top of his shiny dome, his little nose which always looked to him as if someone had glued a toadstool to his oval face, his deep-set eyes which were always timid even when he was angry, his small mouth which always puckered like that of a whimpering eternal child regardless of what emotion he was trying to convey, and his tiny moustache which somehow detracted from rather than added to the character of his features, he realized that for a wimpy person such as he, asking for anything, even for a smile, was making an outrageous demand. No wonder women treated him with such callousness. Or, no wonder they *had* treated him with such callousness, for he had summoned something from his soul, a self-assurance he had never suspected which attracted women to him, which made him interesting to them. He did not care to dwell upon current events, however, for his crimes, including those of the night before and the rather gloating note he had sent to the consulting detective, were like dreams; and he had difficulty associating the person who had accomplished those deeds with the man he saw now, in his mirror, the man who had been defeated by women before he had even asked them to consider impaling themselves on his mighty root, because they sensed a man who could not deal with social conventions, who could not pretend to love them for the sake of their shabby delusions, and consequently they hated him for it; and they treated him with the ultimate contempt only the greatest amount of hatred can summon:

indifference. No, the ripper preferred to think about the godlike man he had been in years past, rather than the godlike man he had been during the past week, for somehow his sleepless body was unprepared to cope with the weight of his deeds and his mind refused to cope with their convoluted implications. In those days he had altered his appearance slightly whenever it seemed that people were putting a tag on him, a name by which they could identify him, but he had never dared alter himself in such a way that women would notice him, for he did not know what to do about his drab personality (though he knew many handsome godlike men had the drabbest personalities of all); the thought of changing himself, and therefore once again changing his concept of who he was, however insignificant he was, filled him with fear; and the thought of it made him sweat and tremble until he turned his mind to other things and wondered why he should alter himself to suit society, when society could just as easily alter itself to suit him. Recently, a year or two before this nameless godlike man became the ripper, he had wondered why society had allowed the demon, the lawyer, and the fat man to depress everyone. Godlike mankind was suddenly granted knowledge, and it had not the experience to support emotionally the added insight into the workings of the universe. In many cases, people were finally allowed to comment openly or to admit a situation which had existed since the birth of godlike man, but which had been suppressed due to a tacit agreement. Even the demon, the lawyer, and the fat man, quite a brilliant trio in their own peculiar way, were victimized by the tacit agreement, and they had expected accomplishments they never would have realistically considered if they had not been so ignorant. Bringing depression out into the open worsened the ripper's emotional dilemmas, but it did grant him one important insight: many were no better off than he. They concealed it in incredibly complicated ways, one of the most obvious being burying their fears and doubts so deeply into the subconscious that the evidence of them was flimsy at best—but never completely concealed. This knowledge had brought to the ripper what little comfort he could nurture as he wallowed alone in his apartment where he had wallowed for eons; he nursed a flourishing depression that slowly, steadily chipped away the few fragments of his self-respect. Eventually all that remained was his hatred, an undying hatred nurtured by every real and imagined defeat.

However, he had not thought his hatred was clouding his judgment when, one morning when he felt all his senses were clogged, he decided he had been appointed by destiny to lead godlike mankind from the East End, to cure godlike mankind of the annoyance that had grown into a plague. He had sat alone in his apartment as the depressed and lonely people migrated to this sector which once had been sparsely populated, as they allowed their buildings to become crowded and decrepit despite the gay manner in which the bright morning sunlight reflected from the gold. He had stood at the window and watched the listless people clothed in despair wander back and forth, or just sit on the curbs; sometimes he had seen mindless, drunken displays of joy, but he realized the desperation from which the display derived. He knew all joy was transient. One drizzling midnight he had seen a burly man fornicate with a fat slut on the sidewalk, in public, right below his window; and though he had been repulsed by the act, in addition to wondering just what they had been trying to prove, he had not been able to forget it, as he had forgotten all other displays of joy; he could not forget a single detail. And he thought about it as he stared at his reflection and then moved to the bed, where he sat intending to contemplate on how he would pass the day, since he knew he would not sleep despite his body's incessant demands. But he did not contemplate; he could not forget those two bozos fucking in the street. The women were all like that fat slut; they would always fuck in the street for a quick thrill, and his own exploits had proven that to be the case—except for the last one, and she had just been leading him on. The ripper inhaled deeply; his arm muscles trembled as he closed his eyes and lifted his head to the ceiling as if he had been stricken with a massive pain; he had not wanted to think about these things, they hurt him too much, he was not built, emotionally or physically, for this task, but it had been thrust upon him by unseen forces and so he had no choice but to continue. He had been selected to cure the inhabitants of the East End of their depression; by slaying them, he would make the rest appreciate the fact that they were alive, which was something you took for granted if you were an immortal. Of course, to this date his work had not had a noticeable effect, but heck, he had just started; he could not be expected to change everything overnight, he had only been able to work on those sluts, those disgusting sluts who would fuck for anyone and who were dragging the rest of godlike mankind down into the bog. *I hate those bitches. I hate them even though they fucked for me. Hell, I didn't even have to conjure them a dinner; I didn't have to be nice to them; they didn't care what happened to them. I bet they wouldn't care now, if they could.* The hatred cleansed him of his pain, and he was able to stand and to feel hunger. But he could not rid himself of the depression which had seized him now that the second murder of last night was becoming only a memory, another meaningless image crowding his brain. He could not delay his excursion to the Joy Mission any longer. A part of him was afraid of the monster he was so proud of; he wished to suppress the monster, at least during the day, when his weariness permeated his body as if the sun weakened him and the night gave him strength. The ripper dressed in black trousers, shirt and shoes, and then put on his black cutaway coat, though it promised to be warm this morning. However, he sensed an eerie coolness in the atmosphere; his normally limber joints creaked, an irrefutable omen of rain. He picked up the parcel concealing the antimatter knife; the light of the blade was smothered by the special substance he had created especially for that purpose. He did not fear discovery by the consulting detective or any of his minions because he instinctively maintained the vibratory shields which masked him from his foes. Others were not affected by the vibrations; they did not detect them because they did not suspect them and consequently did not exert their powers to that end. The ripper did not fear anyone would recognize him today, for even if the consulting detective did choose to allow any description the universal op might have given of him to appear in the newspaper, precious few inhabitants of the East End would read it; and if someone did recognize the ripper from the description, the chances were that he would be too despondent over life in general to notify the consulting detective. The ripper did not know whether to be grateful or frustrated over this singular lack of response; he also wondered why some altruists, such as the consulting detective, were so tenacious that they would strive mightily to save people who did not care if they were saved or not. *Oh well, the answer is of little importance in comparison with my hatred*, thought the ripper as he stared at his reflection, this time positioning his battered, black felt hat exactly right. Then, holding the parcel next to his chest as if it was in danger of inexplicably

disappearing, he left his apartment and soon emerged outside,
walking past godlike men and women sleeping or sitting on the
sidewalk; these emotional derelicts did not speak or smile or give
evidence of any involvement with life, even when they were
embracing, like melancholy statues chiseled by ancient,
inhuman artists. The ripper felt the worm inside him, the worm
which had become a familiar companion to him these past few
days, the worm which urged him to destroy, which had brought
him to this acme of existence. As he looked at the wasted,
depressed people whose life or death would make absolutely no
difference in the world, his hatred grew to such mammoth
proportions that he could form no coherent thoughts on the
matter. He wished he could hate them all at the same time, so his
hatred would be dissipated, causing him to become an effete
nobody sneering at the majority's intellectual pygmyism. But he
could not envision the lot of them in his mind's eye; he thought
only of the ones he saw, in particular whichever group his eyes
happened to be focused on, causing his considerable hatred to be
directed at a specification. It was the difference between hating a
philosophy and hating a sentence. The ripper seethed with red
anger, as the worm seethed inside him; he ceased to hate only
when he saw a godlike woman who was seductive despite her
crippling depression, or when he saw a pubescent eternal child of
the female variety subliminally displaying her wares via a
see-through blouse and tight bluejeans; and he did not hate upon
those occasions solely because he was suddenly obsessed with
sex. He wanted nothing more than the sheer pleasure of forcing
his will upon submissive flesh, whether or not the flesh in
question was interested in submitting. He was seriously obsessed
with jamming his member in a female pubescent eternal child
playing the guitar so badly that he could barely catch her
intended melody when he walked into the diner; and all thoughts
of sex suddenly ceased as he saw the waitress, who weighed
nearly a hundred kilograms and wore a tacky blue dress that had
been fitted for someone who weighed twenty less kilograms. The
ripper feared he would suddenly hear a tearing as if the oversoul
was ripping the sky asunder and he would be exposed to
magnitudes of pale flesh spotted with large gobs of pink.
Thoughts of sex could not possibly exist while under such a
grotesque threat. *Goodness me! What if she read my mind and
believed I was thinking about her?* The waitress indeed appeared

to be staring at him with an impatient glimmer in her eye as he slowly walked to a booth and sat down. When he put his parcel on the table, he would not lift up his fingers. The hissing of the frying hamburgers, the cracking of egg shells, the slicing of vegetables, the gurgling of the soda fountain—these sounds and others assumed symphonic proportions in his mind, a veritable soundtrack as the waitress lumbered like a beached whale rolling toward the sea; and she lumbered in his direction! He glanced at the chef by the grill, at the other customers morosely eating or morosely waiting, at an idle skinny waitress chewing gum, at anything other than those lips caked with garish lipstick, those eyes camouflaged with makeup, those fuzzy cheeks resembling two tennis balls. He scratched his scalp under his hat as the waitress drummed the fingers of her left hand on the table.

"What'll it be, Mac?" she asked.

"A menu would be nice."

"It's right there, Mac," she said, pointing to a tattered laminated cardboard square standing in a rack behind the salt, pepper, napkins, and turned cream.

The ripper smiled weakly, she smiled weakly by way of parodying his expression, and he read the menu. His mind focused on one item at a time, but as soon as he decided that he would like a cup of coffee and he proceeded to the next section, he completely forgot what he wanted to drink, and he was forced to backtrack until he gave up in disgust and studied the main courses; but when he proceeded to the side dishes, he forgot what he had decided upon. Of course, the fact that the waitress was still standing at the table, staring at him, tapping her foot, her arms folded below those gigantic bulbs, accounted for much of his inability to make up his mind. Her very presence negated all thinking processes. Perhaps if he engaged her in conversation. "Hey, babe, is this grub direct from the North Pole?"

The waitress looked very indignant, frowning as if he had piddled in the middle of the floor. "Yeah. We get our stuff from the pigs in trenchcoats; the middleman goes through a lot of trouble, but yeah, we get it direct. We ain't got no jerk in the back room conjuring this stuff in secret. When you taste the genuine natural flavor, you'll know I'm telling the truth. Now what'll it be, Mac?"

"How about a blow job?"

"Do you want me to show you the door?"

"That's very kind of you, but I saw it on the way in."

The clever banter gave the ripper the opportunity to look from his menu and to peek at the customer morosely eating in the next booth. He would have what the customer was having; the decision was such simplicity that he actually anticipated the meal as he rattled off its ingredients. "I'll have a tall glass of milk, two cheeseburgers hold the pickles, an order of fries, and a scoop of cottage cheese."

"Got it, Mac." The waitress turned her head toward the chef. "Two burgers hold the pickles, fries, and cottage cheese. Oh yeah. And a side dish of grease for the big spender."

"Thank you; you're so kind."

"Don't get your bowels in an uproar. It'll be here in a minute."

As the ripper waited, his fingers still resting on the parcel, he feared someone on his trail would pass by, or that someone would idly peer into his parcel, as he waited for his food. The ripper realized his nerve was failing him, as it had failed him so often when he was acting like an average godlike man, and unlike what he truly was: a superior creation asserting his will to power after eons of unnecessary subservience. Yet, despite his attempts to squelch his smugness, he felt a thrill; it amused him to think that he, the most dangerous godlike man history had ever known, was quietly waiting in a public diner for two cheeseburgers, as if he was an ordinary citizen. The aggressive side of his personality, which was fed by his overwhelming hatred whatever his mood, was ascending; and now he fervently wished the consulting detective or the universal op would pass by and notice that a waitress was serving an apparently empty booth. Or that a morose customer would notice his reluctance to draw his fingers away from the parcel, even for the joy of two steaming cheeseburgers, and that the customer would peer into the parcel...espying the antimatter knife which thus far had claimed four victims. Then things would really start to happen; life would become really interesting; and all these people, who had either ignored him or treated him callously, would experience the numbing fear of the helpless who know that their greatest strengths and resources will not suffice. And he would be proud of himself. The few seconds of his utter power would last forever before circumstances forced him to flee. However, as he basked in what he wished was his personal glory, he was afraid of being caught; he recognized his fear, he was honest enough to admit that, at the moment, no amount of bravado could conceal it, and he wondered exactly what sort of monster he had become. He did not regret his deeds, for they seemed very natural and logical; his sexual satisfaction required victims, and so he sought them, and society was fortunate that his sexual requirements would spark a radical alteration in the environment which, after all, had been partially responsible for his desires in the first place. He accepted himself as the ripper, but a portion of him did not want to continue being the ripper because it was too risky. Though he had no faith in the ability of the consulting detective or any of his minions, he was aware that sheer good luck had played its part in his elusion of his trackers and luck would not last forever; in addition, the consulting detective was determined, the ripper had seen fit to increase his determination, to goad him, and a truce was by now impossible, even if the ripper foreswore his sexual proclivities and willingly fled to the most remote corners of the universe. Life could not continue as it was, this the ripper knew, because though he controlled many elements simply by asserting his power, he could not control all the elements; and change, which was the only thing he ultimately feared, was inevitable. These thoughts, along with the fading dreams and sensations of his sexual conquests, the ripper dwelled upon as he ate his cheeseburgers, fries, and cottage cheese. He surprised himself by stuffing his face, hardly pausing to chew before swallowing; he had not noticed the extent of his hunger, he had not noticed that the chef had forgotten to hold the pickles until one of the reprehensible green things slipped out of his second cheeseburger, and he was a man who prided himself for noticing all the nuances of his physical feelings, so that he might better understand himself and his emotions at any given moment; his lack of insight disturbed him, for it was an indication that he was taking too much for granted; despite his lack of respect for the consulting detective, he knew too well the folly of error. Regardless of the speed in which he consumed his meal, the ripper noticed the food was bland; his hunger had not titillated his taste buds and it had not pained his stomach. The ripper was once again losing the ability to experience sensation, as if an improbable cold had closed down all his sensory organs, including the nerves in his fingertips. He dreaded the solution to the problem, though he knew eventually he would anticipate it. He smiled at the waitress as she lumbered toward his booth; for once he was thankful his senses had closed down. She stood beside the booth and cocked her head as if it was the hammer of a giant pistol; she waited, the ripper smiled, and finally she said, "Well?"

"My compliments to the chef," said the ripper by way of payment. He stood, walked past her, and prevented himself from bolting toward the door and freedom from her grotesqueness.

"Hey! What about my tip?"

Despite his better judgment, the ripper faced her; he felt victorious, his senses broadcasting to his brain all manner of sweet sensations. "Get out of the business."

"If I want any shit out of you, Mac, I'll squeeze your head."

The ripper's eyes widened in shock; the morose customers, who had previously ignored the devastating duel of wits, broke out in laughter, many of them holding their stomachs and trying to stop before they vomited their meal. The ripper stared at them, at their pale faces, at the tears streaming from their eyes, at the yellow teeth exposed by their smiles; and their laughter sounded like the laughter of thousands in the tiny public diner. It did not matter that the ripper considered the waitress's rejoinder classless and much inferior to his witticisms; this game had been played for the audience, and from the manner in which various individuals pointed at the ripper, totally unaware of his true capabilities, it was apparent society had decreed a victor. The ripper had no choice but to accept his defeat, though his blunted mind desperately tried to think of an appropriate reply. He was still thinking as he neared the Joy Mission, and he still felt the heat of his humiliation. They had laughed at him; they had drawn upon their frustration and their overpowering need to escape their mutual depression and they had laughed at him; he was the object of their relief, the means of their escape, and they did not know he was the very one who would lead them from their depression, this was the way they had treated him in return. As he walked to the Joy Mission, the ripper wondered why they did not just commit suicide, since they admitted they had nothing to live for. He wondered why the average depressed godlike man moped through eons of days as if he expected something constructive to develop in his existence. He hated each man and woman he saw, they had all played their part in

humiliating him though they had not been in the diner, he would
have killed them all, one by one, starting with the bum sleeping
on the sidewalk that he had stepped over outside the diner and
concluding somewhere in the throng of standing bodies waiting
for admittance into the Joy Mission, yes, he would have killed
them all if only it had been night and they had been several
blocks apart, each of them solitary, he imagined a hundred
solitary spurts of blood cascading from falling bodies in the East
End, along his route to the Joy Mission; and when he began
standing, waiting for admittance, among the silent godlike men
and women who felt so sad they could not summon a frown, the
ripper realized how much he needed joy in his life, a permanent
joy, a joy that would not pass forever like a lost dying moment.
There was no continuity in his existence, nothing that could
comfort him, however minutely, when his disposition was at its
lowest ebb (which was most of the time). Satiating his sexual
desires was ultimately a transitory benefit, and he wondered why
people (including himself) depended so greatly upon sexual
satisfaction, seemingly to the exclusion of aspects of life with
permanent value (offhand, he did not know what those aspects
were). He wondered why people did not just ignore their sexual
impulses (as had he for several million years; it had been
difficult, of course). However, even the memories of the
tremendous joys of sex could not withstand the terrific
radiations of despondency the ripper felt from the crowd; each
individual felt as he, and the combined depression, unrelieved by
smiles or even by resignation, increased until it seemed the
emotions of the throng could not reach a lower state, upon
which time it appeared to arbitrarily set a lower goal and
proceeded to reach toward it. Over five hundred godlike men
and women, the sediment of the East End, were crowded in the
courtyard before the Joy Mission. Some leaned against lamp-
posts or the sides of buildings for support, but in some areas
the people were so thickly packed that movement was next to
impossible, and the ripper spotted several individuals who were
asleep standing up, who would not fall due to the bodies pressing
against them from all sides. He used the term "individuals"
loosely; though the people had separate, distinct identities, the
dreadful sameness of disposition made it hard for him to
distinguish one from the other. Or perhaps he simply no longer
cared. The uniqueness of each was an illusion anyway; each had

selected a different shell to conceal the similarity beneath. A
hulking green man with purple frayed trousers idly chipped a
wall with his incredibly hard forefinger until a dude who was hip
like a zip, wearing a white shirt with a Mr. B collar, informed
him that the building might collapse on the crowd. A delicious
slut wearing nothing but a strategically placed leopard skin
allowed a godlike man with the face of a mandrill to finger her
cunt; both pretended to pay no attention to one another; judging
strictly from their facial expressions, nothing particularly
interesting was transpiring. A monarch in yellow robes
mumbled commands to illusory subjects he hoped would go
mad. A knight with a silver hand spoke with a beautiful
depressed woman who obviously was in love with him, but he
did not notice her love. A surfeit of red-headed men played
marbles in a corner. The cubical man, whose face was comprised
of rectangles, squares, and other geometrical figures formed by
straight lines, leaned against a wall and stared at his cubical feet
in cubical shoes. A dashing blond swordsman, a grim man with a
mace, and a fat buffoon wandered about, pretending to search
for a fight; but they could not summon the necessary emotion to
begin one for the sheer joy of it. Despite the tremendous external
variety, these people were not interesting; there was nothing
fascinating about any of them, the ripper noted, as he sought to
find a place where he could await his entry in privacy. He hoped
he had not come too late. Only a certain number were allowed
into the Joy Mission each day, and the demand far exceeded the
capacity. So many people came to the courtyard as early as
possible, to position themselves near the door, to ensure
themselves of a few fleeting moments of joy. Of course, the time
of their arrival did not ensure them entry; they might be pushed
too far away, especially on days when the crowd was most
desperate. Once a system had been instigated which attempted
to see to it that the godlike men and women stood in line, but the
line went on for several blocks, and when the doors to the
mission opened, the line disintegrated anyway, the people
fought to get inside; one even attempted to teleport inside,
though the walls had been protected from the penetration of
foreign atoms, and only the efforts of three officials prevented
the individual from expiring when his atoms regrouped
belatedly. No one knew why the Joy Mission was open to only
one crowd a day; no one knew just what it was about the

program that (ostensibly) required so much preparation; but no one was inclined to question the regulations of the Joy Mission. The officials were totalitarian; they interpreted questions as interference; and they tolerated no interference. Even the ripper, who considered himself a man to be feared, would not cross the path of an official of the mission, not during the day anyway, not when he so desperately required joy, joy he was afraid would never be his, not until night, when he could no longer prevent himself from asserting his will, from succumbing to the worm inside him. It would seem that the presence of the will and the worm were contradictory, but it was quite the opposite; the will required the worm, the worm required the will. *Legions of them*, thought the ripper, *definitely legions* as the wooden doors were opened from the inside by a dour, bald individual. The ripper pushed and shoved his way through the throng. Despite his listless attitude, he was more aggressive than these people he detested so; desperation caused them not to care, to accept their failure, while it caused him to fight back recklessly, at least until he neared the entrance and composed himself for fear the dour individual would not allow him inside for disturbing the emotional equilibrium. Once he forced himself to stop shoving, the ripper realized that only the physical activity had prevented him from totally submitting to the utter negativism of the legions surrounding him. His anger remained, but it was suddenly dormant; he no longer possessed the will to resist. He felt very tired; these emotional ups and downs were beginning to take their toll; he had never been so weak when he had been able to eat peanut butter sandwiches regularly. He passed the dour individual; he wondered how a person could be so short and yet exude such a suffocating sense of self-importance. Inside the mission, a soft blackness seemed to descend from the roof many meters above, and when the house had been filled, the doors were closed, leaving just over a hundred godlike men and women without their daily ration of joy, a ration they could obtain nowhere else in the East End. (Some wandered away, but most remained in the courtyard, under the rolling gray clouds; and they hoped for a miracle—they hoped the doors would creak open and the dour individual would politely inform them there had been a mistake, there was room for them after all.) The ripper tried to get a seat near the front, but he failed; he was forced to sit in the center left; fortunately he was not behind tall godlike men, which was his usual run of luck. The folding wooden chairs, besides being exceedingly uncomfortable (often thanks to rather tenacious and resourceful splinters with an uncanny talent for placing themselves in an unsuspecting buttock), were arranged back to back; and the floor was flat. Consequently, unless one sat near the front, the lowermost area of the huge holoscreen was not in view. When he first began attending the daily showings at the Joy Mission, the ripper wondered who was responsible for the care of the premises, the show, and the schedule; he could not imagine the few dour individuals about taking responsibility for any of those tasks, since when they were not exercising their power over the helpless they appeared to be straining their mental might merely by opening and closing the doors. He had often been horribly indignant that the authorities, whoever they were, had decreed the episode could be run only once a day; he expected the excuses he had heard were subterfuge; the authorities probably feared if their formula for joy became too commonplace, and the access too convenient, then the results would be proportionately diminished, thus forcing them to think of another formula. And if the quality of their help was any indication. . . . Well, now the ripper no longer cared for such matters. He felt impatient, as if he had been forced to wait an unconscionable amount of time, when in truth he had been sitting in the darkness for only five minutes. He felt the anticipation of the audience too, as members spoke nervously and fidgeted loudly; today's desperation was greater, if more subtle, than usual, and the dour individuals appeared not to notice, as if they were deliberately teasing the audience. The ripper wondered what the delay could possibly be; the ration of joy always began earlier than this, or at least it had seemed to. However, so gradually that at first the agitated ripper did not notice, the holoscreen glowed a dull yellow, indicating it was warming up. Though the desperation did not actually decrease, many members of the audience sighed and outwardly composed themselves. The additional anticipation, as far as other members were concerned, was excruciating. Even the ripper, who did not fear violence (so long as he was reasonably safe), shrank inside as his nerves were adversely affected by the tension which seemed to disrupt the steady beating of his heart and to increase that damned film over his eyes. He thought he would collapse with relief when the holoscreen unexpectedly glowed with considerable brightness, aching his eyes despite the film. Then the brightness diminished to a reasonable intensity, only to be replaced entirely by the vision of a curtain rising on a nondescript stage. The applause of the emotional derelicts was added to the canned applause. The ripper relaxed to watch the ration of joy. The host was known as the wizard of whoopee. If he possessed another identity which he used outside the function of rationing joy, it was unknown; the ripper had never seen anyone remotely resembling him. The wizard of whoopee was over two meters tall, though his body was proportioned as if his height was average; the ripper remembered this with amazement, for now it was impossible to tell since the wizard was alone on stage, waving at the holocameramen as if they were the audience of derelicts. The wizard wore a black robe, a black triangular hat with red stars, and a black cape with red interior lining; he carried a thin black wand with a white tip. Although he could have appeared impressive, imbued with a frightening other-world mysticism if he chose, he smiled as if he had just brushed his teeth for the first time in a million years and was very proud of it. His narrow face, with hollowed eyes and large cheekbones, seemed as if it had been victimized by a terrible muscular disease during the nonstop smile. The wizard said, "Hey, it's great to be here, ladies and germs. We're going to have some fun! Hey, let me tell you about my girl friend who's so bowlegged that when she sits around the house, she sits *around* the house! Hey, too much. My girl friend has the most beautiful silkiest longest black hair I've ever seen—but under her arms? On her chest? From her nose? Hey, I've got a million of 'em! Hey, how do you break the fat man's finger? You kick him in the nose!" Much to his surprise, because he had enjoyed the ration in the past, the ripper covered his eyes and wished he was somewhere else; but, just as the walls prevented people from entering, they prevented people from leaving. The dour individuals would not allow protocol (that is, keeping the doors closed during the rationing) to be violated solely because a person had unexpectedly tired of joy. *Is that what's happened to me?* thought the ripper as he forced himself to watch. *Is there no hope for me? Have I brutalized my sensibilities so much that high-quality material like this is too low-key for my tastes?* The notion that the fault might lie within himself brought to life the dormant hatred; for the ripper, upon

self-reflection, could not discern where he had taken a wrong
step on the path of life. The steps had been mapped out long
before he had begun the journey, and now he suffered due to
circumstances he could not control. He had not asked to be born
a man, he had not asked to be changed into a godlike man; he did
not want *to need* to eat and sleep and shit and fuck and yet it
seemed every moment of his existence was occupied with
activities relating to these requirements and every time he could
no longer ignore one and he fulfilled it, at least for the time
being, the urge to fulfill another would itch at his insides and he
knew that even if he could satiate them all at once, he would be
too tired, or too bored, to do anything because these
requirements of existence had left him no time to learn what else
he might accomplish. And he had lived for eons this way! No
wonder he had become the ripper. No, it certainly was not his
fault. *The ration is shit, that's all, it's always been shit and I've
always known it but I didn't want to admit it because I fervently
required the opportunity to laugh at something unspeakably
demeaning just like these assholes need to laugh though they
don't know, those stupid shits, that they're demeaning
themselves just like being around them demeans me.* And on the
holoscreen the wizard of whoopee introduced the unknown
comedian, a thin, godlike man who wore a tacky pinstriped suit
and a paper bag over his head. The unknown comedian said to
the wizard looming over him, "Hey, I know a joke that'll make
you look stupid! Hey, you've already heard it!" *Holy moley*
thought the ripper as he covered his eyes again and shook his
head. The laughter, both canned and live, offended him so
greatly that he imagined his bones tingling in ire. Though he sat
in the darkened Joy Mission, though he was surrounded by his
fellows of the East End, he renounced his entire life and feelings;
he believed, with all his soul, that everything was a dream; the
Joy Mission, the laughter, and eons of thoughts and deeds and
dreams he wished he had realized and nightmares he had
realized—all were illusions, but another prank of the universe;
and he also believed if he summoned sufficient will he would
shatter the barrier of illusion and perceive the universe as it truly
existed. And while he was making this effort, he happened to
glance at the pitch-blackness enshrouding the ceiling, which not
even the glow of the holoscreen could penetrate, and he saw a
flickering white light that caused a part of his heart he had long

thought dead to respond with a yearning threatening to create intangible fingers reaching for substance and emotions and vague mystical constructs whose collective existences he had only suspected throughout the eons. What he saw, creating this unprecedented response, was a tiny luminescent butterfly attempting to conceal itself in the rafters. He felt a cool stream of air hiss into his mouth, totally without voilition, fortunately at a moment when the derelicts were practically rolling in the aisles at some nuance of the unknown comedian's antics. He wanted no one to notice this remarkable thing, this creature which had affected him, perhaps because he was the only person in the mission or in all the world privy to this beauty which brought him . . . joy. The ripper had never known such joy; he had seen beauty before, but it had always been the beauty of some slut's tits bouncing up and down as she walked down the street or of an especially succulent meal, in any case an object which was beautiful only because it would go a long way toward satiating one of his desires if he had the opportunity to use it; but this butterfly was of no practical value to him, and yet it surpassed all the beautiful tits in the universe. He realized that having seen this butterfly would in some mysterious fashion allow him not only to appreciate tremendous jugs to a greater extent, but the whole of life as well. The ripper experienced so much joy that the godlike man who had ruthlessly slain four women became more than just a distant phantom; he remembered the murderer as if he was thinking of a character in a book by the Big Red Cheese. It was extremely stupid of him, in his opinion, to allow the sight of an insignificant creature to have such an effect upon him; but he could not deny the effect, though a part of him insisted on it. He perceived the black chips of a cocoon near the butterfly; it had emerged sometime during the rationing; it had not taken flight yet. With horror he saw a cocoon chip fall from the rafter; it would surely land on someone's skull, the resulting irritation taking that someone's attention from the ration and possibly causing him to look to the source of the distraction; and then another would see the luminescent butterfly, the beauty would no longer belong solely to the ripper. However, panic did not dull the ripper's mental reflexes; a godlike man in his business had to think fast. He disintegrated the falling cocoon chip, and then the chips still clinging to the rafter, concealing his mental vibrations so the dour individuals would not detect anything unusual occuring within the midst of their normally listless charges. Then, with a minimum of trepidation, he relaxed as much as he dared to watch the butterfly. He anticipated eagerly its first tentative flapping of those bright fragile wings and he prayed no one else would see it as it made its way to the grill at the roof behind the holoscreen, where it could easily slip through the wide spaces between the wires and fly over the golden city. But the ripper was seized by a numbing sensation which simultaneously created an incredible nervousness threatening to overtax his already blunted brain. When the butterfly spasmodically flapped its wings, it was clear the creature was not struggling to fly, but instead it was attempting to cling to its position; it was weak, in danger of falling. And the ripper distinctly received the impression of fear. The butterfly was afraid of the darkness, the loud chaotic sounds; it had escaped from the confinement of its shell, but it had escaped from quiet and security as well. The ripper knew it was ridiculous to anthropomorphize the butterfly; it was only an insect of unknown origins, whatever its aesthetic qualities; however, he had no basic objections to his recent leanings toward the ridiculous, especially if being objective meant that he must deny his vision of a mindless caterpillar struggling up the walls of the Joy Mission. The caterpillar had not been spawned, nor had it been created by a godlike man, strictly as a lark; one day it had simply existed, a creature without origins, without precursors. It did not question why it struggled up the wall, because it did not possess the mind to formulate basic and realistic questions concerning its existence, a characteristic shared by a vast majority of godlike mankind. The butterfly followed the dictates of some unfathomable prodding; it climbed because it had to climb. It was surrounded by an incomprehensible universe, populated by incomprehensible (and very stupid) beings. On the rafters, it felt safe and secure; it had discovered the small, insignificant, untraveled location where it could realize its full potential. And now it had emerged from its shell equipped with an intelligence dwarfing that of the caterpillar. Now it could pose the proper questions. Now it arrived at the proper insights. Now it perceived the universe as it truly was. Naturally it was petrified; who could blame it? But, as if the accuracy of its perceptions was not causing it enough pain, it was realizing just how brief its existence would prove to be. The energy from the ultra-violet range, which had provided its subsistence during its metamorphosis, had lifted electrons into higher orbits; now the electrons were falling back into their proper orbits, setting free the energy responsible for its luminescence. However, the butterfly's system was not strong enough to cope with the energy. The ripper watched it cling painfully to the rafter as its beauty destroyed it. The wings withered, the tips of its wings burned like the wicks of tiny candles, a wisp of black smoke curled from its thorax; and before the ripper could reflect a course of action which would enable him to preserve the creature, its wings crumpled over its body, almost like those of a bat sleeping in the darkness; but this butterfly quickly folded in half, its combustion causing it to bend like a leaf. And still it clung to the rafter. It clung even when it was a charred lifeless lump, beneath the notice of the lowliest person in the East End. At the moment of the luminescent butterfly's death, the unknown comedian said, "Believe me, you have to get up early if you want to get out of bed," and the audience awarded the two gentlemen on the holoscreen a standing ovation which drowned the wizard of whoopee's wacky dialogue punctuating the unknown comedian's exit from the ration. The ripper sat staring at the rafter with tears in his eyes as the loathing for the derelicts surpassed a hatred which he had foolishly believed was insurpassable. *Those fucking nurds, they wouldn't know genuine beauty if it came up and bit them on the ass, how I hate them, how I wish I could kill them all right here and now, how dare they stand and applaud shit like this when they missed the most remarkable thing, how I hate them for being stupid*, he thought, although perhaps his insurpassable hatred would have been exceeded if another person had seen the luminescent butterfly and if the ripper had known. His hatred was not affected in any way by the fact that he had sincerely not wanted another to see the butterfly; no chain of circumstances or maze of desires could have prevented the white hot outpouring of emotion, which had become inevitable upon the butterfly's death. And when the interminable ration had concluded, and the emotional derelicts, their hearts already plummeting to the dreary depths from which they had briefly soared, shuffled outside; the ripper pushed and shoved his way through them with more violence than he had utilized to gain his entry to the Joy Mission. The venom in his heart was so acidic that he, though accustomed to poisonous emotions, feared he would expend himself, as had the butterfly. But once he had turned several corners and had walked a good distance from the Joy Mission, he felt that the venom was a source of strength. Indeed, since he had become the ripper he had never been so drunk on the nectar of his own emotions; his earlier timidity and fears of apprehension seemed totally ludicrous. The brisk coolness of the air pricked him with a thousand pleasurable needles as he nestled his parcel to his breast and reflected upon the coming activities. Thunder rumbled behind the thick dark clouds and the winds nearly blew his hat from his head several times; the weather only served to accentuate his presence. The flashes of lightning, the roars of thunder, the billowing clouds, and the shrieking wind—from them all he seemed to draw strength and sensation that enabled his frail frame to support the tremendous hatred inside him which paled the fury of the storm. The strain was increased by his inability to express his hatred; no one could suspect it or feel its negative vibrations if he was to fulfill his ambitions; to the average observer he had to appear like just another soulless derelict, a victim of the times. *Damn them damn them damn them* he thought of the secret authorities who regulated the Joy Mission. *Why do they give us shit when they could give us butterflies?* Only the greatest control prevented him from sneering at an emotional derelict sitting on a curb and sucking a lollipop. It would not do for anyone to notice, however in passing, that he had anything but the normal indifferent attitude toward his surroundings. After having made that cautionary observation he wondered what difference it would make if something strange concerning his manner was noticed, whether or not it was noted in passing. He was the ripper, he had slain four women, and though he once had been an individual of supreme unimportance, as faceless metaphorically as the universal op was faceless literally, he was now the godlike man who would lift these good-for-nothing fuckers from the East End whether or not they wanted to be lifted because altruists traditionally did not care what the people really wanted or needed, because altruists make up their minds independently and any conflicting evidence is fabricated by poor misguided bastards. The ripper was an altruist and proud of it. The rain suddenly descended with incredible force, the drops plummeting into the puddles like fragile suppositories tossed from on high. The noise of the rain's violent descent seemed to grant the ripper strength, and as it continued unabated, as the night also descended, the ripper stalked the East End. The worm, too, seemed to have descended upon him, more violently than ever, though in truth it had always writhed inside his soul. The ripper could not accept that his sense of being originated totally within himself; disregarding his great powers (which at the moment he considered of no consequence), he could not believe the miracle of his mind and personality was the result of blind evolution, electrical impulses, chemical reactions; somehow, some way, he had to discover a common thread to his existence, or failing that, he had to do something to take his mind off things for a while. He glorified in his sexual urgings, which were vaguely defined in his mind though their manifestations were always rather abundantly clear, at least while he was immersed in the actual act or any of the variations he had developed a taste for. And the rain plummeted and plummeted, the drops striking the puddles with what he easily imagined as anger, the streams of water loudly proclaiming their presence as they flooded the alleys and curbs; he seemed to draw a strength from them, for they were elements raging at godlike mankind and his civilization, as the ripper himself raged. And that raging brought him purpose and aided him in defining himself in his own eyes, even as the lack of definition in other areas confused him; for if the ripper contemplated anything but anger, for instance if thoughts of sex brought forth thoughts of love instead of anger and power and revenge, then he simply could not conceive of himself taking part in a sexual encounter, or in any activity requiring love and devotion. His had been a life of neutrality, devoid of sensation, including hatred, until he had become so depressed that he was forced to act to salvage an existence which had become meaningless to him. He stalked the East End like a phantom, easily avoiding the consulting detective and his minions whenever he sensed their presence; and sensing them had nothing whatsoever to do with his godlike powers, it really was as if the elements were aiding him, as if the oversoul had selected him to purge its cancer, as if he was not actually so alone, so hideously alone as he had been all these long eons. He found it difficult to dwell upon those years as he huddled near walls so the gutters and the patios overhead would partially protect him from the onslaught that frightened him even as it nourished him. He feared the elements would do his job for him, the wind would surely blow the golden buildings like artifacts of straw across the earth. He wished to dwell upon some aspect of his personality other than his sexual desires (which after all were derived from a lust for power—or from the worm), but when he tried to think of those lonely eons, or even of that fat slob of a waitress, he perceived them as dreams, as if all he had ever been and what little that had ever happened to him had become as unreal as the murders, which only another murder could make real again. He had become the ripper, but he was the ripper and the ripper only, and not any of the million nuances that formed a full-fledged three-dimensional godlike man. All his carefully considered rationalizations and irrationalizations, justifying his intentions, became mere wisps of the dreams, their substance nebulous, their meanings trifles. At certain moments, when the light from the streetlamps struck him in a particular way and he turned his palm at the right angle, the raindrops fell through his hand; and not even that knowledge jolted his memory; he became intent upon his ignorance so long as he was the ripper and only the ripper. As for those other aspects of his personality—well, evidently if he forgot his place in the universe, then the universe forgot his place in it. This phenomenon had startling implications—perhaps it explained why a member of the race was forced to assume a distinct identity, so that any doubts would not descend beyond a certain depth; perhaps the disappearance occurred gradually, over a period of eons, and the rest of the race was unaware of what would happen to it if they lost their self-images. The speculations were irrelevant, however, in the wake of his desperation, which fed his sexual desires. It was doubtless this desperation, this craving need for sensation to overwhelm a body rapidly becoming incapable of touch and, consequently, of feeling, which had initially forced him to take such radical measures. Yet, as he reflected back, he could not recall exactly how he had arrived at the choices which were to lead to four events of devastating sensation. True, he had made the choice to become a monster, and he had embarked upon a specific direction at the choice; but he could not recall the particulars and the emotions and the rationalizations behind the first steps. *At least it had to do with women. If it had had to do with men, I would have packed it in and disappeared. I may not know what I am, but one thing's for sure: I ain't no fag.* And his imminent disappearance (which was by no means consistent; most raindrops splattered on his hand) had at least one advantage: it increased the mysterious quality about his person, the quality being that of his sexual magnetism, his ability to attract certain women who sensed his will to power, his desire to dominate women almost as lost as he; these women desired to lose themselves to their passions for a time, they wanted another to decide their pleasures and to tell them what they would do next; perhaps they feared subconsciously, that if left to their own devices for too long, they would also fade. They would not know who they were. Their identities were reinforced and, sometimes, created by what others felt their identities to be. They sensed in this nebulous man someone who would reinforce their identities to their liking. The irony of it amused the ripper, even as he felt himself weighed down by his desperation; indeed, he effectively resolved their dilemmas for all time, though hardly in a manner they would have approved if he had given them the opportunity to voice their opinion. And the sexual magnetism he felt surging in him—that mysterious power many godlike men, who did not possess it, believed to be a myth fostered by the immature— provided him with a sense of identity potent enough to counteract many of the unfortunate side-effects of his other problems. His personality, reduced as it was to an instinctive drive somewhat tempered by civilized habits, was devoid of free will; the ripper would do nothing which would delay his ultimate satisfaction. He had entirely lost what he believed his most valuable ability—that of examining his emotions and feelings, or lack of them, enabling him to pinpoint if not solve his problems. If the question had been posed to him, he would have denied his godlike humanity, for he would have been able to perceive no connection between the shadow in his head and the manifestations of reason in another eloquent (and brave) enough to speak with him. Only the women who needed him, who needed him so desperately they were drawn to him, would willingly confront him as he stalked the thundering and bellowing East End. Occasionally he paused, as if expecting to see a delicate light in the darkness, but all he saw was the lightning and the darts of rain as they passed through the beams of the streetlamps. And then he continued his remorseless journey. His determination increased whenever a raindrop passed through his body or when he saw the hazy outlines of his reflections in a huge puddle. He had no doubt he would succeed; for had he not already succeeded in three previous nights, though the remembrances were vague? Nevertheless, as time passed, as he walked deserted alleys and near-deserted streets, he wondered if he would find someone before it was too late. Would he live until tomorrow night if he found no one? What would his final hours be like? Or would the process of his disappearance take a thousand years? These questions and many others plagued his mind until he saw a godlike woman of just the type he was searching for—the seller of speculations. He recognized her immediately. Once, before he had become the ripper, he had entered her shop in the hopes that he might find some escape from the relentless persecution he sensed; and he had watched her talk very knowledgeably to two handsome godlike men, and he had studied the blonde curls concealing delectable earlobes and the singular curl of extra length falling onto her forehead, and he had thought, *Why, she's almost beautiful*. Now, as then, he wondered just what it was about her psyche that prevented her from perfecting her beauty; he sensed, with the added insight into the feminine condition derived from the practical application of his sexual magnetism, that a great deal of sensation was required to burst through the film of her constant pain, a film she ensheathed herself with not due to circumstances, but due to the awareness that without her pain she would fear she was not alive. If pleasure could not convince herself of her existence, then pain would suffice. The ripper would have smiled if there had not been the possibility she would perceive his utterly ungallant satisfaction through the haze his self-doubts had created upon his features. He stood noble and proud, though slightly self-effacing, as she walked to him with that unmistakable joy in her eyes. If he could have shut off his magnetism, she nevertheless would have still been under his spell, wondering exactly why she desired this unattractive, bland man so, vaguely remembering the staggering intensity of emotion she had experienced upon her first sight of him, instinctively striving to summon anew the powerful tonics of her chemicals running amok. She tilted her head to the left like a baleful cur as she took his hand (he prayed to the oversoul that it was tangible). He was repulsed by the darkened hair dropping straight in thick soaked clumps over her shoulders and those stray strands sticking to her face; surely she might have possessed the foresight to protect those curls. But, then again, like all women, she was just as self-destructive as she was destructive. And even as the ripper was repelled by her timid smile, as he desired with all his heart to ball his hand into a fist and to bash out those white straight teeth, something inside him urged him to press his mouth against hers; and he was tormented by the conflicting desires, and he hated her for causing this confusion. His predicament was heightened by the civilized shackles he could never totally escape; he had to be nice to her for a time, undergoing the torturous meaningless preliminaries, for the sake of her delusions; and besides, there were others on the street, two others, in the distance, and he feared they would not turn a corner until they had passed them. There was the remote possibility they would provide the consulting detective with a clue, regardless of the success or failure of the ripper's more immediate ambitions.

The seller of speculations introduced herself, adding, "I don't want to know your name, not yet. I . . . I just want to love you, not only for a night, but for a long time, if you know what I mean."

"What you're trying to tell me is that you want to go somewhere and screw, right, toots?" said the ripper, his attention distracted, forcing him to fall back on the technique that had worked most often for him.

"I think it's probably the best place to begin, but you must bear in mind I don't foresee an ending in the near future."

"That's all right," said the ripper, not looking at her but at the approaching figures. Holding his parcel to his chest, removing her hand from his so he could grasp her upper arm, he scanned the area; he knew already, through the thick blackness of his resolute instinct, the purposes of the non-residential buildings and the identities of everyone who lived in the immediate vicinity; he scanned for empty apartments. And he could not prevent his hazy eyebrows from raising despite the sleepiness which still weighed him down as he learned of one very interesting deserted apartment, not twenty meters away. "I know a place where we can get it on in style." He led her toward an alleyway.

"Hey, I'm not that kind of woman. I don't do it in public," said the seller of speculations, the lightness of her tone being only slightly forced.

You would do it wherever I insisted, thought the ripper, knowing the correctness of the reflection. He guided her through the debris—the overturned trashcans, the broken bottles, the soaked paper with runny streaks of ink, the cardboard, the rotting scraps of food. The odor, which offended her if the way she wrinkled her nose was an indication, imbued the ripper with euphoria, as if it required a surfeit of refuse to convince him that the East End was his proper element. Filled as he was with the knowledge that he would wipe this filth out of existence, he believed himself innately superior to it—and to everything, as if he would one day be the sole matter in the universe. Only in the environment he detested with the greatest fervor could he feel anything approaching peace. He felt a surge of heat tingle in his fingers at the seller's arm, body heat undiminished by her blouse and jacket sleeves. He wondered if the heat was real or if it originated in his imagination. He wondered why he thought it delightful when it also revolted him. He strode about the garbage like a jungle explorer. He imagined he was guiding the seller on a dangerous journey, fraught with unparalleled menaces. He imagined this thing and others very lucidly, despite his fears of disappearing, of dropping his parcel through intangible fingers, despite the relentless pounding of his heart which he feared had become an alien object somehow implanted in his system. The seller appeared puzzled, her face silently asking innumerable questions, particularly through those confused, bovine-like eyes; and as the ripper wished he could tear them out, right then and there, as he would have if there had not been too many emotional derelicts about forcing him to seek concealment, he wished he could terminate the confusion for all time, but not in the method he normally used; he wanted her to trust him implicitly, and he wondered what was happening to him that he would wish for the trust of one of those supremely untrustworthy creatures, sluts, they were sluts, all of them, and yet perhaps he was only imagining this desire for trust, because he had not slept for so long, even his most casual movements were ponderous to his dreary perceptions, because he had not really looked at things in quite the same way since he had seen the butterfly, because he felt through his sexual needs and his fears and his urge for power an alien spirit inside him, or at least a spirit of which he had previously been unaware, a spirit that longed to embrace an object outside of him even as it remained inside him. Or perhaps he was merely beginning to feel intimate with womankind in general, not an unlikely explanation since he had been examining women in ways unimagined for eons. At any rate, he was being drawn toward this seller of speculations he was guiding through the clutter. He did not exactly picture sticking his dick up her cunt, not in so many words, but it was an aspect of the desire overwhelming him, and he began to understand what she had been trying to tell him though he adamantly rejected her sentiments since they were, at best, delusions he had gained some insight into.

"I don't want to know your name because I want to picture you as an essence of godlike mankind," said the seller of speculations as she tiptoed through a particularly deep puddle laden with tiny floating debris. Then she paused, not allowing the ripper to take her further until he had heard her out. "I think that deep-down inside you're the type that'll truly love me, despite your surface mannerisms. I think that through that haze is a kind face belonging to a man who truly understands my need for love. I need someone who believes in my worth, who appreciates my existence. I need a love that'll last forever. Do you understand?"

"Yes." *Of course I understand you need some poor simp to delude you into thinking your shit doesn't stink.* And he took her arm, feeling again the heat through his weariness; and as he gazed into her eyes, knowing she could not see his, he was overpowered by the need to love her in the manner she intended even as he wanted to fuck her until she walked bowlegged all the time, he wanted to fuck the living daylights out of her, what did he care for her "need to love," she just wanted to impale herself on his dick, that was all, women did not care who they were with or what kind of promises they had made and/or were breaking just so long as they had fifteen centimeters jammed up their cunts, or up their assholes depending on how degenerate they were and this bitch was undoubtedly degenerate, he hated her, the pig, because she aroused both terror and pity in him, thwarting his ultimate ambition of realizing his power over her. It was wrong for a superior being such as he to be in awe of anyone; people always preyed upon him, chafing his anxieties, and it was wrong that he had accepted it for so long, but maybe there was nothing he could do about it, it was too deeply ingrained in his system, he remained in awe of her despite the fact that she was nothing but a slut, an emotional derelict just like the rest of the scum in the East End and he was going to fuck her in this basement apartment now that they had arrived, they had finally fought their way through the fucking trash, and though the journey had not taken two minutes he felt like he had just been released from purgatory as he turned the dirty doorknob only to find it did not work, a few screws were loose somewhere, screws which would have taken but a second to mend with godlike powers, but what was he thinking about beneath his smothering instincts, he should be thinking about doing in this lusty wench and besides he should keep in what was left of his mind just whose apartment this was, an apartment where loose screws in the doorknob were not an annoyance, instead they were an inestimable treasure. "Damn it!" he said with such violence that even the seller, who had been known to utter vehement exclamations herself, was repelled by those simple words; and the ripper turned the doorknob this way and that several times, not thinking to mend the screws himself because he was, after all, a beast and proud of it. However, he pushed the door and it creaked open a centimeter, stopping, requiring a second stronger push before the rusty jambs would allow it to open wide enough for their entry. They were immediately struck by a gush of tepid stuffy air in contrast with the cool wind; yet the warmth was preferable, and so they entered quickly, the ripper closing the door with an effort, and closing it twice more when the latch slipped from the lock, before he took stock of his surroundings. He had never before imagined a place such as this, not in his most vivid fears about the East End, not in his most degenerate nightmares (and there had been a few, as loathe as he was to admit it). He staggered against the door, thankful that the seller of speculations was more stunned than he and therefore did not notice his moment of weakness; for a time all sleepiness, all animal passions, all base instincts were banished from his mind and body, and he sought to confront the vision as a reasonable godlike man might. But in the end reason was negligible and he could only absorb the vision to the best of his superior ability. The door behind him was riddled with knife-marks; the knife had not been thrown at a specific target, or if it had, the thrower's aim had been excremental. Piles and piles of laundry were stacked up on the chairs and sofas and coffee tables and on the floor surrounding them; the highest pile on the floor was over half a meter tall; and there were paths through the laundry except where the piles had been tipped over. The laundry itself was comprised of all types and sizes; the discarded smoking jacket for the extremely obese laid on top of what was once a provocative red negligee; blue towels mingled with white-and-green towels, and there were boxer shorts, white briefs, polka-dot socks, striped socks, solid socks, knee socks of all three designs, torn and faded bluejeans, corduroy trousers, in fact trousers of all fabrics sizes and colors, including a garish orange and another of bright yellow that particularly stuck out in the crowd, offending the ripper because he could well understand why someone would throw trousers of those colors away, but not why anyone would make them in the first place. There were used rags, still greasy, torn strips of cloth that once might have been intended as patches, pillow cases, a few blankets, panties (black or white), a tacky scarf with designs of people in various fucking positions, four umbrellas including a broken one that would not close, sheets wadded rather than folded, there was so much, but though there was a lot of color, a dim brownish haze masked most of the laundry (with the exception of the two pairs of trousers) and besides, after a moment the ripper did not pay much attention to the laundry, it was merely the first thing that had caught his eye, because his sensitive nostrils had detected the unmistakable odor of cat shit, and sure enough, over there in the corner, where notebook paper had been casually tossed, there was approximately two kilograms of dried cat shit with white flakes just waiting to fall to the floor and make an even bigger mess, but that cat shit was so old it could not possibly be causing the odor, and when he made that observation the ripper's superior olfactory system pin-pointed the odor which originated right below his reeling nostrils; and he looked down to see that the source was his left foot, he turned to see that immediately upon entering he had stepped in a big heaping fresh gob of cat shit. And the knowledge filled him with ire at the callousness of the universe, if only he could blame someone personally, but he learned from a quick scanning that the resident's cat was not in the apartment, it had set its trap for the unwary and then departed, leaving the ripper with but one recourse, which was to exclaim, "Fuck dogs!" though offhand he could not see much difference between fucking dogs and fucking the seller of speculations who was nothing but an old bitch anyway, he knew this from her snobbish manner as she inspected the premises, at least he was righteously indignant but she was just condescending that was all there was to it, if he had brought her to his apartment she would not have acted any differently; she would have examined the dehydrated peanut butter on his bracket exactly as she examined the prize articles of worthless trash that adorned the wall-to-wall shelves. Though he could not blame her, he admitted to himself as he sent all the fresh cat shit to the antimatter universe. Broken trophies, chips of glass, rusty nails, lamps without switches, a stereo without a tone arm, warped unprotected records, a cracked saltshaker, a rotted birdhouse, old newspaper clippings in frames with shattered glass, an early holoscreen model, needles, thumbtacks, nails, screws, hammers with broken handles, a rusty saw, torn and water-damaged dolls of all types (including one that pissed when you pushed it on the belly, but it was busted and so it peed constantly—the water deriving from an unknown source—causing a stain on the back of the case and the shelves below it and a steady irritating drip), glass replicas of fat holy men, centaurs, horses, dogs, cats, and other animals, none of the replicas whole—all these and more were jammed on the brimful shelves, the result of eons of serious collecting. The furniture was also in a sorry state; springs stuck out of the chairs and sofas, and where there was no laundry, the ripper saw holes exposing the cotton padding; there were also holes in pillows and cushions. The seller of speculations wrinkled her nose, very characteristically the ripper thought though this was but the second time he had seen her. "Who lives here?" she asked haltingly, as if a verbal acknowledgment of the apartment's existence was taboo.

"Why, the tatterdemalion of course."

Her eyes widened, becoming more like those of a bovine than ever, if that was possible. "I remember him; he wanted beat-up first editions of books by the doughnut-mix specialist; he was very insistent that they were beat-up. I remember feeling very sorry for him, though I confess I haven't thought of him, not even once, since then." She turned and looked down at the ripper. Her eyes remained wide but there was a more animate quality to them, as if she was prepared to be violently dull. "I confess I've thought too much of myself and I haven't thought enough about love. I think love is the most important thing in the world. I used to think love was a myth and only sex was important. I wanted to have sex with men but I never wanted to give myself to them; I wanted them to offer themselves to me. But now I feel so bright and gay inside. I know you'll make me happy. In fact, I'm so happy right now I'm afraid I'm going to cry." She bit her lower lip. "Are you happy? Please say you are."

"I am very happy. I don't know when I've ever been so happy," the ripper said slowly, feeling as if his voice originated with another. *Sure I'm happy. I'm so happy I could just shit.* However, part of him was happy, that was what he could not understand, part of him did want to form a permanent union with the seller of speculations, to settle down, as it were, to renounce his uniqueness though it could never be renounced, not since he had slain the woman without a nose, the ugly old hag. "The tatterdemalion's a good buddy of mine; he lets me crash here when he's away."

The seller of speculations smiled. "Is he supposed to return soon?"

"Nope. You know how it is when you're out collecting trash. He's gone for weeks at a time. His last few trips have lasted for months, in fact, because he's taken up alien trash. Got a little place below the surface of the moon where he stores it." The ripper nodded; he pursed his lips knowingly though he wondered why he did so since she probably could not see them clearly; his face remained hazy and he still feared disappearing, despite his impending victory. What if his hand became intangible and his parcel, which he had been holding with a casual air, fell and broke apart despite all the odds? What would she do if she saw the antimatter knife? Would she then know who he was? Or would she think *What a cute artifact; he must be a butcher* and let him go ahead and fuck her? She was so blinded by love that she would accept any explanation as long as she did not already know the truth. He quickly scanned the apartment to ascertain more accurately the layout. "This way to the bedroom, babe. Don't worry; I'll create some clean sheets."

In the bedroom he pushed laundry from the solitary table and set down the parcel; it was the first time it had left his hands since he had eaten the cheeseburgers in the diner. The room was sparsely furnished; the William Morris chair appeared in excellent condition save for the missing right hind leg causing it to rest at an angle; there were no shelves of choice trash; and the only light radiated from a naked light bulb from a fixture in the ceiling which he had flicked on while entering. The ripper could not attempt to suppress his anticipation when he saw the circular cracked mirror on the dresser. A huge lower piece had been removed from the mirror; nevertheless he would still be able to watch himself fucking her, a fantasy he had not been able to indulge in since he had done his only fucking in the streets. The floor was remarkably, but not entirely, free of laundry and other debris; apparently the majority was crammed in the dresser, for bits and pieces protruded from the tops of the drawers. There was no blanket on the bed; the two sheets had been white in their better days but were now yellow and smelled like they had been dipped in sweat. The odor of the sheets paled next to that of the kitty box beside the dresser; having missed the box several times, the cat had seen fit to pepper the wayward shit with litter, thereby increasing the mess; what litter remained in the box either clung to tiny bars of shit or was dampened with cat piss. The seller of speculations wrinkled her nose snobbishly, but this time the ripper had no objections, since he basically agreed with her sentiments. In no mood for moderation, he sent the kitty box and everything associated with it to the antimatter universe; he scented the air with the odor of fresh roses (an odor he barely remembered; it returned to him with a feeling of inspiration); he cleaned and pressed the sheets with godlike perfection. She smiled at him, and somehow he knew she saw his smile through his haze. The ripper now lost all trace of weariness; his anticipation was excruciating, he could not wait for the event to begin, it was all he could do to resist tearing off her clothes, throwing her on the bed and mounting her without prelimina- ries. *Heck, why not?* he wondered to himself *she's nothing but a hot bitch anyway; she would probably like it* yet simultaneously he was afraid to indulge in this particular fantasy not only because of the possibility that it would ruin everything but because he remained in utter awe of her though she was just a woman and because she was a woman, she was almost an alien being, there was something forever mysterious about women, especially as far as he was concerned since he had been apart from society for eons, especially since the seller of speculations had turned her back to him, asking him to zip down her dress which he did awkwardly, as if it was part of a secret ritual, though he hoped and prayed to the oversoul that she did not notice his awkwardness, especially since she smiled so strangely to herself, thinking he could not see, forgetting about the mirror, as she walked from him, pulling her dress from her arms and then standing next to the bed as she let her dress fall. And now she was naked except for her panties and the ripper was vaguely embarrassed, he had only taken off his coat and shirt and he was thankful that he was hazy so she would not notice how flabby he was, and for a moment he stared at her and she looked back shamelessly and her breasts looked so strange, he could not get used to the sight of them because it was as if women had to go overboard parading their mysteriousness. He reached toward the light switch and she nodded no, implying she preferred doing it with the lights on; that was fine with him, it meant he would not have to use his powers to watch himself in the mirror, but it only confirmed his low opinion of her, he was a fool for ever remotely respecting her as a human being, she was just another specimen of the scum infecting the East End. When he was naked, she took off her panties and they faced each other from opposite sides of the bed. Now the ripper was embarrassed, not at his nakedness or at hers, but at his dick which was half erect when perhaps protocol would have been observed if it had been totally flaccid. The seller of speculation licked her lower lip. She said, "I don't want you to just fuck me."

The ripper said slowly, almost shyly, "I've never done that and I never will."

The seller sighed. "I think I might have been a lot better off if I had respected myself as much."

The ripper shrugged. "Just fucking someone isn't satisfying. There's a great deal more to love and life than just sex. Sex is meaningless by itself. What the mind brings to the act is the most important thing. Don't you agree?"

"Definitely," she said, no longer able to restrain herself as she got on the bed and pulled the ripper to her and they kissed, she stuck her tongue in his mouth, the ripper was taken aback by her unabashed passion, this was the first time he had ever begun in the more-or-less traditional fashion, and so his caresses were at first awkward but as he played with her left nipple, feeling it rise and harden, his confidence increased and he no longer feared he would become intangible, for a moment there he had feared his dick would become intangible just as he was about to stick it in but now he did not worry, it felt so hard (if a little hazy) as he leaned over top of her, supporting himself on his elbows, both his hands on her breasts playing with her nipples, ramming his tongue in her mouth feeling her palate pressing his tongue against it as hard as he could, as she spread her legs enabling him to caress her sweet cunt with his dick which tingled with the touch of every pubic hair and every drop of her wonderful love juice. Already the sensation penetrated the veils which had diluted the range of his experiences, and already he pondered how amazing it was that such comparatively small portions of the body could rack the whole with such force; he considered it incredible that his breathing was loud and harsh, as if he had suddenly become the passenger on a sensual journey in a mystical plane where communication was achieved by providing others with physical pleasure; he considered it stupid that as he was about to ram his throbbing member into the cunt of this hot bitch, he was analyzing the act to the best of his ability, why could he not just fuck her and concentrate on enjoying her while he had the chance? He lifted his head up so he could catch his breath and gain a brief respite from her halitosis; and he watched her open and close her eyes, when they were open they appeared blank as if she stared at blackness and as if he was nowhere, or as if she stared at him and he was everything, he could not decide which of the two observations was the correct one but it was certain that when she closed her eyes she appeared at peace, as if she had reached an exalted plane where she would no longer be forced to distract herself with purpose or needs, she had achieved that appearance despite the rippling of her pelvis as he ran his dick up and down her juicy cunt, she was at peace despite the passions surging inside her, perhaps because she was not giving much thought to what she was doing she was concentrating entirely on her pleasure, what the heck else could he expect, she thought with her hips anyway. Nevertheless, he could relate to her point of view as he succeeded in concentrating, for the moment, on the sensation in his dick which reacted so sensitively to the prickly pubes and the soft damp lips that he feared he would start bleeding somewhere, somehow, surely his skin could not withstand such pressure for so long, whatever its origin, he now understood why people enjoyed this method, why they preferred it to raising a skirt and penetrating the orifice of your choice from the rear, somehow the long preliminaries perpetuated the illusion that sex could mean more than the sum total of its events and then, suddenly, his dick began to worm its way into her hole, she had been fucked so many times (and had paid so little attention to her body) that an elephant could have worked its wang up there with ease and ease was not the word to describe the effortless movement of sticking his dick in that yawning throbbing incredibly damp and hot abyss, he had not expected it to be so damp and hot but then again entry had been a lot easier than it had been on the street so maybe there was something to those preliminaries after all. The intensity of the sensation increased severalfold, he plunged without reservations into her Stygian depths and he became afraid that he experienced sensation only in his dick, he had become nothing but a giant dick willingly submerging itself in darkness, he perceived his hands gripping the sheets just above her shoulders only with effort, but it required no effort to feel the seller of speculations grasp his buttocks and rub her legs against his and then wrap her left leg over his as he pounded her, pounded her, pounded her, but the heat of her touch on his buttocks and legs, even the damp heat of her mouth, was merely a subordinate almost subliminal sensation compared to the joyous freedom of balling this bitch, he did not even have to think of her as a person to enjoy it, in fact thinking of her as a person detracted from the enjoyment, he could not understand why she had insisted on it, it had not taken too many words to convince her before she spread her legs, she wanted his dick, she did not know what he really thought of her and if she did care, she did not care very much and certainly at the moment all she cared about was his dick, he knew this because she had been seized by an orgasm, she lifted and ground her pelvis against his while her body shook as if it was trying to relieve itself of her spine, what the heck, she did not need its support, bitches like her spent most of their time on their backs anyway and she was no exception and he knew this because of the way she was enjoying herself and though he was enjoying himself too, pounding her quim into mud, he was afraid too because the times on the street he had been forced through necessity to keep his mind on his ultimate objective but now he had the opportunity to lose himself to his passions and that was the problem, the very essence of the problem—he was losing himself. Earlier circumstances had forced him to take her off the street, to avoid discovery, but there had been no reason to bring her here so he could do it, more or less, like a normal godlike man. It had been a mistake to bring her here. Previously he had been unique; he had been himself; he had been the ripper. But sex freed him from his identity, what he had been or what he was planning was of no importance, the moment, the jab in question, was all that mattered; each moment lasted forever and he was, therefore, not the ripper. And when he was not the ripper, he was not much of anything. When he glanced at himself in the mirror, he saw that his haze had become more developed; he could not discern his own features for the blur. He imagined himself as some sort of personification of the masculine desire; he pounded her with the rhythm of a dog, attempting to consolidate all sensation in his dick so he could come and get it over with, but perhaps he was too shy, perhaps if he relaxed enough to come he would disappear completely and the sperm would fall from inside her body and through the bed, or perhaps fucking like a normal godlike man was not good enough, it simply was insufficient, he was unique therefore he had to fuck uniquely, fucking this way, losing himself to his desires this way, simply did not restore his self-image, he could not imagine himself doing this though he undeniably was, he felt like he had been swallowed by her cunt, she would never let him go. Besides, what was he doing fucking her this way, if coming was sufficient he would just beat off and forget this woman jazz, he could create an orifice this hot this snug this soft this enveloping if he really wanted to, thereby relieving himself of the necessity of being civil to this bitch, but mere coming was definitely insufficient, sex was unimportant compared with what he really wanted, he needed to feel superior to her and though this was in some part accomplished by her spreading her legs and waiting for him he still believed he was treating her too much as if she was his equal though she was nothing but a hot bitch, no, what he needed, what he most desperately required was the sensation of power, he wanted to be in control, he could and would do whatever he pleased with this sow and her juicy cunt just as soon as he got around to it, but they had begun grounding their pelvises together and he was reluctant to interrupt the successions of moments, he felt like his whole body was in a spasm despite its impending disappearance, he grabbed her buttocks, resting his chest upon hers, and then he rearranged his hands and arms so the crooks of her legs were being held in the crooks of his arms and he imagined himself falling deeper deeper who did this bitch think she was anyway doing this to him deeper deeper yet he felt so insubstantial, this was not himself fucking, he had lost control of himself, he was not responsible, there was nothing he could do, he was ensnared, he wondered if their pelvises would inadvertently crack if they kept it up, if he did not have to concentrate on the act itself then he could try to maintain what was left of his self-image and his corporeality, if only he would come but he could not relax enough for that, maybe he thought about it too much, well there was nothing left to do but get to work on that self-image, so he said, panting heavily, "My dear seller, I would appreciate it greatly, in fact I would consider it an honor, if you would grant me permission to pop your pooper."

"That would be wonderful; it's my favorite," replied the seller, and the ripper smiled to himself, her eyes were closed so she did not see his smile, somehow he had known that her answer would be along those lines though he had not expected quite so much enthusiasm, usually women on the street pretended not to like sodomy that much, at least not on the first date, but there was no point in dwelling upon those poor departed bitches now, not while he was turning her over by lifting her right leg and using it as a guide to place her in her new position, trying to keep his dick in place, but when the right leg had nearly completed its half-circle and she had nearly turned over, his dick inadvertently slipped out which was okay with him, now that he had received her permission to perform this act upon her person, he did not want to waste time with a slippery loose old cunt not when there were tighter avenues to examine. He rubbed his dick up and down her crack, then he inserted his forefinger into her asshole and his thumb into her cunt, his forefinger penetrating as far as it would go, his thumb cocked and rubbing the shaft of the forefinger through the posterior surface of the vagina, in the process contracting the tain't region ("tain't one, tain't the other"). He rotated his forefinger in a tiny circle, gradually dilating the sphincter until it was wide enough for his purposes; during this time the seller of speculations writhed, breathing heavily, gripping the sheets between the fingers of her fists, her butt poised, waiting to be impaled, she was primed and ready, he was going to fuck her in the ass, this would definitely be the highlight of his day. He did not plunge into her, instead he held her by the hips after positioning the tip of his dick just inside her asshole, he drew her toward him, his dick gradually working its way inside, and her head was turned on her cheek so he could watch her bite her lower lip as the sweat rolled from her forehead, he felt supreme, he finally felt supreme as his dick completed its entry and he leaned forward, placing his hands on the bed and he began moving in and out of her, savoring the sensation, it was a good thing he did not breathe through his dick otherwise he would be choked to death, but the sensation was still insufficient, he looked at himself in the mirror, he saw the reflection of her face contorted due to anal ecstasy yet he sensed himself still at the mercy of chemical reactions beyond his control, reactions which affected his soul but only for the worst and which ultimately had nothing to do with it, and as he stared at his hazy face in the mirror, as he slowly oh so slowly worked his will upon her rectum, he pondered all the events which had led him to this moment of his life and he pondered the sum total of the fragments of his personality and he pondered the philosophical insights into the ethical structure of the universe that he had made over the last few eons and he decided they were all worthless, he did not add up to the sum of his parts, much less to a total greater than the sum which was the achievement of most godlike men and women, in fact he was next to zero, in fact he was a worthless piece of shit, not even four murders and his ruthless pleasure derived from this mindless hunk of meat disguised the fact that he was a worthless piece of shit, no wonder he was disintegrating, it was a fucking miracle he had lasted this long, and as he watched he seemed to become transparent, even fucking her in the ass was insufficient but of course he had known it would be, only he had not known the reason for all this, only he had not known why he had had to suffer so much to reach this point, but the immediate fact of his disappearance which was no longer a fear but a definite reality forced him to examine the cosmos as he had never before examined anything not the luminescent butterfly not this pert little asshole not anything of genuine importance, however this time he was examining the entirety of reality and of his disappearance and for once he examined all these things and more without hatred, he was filled with so much pity for himself and consequently for the whole of godlike mankind that there was no room for the hatred which had previously influenced his tiniest gesture, there was no room for love either certainly not while he was conducting this inquiry into her anal regions, there was room only for a curious objectivity that enabled him to see himself as if he was outside his body, as if it was a doppelganger and not himself butt-fucking this lusty bitch; and he believed, if for a fleeting moment, there had been no reason for him to hate the denizens of the East End or himself, there was a purpose to everything, though he was but a pawn there was no reason for him to rail against his servitude to the oversoul, because there was really nothing to rail against, it was the natural order of things; and in that moment of realization he knew that ultimately he could do nothing evil, he could do whatever he wanted, because whatever he did was predestined despite his delusions of free will, and yet he remained free, though he remained outside society and would once again hate detest loathe society when this moment passed, he would know that he was not outisde the natural order of the universe, he was indeed part of the oversoul, a dark and perverted part yes but a part nevertheless, and he had always been this part; and this knowledge filled him with an overwhelming illusion of white light radiating from the center of his heart as if his soul resided there, as if he was becoming whole though he remained hazy, and then the moment passed taking with it much of the light and the knowledge but still enabling him to enjoy to a greater degree the asshole wrapped around his dick and the power that *the oversoul had granted him*, this was what he remembered, this is what justified him, he no longer took this power upon himself, he no longer violated natural laws, he was a natural law and it was proper that he was drilling this chick's behind, everything was proper and wonderful but he still could not quite come but that was okay, he would go ahead and conclude the act as he had intended but this time his security and comfort would be increased, he could not believe how good and warm he felt inside. He caused the parcel to unwrap, he was sure the seller of speculations would not notice it, she was too busy savoring the experience of breaking apart at the behind, she would not care what else he was doing besides fucking her in the ass though she might have been slightly offended, inflicted as she was with the feminine ego that makes them think the world turns around them. Nor did she notice the glow, the cold nearly frigid heat of the antimatter knife as it lay naked and exposed on the dresser, pretty much as her naked back lay exposed on the bed beneath the hazy stare of the ripper who imagined the smooth pale back's expanse larger than it was in actuality, he had never before had an opportunity to gaze at a woman's back, so flat and nondescript, like that of a regular person, concealing the mysterious organs and chemical reactions below the surface, reactions manifesting themselves in all sorts of peculiar and hypnotizing ways, not the least of which was the illusion of something about to burst from his nuts, the kilometer of sperm-producing tubule in his nuts working overtime but still not quite working hard enough, he felt dizzy as he stared at her naked back, knowing of the knife on the dresser, and then thinking of the knife floating to his right hand as his left hand dug its fingers deeper into her left buttock as if his fingers could draw out her mysterious femininity for sport and then holding his knife in his right hand as the fingernails of his left dug like wedges into her soft skin and the resulting pain not causing her trepidation, no, somehow the pain excited her even more, what else could he expect from a woman, and she swung her rear back and forth a few centimeters as if she was attempting to have her pelvic bones directly (impossibly) stimulated without the interference of her skin, and the ripper was nearly mesmerized, nearly so distracted that he neglected the all-important pulsating rhythm of his lower torso, as he stared at the black fires of the blade, forged in a sun of the antimatter universe, the black fires burning coldly so coldly, he wished all life could be so cold, yet he dared not touch the blade though he yearned to, it had magnetized his heart, he loved it as he could love no one but himself, it had become an extension of himself, he recalled how its creation racked his mind as he drifted in a vacuum, not daring to come into contact with stray matter for fear of the results (which though known to others were unknown to him), forging this blade with his godlike powers though the task exhausted him so he felt not godlike but menial, then teleporting himself and the blade a safe distance from himself to his own universe, fearing it would cause the atoms of the air to explode, and when they did not explode but gradually burned causing thin wisps of black smoke to curl upward, throwing the knife to the ground, fearing the ground would explode, and when the ground did not explode, noticing that the antimatter blade had somehow negated the atoms' energy, consigning them to true nothingness, and simultaneously singeing the ground about the blade; and he thought of all this as he looked at the black blade and at the pale back and then, guided by a knowledge derived from he knew not where, perhaps from his long-forgotten days as a mere men, he unerringly plunged the blade through the inferior lobe of the right lung, burning skin and muscle and blood and bone into nothingness. He thought of all this as the seller's eyes widened, perhaps not in pain because undoubtedly the shock was too great for her to experience it, instead perhaps due to the utter negation of sensation, the coldness of the blade numbing her entire body, including the sensitive asshole that had given him so much, the asshole he was not reluctant to pound as he withdrew the blade and then, gripping the specially created antimatter-resistant handle tighter (fearing the sweat of his palm would reduce his cutting skill), he plunged it through the superior lobe of the left lung, tearing also the lower half of her left breast and ripping into the bed, the hilt striking her ribs and stopping his thrust, the frustration of it (he had wanted, suddenly, to penetrate her entirely) causing him to lose the vestiges of his control and to stab and hack and stab madly at the formerly smooth back, slicing her heart and sterum into pieces, even before the full implications of her situation could reach her diminishing consciousness, before she could choke and expel forcefully the blood which now slowly flowed up her esophagus and trickled onto the formerly clean sheets which were now splattered with the blood droplets that had spurted from her back like tiny geysers when the ripper had withdrawn his knife; and the blood flowed, the wounds were too great for it to begin to congeal, as the ripper paused to assimilate the new details he had given the scene, as his powers prevented her legs and the lower half of her torso from going entirely slack on him, and he realized her asshole was still warm, as if her lower half was still alive, and so he fucked it as savagely as he had slain the upper half, allowing the knife to slip from his fingers; and he did not know if it was the sensation of her asshole wrapped around his root, or the bloody evidence of his power, or a combination of the two, that finally enabled him to come, but it could not be denied that the nerve spasm resulting from his endeavors blanked out his mind completely and lasted forever and provided infinite escape and cemented their union for all time and fulfilled the qualifications for many other romantic metaphors despite the fact that her body was already decaying and becoming cold with the chill of antimatter despite the ripper's warm and tender feelings toward her and her still warm and tender asshole now that he was satiated, now that he had discovered his true place in the universe, now that the touch of her did not seem foreign and distant to his fingers, for he now appreciated the universal truth that only womankind could have given him so much, so freely. He would never forget the seller of speculations. And as if to insure the sanctity of her memory, he withdrew from her asshole and allowed her lower torso to slide gracelessly to the bed; and he picked up the antimatter knife before it set the sheets afire and he deftly removed her left breast and her right kidney, setting the trophies on the dresser; he slashed her right inner leg to the bone; he sliced open her nostrils and cut off her eyelids and nicked her ears and then he took a second close look at her eyes and thought she was staring at him tenderly, expecting words of love or some other sign of his eternal devotion like women do, so he cut out her eyes and crushed them in his fist and felt better as he wiped the remains on a clean section of the top sheet at the bottom of the bed; then he started working on her cunt, real work this time, he cut her carefully, studying the lips, the vagina, the uterus, the ovary, and the Fallopian tubes, as if it was actually possible for him to fathom their mysteries, he believed that if he could understand this woman he could understand them all, but of course he could not understand this woman, he realized as he stared at her parts laid out between her opened and bloodied legs, she would have always withheld information from him, just as she was withholding information in death. It did not matter, not really. He was free to study them all, to inspect all their cunts as if he was searching for an organ that would immediately, upon its discovery, explain the mysteries of the eons. If only someone had explained to him the general perimeters of the mysteries; then he might have some idea of what he was doing. *Wait a minute,* thought the ripper. *What am I doing? This bitch is dead, I'm standing here in the buff, and there's no telling when the tatterdemalion will show up. I may have been granted permission by the oversoul to operate outside the narrow-minded, preconceived laws of those insufferable legions, the consulting detective included, especially the consulting detective, but that's no reason to push my luck.* He saw by his reflection that he remained hazy; even the blood of the seller of speculations on his naked body had become hazy. But the ripper did not feel threatened. What he had done insured his position in the universe, and his mental picture of himself was anything but hazy. He sent the blood on his body to the antimatter universe. He wrapped the antimatter knife in its special parcel. Suddenly suffering from his lack of sleep, he stared at the corpse until he fought off the weariness; but the weariness had already made the incredible sensation of coming into the asshole of her mutilated body seem like a dream, like an insane fantasy he lacked the courage to make an actuality. He felt the beginnings of fear; so soon after his triumph and he was already becoming afraid; but he squelched those fears by ignoring them. Then he became embarrased at his nakedness; he slowly dressed, not paying attention to what he was doing, his awareness of location and situation slipping into the back of his thoughts. As he turned to leave, his eyes left the floor, he looked to the bedroom door and he saw—the tatterdemalion!

Although the ripper had known of the tatterdemalion for eons, though he had known the location of this apartment since the East End had assumed its distinctive identity, he had never before seen him—at least, not that he could recall. And the memories of half-whispered threats to annoying eternal children buried away among more interesting information were inadequate to prepare the ripper for the shock. The colorful, filthy conglomeration of rags, accompanied with an odor that made the ripper wish he had not broken through the barriers of his perceptions, shattered the order that had been imposed upon the universe since the slaying of the seller of speculations. The ripper's hazy eyes widened until he could not focus clearly or for very long upon the tatterdemalion, as if he could transfer the blur he had become upon the creature (he could not conceive of him as a godlike man) and thus achieve some of the objectivity required for him to act correctly while under the onslaught of this unexpected complication. It was almost too fanciful to believe—as if reality had not only given away, but opened the door to the surreal as well—but there was an unmistakable sadness shrouding the tatterdemalion's features; the creature begged for concern and pity even as he screwed up courage to demand to know the reason behind this unwarranted invasion of his quarters, consequently offending the ripper to a greater degree. Then, just as the ripper thought him about to speak, the conglomeration of rags turned its head, placing its line of sight in direct accord with the mutilated corpse on the bed. The ripper had of course known at once that his deed would be discovered by the tatterdemalion before he had anticipated, but he had not prepared himself emotionally for the inevitable. And now that it had arrived, so soon after its heralding, the ripper acted without his usual reflections; he merely screamed, an ultrasonic scream whose waves plummeted the tatterdemalion, not providing him with an opportunity to recover between impulses. For whether it was due to luck or skill, the ripper had hit upon the most effective way to murder the tatterdemalion. Struck by an ever-increasing frequency of brief, powerful sound waves, the creature's mind was battered until (after only twenty seconds) it could no longer hold together his body. And as the ripper's scream continued, as he sensed his triumph, he created a wind, delivering the *coup de grâce,* casting the rags into a hundred directions. The ripper gave the rags the temporary property of passing through objects, so that they shot through the walls and the ground and the macadam alley and scattered themselves about the East End.

The scream concluded, the air at peace, the ripper stood still and contemplated his deed. The individual responsible for the air of unreality was gone, but the ripper could not piece together the puzzle anew; it was not quite the same. *No matter,* he thought. *It's just the apartment. Once I'm outside, I'll feel like I'm a part of the universe again. Besides, someone probably was aware of my ultrasonic scream; I've got no time to fuck around.*

The ripper briskly walked through the apartment, barely watching out for the cat shit. He wished he could teleport away, but he feared the trail of sluggish atoms or the discharge of energy or both would prove to be too valuable to the consulting detective, hastening the time of their inevitable confrontation to an inconvenient moment—such as any within the next sixty minutes. The cool air outside came almost as a shock, a welcome one; the rain had stopped, it seemed all the dirt had been washed to the ground where it could be easily ignored, the wind was blowing apart the clouds above even as it carried the stray rags below, and the moon shone like an impassive silver being. The ripper stared at the moon as he walked through the alley. He was aware that his pace was perhaps too leisurely for a godlike man in his predicament, but he was unconcerned; he thought of his

notion of the moon as an impassive being; it was a notion new to
his mind, and he realized that at this moment he was like his
anthropomorphism of the moon; he felt himself imbued with
impassivity, and he perceived the night's events as an alien
studying tiny creatures in a culture must perceive them—with an
indifferent confusion. Despite his nagging sleepiness, the ripper
felt larger than he had ever felt, as if the planet could barely
contain his spirit. The silver moonlight and the dim auras of the
streetlamps shining on the cobblestones and the clear fresh
puddles embraced him into their unrealities; he accepted the
unrealities gratefully, accepting them (for the moment) as other
aspects of his proper role in the scheme of things. But no degree
of acceptance prepared him for the melodious shrieking creature
bolting in the air toward him. It was a shrike. Its path, if
unchecked, would lead its beak into his right eye, where it could
proceed to penetrate his brain. The ripper did not know if his
godlike powers would prevent death from embracing him if such
an event occurred, but at any rate, he was disinclined to take the
chance. Without a thought or an inkling of hesitation, he
avoided the shrike, took control of its wings with his mind, and
veered it toward a golden wall. The shrike's call was hardly
melodious in those brief seconds remaining to it as it realized its
fate. The call ended abruptly, there was the scent of brimstone
and a black puff of smoke, as the shrike smashed into the wall;
and when the smoke cleared, leaving behind merely a trace of the
brimstone, all that survived of the shrike was its black outline in
the golden wall, as if it had been a fossil, and not a living
creature, during recent memory.

The ripper smiled. He wanted to congratulate himself, to
access his feelings, but he had not the time and he knew it. Before
he could even begin to contemplate his best course of action in
this situation, he heard the rustling of wings behind him. He
turned and saw the Batelur flying above the alley, in the
moonlight, toward him, just beginning to swing its feet upward
and thrust back its wings, so it could claw the ripper's hazy face.
But the Batelur had betrayed its presence too early. When it was
twenty meters from the ripper and ten meters from the ground,
the ripper set it afire with a thought. It burst into flame
instantaneously, its momentum carrying it like a tiny meteor
toward its intended victim. It landed hard at the ripper's feet, in a
puddle which extinguished most of the flame. It was still alive,

its feathers ashes and its body charred, barely able to thrash, caring not for the fire and for its pain but for its prey. Then it ceased to move, and the ripper stared at it, also ceasing to move, until he heard another rustling behind him.

This rustling caused a trepidation so deep that it nearly incapacitated him; for he could see nothing, he heard nothing but the rustling, the movement of feathers and wings though he suspected it was something else entirely. And it was not an attack, of that he was sure, and it was that one indisputable fact responsible for his fear. Sitting on top of a weary lamppost across the street was the bird of light. It had always been there, perhaps since he had led the seller of speculations into the tatterdemalion's apartment, and now it was divesting itself of darkness as casually as the ripper would drop a cloak. Its light was incredibly bright, but it did not hurt the ripper's eyes; he had expected to be temporarily blinded at the very least. It soon became apparent that the bird of light would not take part in the imminent drama (for the ripper knew now he could not flee; the oversoul would not permit it); the bird of light's only task was to cast its eerie illumination upon the scene.

The ripper drew himself to his full height, wishing that he could mold his self-image to his choosing so he could make himself taller or that he had bad taste in addition to his degeneracy so he could wear elevator or platform shoes. Nevertheless, he felt confident as he awaited the individual he knew he would be facing next—the bird woman. He paced back and forth, nearly strutting his stuff as a soldier would, in front of the alley's entrance, betraying only the slightest nervousness. He gradually became aware of an almost unbearable beauty in the darkness beyond the bird of light's range, in the shadows between the buildings, in the blackened sky, perhaps even in the billowing clouds. The wind seemed to carry this beauty toward him; he seemed to inhale it. The whole world's purpose was suddenly to bring him this beauty, to make him aware of a spiritual and physical poetry that, in comparison with his own feeble efforts, would reduce him to shame, reduce him into a being whose only emotion was awe tinged with jealousy. The power and justification the ripper had obtained during the past few days seemed meager and insignificant; he was overwhelmed long before he caught the scent of flowers he had never seen merged with the scent of hair, as if the beauty was a disembodied animation; he was despondent, knowing he could experience such beauty only for a brief period, indeed, if he was worthy, if he was capable in the first place. His heart thundered and his stomach roared; the noise of his every wheezing breath seemed an affront against the genteel manners of the universe; he felt the blood draining from his hazy face, increasing his eternal drowsiness; if only he could sleep—then perhaps he would not be so susceptible to these things.

However, no amount of sleep could have prepared him for the beauty that slipped from the alley between two golden buildings across the street and into the edges of the aura of light cast by the white bird. This seemed to be his night for facing those he had never before seen, and though he had long heard of her, though he had recently avoided her as he had avoided the consulting detective, he was dumbfounded by the reality of her. Her beauty was so great, so fragile, affecting him so quickly, that he was almost as repulsed as he had been at the sight of the tatterdemalion. Her white hair like mercurial moonbeams, her slender pale body, her long bare smooth legs, her bodice of spiderwebs—all were lovely, lovelier than the ripper ever could have expected, but they were unspeakably ugly compared to the fires burning in those dark eyes and hidden meanings behind the almost imperceptible smile gracing those red lips, fires and meanings the ripper could see and understand (or so he thought) even standing across the street. The bird woman leaned against a lamppost as if she was standing against a doorway leading to a bedroom where the ripper, naked and under the sheets, waited for her, subtly exuding the sexuality the ripper hated loved detested needed. Then she straightened and took one step toward him, and his knees weakened, his blood pounded, he thought he had eaten lightning and crapped thunder. He had wanted to hate her for being so beautiful, for reducing him to a pawn when he had previously never been happier, in control of his destiny. But he could not hate such beauty for long; instead, he wanted to worship it. In this respect, her beauty was more potent than that of the luminescent butterfly, which had required at least an iota of viewer participation to be effective; the bird woman required no such participation, not from the ripper; he was already ensnared. He tried to think of her in the basest terms, to see her in his mind's eyes as he had seen the seller of speculations, needing a certain segment of his anatomy so desperately that she would throw away all her dignity and self-respect to get it, spreading her legs, allowing those fluids to dampen those pubes, opening the lips of that suction device euphemistically referred to as a sexual organ. The attempt failed; thinking of her as a normal godlike woman, with the normal needs associated with the despondent scum dragging the race down into the dirt, only increased his crippling need to supply her with whatever part of his anatomy she chose. Beads of sweat, hazy but no less salty and hot for that, oozed from the pores of his face and of his armpits; he felt a huge drop roll down his back, less than half a centimeter to the left of his spine. Mucous clogged his left nostril. He knew that if he ever got the opportunity to make love to her (he could not think of it as fucking her) that he would never slay her to rid himself of the vision of her humbling herself before him; for he would gladly humble himself before her, admitting for the first time completely, totally, and not in passing as if referring to an inconsequential fact of life or to one of his programs for social improvement, divorced entirely from his will to power, his all-encompassing need to plug himself into her warmth and dampness which would then flow through him forever. He considered her an extension of his personality and his body; if she left him, it would be paramount to undergoing an amputation, though he really did not care to dwell upon the specifics of that metaphorical operation. As he worshipped her, he required from her, if not actual devotion, then minor gestures and unthinking kind words indicating her approval of him, anything which would justify an existence which would become quite meaningless if he did not have the exquisite pleasure of groveling at her feet. He trembled violently; his knees threatened to collapse under his weight. *Oh may I have the pleasure of eating the peanuts from her shit*, he thought as he rolled his eyes toward the silver-edged clouds in a futile attempt to draw his attention from her, if only for a moment. He imagined them forming a union outlasting the stars concealed by the clouds. But when he thought of himself as part of that union, as an individual and not as a symbiotic being, he became frightened. What was this woman doing to him? He had never before considered himself a partner in a relationship lasting longer than, say, an hour, because thus far none of his partners had lasted half that length. She had cursed him, and though he knew what she had done and exactly how she had accomplished it, as she slowly walked across the street, her dainty feet appearing to float rather than step across the cobblestoned road, he resisted the urge to worship her. (He would have resisted the urge to take her, kissing her violently, whatever the case, for successful results—which she probably would not have permitted—would have needlessly offended her or placed him in unnecessary jeopardy.) He bit his lower lip, not lessening the pressure until he feared he would soon taste blood, as she held out her hand to him, as her smile became more pronounced, the hidden meanings more apparent. When she was not three meters away from him, when he was leaning against a wall for support, he realized—forcefully, as if he had received no preliminary indication though an eternal child would have guessed the truth—that her plans for him were in no way similar to those he had formed for her. He had accepted her curse as long as he had believed she had his best interests at heart, providing him with incentive to do away with his hatred for society and to become a faceless member again. Indeed, the price would almost have been worth regularly balling this savage bitch masquerading as a civilized person, or what was worse, as a noble savage whose shit inherently did not stink and consequently did not perform the redeeming function of fertilizing the earth as well, but his hatred had suddenly overwhelmed him, how could she dare manipulate him, the audacity of it all, nevertheless he felt like he was betraying himself though he was quite aware of his true motives as he balled his hand into a fist and lashed out at her, surprising himself as well as her and accidentally allowing his parcel to slip from his other hand, striking her just below the right cheekbone, sending her flying backward until her trajectory led to her inevitable and ignominious landing. Her legs rested on the sidewalk, her torso on the cobblestones; she looked like a broken scarecrow lying there in the puddle, in the dirt where she had always lain, the slut, the whore, the bitch, he hoped she had bashed her brains out, if only he had the time to tear off the bodice of spiderwebs and drop his trousers, he would mount her right then and there, *the bitch would probably like it*, but he did not have the time, he had to be satisfied with the blue swelling beneath her cheekbone, she was a delicate creature for such a conniving bitch.

The ripper retrieved his parcel, then glanced about, sneering at nothing in particular and at everything. The vision of loveliness lying at his feet was inconsequential at best, he told himself, ignoring the needles piercing his heart. Without actually giving the matter serious consideration, acting on an instinctive level, the ripper violated his *modus operandi* by diverting a portion of power from shielding him, sending out vibrations directly in search of trackers who might be near. He had no idea how many had been deployed to investigate the scream (the consulting detective would not think that he would have been so careless), and he sincerely believed the bird woman was egotistical enough not to notify her comrades that she had found him; women could never be trusted to do what they were told. His mind touched several others, so quickly he was nearly too surprised to act; but act he did, scowling, sneering anew, slamming all his mental might upon the gunsel, then the demon, then the lawyer, then the fat man; they had each been a block away, each stalking the source of the scream from a different direction. Now the ripper did not sneer, he smiled, smiled at his effortless victory, at the impassive bird of light; he had a few minutes of relative safety in which to flee. He said aloud, "The time has come for me to split the scene."

"The only scene you're splitting to is a dungeon beneath the demon's castle," said a muffled voice which at first the ripper thought originated behind him but which upon further reflection seemed to originate everywhere. The ripper spun about, jerking his head this way and that, almost as if he was the victim of a nervous spasm, in search of the muffled speaker. There could no doubt as to the speaker's identity. The ripper searched with infrared vision, into vibratory planes close to his own, into the ground below; he even deduced that the speaker might be a second out of phase with true time, so he inspected the temporal stream; the search, like all others, was to no avail. He told himself the voice had been a figment of his imagination. He straightened his posture and, actually believing his explanation, took three steps before he was flattened by a remarkably fast, remarkably heavy object striking him, hurling him into the air while it remained on top of him, indeed, remaining on top of him as he slid across the wet sidewalk, soaking himself in a puddle, tearing his shirt and coat, bruising his hands which he used to protect his face, failing in that last pathetic ambition, his left temple rapping the sidewalk, causing him to feel dizzy, almost

causing him to pass out. Fighting the need to give up and rest
was especially difficult due to his sleepiness, but he fought it
successfully, regaining his full consciousness and equilibrium
with a tremendous, satisfying effort, ignoring the series of blows
the object sitting on his back was raining on his shoulders and
neck. The object moved backward so it could pummel the
ripper's kidneys. The ripper attempted to send the object to the
antimatter universe; failing that, he attempted to send it to the
other side of the street; failing that, he realized it had deadened
most of his godlike powers, a feat requiring a vast quantity of
power in itself, reducing their battle from grand and glorious
heights to a hand-to-hand slugfest. The ripper retained sufficient
might to deaden the pain caused by the rain of blows, though he
could not negate their ultimate effect, not until the fight was
over, perhaps not at all, depending upon the extent of his
injuries. The ripper fought to his knees, despite the object's
attempts to prevent it; then it was a comparatively simple matter
for him to stand, breaking away from the object, and to turn,
two meters from it, giving him the opportunity to assess his foe.

The object regarded him stoically. Of course it would.
Nothing else could be expected of the universal op. His suit was
a tad ruffled, his tie loosened, his shirt a bit grimy, but those
signs of uneasiness lurking beneath the cool facade aside, he was
his usual unflappable self. *Another asshole. Will I never be rid of
them?* Before the ripper could answer himself, the universal op
stepped up and swung his right; the ripper blocked it deftly,
breaking through the op's guard and landing three blows to the
gut, his fist nearly becoming completely enveloped by skin and
fat upon the third blow. The op doubled over. The ripper struck
him with an uppercut, tearing the skin of the smooth chin.
Contrary to the ripper's expectations, the op did not fall over.
He did not even stagger. He just stood there, stunned. The ripper
waded in, raining a series of blows to the stomach and kidneys
which the op ineffectively blocked. After thirty seconds the op
staggered, the ripper gained confidence, and the op broke
through his guard and smashed him upon the hazy nose. Hazy
blood splattered through the darkness, illuminated by the bird
of light; its fall to the sidewalk seemed to last a long time as the
ripper tottered backward, tripping over the parcel which he had
dropped and forgotten, nearly falling, steadying himself just in
time to protect himself from the op's renewed onslaught. The op

beat upon the ripper's face and chest with an animalistic frenzy. The ripper kneed the op in the balls. Groaning in a peculiar muffled way, the op backed up and shielded his nuts with one hand to prevent a follow-through attack. When the ripper tried to hit him, the op struck him in the face again. The ripper reeled back. They stared at each other, breathing heavily, for two minutes, trying to recover quickly though they could not use their powers as long as the op was deadening those of the ripper; and now they could not deaden their pain, they fought as mere man must have fought. Blood flowed from the ripper's nose and his lower lip; he tasted the blood gradually ebbing from the gums around his front teeth. His knuckles bled, he could not recall having been so dizzy before, the cool bruised-and-swollen visage of the universal op before him was like a nightmare personified, a crushing, smothering nightmare. Which did not prevent the ripper from slowly stepping toward him, his fists clenched as if his fingers had been stitched together, his legs bent and spread apart, his stomach muscles tense; the op lumbered toward the ripper like an eerie drunken slug. They struck one another. For how long, neither could say. But now they did not stagger backward or pause, and soon they did not attempt to block the blows; they swung, connected or not, felt their arms nearly wrench themselves from their sockets, and waited for their opponent, in his turn, to strike. Eventually the op's mug was reduced to a festering bloody pulp resembling an ill-treated cantaloupe. In addition to the wounds previously noted, the ripper had a cut on his forehead, blood flowed over his swollen right eye, mucous dripped freely from his nostrils, and his lower lip felt heavy and encumbered with its bruises. It seemed that the op had not actually hit him for a long time. He was nearly unaware of swinging his arm; he did not feel his fist strike the op, though he knew it had. Suddenly—impossibly—the universal op fell to the sidewalk and did not move. The ripper backed up to a golden wall and stared at the op; he expected the op to move, it was only a sham, a clever ploy, surely he could not have defeated such a tough guy, but of course he had; had not the oversoul granted him power, power even now returning to his brain, surging throughout his weary body?

The ripper repaired himself; he caused his nerves to cease throbbing, he sealed up wounds, he sent the blood on his skin and clothing to the antimatter universe. As he retrieved his parcel, he felt his triumph tingling throughout his being; only the glow of satisfaction he experienced upon the completion of a murder was comparable. He said aloud to the universal op, "That'll teach you to mess with me." Then he turned toward the bird of light which remained unmoving, perched on the streetlamp. "*Now* the time has come for me to split the scene."

"The only scene you're splitting to is a dungeon beneath the demon's castle."

The ripper blinked several times. "Is there some kind of delayed echo around here?"

Again the ripper backed against the golden wall, and he considered walking through it when he learned the identity of the godlike man now standing beneath the glow of the bird of light. For it was none other than—the consulting detective!

6. *An account from the good doctor's notebooks:*

When the consulting detective and I heard the ultrasonic scream, we were of course alerted to the possibility that it might have been the ripper's. But as the consulting detective was engaged in the interrogation of a particularly promising suspect, and as he was of the opinion that any noise made by the ripper would be of a much subtler nature, he sent our comrades, with the exception of the universal op, to investigate it. I suspected the person responsible for the scream was the man in the yellow suit; a nauseating ultrasonic scream signaling his return to duty would have been just his speed. I was unconcerned for the man in the yellow suit, believing he had decided not to join us this night upon a whim, but my friend the consulting detective, though he had feigned indifference when our enigmatic comrade did not arrive in the locker room at the predestined hour, betrayed his concern, after satisfying himself that our suspect was not the ripper, by asking him if he had perchance seen a rather whimsical man wearing a tasteless loud yellow suit. Before the suspect could formulate a convincing lie, we received a communication from the universal op informing us that the ripper had defeated the bird woman and waylaid everyone else; there were no fatalities, at least there were none in our little group. The op had had no legitimate reason for deducing it was the ripper who had screamed; he had simply followed his instincts.

Ignoring the confused and annoyed suspect slinking away, the consulting detective emptied his pipe and smiled, his eyes glowing bright with anticipation for the first time that night. "Remind me never to criticize the universal op again for his lack of imagination," he said. "He appears not to need it."

"What?" I exclaimed. "Are we just going to stand around here jawing while the op risks his neck battling the ripper? What if the op suffers mortal harm? Or even worse, what if he captures the ripper and we aren't on hand?"

"That should be the least of your concerns, my friend."

"It should be, but if the op captures the ripper by his lonesome, it's going to look pretty bad in my memoirs. It would be rather anticlimactic after all this buildup, I should say. Well? Let's get cracking!"

The consulting detective put his pipe in his pocket; to me, it seemed the action took up an unconscionable length of time. "The universal op has just assured me that he has everything under control—for the moment," he said briskly. "However, that communication, which he could direct only to me, has cost him the last of his spare power, which has been diverted to other matters. Here are your instructions: instead of teleporting directly to the site, as I will, you will teleport to the sides of our friends and see that they are well. Then, after you have done all you can for them, remain in hiding near the site, in a location where you can see and hear all. You will shield yourself completely, using every trick you know. Under no circumstances must the ripper suspect your presence, and you are not to act or to aid me in any fashion unless it is absolutely necessary. Is that clear?"

"Why, surely you've become pixilated! My place is by your side, whatever the circumstances! You need not be concerned for my safety!"

"I'm not concerned for your safety."

"You're not?"

"You're my ace in the dirt, as I believe they say. If something goes amiss, you'll be able to correct it before the ripper can take proper precautions. Of course, the ripper'll be very angry if you interfere, but we shall worry about that only when we must."

"Uh, I would prefer if we worried about it now." But it was too late; the consulting detective had blinked away; his mirthfulness, manifesting itself at the most inopportune times, was certainly becoming an annoyance to my overtaxed posterior. Nothing remained for me to do but to seek out our fallen comrades, which I did successfully except for the gunsel. They were all unconscious and, left alone, would be for at least an hour. I would have awakened them, but the nature of the consulting detective's instructions led me to believe that he wanted to face the ripper alone, if at all possible. When I saw the consulting detective standing near the bodies of the universal op and the bird woman, I was sure of it. I watched them from atop a roof overlooking the tableau. I rearranged my moleculear structure so the moonlight and the wind would pass through me, effectively making me invisible and intangible. I could go no further in that direction and remain corporeal, so I deadened my mind to such an extent that my personality became almost nonexistent, reducing the possibility the ripper would detect the vibrations emanating from my admittedly excitable gray matter. I programmed my mind to remember all details, enabling me to reflect upon them as if I had been whole before writing these memoirs, and to reactivate itself the instant my subconscious (which would be its usual perverse energetic self) deemed it necessary. Perhaps I took matters a bit too far, following the consulting detective's instructions too zealously, but I determined if I was to hide rather than stay at his side, I would do so with the thoroughness I would have expected from him. And once my concealment was complete, and my subconscious deemed it adequate, a very strange sensation enveloped what was left of my ego, and I experienced life as if I had never truly been a part of it. I saw the sights and heard the words, but the distance divorced me from all intellectual and emotional involvement. If the consulting detective had met the most ignominious end, I would not have been affected in the least; I cannot say I would have shrugged mentally, for my indifference in that state was so pronounced that I could not arouse enough interest in something to learn if I was actually disinterested. In a manner of speaking, I felt like the author I had been pretending to be throughout the events of the past few days and nights. Everything which transpired before me seemed like a sham played out for my benefit, a sham I viewed with such frightening objectivity that I lost all pleasure and curiosity; what little imagination was left to me did not allow me to think of myself as a participant; instead, I had once been a shadow, of less consequence than those before me, because they at least were acting *now*. It seems that I should spend several hundred words describing my condition, and perhaps I would if I had not reached this thrilling section of my narrative. (Though I know how it ends, still I anticipate writing it as an eternal child anticipates dessert!) Yet I would hesitate, even if the expectation I trust the reader feels was minimal, for how can I, who deals with words and therefore with emphatic statements, describe a state of being where there is no emphasis to be placed? If I described myself as despondent, I would be placing my emotions within the realm of godlike experience; and upon the rooftop, invisible, intangible, I reached the epitome of negative experience. Any word which could be attached to it, even to indicate it was "not such-and-such" or it was "close to this but not really" would be distorting the truth. I did not fear for myself. I did not fear for the consulting detective. I did not fear for our companions. I did not grieve for Kitty. I did not anticipate my future, for all time ceased while I watched the sham before me, only vaguely paying attention because some nagging element in my subconscious insisted I did so without my realization of it.

Below my indifferent self, the ripper moved from the wall and rubbed his chin, holding the parcel near his chest. He stood at the edge of the impassive bird of light's bleaching glow. The consulting detective stood between the ripper and the bird, one foot on the cobblestones, the other on the sidewalk, near the bird woman. He packed tobacco in his pipe as casually and as unself-consciously as if he was alone. He said, "Well, my diminutive hazy friend, we meet at last." He put his pipe into his mouth and turned on the cold steely glare of his eyes. "Now aren't you ashamed of yourself?"

"What kind of question is that?"

"I'm asking if you regret in any way what you have done, if you feel it was right and proper that those women met their deaths to fulfill your needs."

"Of course it was right and proper. They were nothing but sluts, you can't trust them, any of them, they would drag us down into the muck with them if we gave them the chance. What does it matter to you anyway? I didn't cut up your prize cunt, did I?"

"Well, no."

"Then what are you complaining about? I knew before I started this caper that you would be on my tail, sniffing about like a dog looking for his favorite shitting spot, but I've never understood your interest in it. What can the fate of some poor bitches in the East End possibly mean to you?"

"I've often wondered what their fates mean too, though I've never doubted that they mean something. Call me a sentimental old fluff if you will, but every time I've contemplated the hideous pain and suffering I've felt, the interminable hours of loneliness and boredom, my dreary expectations, the daily promise of only study, study, study, without rewards, and the undeniable truth that even as I fear my death in the final hours of the universe, I have a greater fear of life, consequently allowing a part of my soul to yearn for death, but I cannot rid myself of the notion that my pain must mean something—despite all the evidence to the contrary."

"It means nothing. Your attempts to draw meaning from hopelessness and degradation of it all are pathetic. Somehow I expected better of you."

"And I expect nothing from you," said the consulting detective, kneeling at the bird woman's head. "Now I can't be disappointed." He scanned her skull, searching for bumps, cuts, or fractures. Assured that her condition was satisfactory, he stood and said, "Like many godlike men, I perceive myself as an individual somehow outside, apart from society. The discoveries I've made in the last few days have convinced me that more people feel likewise than I ever could have suspected, leading me to believe that the majority of society is comprised of people who see themselves incapable of fitting in, who conform and unconsciously follow the wishes of those who *are* society simply because they know not what else to do. Whether or not that is true is at the moment immaterial, because I've always known what I must do. Of course there wasn't any work, only preparation, until the demon, the lawyer, and the fat man engaged my services, but in all those tedious millions of years, despair as I might, I knew that one day I would have the opportunity to fulfill my destiny, to live at my full capacity, to occupy myself every second of the day, rendering personal suffering immaterial, secure in the knowledge that I was relieving the suffering of others. For my pain was not unique. Every godlike man and woman on this planet has undergone similar pain, at one time or another."

The ripper yawned. "You're the best cure for insomnia I've ever encountered."

"And you make me want to barf," said the consulting detective, holding his pipe between his teeth.

"Very witty, sir! Men such as you will never be happy."

"I don't want to be happy; I want to be alive and active."

"How disgusting you are; how unoriginal."

"No, sir, it is you who are unoriginal, you who are the slave. You seek to make all godlike mankind as low as yourself. You would drag us down, rather than allow us to experiment so that we may one day experience true freedom. You would perpetuate an environment where it is impossible for meaning to be sought. I oppose you; I oppose you with all my will, and my will is greater than yours; it can overcome all obstacles. You are death, and death is stagnation; there can be no originality in stagnation. Despite my weakness, my foibles, and my addictions, I am life, and there is nothing I cannot accomplish if I live with all my will."

"And what do you intend to accomplish?"

The consulting detective smiled. "Why, your removal, of course."

"And, assuming you succeed, which I very much doubt, what do you intend to do with the rest of your life?"

"That is immaterial. Doubtless I shall relax and await the next time my services are required."

The ripper snorted. "If that time does not arrive, would you then sit in your apartment for eons, as you did while awaiting my coming? The rest of your life would be as wasted as if you had spent it lost in the East End."

"Never. For if I cannot live at these heights again, free from the waste characterizing most godlike men, then at least I will be comforted by the knowledge that I've given others the opportunity to be free from the dreary abyss of existence. And perhaps another will be as free as I am tonight, another who might lead me from my slavery. You are too pessimistic, ripper; you are too negative, though I suppose that is to be expected for an individual who is so obviously composed of second-class stuff. There is always cause for hope, however unrealistic. There is always the possibility of salvation, however improbable."

The ripper sneered, emitting the faintest trace of a growl. His hatred was so apparent, even through his haze and the veil of darkness covering his face, that the consulting detective stepped backward, until he was fully a meter and a half from the bird woman. The hatred, which had been stilled somewhat while the ripper had tried to adjust to his present situation, now swept over the area (a portion of it affecting me despite my apathetic condition), giving him the courage to retaliate against the consulting detective's moralistic onslaught. "What a hemor-rhaging thumper you've got; how I loathe scum such as you. There's no way you can improve the lot of these pigs; they like it here, they enjoy it, they love their misery, and all the women want to do is fuck so they can taint us and think they're better than us. The only way you can improve the lot of the race is to eradicate these swine. Death and destruction—that's your only solution—death and destruction! Let the fires fall from the sky and fry them into so many crisps!"

The consulting detective removed his pipe from his mouth just in time, otherwise his slackened jaw would have allowed it to clatter on the street. "How can you say that? Are not all godlike men brothers? And if not brothers, aren't they at least related?"

"You know my answer," said the ripper, a hazy grin distorting his features as he realized the extent of the consulting detective's shock. He began walking the edge of the circle of light, facing his opponent, clearly not intending to run or to teleport; he had begun to relish this confrontation. He possessed what he had lacked at my arrival—confidence. "What possible relation, blood or otherwise, can anyone have to me after my eons of isolation? I might say the same is true of everyone. The deaths of a few lonely bitches here won't detract one iota from my enjoyment of peanut butter sandwiches; in fact, their deaths will enhance it; every moment of enjoyment I ever experience will be augmented by my past moments, by the memories of the power I wielded and the use of those deceitful sluts. The only reason they had for living was to die at my hands."

At first the consulting detective had been taken aback by the intensity of the ripper's hatred, but now he had regained his composure, and he returned the ripper's hazy stare with equal rigidity. The ripper had ceased walking the circle at the conclusion of his speech—he was standing in the street—so the consulting detective had stopped turning to meet that dark stare. They were immobile, eternal, and even in my apathetic state a part of my subconscious reflected upon the millions of years of chaos and pain that had led to this stark moment, the complexities of emotion, motivation, and intellect that had led to this simple tableau of two men standing on a dirty street beneath a bird of light in a golden city. The fallen bodies, the wisps of fog creeping into the atmosphere since the rain had ended, the silver moonlight fighting its way through the breaks in the clouds—all were inconsequential compared to the image of the ripper and the consulting detective confronting one another, each knowing only he would emerge victorious.

"Now I know why I created an image to oppose godlike men such as you, ripper," said the consulting detective casually, puffing his pipe as if they were discussing how pleasant it was to take a stroll in the wee morning hours, though the fire in his eyes did not diminish. "One of the curses lifted from our race on the day we became godlike was the ever certainty of death. Perhaps we've paid for our immortality in a thousand other ways, perhaps we would be content to die if we knew for a fact what lay beyond the shadow of life, but endless time is a gift, and whatever limitations of the godlike condition sidetrack us into wasting millions of years in idle 'innie' and 'outie' contemplation, we have the ability to expand beyond those limitations, because we have time. Mere man did not have that blessing. Whatever error a mere man made in dealing with the peculiarities of life, or whatever goal he regretted reaching, was final; he did not have sufficient time to backtrack and rectify his errors, or even to learn if he had actually made an error; he would never know if he was as happy as he could possibly be; he would never know if he had savored to the fullest the pleasures, both physical and spiritual, life had to offer. Every day, whether or not he was aware of it, he faced his inevitable physical decline; the body which walked tall and straight would become stooped, its muscles weakened and their strength dwindled, the fat mysteriously appearing and packing itself in embarrassing places, the bowels demanding an inordinate amount of attention, and the libido either changing in all sorts of peculiar ways or just giving up, decreasing into nothingness. While our culture might bear some surface resemblance to that of mere man, his culture was more than tinged with darkness—it was obsessed with the darkness of death. Mere man was forever trapped in the birth-rebirth cycle. His childhood seemed eternal;

his mind was bright and innocent, and despite his fears, the world seemed preposterously large and wonderful; his parents protected him, fed him, clothed him, perhaps trying to raise him too much in their image but after all, that was only human, the kind of thing you have to expect when dealing with mere man. However, despite his shelter, the child invariably sensed the darkness of the world stealthily worming toward him, that nothing he could do would prevent the inevitable from occurring whenever the oversoul decreed. The child might grow to become an adult, and he might leave the world of lightness his parents had created for him even as they feared the darkness, and he might ignore the specter hovering over him and all he loved even as he watched and heard about and read of others being engulfed by it every day of his brief youth. And then one day his father, shall we say, dies, unexpectedly engulfed, and this child—who is no longer a child except perhaps in some secret chamber of his heart—knows he can never afford to ignore the darkness again. He knows that like his father, everything he has learned in his heart or accumulated outside will slip away, his mind will cease to exist, and he will not even be able to regret what he has lost. Nothingness suddenly becomes very real and cold to him, though he knows he will not be able to feel the coldness his mind imagines. And you have brought back that curse, ripper. Once we feared death as an abstraction, now we fear it as something very close and abhorrent to us. That is why I must oppose you. I cannot eradicate the curse you've returned to us, but I can make you regret the forgotten day you were born. I am your opposite in every way, and I am your superior. Now that I've finally met you, I see there is nothing about you to inspire mercy in my heart. There is nothing about you that resembles me, nothing that makes me think of you as anything other than a pustulous maggot."

The ripper shrugged; he had appeared very bored. "Well, you see, that's where we disagree. The oversoul didn't place you here to destroy me; it placed you here to create me."

The consulting detective blinked, his head snapping as if he had been stung by a bee. His complexion paled as if I had accidentally turned his blood intangible and he was unable to deduce the cause of his asphyxiation. "Why, that's the most ridiculous thing I've ever heard. What kind of madman are you?"

"I'm not mad; unlike yourself, I see things the way they really are. You're just too deluded to accept it, that's all. Face facts, buster, you're an asshole."

"Am not!"

"Are too! I was nothing, a veritable nobody, until four nights ago, when I overheard a certain noted, unemployed detective telling a certain doctor about their mutual destiny. He spoke of a lost downtrodden common man who had nurtured seeds of resentment for eons, a man who would soon act to satiate the hatred he felt in his heart. Well, I certainly identified with that individual. When I heard you speak of your other goals, particularly those in relation to love, I knew you were loony. Love! Love's only a disguise for the lust seething within us, a lust women perpetuate. As for the race's new and glorious heights, well, we're standing in them right now. Our race is the shits, it's headed for the dumper, and it'll stay in that direction as long as assholes like you are the ones feeding it crap about love. Ha! Fuck 'em in the ass, that's what I say, that's all they're good for. And when we run out of women, we can tie up jerks like you and fuck you in the ass instead, it's all the same. But you were right about one thing: godlike mankind needed a monster to cleanse it of scum. My work's just started, I don't know where it'll end, but I know this: I never would have gotten the idea to become the ripper if it hadn't been for you. You created me."

"Did not!"

"Did too! It never would have happened if not for you, do you hear that? All those bitches I killed—it's your fault!"

"Is not."

"Is too! You must believe me. It's important you know you're as much of a monster as I am. You must realize that if you hadn't hit upon your idea of becoming the consulting detective, you might have turned out just like me—a murderer in potential, requiring only that final nudge. You're my soul and inspiration."

"Am not."

"You must believe me!" the ripper screamed, his hazy face to the sky, his hazy mouth open wide. The muscles of his neck trembled as he jerked down his head to renew his stare at the consulting detective. "You must take your share of the responsibility!"

"I will not."

The ripper spat the word: *"Putz!"*

The consulting detective snorted. *"Momzer!"*

I know now, though I was unable to perceive it adequately in my apathetic state, that my subconscious feared my friend was becoming grossly over-confident, admittedly a common failing among geniuses. Already my subconscious radiated tiny, annoying messages urging me to return to my normal self. Before I had the opportunity to ponder the pros and cons of transforming myself into the dashing good doctor of old, the ripper threw his parcel at the consulting detective, screamed, and attacked.

The parcel had been thrown as a distraction. As my friend sidestepped it, the ripper stopped time.

The border of the limbo he created was six centimeters from the consulting detective's body, enclosing my friend in a static area where there was no air and no need for air, where he did not think because his thoughts were what they had been the instant before the ripper acted (though I surmise some instinct was very aware of what was happening), where his blood did not flow and where he experienced no sensation. The six centimeters of limbo was pitch-black, and the air which came into contact with its border disintegrated with a crackling shower of yellow sparks, creating the eerie effect of the consulting detective eternally frozen with a defiant expression, while all about him was a flurry of meaningless activity which could neither touch nor affect him.

At this point my subconscious broadcast all manner of annoying proddings, so that my conscious had no choice but to acknowledge that its vacation, its period of freedom from all the trials and tribulations associated with thinking, was finished. Nevertheless, it was reluctant to assert itself. I had done my work too well. I knew that my friend was in mortal peril, but my apathetic condition did not allow me to care very much about the implications. The thought of facing eternity without the sage wisdom and unpredictable shenanigans of the consulting detective caused no anxiety whatsoever. I did not even grieve for Kitty. I imagined her death and his impending death to be of absolutely no consequence in the ultimate scheme of things. Of course, there was always the possibility the ripper would search for a certain good doctor, conspicuous by his absence; and there was always the possibility my concealment was not as effective as I had supposed . . .

I became whole in an instant. I walked on my knees to the edge of the roof, peering over the railing. I felt fairly confident the ripper would not see me. And if he did look up, perhaps he would not be able to see past the glow of the bird of light. I wanted to act immediately, but the ripper's attack had been devastating and imaginative. Small wonder that the consulting detective had been caught unaware. I knew, however, that a premature defense might also put me in jeopardy; I had to select carefully the proper moment, if I was to catch the ripper off guard while I saved my friend.

Then the ripper caught me unaware. He snapped his fingers and the epidermis disappeared from the consulting detective's body. The ripper did not strip his clothing, so that the effect was visible only on his face and hands. Exactly where the ripper had sent his skin, to this day I do not know. I only know my mind followed it through darkness and heat and through matter that clung to my energy as molasses clings to fingers. Sweat broke out on my brow as I strained to hold together the epidermis, an effort which was compounded when the ripper sent the derma and the fat cells to the same unknown dimension. I noticed that the ripper had thus far left the consulting detective's hair in its proper place, as if he had no intention of allowing it to fall to the lower borders of the limbo, as if the crowning nuance of his deadly prank would be the vision of a consulting-detective skeleton fully clothed, with all its hair (and possibly its eyes) where one would normally expect them to be. I became convinced my supposition was correct when, after the ripper had removed the nerve tissue, he began systematically unraveling the muscles of my friend's face, miraculously leaving the blood vessels undisturbed. The unraveling began slowly with the *dilatator naris anterior* and *dilatator naris posterior*, and then moved up the nose until all the muscles on the head were spinning off into several directions at once, the ends disappearing into that other dimension. The same process began on the hands when the face was fully stripped. When that stage of the ripper's fun was completed, the organs held into place only by his power and his desire to control the consulting detective's spark of life as long as possible, I began to fear for my friend's mind. Though it felt nothing in the manner we normally mean when referring to feelings, surely upon some subliminal level it understood the agony of being taken apart alive. The ripper acted more quickly, teleporting the lymph glands and all associated vessels, the digestive and excretory organs, the respiratory system. The ripper paused to jump up and down and to shake his hands as if he was playing an eternal child's game. He laughed gleefully at his impending victory—providing me with the opportunity to retaliate.

I returned all the wayward cells of the consulting detective instantly; there was no hesitation between my decision and my action, for the ripper might have detected my vibrations of anxiety. The effort of teleporting the cells across those unfathomable distances nearly caused me to faint, and I wanted nothing more than to lie down, resting my head on a soft lap, and close my heavy eyelids. But one more task remained; I had to counteract the limbo surrounding the consulting detective. To this day I have never understood how an individual as lowly and as worthless as the ripper could have summoned such puissance; the act of creating a limbo requires the absolute limit of mental might a singular person can assume, and the act of sending the cells to that distant dimension required considerable will, as I can attest. The strongest mental energy I could summon caused only the tiniest, most infinitesimal crack in the limbo. I could direct no spare power to grant me the added strength to remain alert, not if I was to save the consulting detective. The ripper, apparently quite stunned to see my friend's body all in one piece, did not react immediately; he had been so confident of his victory that he had difficulty accepting evidence to the contrary. But it would not take long for him to act, this I knew; I redoubled my efforts, grasping the railing weakly, my fingers feeling as if they had lost all strength forever, and yet it was to no avail; the crack did not widen. The ripper would surely repair it as soon as he recovered from the shock of seeing his will contradicted.

However, a wisp of air seeped through the crack without being disintegrated. It colored the black red, and the red swirled about, enveloping the consulting detective. I could no longer see him. I feared I had muddled everything. I feared I had smothered him. I feared for all that I had been and all that I had known. In that instant of desperation I realized on what a flimsy base the transparent structure of my life had been built, and I saw the structure ripped asunder by powerful forces I could not hope to withstand. I did not cry, I did not give evidence of any despairing emotion, I felt only numbness; even the despondency I had felt upon seeing the mutilated corpse of Kitty on the street was preferable to this. I had fooled myself into thinking I had previously descended to the depths and survived. *This* was the depths, and survival was out of the question.

Perhaps then the reader will forgive me when I state that my zeal was positively euphoric when the consulting detective shattered the limbo with a sound of thunder that rang in my ears many minutes after it had ceased. In fact, during that infinite moment, it seemed the fabric of the universe itself had severed. I had saved the consulting detective! Once again I had crawled from the depths of despair and degradation!

Even in my near somnabulistic state, I was frightened by the glare of the consulting detective's eyes. Directed at the cowering ripper, the glare indicated that in one brief moment the consulting detective had recalled all the pain visited upon him, and his hatred of the ripper had reached a corresponding fervor. My friend carried his pipe casually in his left hand, but his right palm was held out toward the ripper, and above that palm crackled tiny red-and-yellow bolts of electricity, bolts dancing in anticipation, bolts through which my friend directed his anger.

The ripper did not have time to draw himself to his full height as the consulting detective hurled the bolts at him. The little man did not even attempt to avoid them, as if he had already accepted the hopelessness of struggle. When the bolts struck him, he screamed and fell to his knees, his eyes staring at the great arc of light above him. His scream became shriller and shriller during the two minutes it lingered. Then, exhausted despite the pain remaining inside, tormenting him, the ripper went limp, his head and shoulders drooping like those of a soaked scarecrow.

The consulting detective stood over the ripper and said, "Now you know exactly the pain I suffered, ripper. Now you know exactly the pain you've hidden from yourself for so long. You can't hide it anymore, ripper. It will be free forever."

The ripper whispered, "Nose, nose, anything goes. What can I do to end my woes?"

"Destroy that which is responsible for your pain," said the consulting detective sternly. "Destroy yourself."

The ripper answered with a barely perceptible nod. He remained motionless for several seconds, then his degree of haziness increased. Soon he appeared to be wearing gray clothing instead of black; soon he appeared to be wearing chalky white clothing instead of gray; and soon he was but the faintest of outlines. Through him I saw the cracks in the sidewalk, the weeds growing beside the golden walls. Then, quietly, he blinked out of sight. His passing from this life was not even noted with a brief twinkling of light; there was not a trace of prettiness to be associated with his exit from this plane. Having pulled myself to a standing position on the roof, I examined myself for the feelings of satisfaction or vindication I had been sure would be mine upon victory; but I felt nothing, save a grim hope that the ripper's soul, wherever it was, had only just begun to suffer.

If I had waited until I regained sufficient mental might to teleport, it would have been many minutes before I would have been able to join my friends. So I walked through narrow corridors, down narrow stairways in a golden building. I searched for some sign that the texture of life had changed, some indication that the grime on the walls and the dust infesting the atmosphere were on the wane. I could find no such sign, though their effect on me was less pronounced, as if I had suddenly grown above the painful perplexities of my environment. As I emerged from the building, I saw the consulting detective and a plainly weakened universal op help the bird woman stand. She held her occipital bone with the hesitant air of a patient afraid she might cause additional injury while attempting to avoid undue pain; she walked a tad more unsure of herself than did the universal op; but a quick mental examination (which was never beyond my resources, regardless of how depleted they were) assured me the consulting detective had been correct when he had assumed earlier that she had sustained no damage during her skirmish with the ripper.

When I joined them, we said nothing. We were not even in a hurry to awaken our comrades and tell them the good news (though I admit I was already composing a lead for the fat man, and preparing provocative statements for my inevitable interview with the ace reporter). The consulting detective put his hand on my shoulder and nodded, his eyes reflecting his gratitude; and I nodded in return, slightly embarrassed and humbled, until I once again thought of the ace reporter.

I dared to break the silence by speaking to the universal op; I offered to help him heal his wounds. As he muttered his refusal, I felt a warmth to which I had become accustomed suddenly forsaking me. The bird of light, which had been perched on the lamppost, now hovered in mid-air, its wings stationary, waiting for a signal from the bird woman. She nodded her assent, and the bird of light slowly rose toward the clouds, until its glow was but a tiny speck, no larger to my eyes than a star; and then a great black cloud rolled over the sky, concealing the mysterious bird of light, which I have not seen again to this day.

And when I once again returned my attention to the earth, I saw the consulting detective walking away from us, toward a trash can which was engulfed in shadows now that the bird of light was gone. He knelt a meter before he reached the trash can and picked up something. Increasing my visual abilities, I saw that it was a grimy red cotton rag, tattered and worn; and though there was seemingly nothing unusual about it, upon closer examination it became clear that it possessed a magnetic aura issuing forth from its fibers, as if it had once been something more than a mere cotton rag. Standing alone under the conical light of a streetlamp, the consulting detective stared at the rag for over a minute, until he nodded, making a private, undoubtedly melancholy observation to himself, and placed the rag into his coat pocket.

7. *An account from the good doctor's notebooks:*

Whatever victory celebration we may have planned was, of course, out of the question when we discovered the corpse of the seller of speculations in the tatterdemalion's apartment. How the ripper coaxed her there is a mystery I do not care to dwell upon. In addition, though I am reluctant to do so for obvious reasons, I now concur with the consulting detective's deduction that the ripper murdered the tatterdemalion.

As I prepare these memoirs for publication, I worry too over the fate of the man in the yellow suit. I fear he also might have met harm at the fiendish hands of the ripper. My concern perplexes me, for when I reflect upon my encounters with the man in the yellow suit, I recall mostly confusion and annoyance. Yet I stand fast by the hope that the man in the yellow suit left us merely upon the urging of one of those damnable whims of his. I sincerely believe he will return to our little group one day, and through these memoirs, I wish him well.

Now I am faced with the difficult task of concluding my tale.

I have consoled myself a hundred times by remembering that I am not, after all, writing fiction, as does the Big Red Cheese; loose ends can be tied up neatly in a story. Instead, I am dealing with real life, where stories never end and plot lines are left dangling until picked up by a new inspiration of the oversoul. In other words, I apologize to the reader for any arbitrariness he may perceive in the conclusion of this book.

Three days after the ripper's demise, we sat in the locker room of the demon's castle. We had long since sent Kitty's corpse to the antimatter universe, but the flowers remained, tingeing our dispositions with melancholy. That is, save for the disposition of the consulting detective, who was gayly lecturing us on the finer structural qualities of the ripper's antimatter knife, which he insisted on brandishing about, as if to cement his unfortunate monopoly on the conversation. The bird woman had returned to her African jungles, so the demon paid little attention to the consulting detective's words, despite their ironic connotations; the demon's thoughts were obviously elsewhere. The fat man sat with the shrew by his massive side; they too did not care for the lecture; they constantly muttered asides to one another, giggling at insignificant matters. I confess I did not and do not understand the attraction between them. At first I suspected it was the common solace of the extremely ugly, but then it occurred to me that the fat man might have finally found a permanent partner who was satisfactory on levels far more important than that of physical appearance, a deduction reached from my observation of the tip of a brown paper bag protruding from the flap of the shrew's purse. The lawyer appeared to be the most annoyed at the consulting detective; each time he glanced at the antimatter knife, he shuddered and looked away as if he had formed for the first time a mental picture of the ripper slashing Kitty. I should add that the lawyer bore his grief rather well, though he remained his usual over-demonstrative self. Finally he could contain his irritation no longer and, brandishing his sword cane as the consulting detective had brandished the antimatter knife, exclaimed, "All right, we've heard enough about how cleverly you've been figuring out how the ripper accomplished everything; let's talk about what it means! Let's hear your conclusions about the sociological and philosophical implications of the case. How does this remarkable little caper apply to life itself?"

"What?" asked the consulting detective, apparently confused in the extreme.

The lawyer paced about a bench, ostensibly because it was there. "You've just led us on a journey we never could have conceived before we began our crusade. Every time we've been the slightest bit confused over a matter, you've had the right answer—or at least the right question. Now clear up our confusion over the biggest question of all: what was it for?"

"Precisely the question on my mind," I said.

"I really don't know what you're talking about," said the consulting detective.

"Come, come, it's a little too late to play stupid," said the demon.

(The fat man and the shrew were lost in a world of their own devising.)

"What does it mean?" asked the lawyer, standing on the bench so he could look down at the consulting detective, for a change. "The East End, the ripper, Kitty's death, the disappearance of the man in the yellow suit, those disgusting lovebirds over there—they must mean something. Surely we can pause occasionally in our eternal journey, take stock of what we've seen and done and learned, and then draw some conclusions. I've lost the one thing in my life that gave it meaning, I can't conceive of myself ever loving another woman; and yet I want to live. Damn it, man, you promised us some answers!" He leapt from the bench and grabbed the consulting detective's elbow as if he was angry, prepared to embark upon a violent exchange. But they stared almost tenderly into one another's eyes, as the lawyer said, "You didn't come right out and say it, but you promised us some answers. We were supposed to discover something important. Well...it's over. What have you got to tell us? What are you going to say to me that will ease the pain here, in my heart?"

The consulting detective blinked rapidly several times, fighting to contain some sentimental emotion. After a few moments, he prepared himself to stammer an answer—his expression indicated it would be totally inadequate—when blind circumstance saved him.

The universal op entered the locker room. The demon

noticed him first, and he inhaled sharply, his green skin paling considerably. We turned as one and looked at the op standing there in the doorway.

The op wore his usual blue suit; his hair was its usual short black self; he stood with his hands in his coat pockets, so he was not carrying anything strange or enticing, such as one of the fat man's former cheerleaders. An indolent writer of fiction would have described his face as smooth, but such a convenient description would have been erroneous.

The demon rubbed his right eye, near the duct. The shrew, who was but passingly acquainted with the op, silently shed several tears. The fat man placed his hands on his knees and smiled as if he had been personally responsible for the phenomenon. The lawyer's expression was a peculiar mixture of sadness and gaiety; his mouth twitched too frequently for me to decide which emotion was predominant. The consulting detective's larynx bobbed twice; he held his hands behind his back, unaware, I think, of the tears glistening in his eyes. And as for myself, well, I rushed to the op and clasped his hand in mine, placing my left hand on his shoulder. The tears flowed freely down my face.

The universal op held his mug toward mine, as if to stare quizzically at me despite his lack of eyes. But I prefer to think he was instead providing me with a better view of the tiny ridge in the center of his mug, of the two indentations just below his forehead, of the thin strip of pink above his chin. The embryonic face was not an artificial additive, this we all knew at once; it stemmed from a fundamental alteration in his emotional profile, from the wealth of humanity we had always sensed in his soul. Something had indeed happened to the universal op on the course of his journey, something which gave us the hope that our respective journeys would not be in vain.

Whenever I think of this extraordinary development, the warmth I felt then rises anew in my breast. It is in this compassionate spirit that I submit these memoirs of tragedy and achievement to the public. It is my intention that they play their part, however minor, in the collective journey of our race, in the great mysteries of the cosmos which, once unraveled, will eradicate the misery that has been preventing us from realizing our full potential for eons.

But I feel compelled to add that there are times when I become rather realistic and I cast off my romantic delusions. I realize then that we have been born to stupidity, that life indeed has no meaning. No book can alleviate this situation. Our pain and suffering will never end, and the entire race should be consigned to the fires of the antimatter universe for all eternity.

16